Fester

Donated by:
Shantella Y. Sherman
Washington, D.C. - U.S.
♥♥♥
In loving memory of:
Lee Andrew & Hattie Hall Ross

Fester

Lilies that fester stink worse than weeds

A Novel by

Shantella Sherman

Copyright © 2008 by Shantella Sherman.

ISBN:	Hardcover	978-1-4363-0929-5
	Softcover	978-1-4363-0928-8

All rights reserved. No part of this book may be reproduced or transmitted in any form or by any means, electronic or mechanical, including photocopying, recording, or by any information storage and retrieval system, without permission in writing from the copyright owner.

This is a work of fiction. Names, characters, places and incidents either are the product of the author's imagination or are used fictitiously, and any resemblance to any actual persons, living or dead, events, or locales is entirely coincidental.

This book was printed in the United States of America.

To order additional copies of this book, contact:
Xlibris Corporation
1-888-795-4274
www.Xlibris.com
Orders@Xlibris.com

For Lee.

August 24, 2001
3:23am

    Lillian pulled the scrunchy from her hair and fitted it around her wrist as she tipped down the side steps and entered the foyer. Seeing two uniformed Mosse Point police officers and a trench coat clad fellow standing alongside them through the glass door; she fastened her silk kimono around her naked body. Bare-foot, the cool night breeze caused her to curl her toes under as she opened the door.

    "Mrs. Lillian Holland?"

    She recognized Sean McAfee in the trench coat as a former high school classmate, now a Lieutenant with the Mosse Point police. He wore the same stern-lipped, beady-eyed look tonight as when he'd informed her of her father's passing years ago. Lillian stood blocking the entrance, a slight panic gripping her, until she remembered her manners.

    "Yes, I am Lillian Gottlieb Holland. Officers, Lieutenant, please come in," she half smiled. "Is there something I can do for you?"

    "Ma'am we—", one of the uniformed officers began, but was halted by the furrowed look of his superior.

    "Lillian, how you been?" the Lieutenant asked, leading her by the arm into her parlor.

    "Okay I suppose, though I am getting a bit uneasy with you all standing in my parlor at 3 o'clock in the morning. What's wrong Sean?"

    "We pulled your son Chasen over around midnight. He was driving erratically along the interstate in a vehicle that had been reported unreturned by Phoenix Car Rental. We identified ourselves and asked that he step out of the vehicle. He did. We asked if we could search the vehicle, thinking maybe he had open bottles or something in the car and we could pull him in to sober up. Instead, we found explosive-making materials and a handgun under the passenger seat. Once he realized we were about to arrest him, he started yelling and screaming about how we'd come to stop him. Said that we'd been sent to intercept him by the mighty Gottliebs. Said he could no longer live a lie and that he would have the last laugh. Before we could cuff him, he . . . he wrestled one of my officer's guns from his belt and put it to his head. He kept saying his mother would not deny him any longer. We tried to stop him. But before any of us could react, he put the gun under his chin and pulled the trigger. He's at Mercer Hospital," the Lieutenant sighed and gathered his breath, relieved he'd gotten it all out.

    Lillian sat silently for a few seconds before announcing stone-faced, "There's just one problem Lieutenant, Chasen is my nephew, not my son."

    "That's pretty peculiar, as we just left your sister Lindersyl, and she said the same thing and sent us here."

Chapter One

Three months earlier

To be invisible would be my claim to fame,
A girl with no name—that way I won't have to feel the pain.

To Be Invisible, Gladys Knight

johnathan & lillian
Gottlieb Grove Estate
May 10, 2001

"Say 'cheese'!," Jasper Dean said to the most pitiful couple he'd ever come across. Usually his assistant handled the Holland family, but for what was now an obvious reason, he'd canceled at the last minute. One of the wealthiest families in Connecticut, the Hollands were expected to be somewhat eccentric, but this was ridiculous. Since the photo session had begun, an hour earlier, there had been six interruptions—signaled by the wife, Lillian's, delicately raised hand. Each time she would mumble something tacit in the ear of her husband, Johnathan, and then walk from the room with tears in her eyes. Lillian Holland was one of those refined, shallow nut-jobs Jasper hated to deal with. Something was always against her taste. She had a reputation for being quick-tempered and nasty with the help whom she counted Jasper among, but today her agitation was clearly directed at her husband. Lillian had only just returned from her last walkout and been repositioned on the platform, when the house phone rang. Neither Johnathan nor Lillian moved to get it.

With plastered politician smiles, the "happy couple" mumbled a delayed 'cheese' for Jasper.

"Great!" Jasper smiled, hoping to finish and leave before the tension in the room suffocated them all. If they didn't like the shots, he'd send someone else out to re-shoot. "Now, hold that pose a second so I can adjust the lights."

"Would you get your hand off my behind?" Lillian screeched between clinched teeth.

"Petal, my hand is on your waist, exactly where Jasper placed it. Trust that as soon as this session is over, it won't happen again," he whispered in her ear.

"My waist is here!," she shouted, jumping up from the platform seating and pointing feverishly at her side.

"Oh sit down Lil . . . . I'm married to you for half my life. You think I don't know where your waist is? Besides, it's not as if I haven't touched you before," he stammered.

"I don't know where your hands have been! You sleep with ten-dollar whores . . ." Lillian retorted to Johnathan, then turning to Jasper, repeated, "He sleeps with ten-dollar whores!"

Jasper unplugged the lights. This was about to get real ugly. If any portion of the Johnathan Holland he'd known twenty years ago was still in his graying buddy, Jasper needed to evacuate and quickly. Jasper did his best to ignore them, letting down umbrella shades.

"Oh, you are a mad woman!," Johnathan laughed, brushing her off with a slight of his hand.

"Where were you last night? Hey, Mr. Rutherford Studios man, ask him where he was last night," she screamed.

"Lillian, what is the matter with you? What brought this on all of a sudden?" Johnathan said with deliberate restraint. The last thing he needed was to turn his wife out in front of an old buddy. As good as he was, Jasper would be telling everyone with ears how "Old Holland smacked the piss outta his wife."

"Don't you stand there pretending I don't know what I am certain that I *know*! You were with that goddamned Anastasia weren't you? You dirty old pervert! I'm going to tell her father so he can come over here and whip your sorry ass!" she screamed.

"Perhaps I should come back some other time and finish this . . ." Jasper finally said, striking the camera stands.

"Yes, I think maybe you should," Johnathan said. "I'm sorry about my wife, man; she gets these . . . sick headaches."

"It's not my head that aches Johnathan!" she said, walking from the room and stomping up the stairs to her bedroom.

"Honey? Lil, yeah, go on up and lay down. I'll come check on you in a second," Johnathan called behind her. When he looked at Jasper there was fury in his eyes.

"Handle your business, man. My name is Jasper and I ain't in it," he said, with saucer eyes.

"That shit don't rhyme!" Johnathan laughed, walking out into the driveway behind Jasper, where the Rutherford Studios van was parked.

"It ain't gotta rhyme cause it's nothing but the truth." Jasper said, climbing into the van.

"Uh, look Jasper, man, I'm really sorry about that," Johnathan frowned, pulling back three one hundred dollar bills from his money clip and handing them to Jasper through the open van window. "You still stuck in the Sixties man. This should help you forget what you just saw."

"Ain't nothing wrong with the Sixties and I'd rather be stuck there than where *you* stuck! Dig?" Jasper said, slapping Johnathan a vintage 'five on the Black hand side'.

"You got it." Johnathan smiled.

Examining the bills under the mid-day sun, Jasper decided the day had just picked up. "Shit! My name is Jasper and that's between y'all".

"Man, whatever!" Johnathan laughed, shaking his head.

Johnathan Holland watched as the van turned onto the main road. He could kill Lillian. He replaced the humiliated, hen-pecked husband face, with that of the one he wore most often when interacting with his wife.

"Lillian! Lillian! You hear me woman?" Johnathan yelled, making a mad dash up the stairs to what was once their shared bedroom.

"The whole of Gottlieb Grove can hear you," she grimaced, stepping from the master bedroom's bath area. She'd tossed a dressing gown over her slip, throwing her photo suit onto a brown recliner in the corner of the room.

"Now just what in the hell is your problem? Did you think that little scene was funny?"

"No, but then it wasn't meant to be. And don't take that tone with me or bring that street language into my house! What you witnessed was a reality check. And from now on that is the way it will be between you and me, dear husband," she smirked.

"Have you been drinking?"

"I'm plenty sober, thank you. How dare you go jet-setting off all over the country-side with whomever you went with and then find your way back home just in time to take "family photos" with your wife and kids. Notice, your children didn't bother to show. Why don't you get Betty or Anastasia to pose in your damned family photos?" she asked, pushing hard against him with the palms of her hands.

Grabbing Lillian by one arm and swinging her around until her back was to him, Johnathan held her captive in a bear hug with one arm and groped at her breasts with the other.

"Is this what you want? I don't give you enough attention, huh? Well?"

"Let go of me!," she screamed, breaking his hold.

"No, no" he growled, grabbing at her until he'd backed her into the bed. "See, Anastasia likes to be spanked, and Betty . . . well Betty likes the group thing and since I'm a sociable person, I like Betty. Lillian, after thirty-four years all you can say is 'real ladies just don't do certain things?' What kind of bull is that? What we have here is a failure to trust Lil. You don't trust me . . . and I'm not about to suffer because you won't put out."

"You've proven yourself to be utterly untrustworthy and irresponsible! How else was our home invaded by disease?"

"Lillian that was twenty years ago! And . . . and the verdict is still out on who gave what to whom!"

"I know where you got it Johnathan, so before you go retreating into a corner you know I can devour your ass up in, change courses." Lillian said, her voice cracking under the emotion.

Silence.

"You've not been faithful to me during any portion of our marriage," Johnathan retorted somewhat deflated by his wife's knowing. His tone became bitter. "You don't have the right to carry an attitude caused by your own shortcomings . . . and you damn sure don't have the right to make scenes like the one you just made downstairs. If you don't like what's going on in this relationship Lil, then do us both a favor and vote with your feet . . ."

Lillian turned her head away from him.

"Do I make myself clear?," he asked, grabbing her by the collar and yanking her forward.

"Crystal clear," Lillian whispered.

Johnathan released her, plopping her down on the edge of the bed.

Point.

Game.

Match.

Johnathan's conscious was getting the better of him. For some reason he really felt bad. Years ago he'd have smacked Lillian and locked her out of the house for a few days. But now, he just felt sorry and ashamed. Lillian was right; he *was* an inconsiderate bastard. He didn't deserve her, but he also didn't want her. If she could just leave him alone now, he could think of love and loss and try to forget she was even in the same house with him.

When Lillian began to speak, Johnathan was less shocked than disappointed. No matter what he did to her, she would take the responsibility and blame onto herself. She wouldn't leave him alone. He half listened, folding his arms and leaning his back against the wall.

"You know that I would never leave you Johnathan. But I can't pretend not to notice you being able to love every woman you meet, but me. What about me? What am I suppose to do? Feel guilty because I don't like putting my lips on something you've had God knows where? How do I turn my mind away from thinking "this is probably what he does to 'so-and-so', while you're down there pokin' and proddin'? You won't even look me in the face when we make love because you're miles away. You're using me as a stand-in and that's just not fair. You're my husband, and I don't think it's too much to ask for you to make love to *me* on occasion without causing either of us some major emotional trauma," she pleaded, tapping herself against the chest.

"Lil please! You spend more of your time in the poolhouse in your lover's bed than you do with me in mine. I'm not complaining. In fact, I'm grateful," Johnathan spat.

"*He* is not my husband. *He* has nothing to do with *us*."

"You really are mad! How is it that I'm some "Johnny-Out-Of-Control" because I get my needs met, but you're this poor deprived housewife? Does your little Haitian lover call you "gal" and make you giggle? Does he woo you with pineapple juice before he sticks it to you? I'm unclear on the difference between what I do with whomever and what you do with 'Mr. Chlorine'."

"You're incorrigible! For thirty years I've laid up under you while you grunt and moan and collapse into me and you've disgusted me since the first time."

"Make up your damned mind! Do you want me to do it to you or not? In one breath I'm a beast; in the next—"

"So why don't you divorce me and marry one of the others?" Lillian asked. Now it was her turn to drive the nail in. They both knew that the one he desired most, he could never have.

Divorce was the furthest thing from Johnathan's mind—even if he had been unhappy and restless since they married, Lillian presented a kind of comfort he had only experienced once before in his life. His wife's old-school polish was a turn-on for the mind in public and a business necessity. Dealing with that polish inside his home, in their bedroom, though, was another story altogether. And just like the changing of seasons, they both came repeatedly to the same fork in the road that led them back into each other, instead of out the front door.

"Divorce you for what, Lillian? Your face is all twisted with jealousy, but I don't want you and you—so you tell it, don't want me," Johnathan said.

It was an ultimatum; a challenge, but no more.

It was logically illogical that they wanted one another for wanting's sake. Her ego: How dare he overlook my beauty. His ego: the pool man has got nothing on me!

Lillian couldn't argue his point and in frustration sucked hard on her teeth before mumbling, "Forget you."

"Lillian, c'mere and gimme a kiss," he laughed. These upheavals, though fewer and farther between than years earlier, were becoming more and more intense. Johnathan found the easiest way of handling Lillian when these moods struck was to adhere to her demands. If she wanted love, Johnathan would find what he could of it. He'd manufacture some semblance of love and pretend where his imagination fell short. He would not have her moping about and slamming everything not nailed down for the next few days in search of affection when sex was all that the situation required. The sacrifice, he determined, had to be made. He reached for her and she sidestepped him, not wanting to accept too quickly his surrender.

"No!" she said with that teenage shrill that told Johnathan she was playing hard to get.

"Come on girl and stop playin'. I *have* missed you, you know!" he smiled broadly, lying back on her bed with his hands tucked under his head.

"I am not playing!"

"If you're not playin', then why are you grinnin' with your fresh ass?" Johnathan laughed at his own cunningness for the game. If memory served him correctly, that was the exact same line he'd used on her in 1967.

Johnathan reached for Lillian again and caught her arm. This time she did not turn away from him. She looked down at Johnathan, reclined across her bed and gave him a peculiar look, rather sinister it was. Her eyes penetrated Johnathan and almost caused him to run back to his own room and lock the door. Almost. In his dreams that was the face his wife gave him just before she hacked him to death. Perverse, but oddly seductive. Instead of leaving, Johnathan moved from the bed and being sure not to turn his back to her, searched for something in Lillian's face that would let him love her. He found enough. Just barely.

Johnathan removed his shirt and slacks, while Lillian drew the curtains (it was after all still daylight!), turned the bedside lamps to a dimmed setting and pulled the covers up to her waist. He had forgotten how beautiful his wife was. With a bevy of women occupying his mind, it had been years since Johnathan had looked upon her as much more than a good friend. But there she laid, a living testament to the phrase "black don't crack", and in love (or something) with him. Lillian's middle-aged spread had been more a cause for celebration than concern. He had always hated the way she bird-necked her food when she ate, afraid she would gain weight with the slightest indulgence. Fortunately as she had gotten older, her body began to settle into that 'Southern Comfort' body—wide hips, thick buttocks, noticeable waist and a great pair of boobs. Johnathan yanked the duvet and sheets back, exposing his wife's nakedness. Her body reacted first to the chill in the room, then to his touch.

"Lillian," he said, pulling her as close to him as she would fit. "I wasn't just saying it, I really have missed you."

"Yeah?"

"Yeah."

Johnathan moved to kiss Lillian, closed-mouthed and innocent as though coaxing a virgin lover through the motions. He felt her lips quiver against his and found himself aroused by the newness of her. His eyes met hers and for the first time in three decades, they welcomed him. There was desire and hope there instead of the suspicious and frosty glare she held on reserve for him.

Johnathan kissed and nibbled at her neck, taking his sweet time around to her ears and down her cleavage, finally supplanting himself at her nipples. He removed his boxers and kicked them down to the foot of the bed, pushing his hardness against Lillian's thigh. She opened her legs only slightly, teasing at him, forcing him to finger her clitoris with her thighs cinched tightly around his hand. Johnathan felt like a new man or rather the one he'd once been. With his sensuous stroke against her, he felt Lillian slowly part her legs to receive him. He drifted in the moment, wrapping her hair around his hands and tugging her head heavenward as he entered her. He felt her muscles lock around him and her breath escape suddenly against his chest. Her fingers sank into his back, as he swung his hips down low and brought them back up rhythmically. Still drifting, Johnathan felt as if he could last in the moment forever. Unfortunately, his romps with the quick and easy had ruined his stamina. What once took hours was down to minutes.

He felt a familiar pinch in his stomach and began talking through the sensations he felt. His pace was closer to that of a "john" than a considerate husband and lover, but he could not help himself. He felt Lillian go limp in his arms, and figured she'd just had her own fireworks go off. Straddling her from behind, he suddenly took note that what he was hearing was not panting, but muffled sobs.

Too close to turn back now, Johnathan fell into her from behind and brought the festivities to an end. He whispered in her ear that he was sorry, but he wasn't sure for what. His heart beat heavy in his chest and he felt a twinge of guilty pleasure. He had just experienced one of the best moments he could remember with his wife in a long time and she had probably been crying through the entire thing. Could these have been tears of joy? Doubtfully. Johnathan didn't feel compelled to ruin the moment by finding out either. He wanted so much to love her, he simply didn't. He couldn't. Disgusted, he kissed her cheek and rolled off of her, turning his back to her and wiping tears from his own eyes with the edge of the pillowcase.

Lillian looked at Johnathan and rolled her eyes hard. Johnathan was like a cow that gave a good bucket of milk and then kicked it over.

What's worse, he never knew when he was messing up until he'd messed up. Lillian was so close to having her husband back. He was bringing her to heights of passion she'd never known, when he called that bitch's name. Said it just as loud and clear as you please. Then, as she tried to recoup her pride and focus on him, he said it again and again and again. Johnathan was making love, touching, kissing, talking to *her* and not Lillian. He was fantasizing about someone else the entire time.

Too ashamed to smack his face and push him off of her, Lillian figured it was easier for two to play at that game than one. To bandage her hurt feelings, she imagined Johnathan was Ving Rhames and set out calling the actor's name. But by then, flat-head Johnathan had lost the ability to hear her voice over his own. Lillian only had two choices where Johnathan was concerned: Pretend not to hear his true love's name when he made love to her or be turned into an amusement park ride to please the perversity in him... *Ladies and gentlemen, watch the man twist and contort his wife for his own sexual pleasure...* This was not the first time, nor would it be the last for her to stand in the shadows of another woman. Thank goodness he was getting too old to prolong her agony. Denying him access to her altogether would only serve to alienate him further, and Lillian couldn't have that. Sooner or later, Johnathan would grow to love and desire her. Sooner or later.

As soon as Lillian heard what she thought was snoring, she went into the bathroom and started the tub to filling. She sat facing her own image in the mirrored walls, until the water from the tub had risen to hip level. Without turning or standing, she scooted herself backwards into the boiling water and peppermint oil. "The bastard!" she yelped, gritting her senses through the sting in hopes of adjusting quickly to the scorch. Lillian soaked and then used a fresh loofah to scrub as much of Johnathan off of her as possible. It was only when she saw the pink of her own blood mingling about the suds that she stopped.

Wrapping a terry drape about her body, she yanked the plug from the bath and started for the bedroom. She could hear Johnathan's locomotive-like snoring and moved to what was once his side of the bed, standing over him. His face was so handsome, even noble; so unlike his sinister self. Settling into the window seat, she looked over the expanse of Gottlieb Grove. The orchard had seen a full bloom, but the branches were now stark and bare. So much of the Grove was stark and bare. But that had been its legacy even before her father bought it.

Gottlieb Grove was one of the most stately New England properties known to man. The 17th century estate was made up of stables, a shrubbery maze, a fruit grove and four houses: the Big House, a guesthouse, a carriage house and the smokehouse (later, the pool house). At the far end of the grove were the servants' quarters. Built by a French aristocratic family, the Gottliebs, who'd made their fortune insuring slave ships and slave cargo, it was fitting that at the close of Reconstruction the family's acquaintances saw the home collapse into the hands of Negroes, no doubt former slaves with the same sir names. Though Connecticut was far removed from the cotton fields and harsh labor of the Deep South, the original Gottlieb's procured several slaves for their own personal use on The Grove. As a result, the Grove had never been a particularly peaceful place. With its gates facing the center of town, the "laborers" were a firm reminder to educated Blacks where their true value rested within wealthy white circles. Officially, the Blacks on the Grove could not be classified as slaves. They were even given wages and living quarters on Squatters Row, an area of dirt road bungalows on the edge of town behind The Grove, but their money was on paper only.

The Grove was owned and operated by Jan Gottlieb, the last of a dying breed of intellectuals perpetuating and touting the Darwinian belief in the eventual extinction of freed slaves. Negroes were savages who, without the aid and benevolence of their white masters and caregivers, would spiral into moral and social decay, until extinct like other genetically inferior species. The sub-humans had to be reigned in though until their demise to keep them from littering the nation with their offspring or hybrids produced from raping unsuspecting white women. Jan could not put the shackles back on them, but he did mean to keep negroes in a position deemed acceptable for their stations in life. Oskar, his nephew was a softer, gentler version of his uncle and mixed freely among black and red people without care. Eventually, Oskar's affections turned to a Negro laborer named, Annie, who worked the orchard. He'd even taken to sleeping in the servant's quarters with her, prepared to live illegally as man and wife. And when Annie gave birth to their son Benjamin, he didn't have the good sense to keep it to himself, but paraded the woman and child outside the gates of the Grove. Jan endured his nephew's delirium for years—it had to be a sickness; after all, what white man of sound mind would claim animals as wife and child? Still, Jan took Oskar's love of Annie and Ben as little more than comic relief while waiting for them to die out. But when the bright and charismatic, boy Ben turned twelve, his bravado and sense of place had foiled him into believing that he was as white as his father and uncle. Jan was being psychologically challenged by Ben's well-spoken and highly versed orations that could no longer be attributed to mimic and imitation of whites. And when, on one such occasion, Jan felt himself publicly humiliated by the boy's acumen, he'd allowed an angry mob loose on Ben and Annie. Their bodies were later found, bent and disjointed, in a metal sorter.

Oskar had been away when the "accident" occurred, and was inconsolable over Ben and Annie's deaths. He returned to the Grove just long enough to say 'good-bye'. He would return to France, by train to New York and then steamliner to Europe. Oskar knew that his uncle was responsible for Annie and Ben's murders, but could do nothing of it even if he could prove it. They were niggers. Just niggers. Perhaps, even uppity niggers to any white person who mattered. They were expendable, but Oskar's feelings were not. Tragedy makes a person rethink a position or two. Surely, Negroes were worthy. They were human after all, even if slightly less human than whites. Oskar was deep in thought concerning the white man's burden, the merits of Negroes and his unpopular love of them when he had a chance encounter with Mitchell Bates, one of the Pullman Porters on the train headed to New York. Oskar found Mitchell bright and well-spoken, even ambitious. He cringed each time another white passenger would call after Mitchell, "Boy, do this", "Nigger, get that." Mitchell was not a boy and, well, Oskar supposed he really wasn't a nigger, given his education. But Mitchell answered, as did his own beloved Ben, each time he was called with "Yassah and Yassam". Oskar watched Mitchell's dialect and mobility protract and retract from their scholarly discussions to the whimsical, head-scratching expectations of the other passengers. The duality was frightening. If Mitchell could pretend to be ignorant to appease white coach riders, perhaps most Negroes did. Perhaps shiftless and child-like on the surface meant safety, if not tranquility. The Negroes' place was somewhere the Negro accepted because it meant he was still alive. Mitchell was alive. Ben was not. Oskar could not replace Ben, but he could give Mitchell what he had planned to give Ben. Mitchell Bates and Oskar Gottlieb left the Northeast Direct Pullman train and headed for France together.

The niggers had not died! They were breeding and infiltrating cities faster than Jan could estimate. What's more, the white women seemed to flock to the niggers, drinking and carousing with them, and even flaunting their animal offspring. They did not scream 'rape' anymore. And when more of the type like Ben began to emerge, Jan had enough. The thought of sub-humans sharing in his lot was too much to bear for Jan, for whom death seemed more reasonable. In late 1929, Jan hung himself in the study of the Grove's main house; the fifth of his Darwinian cohorts to do so. By 1930, a small group of educated Negroes descended upon Downing, Connecticut and purchased most of the property. They changed the name to Mosse Point and created a new Negro-friendly town and government. Among them was Mitchell

Bates, who took his dead mentor's sir name as his own and became Micheaux Gottlieb. With no heirs to The Grove to contest it, the property was turned over to Oskar's "son" Micheaux and it became the wealthiest Black-owned estate in the country. Micheaux and his wife Faye would live in the Big House with their daughters Lillian and Lindersyl until the children were grown. The Big House was given as a wedding gift to Lillian and Johnathan, though Micheaux and Faye remained on the property, living in the carriage house until their deaths. Lillian and Johnathan's marriage, now thirty-four-years old, was as hollowed and void of life as the old house. They both knew why and made only soggy, sporadic attempts at fixing it.

Lillian pulled herself from her thoughts long enough to peer through the pool house window, where Harry Veda, her pool man, her lover, could be seen in front of the television.

Life was so ironic for Black women her age. She'd been taught by responsible parents as a young lady to keep her panties up and her dress tail down. She was taught that the thing dangling between a man's legs was filthy—*Turn her head away! Don't ever put her lips on it*! A respectable young man would see this as her virtue and treasure her all of her life. *A man ain't gonna marry no whore!* No one ever told her that those respectable men may marry women like herself, but they never desired them. They hardly respected them. No one mentioned that men think with those filthy things dangling between their legs and that unless a woman learned to truly love that filthy thing, he would never truly love her. No one told her that the reason young women and whores were despised by other women was because they learned a different lesson. They didn't keep their panties up or their dress tails down. They didn't look away from those filthy things. They learned to love those filthy things as much as the men did themselves. Some of them loved them even more than the men and the men loved them for it. Crazy, toothless, immoral, or penniless, if she was cool with *The Thing*, then she had herself a man . . . or two. Her rent was paid, even if she didn't have a job. Her kids were looked out for, even if they had two or three absentee daddies between them. Virtue meant nothing to a man with a hard dick.

Johnathan had discounted Lillian's virtue until it floated around the rooms of their home like dust. If only she had known then what she knew now, Lillian would have left or killed Johnathan before her emotions got the better of her. No, no one taught her that. That, lesson they let her learn on her own.

Lillian rested her head on the pane of glass before her trying to decide whether to join Johnathan in bed or retire to the guest bedroom, usually occupied by Johnathan. Harry was standing at the balcony doors watching her when she looked in the direction of the pool house again. He motioned for her to come over. She shook her head 'no'. He pushed his palms together, as if pleading. She smiled, then held up her open palm. She would be there in five minutes. She looked back at a sleeping Johnathan and frowned. The irony, she thought aloud. "I married you for security, but all you've ever given me is panic. Harry has nothing material that I desire, nothing that symbolizes security; yet, he is home".

Still draped in a towel, Lillian slid her feet into her house shoes and ambled across the yard to Harry's waiting arms.

I don't wanna talk about it—how you broke my heart,
But if you stay here just a little bit longer, won't you listen to my heart?

I Don't Want To Talk About It, Rod Stewart

lindersyl
Ladbrokes Mews Estate, SW London
May 10, 2001

The Holland Park area of London had always been a favored neighborhood of Lindersyl Gottlieb. So when she made her sojourn from Connecticut, it seemed only logical to supplant herself there. Though she remained the only woman of color and American on her block after nearly twenty years, she found her three-story deco home the perfect mix of modern art design and English manor charm. The weather of late had been typical of London—a lazy mix of cool rain and overcast skies. Unfortunately, it had only lent itself to Lindersyl's ongoing malaise of self-pity and drunken bliss.

Lindersyl walked from her bedroom into the master suites' bathroom and took a deep breath. The day officially began when her bare feet tapped across the cold bathroom tile. She shivered only slightly and took a seat on the bidet, moving her hand beneath the faucet to engage the sensor. The warmth of the water shooting up her backside caused her to wince—she needn't any sexual excitement. Besides, the floor just next to the bidet was saturated in water and her annoyance had easily capped what could have been an otherwise guilty pleasure. She pushed the thermostat on the wall to heat the floor tiles and began to relax.

"Why can't he wipe up the water from the floor when he gets out of the shower? It's a simple enough thing to do, not to mention considerate," she spoke aloud.

It was Olivus Blackstock, her boyfriend, seventeen years her junior, who was dancing on her nerves. It wasn't enough she'd awakened to find her feet knotted up in his underwear beneath the cover, but now the bathroom looked like a lagoon. It was past noon, but she was still tired. She and Olivus had attended a launch party and two after parties the night before that brought them home as the milkman was dropping off supplies. Lindersyl wondered if she looked as tired as she felt. After patting herself dry she began the daily surveillance of her body. Beginning with her hairline and forehead, Lindersyl checked for imperfections of any sort, with a chemist's allotment of crèmes, depilatories, sprays, scrubs, waxes, and soufflés on hand to mend things at once. She removed her nightgown, allowing it to fall around her ankles. Turning the overhead light on and adjusting the magnifiers, Lindersyl smiled contently, amazed that with only minor, unremarkable differences, her body was still curvaceous, sensual.

A dry, calloused hand danced down the back of her thigh interrupting her self-admiration. It was Olivus back from a jog around the square. He had removed his shirt and tucked it into the waistband of his blue sweatpants, revealing a washboard stomach and chiseled arms. She never tired of eyeing his physique, but could not focus on it for wanting to reprimand him.

"Olivus, I ask you, you say you will, but you don't. Am I talking for my health? Am I your woman or your mother? I shouldn't have to repeat myself to a grown man," she snapped, removing his lassoed hands from her waist.

Deflated, Olivus shook his head and smiled. "What is it?"

"Are you wearing underwear?"

"Yeeeeessss," he dragged out his reply, knowing that this cat and mouse bickering was so much more enjoyable for her than just saying what the problem was. His impatience for her exaggerated admonishments had waned some time ago. Now he simply smiled and answered, loving her all the more.

"Then why, dear, are there underwear tied up in the sheets?"

"Oh, well those are from last night. What? Did you put your panties back on?"

"Of course not. I did have the courtesy to remove them from the bed and drop them down the linen shoot. Then, I washed up and redressed for bed."

"Why?"

"Olivus, I will not take ill in the night or Heaven forbid, lay up in here and die and have people think that you killed me in some ravenous sexual romp!"

"Shagged to death, huh?" Olivus laughed at his own funny.

"Oh, you are a right mess this morning. And look at all that water you left on the floor."

"I'll get it. I'll get it," he said in defeat, kissing playfully at the nape of her neck. "I love you."

"I know. Now, please get that water up," Lindersyl half-smiled, turning Olivus by his elbow in the direction of the puddles he'd made.

She watched as Olivus threw fresh folded towels on the puddles and soaked up the water using his sneakered feet to guide them across the floor. Lindersyl could have become annoyed all over again. "Why not use the mop instead of my 1000-thread designer towels? That's what mops are made for," she thought. She held her tongue though, looking smugly at Olivus' bare back, satisfied that she was still able, at fifty-seven to enthrall such a tasty dish. Lindersyl returned the dancing hands down the leg when Olivus stood from picking up the towels.

He smiled, "Your hands heat and chill me at the same time. Is there a word for that?"

"Yeah, it's called having your nose wide open," Lindersyl laughed, tugging him forward by the silver cross he wore around his neck. She craned her neck to kiss his lips. They were thick and wet and tasted of salty sweat and sweet mango juice. Olivus covered both her lips with his, sucking the breath from her chest. He was deliberately intense and passionate, increasingly satisfied each time she sent those shock waves up his spine. Likewise her body's response to him—always soft and abundantly wet. For newness sake, Lindersyl would shave, dye, plait even spike the hairs of her pubis. Like a prize in a crackerjack box, Olivus was pleased and excited every time. Her pubis coif was as it had been the night before, long, exotic gray strands, as thick and waved as an afghan. Olivus wasn't certain, but thought this to be the true nature of her nether-region. He took another look and fell into a clumsy laugh before engaging Lindersyl in a playful game of "catch me" that ended in the kitchen with Lindersyl straddling him on the chopping isle. They were fully bare and covered in perspiration.

"You minks!" he shouted.

Lindersyl gave a coo and growl, extending her legs to rest on the light beam above her.

"Your prey is caught hunter, now feast! Feast!" she laughed, playing caught.

Olivus pounced, convinced that with a bit of effort his penis could ping her heart. He looked at her reflection in the doors of the metallic refrigerator. How perfect she was this Lindersyl. Years his senior but with a body he would never get accustomed to claiming. She had admitted to having her breasts "fixed", lifting taut what gravity had so unkindly sagged, but otherwise was naturally inclined to stay looking twenty-one. Olivus listened to her soft panting, through giggled commands for him to 'feast'. She enjoyed being had and he in having her.

Lindersyl had flipped Olivus to his back for a horse and jockeying game, when her niece Grier's startled face peered around the corner of the kitchen. Both acknowledged her. Neither stopped.

"Grier, what is it?" Lindersyl said between labored breaths. Her breasts jumped and bounced as she dropped down crudely on Olivus' penis causing him to moan out in delight.

"I'll come back . . ." Grier grimaced, totally disturbed by their blatant disregard for her.

"Give us a few . . . Olivus, you ready to end the feast?"

"Yeah, baby" he said through exhausted lips.

"A few minutes then," Lindersyl blew out hard, turning her butt to Olivus and straddling him from the opposite direction. Grier threw a distasteful glance back in their direction, making a mental note to severely disinfect the kitchen.

Lindersyl half-chuckled, secretly pleased that her virgin niece caught an eyeful of reckless fornication. Perhaps she'd long for it enough to partake someday soon, Lindersyl thought. In case Grier was spying from the doorway, Lindersyl performed a near-acrobatic twirl still firmly attached to Olivus. Olivus cried out as if caught in some powerful vice grip, spent, delighted, and only slightly embarrassed that his woman's niece might be hearing him. He lay still, out of breath and dizzy for quite a while. Lindersyl peeled herself from him. She was using the stove burner to light a cigarette and looking at him grinning, when he finally opened his eyes. She bent over him, still lying on the block, and gave him a light kiss on the lips.

"You better get ready for work," she smiled, blowing smoke rings out to him.

The early afternoon had passed, causing Olivus to ponder, as he had in the past, giving up work to become a kept man, running around the house playing cat and mouse with Lindersyl. He admonished himself inwardly for being as 'fickle as some young school girl'. Lindersyl was right. Neither the nightclub or the band would take care of themselves; he needed to get to work. Olivus walked from the kitchen without looking back, yanking a dishtowel from the rack to cover himself as he walked through the living room to the elevator. Grier was seated on the sofa awaiting her aunt, and covered her face as Olivus rounded the corner. He gave her an apologetic smile, but was met with a raised eyebrow and upturned lips. Lindersyl walked behind Olivus, but at a much slower pace, examining his lazy swagger across the living room. She was still naked when she sat down on the sofa across from Grier.

"Would you . . . ?" Grier asked pointing at her nakedness.

Lindersyl sighed heavily, pulling a chenille throw resting on the lounge chair around her. She wrapped it as one would a full sarong before sitting back down and giving Grier a frosty glare.

"Thank you." Grier said, ignoring her aunt's frown.

"You intimated that it was important dear. So, what is it?"

"Well, the firm is sending me back to Connecticut shortly. I'll be gone for about three months . . . And, guess what?" Grier asked excitedly.

". . . I have no clue, fill me in," Lindersyl said with feigned enthusiasm.

"They're allowing me to bring someone along with me! They'll pay for first-class accommodations for me and . . . you, all the way! Airline tickets, hotel, rental car, daily expenses . . . Everything!"

"You and . . . me?"

"Aunt Lindi, why don't you come on home with me? It's been like years since you've seen your own flesh and blood," Grier pleaded.

"Darling, I know she's *your* mother, but Lillian is hardly a selling point to return to Connecticut."

"Aunt Lindi, don't you have friends and . . . What about Eisendorff? I know Eisen would love to see you. Don't you miss any of them? All of granddaddy's old friends . . ."

Lindersyl frowned and smiled, then smiled and frowned. She couldn't make up her mind if returning to the States was a good thing or not. Grier was still talking as she often did when she was trying to bully a response.

"Look here now, girl. I ain't saying I will go or that I won't. Not yet," Lindersyl replied, annoyed.

"Aunt Lindi, I only have until the end of the week—two days from now to give the travel department your name and passport information."

"Then I will let you know at the end of the week—two days from now. Okay?"

"Okay then! You make it seem like I just asked you to do something sordid, rather than see the people you love!" Grier retorted before walking from the room. She thought better of being confrontational even though her aunt had really been getting on her nerves lately. She'd never really figured out why her aunt had left America in the first place. Grier had always heard from her father and family friends that it was something to do with men. Not surprising, given her aunt's lack of intimate decorum. Whatever her aunt's reservations to returning home, Grier had already given Lindersyl's name as the guest accompanying her. Hopefully that would be the case.

Lindersyl watched Olivus' little red Corvette speed out of her driveway then headed back down to the kitchen. She took the stairs this time, slowly counting each one as she descended.

She had been pretty good with her drinking since Olivus had come into her life—only occasional glasses of white wine, mostly with dinner. But the desire for Bollinger champagne, her drink of choice for remembering and forgetting, had begun as soon as Grier mentioned returning to Connecticut. And Lindersyl did not want a glass; she wanted a bottle, or two. Olivus didn't care for her when she was soppy so she'd graciously awaited his departure before beginning her binge. He would not return until sometime around dawn from the nightclub, by which time she should have showered and found her way to their bed. But for now she wanted to get good and drunk on the *good stuff*.

Lindersyl replaced the chenille throw she'd donned earlier with a long Egyptian robe. She climbed the stairs from the kitchen and passed her bedroom to the attic stairwell. She was already out of breath and was happy that she'd thought to bring four bottles instead of two. She would not want to have to go down and come back up again. The narrow passageway up the attic stairwell had no lighting, so she forced herself from memory to make her way. Once her eyes adjusted, she disrobed and locked the door firmly behind her. She stared at the view outside her digs and popped the cork on the first bottle, before pulling the curtains closed. Lindersyl stared off blankly for some time, squatting with her back leaned against a wall. As if entranced, she drank and thought, thought and drank. When she finally took note of herself, two of the bottles were empty and she was in what she referred to as "champagne afterglow" (and others called drunk). Tipsy, and just teetering on the edge of delirium, Lindersyl sank her backside deep into the plush two-inch thick carpeting beneath her. She smiled to herself, enjoying the giddiness and fluttering of what felt like butterflies in her stomach. She would agonize in the morning over this same feeling, when of course it brought up the "butterflies" and the morsels of food she'd eaten with it.

Lindersyl knew it was more than the alcohol that was swelling her emotions. Why had Grier invited her? The child could hardly have known that everything that crippled Lindersyl was in a place she called *home*. First Lindersyl would have to think of her father, Micheaux Gottlieb, whom she'd never stopped mourning. Her father was the Sun, Moon and all constellations in between. She had meant as much to him as he had to her. She was named for his twin sisters, Linda (pronounced Linder by their parents) and Sylvannah, because according to her dad, she had their eyes. He had died in 1966—heart attack—and she still missed him more than she could imagine. They had the kind of relationship that father-daughter relationships were supposed to be—kind, honest, gentle, loving, giving, and protective. More than anything, Micheaux had protected Lindersyl; from men, school administrators, neighbors, and most often, her own mother. When he died, it not only left her without a father, but also without an ally. He would be sorely ashamed of her if he could see her now. Her father was also responsible (or so she believed) for encouraging Lindersyl's affair with a man who had initiated the slow-paced destruction of her life.

Oh, she didn't want to think about *that old love*. Thinking about him meant it wouldn't be long before she had a wanting for him again. And once she made up her mind that she wanted him, it was only a matter of time before she'd have him. Only having him would mean her undoing. It always did.

Lindersyl drifted into a mental lull where she felt right at home. She could see herself, full of life and vibrant, dancing with exotic motions across a field. She was in the arms of the man she loved . . . a man her father claimed was righteous and her perfect counterpart.

"Lindi," the man called out to her in sear sucker trousers and letterman's sweater, "I need you . . . . Don't just walk away." He screamed something incoherent before pointing a gun to his chest and pulling the trigger . . . his insides spilled onto the concrete before her face . . . she screamed but the echoing of the gun blast muffles the sound . . .

"No!" Lindersyl yelled, jostling herself to a sitting position. She shook herself to a half dazed state and whimpered, "Not like this . . ." before drifting back off. This time she realigned the events of her affair as they should have been. Lindersyl shook her head from side to side as her ring, a Bvlgari Cicladi, pinged an unopened bottle of Bollinger she'd cleverly placed next to her collapsed torso. She'd opened the third bottle, but the urge to drink was over now. She tried desperately to conjure images of yesteryear. Why couldn't he love her as he had? How had she lost him? Lindersyl forced her mind to dip again and again into lost moments, searching for answers she knew weren't there.

She could just make out the smell of that country hair tonic and aftershave oil he used, and then it all came back to her again. They had a nameless passion that neither could explain nor hide. Her 'nos' always became "okays" and his "I don't think we shoulds" always turned to "maybe just for a whiles".

Lindersyl pulled her lover close to her, straddling his body in the waist high blades of grass on the backside of the university campus. Rosedale University had only recently erected its new athletic stadium, and to the average onlooker, it was a magnificent showplace, but to Lindersyl, it was an isolated love nest, which no one considered outside of game time. With the scent of magnolia milling undernose it wasn't long before she'd once again lost control: pulling, scratching, and biting at him. Her lover, thoroughly pleased, had, as he'd done many times before, closed his eyes and rocked within her, first coaxing her along, and then talking in deep and incoherent sobs. His body was strong and fit and the power in his movement was forceful, but not intrusive. Lindersyl enjoyed the way he lost control and commanded her, through his actions, to do the same.

Somewhere in the midst of their passion, her palms began to itch. Not on the surface, but somewhere deep within her flesh where she couldn't reach it. Soon her neck and chest too, became flushed and sensitive. So sensitive, that his breath on her skin and the tiny droplets of sweat running from his back and forehead touching her flesh sent waves of excitement through her.

Lindersyl looked up to meet his eyes . . . but instead of pleasure, there was a look of horror on his face. Pulling her body back from his, the blood from his chest had soaked the front of her white sundress.

This time when she woke herself, the pretense was over. She was fifty-seven years old; not seventeen. She was still in her lovely home, surrounded by her lovely things, but totally miserable—even with a man who loved and adored her within reach. Tears ran down Lindersyl's cheeks like small tributaries, darkening the color of the carpeting beneath her as they fell. The incidents were as clear and painful as if they were yesterday, but she couldn't let it go without letting go of him. The possibility of losing him completely was something she couldn't deal with, even thirty years later.

To the world Lindersyl Gottlieb was power Superbitch personified, but to those who knew her well, she was a vulnerable, love-starved woman, with an unhealthy appetite for men, drink and fantastical versions of reality. Early in her career as a journalist, writing stories had allowed her to manipulate and take hold of others' lives in nix of controlling her own. Later, working public relations gave her permission to create acceptable images for unacceptable people—to lie to the masses for the betterment of a few. Most people couldn't handle the truth about life. Lindersyl was among them.

Lindi's smile disappeared as she remembered that she hadn't yet done evening prayers, and in her pissed condition, the likelihood was slim. She loved telling people she was a Buddhist, but it had been years since she'd practiced with any conviction. Her religious conversion came at the behest of her psychiatrist following the loss of the child she counted as her third. The others. Four. Five. Six. She had been pregnant nine times; had miscarried three, terminated two and had bore four. Lindersyl had all but convinced herself that only three ever existed, the others had never been conceived and should not be spoken of. Speaking of them, acknowledged them. Acknowledging them made her responsible for their damaged lives or their deaths. That was a responsibility that she simply couldn't shoulder. The first two were with their father, who would rather walk across hot coals than see her face. He had fathered all nine, but asked her to stop having the children after their third child Ana-Leslie died. The child had died suddenly of an undetermined illness just shy of her second birthday and he blamed Lindersyl for the child's death. He had already taken the others from her, and believed that had he taken Ana-Leslie as well, she'd have lived. Lindersyl buried Ana-Leslie alone, standing graveside in woolen pajamas and an overcoat. No one else showed that day to console her, but like a thief who robs the same house over and over to claim any replacement valuables, Ana-Leslie's father showed that night. Lindersyl cried through his lovemaking, interpreting his embrace as sympathy. The next afternoon he was on a plane out of London. Her fear of children coming to harm while in her care made having them in her space insufferable, despite adoring them. Then too, those she'd abandoned refused to be ignored. They tormented her thoughts and interrupted her dreams. Sometimes she thought she could hear their crying or feel their movement in her belly. She saw their likenesses in others, just as they'd been or should be now. More than anything, the children reminded her of their father. To forget him, she'd laid with as many men as she could stomach. Random sexual encounters temporarily took the children's father from her mind, but made her feel lonely and abandoned afterwards. When the men failed to block his memory, Lindersyl turned to drink. First vodka and cranberry juice, then aged Jamaican rum. Only fainting spells and blackouts caused her to opt for champagne, instead of hard liquor. She'd blocked his telephone numbers, served him orders of protection and secured the property around her to keep him away. Only as soon as he stopped trying to get at her, she wanted him back, and felt sick over any other woman having him. In an act of total desperation, Lindersyl took refuge on foreign soil. But nothing about their relationship had changed in years, except his temperament and her locale. He hated her now, or at least as much as he loved her. He still mattered. And all it took was a reminder of him and home to turn her back to being pitiful. She was unable to claim the children and there was nothing she could do about it except pretend none of it had happened. But it had. Their father would never love her as he had.

    Lindersyl was fully awake now. She wanted to go home. She had to go. Aside from this one slip into the bottle, she was coping just fine, she told herself. Lindersyl thought about having Grier with her these last few years. It had been nice. She had mothered successfully. Her children were grown now. She could not kill them or cause them harm. They would be happy to know her. Maybe. She should at least try. As for their father, he would be happy to see her too—even if just for a little while. She would leave if he became crazed. "He's probably wrinkled, senile and suffering from incontinence by now," she laughed.

    Picking herself up from the floor, she swayed a bit to catch her balance. Lindersyl slowly slid the attic door open, noticing the time on the landing wall. It was well after midnight. She redressed quickly, closing and locking the door behind her. She had to piss like nobody's business and made a mad dash down to the second floor. Her age was catching up with her in strange ways like laughing or sneezing hard and finding urine running down her legs.

The doctor said it was natural, but the last thing she needed was to sneeze and piss two and half bottles of champagne to the floor. Lindersyl barely noticed Grier lying across her bed when she entered the bathroom and sat down on the commode. Her side ached like mad, no doubt her kidneys telling her to cool it. She made a mental note, no more than a bottle at a time. Still carrying the full and empty armful of Bollinger bottles, Lindersyl jumped a mile high upon spotting her niece.

"Aunt Lindersyl, have you thought anymore about going home? I noticed that in three years' time none of our family has visited you, not even your children. Where are they? You don't even have pictures of them up in the house. You didn't drink all of that did you? Are you all right? You don't look well. Do you feel okay?" Grier asked on in her customary way.

Lindersyl raised her hand to stop the barrage of questions. "Actually Grier, I have decided to join you. My children . . . are fine and are of no consequence to you. Photos clash with the minimalist décor and I am fine—just fine and my mood should not trouble you, I am just a bit annoyed with your Uncle Olivus, and I did drink all of this because I was extremely thirsty," she said, giving Grier a taste of her own medicine, before motioning to Grier to leave the room.

Once she was alone, Lindersyl opened the fourth bottle of champagne. This time she swigged straight from the bottle.

I don't need your loving arms around me; all I need is to be free
That's what I keep telling myself and I tell you, you don't need me . . .

I Don't Need You, Kenny Rogers

johnathan and lillian
Gottlieb Grove
May 12, 2001

The crop of green tomatoes Lillian had planted earlier in the year were ripe for the picking and she had spent the better portion of the morning filling a plucker's basket with them. After taking a few moments to sip sweet tea and wipe her brow, Lillian lowered herself into the new soil Harry had packed down and began pulling up roots and turning over soil. She hadn't decided yet on whether to do squash or radish, but given Johnathan's love of squash, she would probably plant radish. She was still upset with him for his emotional torment days earlier. After their failed attempt at lovemaking, they had unceremoniously returned to their separate lives. Only this morning after bumping into each other in the kitchen did they settle into each other's company and sit down to breakfast together. Lillian had given nothing but cold and evil stares over their breakfast of shrimp and cheese grits. Undaunted by her silence, Johnathan had filled the void of her conversation with mindless chatter to some female on the other end of his cell phone. This had upset Lillian something terrible, though she didn't know why. In an effort to pull herself together, she'd taken a long look at the splendor growing across the Grove and decided to work the orchard for the day. The kneading and whisking always proved therapeutic for her, and this was one time she was in desperate need of it, as her emotional well-being seemed to be unraveling by the minute. She could feel in the pit of her stomach that a storm was brewing in the house.

Having wrapped herself in her own world, Lillian forgot all about Johnathan until she felt his eyes on her from the kitchen window. When she ignored him, he tended to get suspicious and territorial. As he approached the screen door, Lillian turned her back to him, determined not to let him interrupt her peace. She bent to pull up a deep running root and he paused to watch her. As with most things, she was undeterred by the root's show of defiance; she would pull it out if it meant having to lie in traction for days. With the bulk of the root embedded in hard earth, Lillian continued to pull in vain.

She listened to Johnathan move slowly down the deck's steps and into the small garden, leading into the Grove. It was his "day off", again, (he hadn't been into the office in nearly three weeks) and he'd decided to don chinos to beat back the unseasonably warm May heat. Lillian ignored the brush of his body against hers, but acknowledged him with a wave of the hand only once he'd patted her bottom.

"Need a hand with that?"

"No, I think I got it," she smiled, grateful he still found favor in her, despite his invective manner. His attention made her jaws relax and her anger evaporate. She felt fickle when the giddiness took hold. When he wrapped his arms around her and nibbled at her ear, she couldn't help herself but to respond. Her heart was still broken, but not so that it would not repair.

"Here," he whispered, reaching down alongside her and giving the root a hearty tug. Without much resistance, the earth released its grip and freed the straggly weed. They both grinned a bit to fill the stretch of silence.

"Well, I am ever so grateful . . . How on earth can I repay you?" Lillian finally offered.

"Well, just to bask in your glory is 'nuff for me, ma'am"

They both smiled, leaning into one another. It had been a long while since they'd shared smiles. It felt good to them both to know somehow, they were of some use to each other.

"Lil, about the other night . . ." he began.

"Oh, don't worry about that-" she scowled, waving him off. It was too good right now to ruin it with talk of that fiasco.

"No, I have to worry about it, Lil.'"

"Really Johnathan, it's all right," she insisted.

"Damn it, Lil, something ain't right between us! You completely shut down on me and I don't know why. What did I do?" he asked, his voice cracking.

"You did nothing to me that I didn't allow. This is not about you; it's about me. Besides, all that matters to me is that you're here with me," she said, embracing him tighter than necessary.

Taking her hand and leading her over to a huge apple tree on the far end of the garden, Johnathan breathed a sigh of relief. He lifted her up onto one of the tree's thick extended limbs, leveling them face-to-face. Lillian was pleased that their "the other night" conversation had so abruptly ended.

"You smell so sweet this morning . . . you nearly drove me crazy, first thing."

"Oh, stop!"

"No, I'm serious. You smelled like those wildflowers I used to pick for you and you'd wear 'em in your hair sometimes. Remember that? And you used to always call me Jumper?"

"Yeah, I do," Lillian whispered, fidgeting a bit to get out of his embrace.

"You'd always say, 'Jumper, you so crazy' . . . in that real high pitched tone," he said, pulling her closer.

She didn't have the heart to tell him that he was confusing her with someone else. She'd never called him anything but Johnathan; never cared much for wildflowers, either.

Johnathan reached out and embraced his wife as gently and lovingly as he could. Intoxicating. Comforting. It wasn't sexual; it was stillness. Johnathan inhaled deeply, still holding Lillian in his arms, and smiled.

The two stayed locked in their embrace, unaware of time, listening to each other breathe and enjoying the intermittent breeze. Johnathan lowered Lillian so that they could stretch out in the grass, gently kissing her forehead and then her hands. They sprawled themselves out in the shade of the tree with Lillian resting her head on Johnathan's chest. Deep in thought, the house phone rang several times before either heard it. It rang a few more times before either stirred to answer it. Lillian pulled herself up onto the porch, walking through the kitchen out of mere habit, and picked up Johnathan's cell phone from atop the microwave, en route to the house phone. She made it to the gossip bench at the base of the stairwell just as the answering machine message began. Slightly agitated by the sudden interruption of her inflated love-fest, Lillian answered abruptly, "Yes?"

"Cheers love! I was just about to disconnect," Grier yelled into the receiver.

"Grier! How's my girl? Is everything okay?" Lillian yelled back. Grier's cell phone connection was better than most, but still required the primitive yelling ritual in which they found themselves engaging.

"Everything's lovely, Mum. Work is good and Auntie Lindi and I are keeping good company . . ."

At the mention of her sister's name Lillian stopped listening. It had been a little more than twenty years since her reckless younger sister had made London her permanent home. Lillian imagined her off living some posh Euro-trash lifestyle. In her mind her sister was an aging socialite turned tart whose penchant for odd men and high living were legendary. Despite her age, Lindersyl was just shy of being a strumpet and no one was pleased with Grier's decision to move in with Lindersyl, least of all Lillian. Lillian turned her lips into a scowl at the thought of her sister. How a fifty-seven-year-old tart frolicking down a rugby field, drinking Bollinger (or as she called it, "Bolli") champagne by the crate, and shagging like an oversexed rabbit could care for Grier suitably, was unimaginable. But what could Lillian do? Grier was grown, even if she was impressionable and utterly biddable in her aunt's space. Lillian's feelings were still sensitive to Grier's move and she kept her phone calls to her daughter short and sweet, rarely mentioning Lindersyl.

Lillian heard her sister's influence over Grier in a Cockney accent and phrasing that kept her squinting for clarity.

"Mum, my office wants me back there for a few months to get their on-line interactive service up to European standard. I'm leaving Tuesday night and should arrive Monday morning," were the first words Lillian heard when she tuned back into the conversation.

"Grier, wait. You're coming here? Why didn't you phone sooner? I hardly have time to make up the house and plan a welcoming party. We need to do something with Brice and his parents, especially with the way you tore out of here."

"Are you listening? I am coming Monday and Lindi and I are staying at *her* place. I could give a bloody bollocks about Brice or his parents and I've made plans with friends I care to see. So just meet us at the Mosse Point airport at eleven the morning of the eighteenth, on the other side of international customs . . . Right?"

"Is that it then, Dear? I'm a limousine service now?"

"Oh, I suppose I've bruised your feelings? Well, sorry—okay?"

Arguing was futile.

Lillian relented, "Okay. So, you say your aunt's coming too. How is she?"

"She's fine. She's right here, hold on . . ."

"No, I don't care to speak with . . ."

"Yes?" Lindersyl's voice called out over the line, her tone quick and bothered.

"Yes what? I didn't ask to speak with you."

"Oh, Lillian, babe, just be at the bloody airport the eighteenth. I don't have time for your foolishness right now . . . I've got company over."

"When don't you have company over? Anyway, who asked you to get on the damned phone in the first place?"

"Hmm, you sound too tense to be gettin' any. I know Johnathan's not giving you *any*. Tell me, is the pool man still floating your boat?" Lindersyl asked, snickering before she could get the words out good.

Lillian removed the phone from her ear in surprise.

"I'll have you know Johnathan and I made love just a couple of days ago. In fact, we were contemplating going upstairs when Grier phoned!"

"Lillian, you were in bed with Johnathan but we both know you were the furthest thing from his mind."

"How dare you insinuate such a thing!"

"When I lie, you correct me!"

"Why do you feel like you have to do this to me Lindersyl? I am your sister and I've tried to do nothing but love you."

There was a pregnant pause in the conversation before Lindersyl answered, "You're right Lillian. I was just giving you the cheek, but it was bang out of order and I'm sorry. I love you too."

"I wish somebody would come love me . . ." an agitated voice called from the background.

There was a muffled silence, but Lillian could just make out her sister saying: "Olivus! Get back in the bathtub . . . . I said I'd be right back!"

Then returning to the phone Lindersyl grinned, "Gotta go Lillian, I left something soaking in the tub that needs my attention. Give my best to Eisendorff and Johnathan."

"I will," Lillian answered, replacing the receiver. She turned her attention to Johnathan's cell phone, doing an impromptu search of his incoming and outgoing calls.

Lillian promised to be on her best behavior when Lindersyl arrived. She walked through the foyer to the kitchen, scanning the obsessive number of +44 calls to England Johnathan had made and said a desperate, silent prayer. Once Lindersyl had been everything in the world to Lillian, but time and circumstance had driven them to jealousy and hatred. Lillian had enjoyed a subtle form of detracted togetherness with her ever since that kept her true feelings at bay and courted peace, but the peace could not last forever. And maybe, just maybe, this visit would finally bring things to a head.

"You sound like you're having a pretty good time in here . . ." Johnathan called out from outside the screen door.

Lillian stifled a crude comment and masked her hurt behind a hostess smile. "That was Grier, darling. She and Lindersyl are flying in on the eighteenth."

"Jesus H. Christ! Lindersyl's not setting foot in this house!"

"Of course she is. She's my sister. Besides," Lillian said tossing Johnathan a curt look, "I cannot think of a single thing to keep Lindersyl out of this house. In fact, I insist she and Grier stay here. I just spoke with her and I think this visit will be like no other . . ."

"Fine. Say that now, but if the two of you get to fightin' and pullin' each other's hair . . . any of that shit that happened last time, I'm not jumping in the middle. I swear before God, I'm calling the police!"

*If I could get another chance, another walk, another dance with him,
I'd play a song that would never, never end . . .*

Dance With My Father, Luther Vandross

grier
Full Gospel Temple Baptist Church &
Ladbrokes Mews Estate, SW London
May 15, 2001

Full Gospel Temple Baptist Church was pretty standard as Black British churches went—a few tongue talkers, fainters and shouters jumping in from time to time, but otherwise pretty subdued services. Grier had attended services at Olivus' church a few times, but found the mix of Caribbean, African and British cultures too pronounced, especially keeping ear to decipher the many thick accents and dialects. Grier had chosen Gospel Temple after months of searching because it had one thing that none of the others combined had: her aunt's ex-husband, Arthur Collier. Grier had heard Arthur's name mentioned only a few times and thought it fascinating that she could see, in the flesh, a part of her aunt's past. In fact, Grier had become almost obsessive about finding out her aunt's secrets, and there were plenty. It's like her grandmother used to say, "Lindersyl is an open book, you just have to know which page to turn to in order to find what you're looking for." Grier had found that to be pretty much the case. Her aunt hid nothing; she simply didn't divulge all. Grier found it odd that after three years of living together there had been no telephone calls, letters or visits from her aunt's children. There were no photos of these mysterious cousins whose names were never mentioned. In fact, it was unclear just how many children her aunt had or with whom she'd had them. No childhood crafts from summer camp or remembrances from vacations decorated the walls. There was only the occasional mention of Chasen and then only if Arthur Collier called and asked about him. Grier was determined to meet and befriend the man with whom her aunt had spent thirteen years of her life.

With a membership of more than five thousand, finding Arthur Collier at Gospel Temple had not been an easy task. He was usually at eight and eleven o'clock services in the morning and three o'clock services in the afternoon on Sundays. Sometimes he was on the Deacon's bench, other times, he was in the counting room above the sanctuary totaling tithes and gift offerings. But this morning, Grier had arrived in enough time to take a seat directly behind him. He didn't look at all like Olivus or any other man her aunt had been known to 'conspire' with. Grier craned her neck over and over again, trying to see around his massive build to any part of his face. His head was big, like a Rockweilers and clean-shaven, but he also looked to have sideburns coming out of his ears. Finally, when the call to greet came Arthur Collier spun around full to shake her hand. He froze, staring deep into her face and tilting his head so as to take her in. Grier stared back with equal intensity. His face was round with high set cheekbones and beady little eyes. He had a full beard and mustache, peppered with gray that surrounded paper-thin lips. Arthur Collier had a handsome smile, though he was not a particularly handsome man. Grier held his hand tightly, her heart beating in her ears. This was the moment she had been waiting for and yet she couldn't seem to get any of her words out.

"Hello young lady," he managed, extending his hands to her.

"Good morning Mr. Collier. God be with you."

"I'm sorry Darling, do I know you? You look very familiar, but I can't place you."

The widow Mrs. Macon, from the usher's board grabbed hold of Arthur's arm, just as Grier went to answer, turning him so as to detract his attention before Grier spoke.

"I'm Grier Holland. You know my Aunt Lindersyl."

Arthur pulled his arm from Mrs. Macon and placed both hands on Grier's shoulders. "Lindersyl's niece, huh? Well, don't that just beat all? C'mere sugar", he said, pulling her into a warm embrace. "You sure are the splitting image of Lindersyl, I'll tell you that. What brings you here? Is she alright?"

"Yes sir, she's fine. I've been coming to this church for a few months."

"No. Why you haven't made yourself known to me before now?"

"I didn't want to overstep myself. I mean, I wasn't sure how you and my aunt left things, so I didn't want to impose myself."

"No imposition at all! I'm still your uncle Arthur whether I'm divorced from Lindersyl or not. And the fact that you up in here instead of hung over or . . . doing what your aunt's done in the past," he gave a knowing look, "says you're a good girl."

"Yes sir."

"Tell you what," he said, patting her hands with his for punctuation, "after service, you come on downstairs and have supper with me and we can talk."

"Yes sir. I'll do just that," Grier smiled big, happy that she was finally going to find out something tangible about her aunt.

Grier returned to her seat. What a nice man, she thought, as she turned her body inward to allow a returning worshipper back their seat. She could barely focus on the sermon after it got started for trying to figure out what could have brought two such dissimilar people together as her aunt and Arthur Collier. By the way Arthur turned around in his seat to look at her and smile occasionally; he too, was having trouble focusing on the sermon. The widow Mrs. Macon didn't like it one bit. She had no clue who this young girl was who had so completely distracted Arthur's interest in her, but the widow was not about to stand for it. Mrs. Macon stared long and hard at Grier to cause her to turn and face her. When she did, Mrs. Macon rolled her eyes at her as hard as she could before joining in with the chorus' spirit-filled version of "No, Never Alone".

Grier sat unfazed by the widow, focusing her attention on how cordial Arthur Collier was and how happy she was that he had been nice to her. As promised, as soon as service ended, Arthur turned and grabbed Grier's hand, leading her through the sanctuary and into the dining hall. Arthur was a big man, well over six feet with a round belly and what her father called "preacher's feet"—flat and heavy. Every time he stepped forward it was like a giant was on the move and the people around him naturally parted to let him pass. His hands were big and fat, but soft. They reminded Grier of her grandfather's. Arthur had never been seen in the company of the fairer sex, including Lindersyl the entire time he had been at Gospel Temple, so the whispers and speculation came quick and mercilessly from the congregation when they saw him with Grier. Those who were old enough to remember Lindersyl were not lost on the young lady's resemblance to her. Perhaps she was a long, lost child of Lindersyl's and Arthur's. The horror! Either way, the members saw this as a bad omen and decided to make their suspicions known.

"Deacon Collier! I say, Deacon Collier," one of the trustees called from behind Arthur.

Arthur situated Grier at a table, pulling her chair out and then scooting her up under the table, before turning to acknowledge the trustee.

"Deacon Collier, who is this young girl you carryin' on with so?" asked Trustee Ray Clark, with five or six bodies ambling behind him in wait of an answer.

"Who talking about carrying on? Ain't no carrying on being done here. This here is my niece, Grier."

"Niece, huh? When you get a niece, seeing as you the only child your mama had?" Ray Clark persisted.

"Since you busybodies must know, this is my niece by marriage—remember Lindersyl? This is her niece."

"Awh, yeah. Now I know why you look so familiar and why the ladies in here are so up in arms. Sweetie, forgive us. We just a bit hard on the young girls staking out churches for pension checks," Ray Clark smiled, backing away.

"I understand, sir." Grier laughed to herself. These old geezers thought she was trying to stick Arthur Collier for his check. How disturbing!

Once they were seated in front of plates of fried fish, spare ribs, macaroni and cheese, yams, fried apples and collard greens, Arthur began to stare again at her. Noticing her shift uncomfortably in her seat, Arthur looked down at his plate.

"You have to forgive me for staring at you like this. I was married to your aunt for a long time and if I didn't know better I'd swear I was seated across from her right now instead of you. One thing is for sure, you may look like her, but you sure don't act like her. She would've ripped these folks a new booty hole—'scuse my language—if they had been questioning me in front of her like that," he said, laughing a laugh that was as much snorting as it was laughing.

"She can be a bit rough, that's for sure. But I guess it's good that the members here are trying to look out for you," Grier conceded.

"They trying to be nosey, Petal; that's all," he said with a wink.

"Uncle Arthur, you might not want to wink like that and hold my hand in front of them. I can handle myself, but they may try and make things difficult for you, especially the widow Mrs. Macon," she smiled.

"You look just like Lindersyl when you made that face. I ain't worried none about these people. Anyway, I need to tear into this cornbread before it gets cold. Sister Broadnax cornbread is beautiful long as it's hot, after that, it's like chewing wads of paper. You start finding these little knotted up pieces of meal in it" he smiled.

They both laughed a little to the annoyance of those watching.

"So, Uncle Arthur, how long were you and my aunt together?"

"Oh, near about twelve, thirteen years, so as I can recall it."

"That's a long time."

"Yes, yes. She was a good woman, just we weren't so good together is all. You know they call that unevenly yoked—she chanting to *her gods* and me worshipping God. We tried everything, but it wasn't meant to be."

"What was she like then?" Grier asked with true curiosity.

"Oh, about the same as now I would suppose. She like to dance and she kept enrolling us in these dance classes—Calypso, Flamenco, West African . . . she even had me learn to beat a Djembe drum so she could do this belly-dancing routine. Oh, she was something else. She's still very special to me. I keep hers and Chasen's pictures with me," Arthur said, reaching into his jacket pocket for his wallet.

"Can I see?" Grier said simultaneously.

"Sure, Petal," Arthur said, pulling his wallet from his pocket and retrieving two photos.

One was of Lindersyl by herself in a white tube dress and matching sunhat. Arthur was right; her aunt did look the same. She was giving "face", her facial features frozen dramatically. In the other photo, Lindersyl wore pink sarong and bikini top reclining on a lounge chair and draped by Chasen in pink Speedos. The Gottlieb genes were strong in Chasen, whose lips were reminiscent of both her mother and aunt's downward curl. It often gave the appearance of displeasure to onlookers, who when asking, "What's wrong?" were surprised to hear a pleasant, "Nothing".

Grier fingered the photos, totally mesmerized by the faces, so distinct and distant, yet familiar. How her aunt could not mention either of them or try to keep contact with them was disturbing to Grier. She pressed Arthur gently, "Uncle Arthur, it's too bad you guys couldn't work it out . . . well at least you had Chasen."

Arthur thought better of lying inside the church, so he arranged his response to say as much and as little as possible. "Chasen was a gift, you understand. He was a gift."

"Is he here somewhere too?"

"Oh, no Petal, Chasen wouldn't be caught dead up in here. You know, Chasen got to liking other boys and carrying on real feminine like. I still love him, but I don't love his ways."

"He's gay? Is that why he never comes to visit his mother?" Grier asked, hoping to connect a few dots.

"Lindersyl don't rightly care for too many folks. Chasen like to whip his neck around and such, which really bothers Lindersyl. She supposed to be his mother, so she'll smack him around good for being feisty with her. I don't know that that's all on account of him liking boys though. I think she just want everybody to do what she say when she say it. But I know you know that."

"Yes, sir, I do. I am sorry you sitting in this church all by yourself. Shame your own family's not with you."

"I can't say that at times it don't get to be lonely for me. I do miss Chasen an awful lot and I don't even mind so much the gay thing, but you see how these folk carry on with you? Can you imagine how that boy would act if they get to handling him like that?"

"He'd be just like his mother that's for sure!"

"Ain't it the truth. But now, I figure if God is the master designer, He knows what's in store for Chasen and me. If Chasen is going to end up here with me, then in time, he will. In the meantime, I just keep my seat and wait."

"Well, while you're waiting, how about every Sunday I take the seat right next to you. That way we can wait together."

"That's all right," he leaned forward and kissed Grier's cheek. "I'd like that. By the way, where you staying? You living on your own?"

"No sir. I stay with Aunt Lindersyl and her . . . boyfriend."

"Is it comfortable for you?"

"Comfortable enough. They are a bit . . . well, you know Aunt Lindersyl."

"Yes I do and that is why I asked you in the first place. Some things a nice young girl don't need to be exposed to. What your folks say about you living with Lindersyl?"

"Oh, you are so sweet, but really it's not so bad. I just have to keep out of Aunt Lindi's way sometimes. My parents didn't like it at first, but they are okay about it now. As a matter of fact, I am headed home to Connecticut for about a month next week and Aunt Lindersyl is coming with me."

Arthur looked up from his plate with a fish bone resting on his bottom lip. "Home? You think that's such a good idea taking Lindersyl home with you? I mean, she fled there with her life and after all the mess . . ."

Arthur realized what he was saying and who he was saying it to too late.

"What do you mean?"

"Nothing really. Just your mother and aunt fight like cats and dogs sometime."

"But you said *fled*. My aunt *fled* with her life."

"*Fled* is too strong a word. Nevermind me, Petal."

Grier did mind, but she decided to drop the conversation and started talking about holidays to keep the vein along Arthur Collier's temple from tap dancing across the table. Not only was something not right, something was very wrong; and if it were the last thing she did, Grier was going to find out just what it was. The two filled the remainder of their meal with nonsensical conversation and promised to make their breaking of bread a regular occurrence.

Grier left the church feeling lighter than air. She wanted to ask Lindersyl a million questions about Chase and a million more about Arthur Collier without letting on that she had met the right Deacon for herself. Grier liked Arthur too much to be forbidden to talk to him anymore, or to have some wickedness of him exposed to her. This was her uncle and he was normal, unlike so many and so much of what she'd known. She had to keep him to herself for just a while longer.

When she made it home and found Lindersyl pissy drunk, in utter frustration, Grier ransacked her bedroom, tossing clothes everywhere. She calmed down long enough to pull her aunt's listless body up from the second floor landing into the master bedroom. Grier grabbed the house-keys and walked out and around the square a few times to relax. Nothing made any sense and the more Grier tried to fit the pieces together, the more confused she became.

When she returned to the house an hour later, Olivus was home and Lindersyl was busy trying to sober herself. Grier entered her room in shock, having forgotten the number she'd done on it earlier. In a panicked hurry, Grier stuffed everything off the floors into the closets and chifferobe so her aunt wouldn't see the mess. Grier asked herself, why those people at the church stared so dispassionately at her. What had Lindersyl done up in that church or to Arthur to warrant the kind of reaction they gave when her name was mentioned? When Grier peered up from her thoughts, her aunt was staring back at her with brooding eyes.

"Do you know what your problem is? Do you?"

"No, but I suppose you are about to tell me," Grier replied, in no mood to have words with her aunt.

'You don't appreciate the things you have," Lindersyl said, pointing a chastising finger at Grier. "You enjoy wearing nice things and having people say 'Oh, aren't you lovely', but you handle your fine things like they're from some Eastend street market."

Grier didn't utter a word, just sat on the edge of her sleigh bed with her head in her hands. She was counting down until her aunt's tirade, such that it was, ended. Drinking was one thing; getting drunk was another. Being a mean drunk was something else entirely and her aunt was leaning more and more into being a cold, calculated *mean-spirited* drunk. Aunt Lindi was the "parental influence" she'd never had, and had guided the thirty-four-year-old through things she should have known, but were taught by neither nannies nor private schools. Grier had learned in the three years' time to sit still when her aunt spoke and be creatively inattentive, nodding when she heard a break or pause in the rant and then apologizing profusely afterwards. But tonight Grier was in no mood to deal with Aunt Moods-R-Us Lindi, who stood before her in Olivus' black shower wrap, which covered her breasts, but left much of the rest of her naked and exposed. Apparently Lindersyl had already spied the ransacked room before Grier came in and she was going on about how 'pretty is as pretty does'. Her aunt's home was immaculate. No dust, no soap scum, everything polished, pressed, ironed and manicured. And all done by her aunt with no "artificial support" from maids and the like.

For as much as Grier had idolized her aunt as a kid, she had grown to dislike her quite a bit since moving into her home. More to the point Grier was confused and marked by the extreme levels of her aunt's femininity, which were only mirrored by the roughness of a mannish disposition. She imagined that if given the mind to do so, her aunt could urinate at a man's urinal, standing. Grier had watched Lindersyl with a despised eye as she coyly leaned her body into men, laughing and pulling at their arms. Raw sexuality found no comfort in the mind of a virgin and was call for total embarrassment when poor Grier had to bear witness to it constantly. Though she certainly had the desire in her, Grier also had the fear. And that fear ran in all directions. Would she in time turn into her aunt, whisking about the flat nude, doing very private pawing in very public spaces? Would she ever coil to her desires as her aunt did, on a moment's impulse—giving her sagaciousness over to bawls of bliss? Grier's parents were always commenting on Lindersyl's inability to deny or restrain her sexual self, publicly or privately.

But for all the foolishness her aunt was kicking up these days, Grier remembered the aunt of her childhood who was at the ready to save her bacon with Lillian and Johnathan. Grier's mind wandered as Lindersyl admonished her, back to the day her aunt arrived at St. Benedict The Moor for a visit in fitted Yves Saint Laurent suit and crocodile pumps. Grier was having a difficult time adjusting to life away from home in her third boarding school in as many years. The school administrators' efforts to get her to eat and bathe had been futile. As a last resort, they called her parents. Johnathan didn't bother to come and Lillian was fit to be tied when she saw the state in which Grier had allowed herself to fall.

"What is your damned problem girl? You up here with these self-righteous white folk acting like you come from a bunch of monkeys. They're sitting in here talking to me like I haven't taught you basic hygiene. I am a Gottlieb Girl! We put the *fine* in refinement! Pull yourself together at once!" Lillian fumed.

Grier had stared at Lillian with the coldest stare she could muster, to which her mother responded with a smack across the face. Grier didn't cry a single tear, but wiped the slobber and blood from her lip and continued staring at Lillian. When the administrators saw this, they asked Lillian to leave and had Grier led to the infirmary bound in a makeshift straightjacket. Lillian left without protest and Grier determined that as soon as she was released from her shackles, she would kill herself. As she lay contemplating the method of her departure, Grier caught a whiff of her aunt's unmistakable Bvlgari fragrance. She could smell it long before she saw her aunt standing in the doorway of the infirmary with her hands covering her mouth. Lindersyl had the restraints removed from Grier and then sat on the floor, mucked with dust and dirt. Lindersyl never said a solitary word; she sat there and balled her eyes out, rocking. Grier forgot all about wanting to die when she saw how much pain her aunt was in. She sat next to her on the floor and cried and rocked alongside her. When they'd both had enough, they simply kissed and said good-bye. Grier heard and felt everything she needed to in her aunt's sobbing and the gentleness of their parting embrace. How beautiful and kind, like a fairy godmother Lindersyl had been to Grier. And now, how not!

When Grier drew back into the sound of her aunt's voice, it was as if a needle stuck in a record album's groove had forced itself to a point of clarity.
"Yes, ma'am," she said instinctively.
"Yes ma'am what? You obviously aren't listening to me."
"Why do you say that?" Grier asked with a slight panic.
"I just said, I hope your raggedy-ass daddy is in a civil mood . . ."
"Please, don't bring him up."
"Well, do you expect to dance around him your entire stay?"
"Can you cover up your body sometime?" Grier asked, annoyed that parts of her aunt's body were closer than necessary.
"What?"
"I mean your womanhood is like flying into my face along with your index finger. That is very rude!"
Her aunt eyed her suspiciously then walked from the room.

Grier sighed and fell back onto the bed when her aunt left the room. Why did she have to bring up her dad? Grier had done a fine job of relegating him to the far recesses of her mind. Her grandmother used to say, 'If you ignore anything long enough, it will go away'. How wrong that old woman had turned out to be about most of what she said. Tormenting people and situations never just went away; they had to be driven off or faced down. And since Grier could do neither with her father, she chose instead to avoid him. Johnathan Holland was as much a standard as an anomaly when it came to fatherhood. Almost from the day she came home from the hospital, her father had maintained a love / hate relationship with his first-born. Some days she was kissed and cuddled by him for hours on end. She loved the little songs and goofy stories he'd make up off the top of his head. Other days, without any provocation or warning, she was the target of his anger and aggression. He'd spank her uncontrollably and then burst into tears himself, crying aloud about what a horrible father he was. Her mother was hopeless in explaining it and helpless in stopping him. Then one winter when other family members, including her aunt witnessed a particularly bad whipping, Grier was shipped off to boarding school and her brother Eisendorff, who was no more than nine, was shipped out to military academy. Over the course of the next seven years, the family came together only for Christmas and summer breaks, and these were less family gatherings, than tense melodramas, playing out over opulent surroundings and gourmet food. Grier's resentment, though residual, had not died.

Lindersyl returned to Grier's bedroom in red Christmas boxer shorts and a Harrods t-shirt. She looked slightly perturbed, like she was about to bemoan Grier's asking her to cover up. She was carrying a bottle and a glass—a bad sign.

"What?" Grier asked exasperated.

Smirking more than smiling, her aunt rolled her eyes and pointed to the chifferobe across from the bed.

"Grier, take all of the clothes you've thrown on the floor and crammed into those drawers and fold each piece individually. Do not ball them up, do not roll them up—fold them. Neatly!" Lindi said.

"Yes ma'am," Grier moaned.

"Yes ma'am," Lindi mocked. She held up the bottle and glass as if offering Grier a taste. "I don't know who you think you're fooling with that goody-goody act."

"I don't know what you mean!"

"You like girls or something? I mean it's nothing wrong with it necessarily, except its sick when so many men are about . . ."

"Aunt Lindi, I am not a lesbian."

"Then why are there no men coming by here to see you? No late nights? No drunken fumbles in the dark? No wet sheets—and I *have* checked."

"You know, you're really doing my box in! You're disgusting! Look when I'm ready, I will. Not before!"

"Ready? I thought you and Brice . . . Ooooh."

"You are such a juvenile sometime! No, despite what you may have believed, we didn't. I wasn't ready."

"Ready for bleeding what? Grier, we're talking about sex for Pete's sake, not skydiving."

"I'm scared okay!"

"Scared of what?"

In a bid to end the third degree, Grier pulled her aunt close. "Scared of ending up like you. An old sexpot too stupid to know she's passed it! Now I've got plenty of work to do in addition to picking up all these damned clothes, so I'd thank you to let me get on with it".

Lindersyl looked at Grier and smiled. The child wasn't completely void of passion it seemed. She could have been a bitch about being tossed from a room in her own home, but couldn't bother. Her drink and her man were on her mind. In a parting thought, Lindersyl turned to Grier and said, "I may be getting up there in years, Darling, but I'm far from passed it."

Grier rolled her eyes, slamming the door hard behind her aunt.

"Make me sick", she screamed into a pillow.

What's new pussycat?
Whoa . . . whoa . . . whoa

What's New Pussycat? Tom Jones

eisendorff
Pacifica Restaurant, Coriander & Maine Avenue,
Mosse Point, Connecticut
May 17, 2001

"Where'd you get a name like Eisen?" a blonde with two layers too many foundation asked before taking a half sip of frothy margarita.

Eisendorff Holland smiled, exposing an enormous, but charming gap between his two front teeth. He paused, allowing the moment to simmer before answering. He was two seconds from ending their interview and sending this applicant on her merry way. Eisendorff and his practice partner Damascus Titan had been without an office assistant for nearly two weeks. They had seen plenty of applicants, but had starkly different styles and needs, and so couldn't decide who to hire. In final frustration, the two had narrowed the batch down to eight and Eisendorff was charged with deciding over dinner with each who the lucky hire would be. This one, one of Damascus' picks, was good on the eyes, but after two previous office interviews and a two-hour seminar on his psychotherapy practice, she had nothing more to ask him than, 'Where'd he get a name like Eisen?' Obviously, his partner, who'd pushed her through to the final round of interviews, was seeing something very different in her.

"Actually, it's Eisendorff and I got it from my mother. What I meant when I asked you if you had any questions, was questions pertaining to this practice," Eisen stared off, clanking the ice in his bourbon.
"Oh . . . uh, no, everything seems really lovely," the blonde responded.
"You are literally boring me to death. My head is beginning to hurt, which means that at any minute, I will have an aneurysm and keel over onto the floor. Please call the paramedics . . ." Eisen mumbled underbreath. He closed his eyes and rubbed his temples for a few minutes in silence. When she started yapping about something else, he only squinted enough to motion the server forward to freshen his bourbon and branch. The drink tasted awful to Eisen, but it took the edge off of a desperate night like this one. With the drink on its way and his guest finally picking up on his "I'm-sick-of-your-dumb-ass-questions" vibes, he figured he'd be rounding the corner to his home in just under fifteen minutes. From there it was straight to bed. Hell, he could shower in the morning.
In one day he'd seen eight patients—all with terribly traumatic and crippling emotional malaise or so they believed. Six were regulars he'd had for over five years and they seemed to show up more to socialize than be treated, the other two were new patients who had taken up quite of bit of

his time, since paper work had to be completed before he could do anything with them and he had to rely on his own poor knowledge of insurance form regulations. His clientele was pretty average; ten patients—three with father abandonment issues, two obsessive compulsives, two manic depressives and a lone paranoid-not-quite-schizophrenic, the two new patients had been referred by Connecticut Corrections and Mosse Point Social Services, both female abuse victims who'd killed their abusers.

Eisen was certain the bells he heard chiming were coming from inside his head and for a split second thought that maybe he *was* having an aneurysm. Instead it was only his mobile. He sat confused through the third ring, unsure if he should celebrate or bemoan his return from near-death.

Eisendorff's chest tightened when he saw the telephone display. The number was the familiar dial of his parents' house. It was either Johnathan or Lillian—he refused to call them mom and dad because they'd not been more than hosts to him growing up—landlords, overseers, but never parents. On occasion, and only to annoy his father, Eisendorff would call Johnathan, Pops.

"Who am I Fred Sanford?" his father would always wolf when called 'Pop', to which Eisen would simply grunt and continue talking. What could either of them want on a star-filled Wednesday night with no sign of trouble? To distress him, no doubt. Eisendorff considered not answering it, but caught his guest's confused look and decided for appearance's sake to engage them. If ever there were a more dysfunctional father-son relationship, this was it.

"Yeah" Eisendorff roared into the receiver.
"Eisen, come by the house on your way home. Wait, where are you?" his father asked hurriedly.
"What difference does it make?"
"It doesn't have to make a difference to you because it makes one to me—where are you?"
"I'm at the Pacifica Restaurant on Coriander."
"Okay, come by on your way home and bring some Goldenseal tea."
Goldenseal? Eisendorff mouthed to himself first, then "Where am I supposed to get Goldenseal tea at eight o'clock in the damned night Johnathan?"
"Try the health food store, Retard, and lower your voice. Don't forget who you're talking to."
"Why is it that you and Lillian sit around the house all day digging up your asses, but can't find time to go half a mile to the health food store? I'm

a businessman, not a flippin' errand boy. You two never need anything until after everything decent is closed!" Eisen protested.

"Just bring the god-damned tea!"

"Yes, sir . . ." Eisen fumed.

As with most of their telephone conversations, Eisendorff sat listening to the dial tone. When Johnathan had said all that he needed, he generally hung up the phone with no 'good-byes', no 'see ya laters'; just a dial tone. Eisen was so upset he went on autopilot, paying for the meal, finishing off his drink and tossing his trench coat over his shoulder. "Bastard!" Eisen mumbled, turning to see the startled applicant red-faced and pushed back from the table.

His tantrum continued, "Old bastard!" Eisen ranted. "One day I'ma rip him to shreds for this stuff! Treat me like I'm two years old . . ." he rambled, kicking at the revolving door. He handed the valet his ticket and waited impatiently. Eisen needed to vent his anger or he was sure to have one of his infamous nosebleeds.

Eisendorff Micheaux Holland enjoyed life to the fullest with the exceptional distaste of two things: his father Johnathan and his mother Lillian. A prominent psychotherapist, Eisendorff had reasonably assessed his own life and had prescribed frequent group sexual encounters, hard work and familial distance as the keys to his success.

Order had been the law of the land for Eisendorff since being sent off to military academy. It was just before his ninth birthday and he remembered crying for days on end when he found that no party, presents or friends were in the works. While he adapted quickly to being on his own, he never forgave his family for abandoning him. By fifteen, he quite preferred his own company; dining, studying and recreating, alone. With the exception of his sister and eccentric aunt Lindersyl, Eisen elected not to deal with family. Even when necessity dictated that he "take a woman", it was of a nameless, faceless variety and from within a domicile of pleasure—a den of swingers, who understood the no-commitment, no contact rule. Relationships were a distraction to common sense and true decency, Eisen had decided and so companionship was deemed unnecessary until aged. His personality could be summed up in a word: excesses. He cursed too much, drank too much, worked too much and utterly dismissed everything from his space that did not on some level make him feel good. To date, this included a son, Avery, who was three or four—he couldn't remember which, a list of clients that he was certain could never be treated for whatever emotional disruptions belayed their lives and a relationship with his parents that forced most spectators to tears.

Eisen circled his black Jaguar twice, looping and doing an about-face, as soon as the attendant jumped out. His fraternity tag holder was cracked and although he'd done it himself, he considered blaming the valet. He surveyed every inch of his vehicle before sitting down in the driver's seat and pushing the power button on the stereo system. Busta Rhymes exploded from the speakers with all levels at full blast. Eisen swiveled his body back around through the opened door with his hand drawn back. He grabbed the valet by the jacket collar and swung him around to face him.

"Put it back the way you found it," Eisen growled.

"Yes sir," the valet said, leaning in and readjusting the controls and volume.

"And put the CD back where I had it!"

"Yes sir, sorry about that. The Tom Jones song was on repeat and I just couldn't hear it again while I was circling for a space. It was like being trapped in a casino elevator in Las Vegas," the valet explained.

"Your job is to park this motherfucker, not to turn it into your own personal joy riding experience. I don't care if the song makes you collapse into convulsions, you don't mess with my system!"

"Yes sir."

"Don't let this shit happen again. Tonight, you forfeit your tip." he frowned, stuffing the bills back into his pocket.

Eisen pushed the Jag to 70mph, rounding Weager's Creek. He'd dropped the top and was enjoying his own suped up version of Tom Jones' What's New Pussycat. "Whoa . . . whoa . . . . whoa. What's new pussycat?" Eisen bellowed, off key, out of pitch and out of range. He decided to go home. Fuck Johnathan. He was tired and wanted to rest, besides, he was a grown man and well from beneath his father's lashes. He'd have to endure a bunch of crap from him later, but well, Johnathan and Lillian both were to him now, what he was to them as a child—a hindrance. And just as he'd been dismissed from their lives and made to feel like he was a burden, so they did now.

Eisendorff walked through the lobby of Koulanger Square Condominiums taking two steps forward and half a step backward, slightly discombobulated from the drinks. The desk attendant looked at him with disdain. He was an older Black man, easily pass seventy, with his white hair long enough to touch the collar of his navy uniform blazer. On rare occasion Mr. Sammy spoke back when Eisendorff bothered to acknowledge him. More often Eisendorff was regarded as an embarrassment. Eisen overheard Mr. Sammy, swollen with anger, tell someone that in his day, Black folk didn't address their elders with the same cavalier rudeness as whites. It was clear that this little rich Black boy had come across some money and thought he was white. *Under the illusion of inclusion*, Mr. Sammy would call it. Had a half a million-dollar condo, a luxury car, and some education. Next, he'd be sporting some trashy white girl on his arm.

Eisen had stood, shocked by Mr. Sammy's relentless talk of the 'coloreds' living in the building. There were only five African-Americans in the entire five-hundred unit complex which Mr. Sammy described as; a Cicely Tyson-type sister married to a Jewish fellow, two 'studs'—Black lesbians who called themselves a couple, an 8-year-old African boy adopted by some white liberals with nothing better to do in Bulawayo Zimbabwe, and Eisendorff. 'Cicely Tyson' was always looking at him like a Smithsonian artifact, the lesbians ignored him and the little boy was too young and 'foreign' to matter much one way or the other. Then there was this damned fool, Eisendorff, who was too smart to believe in God and too weak to believe in himself. Mr. Sammy thought Satan had bred them all.

Eisendorff pulled the mail from his mail slot, leaning heavily against the wall to steady himself. Noting how messed up he was, Eisendorff inwardly acknowledged that he probably shouldn't have driven. He waved to his elder, "Hey Mr. Sammy."

"Hey yourself Black boy."

"Mr. Sammy, why you always giving me a hard time?" Eisen asked for mere amusement.

"My name, Black boy is Mr. Addison Thornbush. Not no damned Sammy!"

"Well, why you got people calling you Sammy?"

"I ain't got *nobody* calling me nothing Black boy! White folks will call you what they want. I been here for thirty years and the owner called me that 'cuz that's what all niggers was called! Times changed, but not enough for anyone to call me by my right name."

"You the damned fool! If your name is Mr. Addison Thornbush then that's what you need to tell people to call you! I have been here six years and everyone calls you *Mr. Sammy* and your nametag says *Sammy*. What then, was I to call you but *Mr. Sammy*?"

"You young people, Black boy, just don't get it. Your name is all you got in this world."

"No, Mr. Thornbush, I 'spec I don't get it, especially since you know my name is Eisendorff Holland and that I'm a grown damned man. But you insist on calling me Black boy. Good night Mr. Thornbush," Eisendorff said, unlocking the elevator and pushing the 'up' button. When the elevator doors opened, he gave a passing glance to his elder, who was deep in thought. Mr. Thornbush was a ridiculous old man and even more aggravating than the two other dim-witted old people he was charged with dealing with, his parents. And just like when Johnathan and Lillian, started talking 'sideways' at him, Mr. Thornbush had upset Eisendorff. Mr. Thornbush made Eisen feel like he didn't have a full grasp of the world around him, when in Eisendorff's estimation, his two degrees, his intellectual agility and his success as a Black man in a cruel white world, proved otherwise. He got that crap from Johnathan all the time, the white man this, and the white man that. Eisen figured, if the white man spent the majority of his time plotting on brothers, then the brother, as broke, inept, and socially crippled as he was, was truly the master of all earthly things. And if that was truly the case, Eisen reasoned, there was no sense concerning himself with white angst, anger or animosity. Rationale needn't be applied to psychosis.

Eisen thought better of going back down to the lobby and cursing Mr. Thornbush out as he exited the elevator on the fourth floor and was whipped in the face by the stench of cleaning disinfectants. The cleaners had doused the walls and rugs with a sanitizer that removed all traces of heavy traffic and pet odors but smelled of industrial ammonia and roses. Eisen held the wall, steadying himself and stifling a sneeze to the end of the corridor. After tossing his keys on the dining room table and removing his shoes, Eisen fell asleep across the foot of his bed. The combination of his exhaustion and the four bourbon and branches had produced a good, coma-like sleep that left him more refreshed than hung over the next morning.

After releasing what must have been a small pond of bourbon pee, Eisen noticed the message button flashing "full" on the answering machine.

"When I see you, I'm gonna whip your little black ass!" It was Johnathan. And boy, was he upset! Eisen leaned back in his recliner and laughed. He wondered what Johnathan's face looked like while he was cursing him out. Was that vein across his forehead about to burst at the seams? Were his eyes bulging in anger? Eisen's side began to cramp, as his laughter became uncontrollable. He was up to the sixth message and it was still just Johnathan's threatenous litany. Eisen gasped for air and tucked his head between his legs as the twelfth message played. But by the time the fifteenth message had played, Eisen's flushed face was not as humored. Johnathan really was furious. Maybe he should've taken him the Goldenseal after all.

Baby you'll find, there's only one love—yours and mine
I've got so much love . . .

You Are, Lionel Richie

olivus tarquin blackstock
Ollie's Nightclub, Southeast London
May 17, 2001

Olivus brushed the crumbs of a roast beef and tomato sandwich from the creases of his gabardine pants and closed the reports ledger for the club. Money was good. Better than he could have predicted. Even this night, a Wednesday, the club was packed to capacity. Though he should have been happy—mixing and mingling freely with the patrons—he didn't feel up to it. He pushed himself back from his desk and moved to a gigantic window that overlooked the dance floor. Once upon a time, *this* had been the dream for the thirty-year-old musician. He was self-employed, a successful business owner, he was rolling in pounds, and he owned a flat in one of the most prestigious neighborhoods in London. Olivus thought of his girlfriend, his woman actually. She was hardly a child or some fresh through puberty femme. Lindersyl. His Lindersyl. Olivus wondered if God could be such a comic genius as to give him what he'd always wanted, knowing full well he couldn't handle it. He'd prayed for a woman like Lindersyl, sincerely, earnestly, honestly. He wanted to commit to one woman and one woman only. After fasting forty days and having some strong heart to hearts with the Lord, Lindersyl came to him. She had long-turned her back on God, though she was smart enough not to flat out deny Him. She still prayed over her food, and had bent easily to his chucking out her Buddhist altar. "This is one thing I will not stomach in a house I enter," Olivus had told her. He could even hear her sobbing mournful tears when he did his Sunday morning devotionals and those old spirituals began filling her home. He laughed to himself. Loving Lindersyl was now his only ambition and returning her to God was his purpose. But like Samson under Delilah's spell, Lindersyl's beauty and that evil temptress inside of her kept Olivus' mind slightly removed from the task at hand. Did that make him a fool or a wise man? The club manager, Moye, a loud-spoken Cameroonian walked in, interrupting Olivus' contemplation.

With a heavy accent that was as much Cockney as it was African, Moye yelled, "Oy, mate! Got some pretty lasses in tonight. Going down?"

Moye had the annoying habit of being always a decibel above normal and smacking the backs of people he spoke with to emphasize his points. The shouting wasn't so bad given the nightclub's sound system, but Olivus did everything he could to avoid the back smacks, to no avail.

"Nuffin' to mi fancy."

"Your Lindersyl's got juju on you. Ain't natural the way you turn away from punanny."

"Sod off, Moye!" Olivus yelled, having officially reached his tolerance for Moye's suspicion of Lindersyl.

"Okay, sorry. Sorry. But what you see in that woman? Seriously. What she got so special?"

Olivus poured himself a glass of water and pointed to a seat for Moye. They both sat in silence for a moment.

"Well?" Moye asked, slapping Olivus' back.

Olivus licked his lips and then wiped them with the back of his hand. "She's beautiful, but you know that. She's sexy and not just in a physical way. It's like she's ultra feminine at times," Olivus said, unable to hide his affinity for her.

"She a woman, man! She supposed to be feminine!" Moye howled, unconvinced.

"How many women you know that are really feminine? Don't spit. Don't curse, don't act jealous and vindictive?"

"That's the mark of most women, ain't it? The jealousy?"

"I know she's got it in her, but not with me. She makes me happy. Like the other day; I got to my flat and she was there. She had a hot bath waiting for me. Afterward, she scrubbed the husk off my feet and cut my toenails. She put my dinner on the table and kissed me good and plenty, then left for a late dinner meeting," Olivus smiled.

"She cheating on you. She wasn't at no meeting. Bet she did that so you wouldn't suspect her."

"Men are stupid."

"Why you say that?"

"'Cuz, I thought the same thing. Couldn't enjoy that meal—Shepherd's Pie, from scratch—trying to remember where she said she was going. Raced out and hid in the lobby of the hotel she was at. Sure 'nuff, she was with a bunch of butt-ugly old women."

"Just 'cuz you didn't catch her that time don't mean she ain't up to something."

"Moye, man, why you say that?"

"She too good to be true! Besides, there has to be a reason your Mum doesn't fancy her"

"You leave my Mum out of it. My father started running around on her while on their honeymoon. She's the last woman in the world to give advice to me on women. So there!"

"Maybe. But how old *is* your lass?"

"Watch it!"

"I mean, don't you want no pickney?"

"Hell no! Never been fond of kids. Too much of a headache."

"What happens if you change your mind a few years from now? She'll be earning a pension by then."

"She's got kids older than me. If I want to play daddy some day I'll look after her grands."

"Don't care what you say Olivus, she working juju or she a witch. By the way, me Mother say she ain't seen you at Bible Study in a few weeks and she t'ink you been turned into a zombie," Moye laughed.

"Man, get your ass outta here!" Olivus said laughing.

"Yeah, alright. I got work to do anyway," he laughed, slapping Olivus hard across the back. "You finished with the books?"

"Yeah, here. Everything looks good and seeing that you don't need me here tonight, I'ma go on home," he tossed the ledger to Moye. Lindersyl and Grier were leaving in the morning and he wanted to be as near to her as possible until she left.

Moye shook his head and laughed. "She got you deep under manners Olivus. Tell Ubu Lindersyl I say 'hello'".

Olivus tossed Moye a passing nod on his way out the door. He could care less what Moye had to say about Lindersyl, especially since Moye's wife and their eight children looked like the starting line-up for Manchester United.

Olivus moved quickly to his Audi parked in back of the club. Talking about Lindersyl had made him hot and bothered. Welled up with desire that was latent, he could just make it to her home before it became urgent. Olivus took the back stairs of the club to his car. His friends, ex-lovers included, thought like Moye, but Olivus couldn't explain his desire for Lindersyl—it just was. Like being able to blink or swallow, his love for her was natural, instinctive. He knew where to touch her. He knew how to hold her. He never missed a beat and she was precisely syncopated to his nuances. They had their own rhythm. Olivus felt he could not live without her and at times in the past had shown he could be wild with jealousy.

Olivus was jealous of Lindersyl's ex-husband Arthur, until he met him. He was a big, bald-headed guy, who looked the part of church elder. How Arthur had got down with his Lindersyl was a mystery. Then too, Lindersyl had a perverse sense of taste at times. Olivus figured she enjoyed making the church guy squirm and run from her. He saw the way the guy still looked at her with that longing in his eyes and felt sorry for him. Lindersyl had obviously turned him out. That day when he popped by Lindersyl's unannounced, the deacon had found Olivus and Lindersyl steaming up the windows of his classic '67

Corvette. She got out bare-assed, wearing £1500 diamond encrusted stilettos, and introduced the two before inviting Arthur inside.

Arthur wiped constantly at little rivers of spittle that kept escaping the corners of his mouth, but Lindersyl paid him no mind. And when Arthur Collier told her that their son Chasen was missing, she had waved him off, saying "He's grown, Art. Let him be", before showing Arthur back to the driveway. "What a woman!" Olivus had said to himself. Lindersyl was bouncing up and down on him before Arthur pulled away. At that exact moment, all of the girls Olivus had dated looked like little more than, well, girls. He had found himself a real, bonafide woman, a lady.

Olivus' father, Martin, constantly reminded him how fortunate he was to be with Lindersyl. His mother, Miriam, was less excited, calling Lindersyl an old slag. Miriam was an old-school Trinidadian, who had zero tolerance for designing older women. She forbade Olivus to see Lindersyl. When he refused to stop seeing her, Miriam barred Olivus from the family home. Olivus had not seen his mother in more than a year, though his father dropped by the club occasionally to check on him.

The women at the club too, treated Olivus with marked difference. Where he used to be open to having casual relationships with them for as little as VIP access, they all wanted some sort of commitment once Lindersyl came into his life. Game recognized game. And they recognized that if Lindersyl's reputation was even half of what it was rumored to be, Olivus would be off-radar until she bored of him. That meant no free drinks, no VIP access, no holidays to Trinidad, no nothing. Lindersyl did not frequent Ollie's once they began dating seriously, and never questioned his relationship with any female with whom they came in contact.

And it was so.

It was just after ten when Olivus reached the Ladbrokes area. He parked his car at the back entrance near the kitchen. The house was dark and he stopped abruptly, adjusting his eyes.

Olivus closed his eyes for a moment, there against the wall, imagining Lindersyl's lips soft and warm against his neck. That spot behind his ear that she found each and every time. He ran his hand down his erection and jogged the two flights up the stair.

Lindersyl's bedroom doors were open. The sheer drapes gave a hypnotizing blue glow to the room. It bounced off Lindi's naked torso. He watched the wind blow against the curtains, shifting the lights, fluttering over her body. She had configured her body in sleep with one arm resting beneath her head, her lower half twisted toward the window, away from him. He undressed, sweat already running down his chest and back. Olivus yanked the covers back, exposing Lindersyl's full nakedness. Stark, stunning. She moved only slightly from the breeze caused by the covers. Olivus watched her sleeping and thought how beautiful it would be to enter her dream and make love to her without waking her. He laid his body atop hers, rubbing his penis gently up and down her thighs. When she sighed her pleasure, Olivus' passion increased. Though she never opened her eyes, she loved him back, wrapping her legs around his waist. Still fast asleep, Lindersyl reached a very audible climax, latching on to Olivus' neck, at that exact spot, causing him an immense wave of pleasure.

Olivus did a body check. His heart was racing, but he was alright. He turned to face Lindersyl, wanting to please her all the more. Her breath, smelling of Bollinger champagne and sick, smacked him in the face. He squeezed her waist and kissed her shoulder.

"Jumper, baby. Put out the fire," she whispered.

Olivus sat up, pulling his arms sharply from around her. "Lindersyl!" he yelled.

She squinted to focus, her eyes red and puffy.

"Olivus? What's wrong?"

"Who the frick is Jumper?"

"What?"

"You just called me Jumper."

"Did I? I must've been dreaming. What did I say?"

"You cheating on me?" he blurted out. It was less a question than an accusation.

"Of course not. I used to know someone named Jumper is all. I must have been dreaming about him."

Lindersyl sat up full in the bed and felt the wet spot beneath her. "Olivus, what's been going on in here?"

"Well, see, what had happened, right, was that we were making love . . ." he said sheepishly.

"What had happened? You were molesting me in my sleep weren't you?"

Olivus laughed nervously, realizing Lindersyl may have considered his lovemaking an act of force. "Lindersyl, c'mon. We were making love to each other! Now I'm asking you again who is Jumper and why was he in this bed with us?"

"An old friend, Olivus."

"An old lover?"

"Don't torture yourself. Jumper was someone dear to me once, but I do not recall dreaming anything about him. What exactly did I say?"

"You said for Jumper to put the fire out."

Grier walked by the doorway frowning, before returning to her room.

"That's it then. Olivus, Jumper and I used to live together about forty years ago. We had a fireplace . . ."

"Did you shag him?"

"Olivus, go to bed! And the next time you decide to ravage me, wake me first. I have no more control over my dreams than you have over yours!" she said before turning over.

Olivus pulled the covers back up over them both. He was only slightly convinced of her answer. Maybe Moye was right when he said that Lindersyl had an unnatural hold on him. Lindersyl turned to look at him with a peculiar look on her face. He braced for a cursing out, when instead, she pulled her body to his.

"What?" he asked, trying to hide his hurt feelings.

"Pervert, was it good?"

"Shit yeah." Olivus laughed, glad that there would be loving and not fighting between them, "You want some more?"

"Noooo. I've got an early flight Olivus. You know that."

"He frowned, poking out his bottom lip. He knew she could not resist him.

"Okay. Wake me early and I'll give you a bon voyage surprise," she laughed, drifting back off to sleep.

Olivus smiled, squeezing her tightly to himself. He squeezed so tightly that his arms became sore and began to lock. "Moye was right! Ubu Lindersyl, you wicked, evil temptress . . . I love you," Olivus whispered, tightening his grip a bit more.

Chapter Two
Who's Loving Whom?

*Lord I hear of showers of blessings thou art scattering full and free,
Showers the thirsty souls refreshing, let some drops now fall on me . . .*

Even Me, Yolanda Adams

lindersyl and olivus
London's Gatwick Airport,
First-Class Guest Lounge
May 18, 2001

London's Gatwick Airport was usually a breeze for Lindersyl, but this particular morning, it was presenting itself as a major pain in her ass. She was hung over. From behind gigantic Bvlgari shades, Lindersyl kept her eyelids at a slitted half-mast and silently wished the world away. How in all hell had she been convinced to take this trip? It had been years since she'd set foot on American soil and even longer since she'd been back to Gottlieb Grove. Home. Home? Could she ever call it that again?

Like an addict fresh out of rehab, Lindersyl wondered how long it would take before she broke down under the weight of being home. Lindersyl's mother had forced her to recite a Shakespearean sonnet that for some reason kept popping into her mind this morning. She'd stood in the bathroom mirror, doing her body inspection and reciting it—line for line the way her mother had instructed in her youth. "Uhm, and without notes" Lindersyl had begun,

> *They that have power to hurt, and will do none,*
> *That do not do the thing they most do show,*
> *Who, moving others, are themselves as stone,*
> *Unmoved, cold, and to temptation slow;*
> *They rightly do inherit heaven's graces,*
> *And husband nature's riches from expense;*
> *They are the lords and owners of their faces,*
> *Others, but stewards of their excellence.*
> *The summer's flower is to the summer sweet,*
> *Though to itself, it only live and die,*
> *But if that flower with base infection meet,*
> *The basest weed outbraves his dignity:*
> *For sweetest things turn sourest by their deeds;*
> *Lilies that fester, smell far worse than weeds.*

It was the last two lines that haunted and chilled Lindersyl then as now. *Sweet things turn sour by their deeds; Lilies that fester smell far worse than weeds.* And how she had festered. And how tired Lindersyl had become of keeping secrets, telling lies, holding unsavory counsel and forging unhealthy alliances. She wanted so bad to tell the truth—and the truth was harpooning its way out, prying its way from jaws that had once been locked tight and leaking from glances no longer blurred by an insane love. Lindersyl had hinted, had insinuated, had done everything but announce to Grier who she was. Wanting so badly for the child's curiosity to pique just enough to ask a single question, which would lead to another and another, until her confession could be made. But it had not come. And now she was about to head back into the belly of the beast. Lindersyl would have to look into Johnathan's eyes and embrace him with love even though she hated him. Lindersyl would have to anchor her emotions to withstand being called every kind of dirty, lowlife whore Johnathan could think up from behind his masked passion and desire.

Lindersyl understood fully that this was a process she had to endure so as not to alarm Johnathan or Lillian. She wanted to ask permission from them to tell the truth because, it was a shared deception. There were repercussions for them all and Johnathan and Lillian had more to lose than she did. And where Lindersyl could sidestep Johnathan, Lillian was another story entirely. They lived like chess pieces, maneuvering and counter-maneuvering each other. Lillian could see her intent a mile away and block everything if she chose. Lindersyl would have to remember the love she and Lillian once had in order to love her now when it only took one indiscretion, utterance or motion to turn Lillian against her. Lindersyl would have to put her own needs aside for the good of the whole—or beg the others, convince them, that she had held up and held on long enough and now deserved some happiness too.

"Tea?" Olivus offered from a few seats down.

"Nope," Lindersyl answered quickly, turning her head and her attention away from him like a camera flash. She'd asked for space to prepare for this trip, but he had insisted on making himself a shadow against her.

Grier was in as truculent a mood as she was and had barely spoken in Lindersyl's direction since they'd left the house. She sat on the opposite row of seats from the others, flipping through Noir magazine, peering up at Lindersyl and Olivus only occasionally and then with noticeable disdain. Lindersyl's nerves were getting the better of her and the Bollinger was only making it worse. That she had mentioned Jumper by name in her sleep was reason enough to panic, but she couldn't help but think it was a sign not to go home at all and to let things rest as they had. Should she cancel out? Grier would be disappointed, but so what?

Olivus could see Lindersyl's eyes blinking behind those damned glasses. She wasn't fooling him one darned bit. In the pit of his stomach his muscles pinched together. Something was wrong and he only had an hour to confront Lindersyl, get it out in the open and then send her off to the States. He didn't want to lose her. What if she didn't come back? Olivus knew who Jumper was. He also knew what putting out that fire meant. Not because Lindersyl wanted him to know or because she had told him. More exactly, she'd shown him. When he went to wake her for their pre-dawn snogging, she picked up with Jumper where she'd left off. Instead of the fire-pistol, Lindersyl was gentle and loving. She was filled with emotion and cried satisfied, joyful tears while she kissed Olivus.

When he pulled away from her sharply, Lindersyl finally said Jumper's given name. She said Johnathan. Johnathan. Maybe that's why Lindersyl couldn't go home. She'd shagged her sister's husband. That's bad, Olivus surmised, but not so as to warrant their break up. No matter what, he would not give up Lindersyl. Not to Jumper, Johnathan or anyone else.

Beautiful, naive, totally devoted Olivus. Lindersyl cracked a smile thinking of how problematic he'd been at the start of their relationship. And how she couldn't imagine being without him now. Olivus was a part of Lindersyl's "settling in" phase, following her divorce from Arthur Collier. Even while married, she'd endured a barrage of indecent proposals from saggy-bummed Englishmen. America had put her on the wrong side of love one too many times and as far as she was concerned, men were worthless to the core and good for not much more than a quick romp. Her ex-husband had been a casual friend who wooed her into thinking he was different. He, too, was found to be terribly disloyal to her when she was fully clothed. Once divorced, she gave Arthur full custody of their son, Chasen and began sampling the men of Europe like a connoisseur of life. European men were classical in many respects: they held open doors, they carried packages, they always showed up at a lady's door with something in hand—flowers, candies, fruit—something. Lindersyl blossomed in their attentiveness and took easily to dating two or three men at a time. Though it was hard on the men's egos, she couldn't seem to help herself. After all, it was the closeness she craved, the touch and caress of love. Olivus was an under-celebrated musician, born and reared in Tottenham, England, who owned one of the hottest jazz spots in East London. His mother was Trinidadian, his father a British MP. He had a face and complexion that spoke to his heritage: thick wavy hair, nougat skin tone, full lips and a sharp pinched nose.

Lindersyl and Olivus had started out really cavalier about their relationship; it was just sex. That is, until the day Olivus decided to end the relationship, because he "refused to stand in cue behind any other bloke over some arse". When Lindi didn't protest through sobs and swears, Olivus changed his mind and took to staking out her estate harassing any man in sight. Olivus wasn't a big man, but what he lacked in physical size and strength, he made up for in cunningness. He'd punch a man in the throat rather than risk getting himself hurt in a head to head bout. And he was a fighter. Against herself, Lindersyl found that she fancied almost everything about Olivus, particularly that fighting streak. She loved his walk, a confident swagger, his head for business, his musical artistry, his way.

The stakeouts were more flattering than annoying after a while.

Nudging forty, (Lindersyl had never bothered to ask specifically his age) Olivus had a tremendous grasp of life and reason, and had easily become a semi-permanent fixture at Lindersyl's estate. They'd met at his jazz club—Ollie's—he on the bandstand checking her out and she on the dance floor, making sure he had something to check. It was just after her cosmetic lift and Lindi had plenty to prove. She wore a sheer black dress with strategically placed appliqué and the dress clung to her every curve as she perspired. As her body jiggled and dipped to Arturo Sandoval's *Candela (Yo Si Como Candela) / Quimbombo*, half the men in the room walked to the dance floor to join her. Olivus, not to be outdone, hurriedly attached a reed to his horn. He didn't want to be a part of her fan club; he wanted her attention, undivided and unrestricted in a crowd of hundreds.

"Good evening ladies and gentlemen, for those of you who don't know me, I am Olivus Blackstock, owner of this fine establishment, and I'd like to welcome you all here tonight. As a rare treat . . . well, I'm gonna play a little something for you tonight. I've been writing this piece for two years, and there's been something missing. But tonight . . . I found that missing component. I was inspired by something . . . someone. Someone so mesmerizing, that, well, I had a moment of eureka! Pardon me, young lady", he stretched out his hand to Lindi. "What's your name?"

"Lindersyl."

"Lin—durrrrrr-seeeel" he droned out.

"Oooh, you do that so well . . ." Lindersyl smiled. She thought he was corny, but enjoyed the spotlight and attention.

"Lindersyl, would you do me the honor of joining me up here on the bandstand." he asked, caressing her hand and guiding her up the stairs to the stage.

"Not at all, Olivus, is it?"

"Yeah."

The stage light shone luminously through Lindersyl's dress, causing every male mouth in the club to pop open. Boy, was she a beauty! Olivus pulled a stool forward for her, but she refused.

"If you blow as good as I think you do . . . I won't need that" she smiled.

"Well, on that, fine people, this song is titled, Sheer . . . Lindersyl"

With that he blew out the sultriest notes Lindersyl had ever heard. She couldn't keep still. He slowly hypnotized her with his riffs, and she, enjoying every minute of it, began dancing about the stage alongside him, like a snake being charmed from a basket. Lindersyl nestled her body against his from behind, sliding her long legs in between his. She could hear his heartbeat quicken as she leaned her head against his back. He jerked up and down to pin point his notes, and she with him. They were one, and only the yells from the audience kept them from "going public". One man yelled from the crowd, "The girl beating poor Ollie without a stick!"

Neither waited for the applause from the audience to die down before they walked off the bandstand. They were off the stage and headed for Olivus' flat within minutes.

Olivus was one of the more competent lovers she'd had, and in one fluid motion, Lindersyl found herself pinned to a wall. In turn, he took her breath from her lungs, and all sensibility from her mind. That night Nottinghamshire police were dispatched twice to his flat under reports that a woman could be heard screaming 'you're killing me' at the top of her lungs. On neither occasion was it Lindi, but Olivus who had done the screaming. Lindersyl loved it! And she began to love him.

That had been almost three years ago, and now, on any given day Olivus could be found traipsing about Lindi's home as if it were his own. He paid the utilities and made minor repairs to the house without any persuasion and even cooked the odd meal. Because she'd allowed a larger public relations conglomerate to buy out her own, Lindersyl pretty much sat back, collected checks and attended openings, galas, and premieres for a living. It was an extremely comfortable lifestyle, and aside from fighting an ongoing battle with depression, (said alcohol), Lindersyl was living the life. Lindersyl was happier romantically than she'd been in decades and a lot of it she owed to Olivus' love and patience. She could barely imagine her life without him. Of course, she wasn't prepared to admit that to him just yet.

The temperature in the airport was above sixty, but to Lindersyl felt like twenty below. She shifted her weight from one hip to the other and rocked from side to side to fight off the chills. She looked at Olivus sitting confidently in black gabardine pants and butterscotch cashmere sweater, and tried to pretend he wasn't there. While he looked immaculate, he was doing an ugly job of assessing her. She could feel his eyes on her even when she could not see his tasty self. Though she was sure Olivus was supposed to have gone back to work the night before, she'd awakened to the smell of frying swine and eggs. She'd felt sick right off, but went through the motions of eating to save his feelings. When she hurried up the stairs to vomit, she thought she'd escaped his scrutiny. Instead, he'd escorted her from the house into the car and down the turnpike, casting his eyes upon and then away from her, as if waiting for her to confess.

"Baby, you alright?" Olivus asked, running a finger across her cheek.

"Yep," she turned her face at his touch.

"You've been drinking—"

"Olivus, go over there and talk to Grier or something," she turned a shoulder to him and leaned her head against the window.

"I think we need to talk."

"No, you need to leave me alone! I want to be left alone," she said just a bit too loud. Grier and a few others turned to see what the commotion was.

"What is the matter with you woman?" he asked between clinched teeth, his patience worn thin.

Lindersyl took the strap of her handbag and wrapped it around her hand tucking the bag under her arm. Without looking back, she stood up and walked swiftly down the aisle to the ladies room. Once inside, she plopped herself atop a baby changing table and began crying. It was a loud, mournful-type sound that enveloped the entire bathroom. She didn't care who heard her or what they thought, until she felt a pair of arms pull her in. It was Olivus.

"Olivus, what are you doing in here? This is the 'Ladies'! Do you want to get arrested?"

"I'm worried about you, Love . . . what's wrong?"

"Everything and nothing." she caved.

"Y'know, you're gonna have to talk this thing out with your family while you're there . . ."

"What thing is that Olivus?" she asked, suspiciously, not willing to divulge any more than was necessary.

"Lindersyl, don't play games with me! Now whatever else we do or don't, we don't lie to one another. You made love to Jumper, pardon me, Johnathan this morning, not to me. Is this your sister's Johnathan?"

"He is *not* my sister's Johnathan—he is mine!" she said sharply, before lowering her voice. "Was . . . he *was* my Johnathan."

Olivus held his breath a few seconds before asking, "You love him then?"

"It's not about love, Olivus. Not anymore. There was a time when Johnathan was all I had in this world. We went through a lot."

"God should have been all you had in this world, Lindersyl, not some man."

"Don't toss God into the mix! *God* and I fell out because of him, and look where I am. I guess God was right."

"How did your sister end up with your man?" Olivus asked, with one eyebrow raised, backing away from her. He had never heard anyone hold such a grudge against God. He was shocked by the bitterness in her voice, and had resisted an urge to smack her across the mouth.

"I let my mother and sister convince me that Johnathan deserved better than me; my sister being better."

"That's rather funky! But how?"

Lindersyl did not consider for a moment that she was in a public toilet before she started talking, "I let him go by pretending I never had him. Johnathan let me go by pretending Lillian was me. And my sister pretends what she did was for my own good. So now, as long as we each hold up our end of the pretense, all is well."

"How does she look you in the face?"

"Hardly. With me here, and she across the Atlantic, there are few reasons to glance over at one another," she sighed.

"Do you still love him?"

"Of course I do; we share children," Lindersyl stopped herself, then shook her head.

"You mean, *he* is the father of your children?" Olivus yelled, grabbing her by the shoulders.

"Grier and Eisendorff, *and* the others."

Olivus covered his face with his hands in an attempt to close his mouth.

"Have you ever done something foolish because everyone you loved and trusted told you to?"

"Yeah."

"When that very thing explodes in your face and you can't do anything to protect the innocent ones around you, it makes you vengeful and angry. Do I love Johnathan? Yes and no. I haven't been in love with him for a long time. I hate the way he treated me when things got bad between us, but then I see him in Grier; the way she eats or holds her head. I hear him in Eisendorff's weekly phone calls to check on me. I know the good of him even though I've felt his sting. Over the years Johnathan and I continued to meet up—once or twice a year, even when I was married to Arthur. I slept with him because I knew it would hurt like hell for him to return home without me. He would in turn take it out on Lillian and that bitch deserved every cruelty. I decided a long time ago that if I was going to be miserable, I'd make sure that we were all miserable together. So, you see, it's not about love at all," she shrugged her shoulders.

"Lindersyl, you can't keep doing that!"

"Olivus, I have not spoken to Johnathan since Grier arrived. He still calls, everyday in fact. But he's the call I always tell you to let the service get. I have had my daughter in my home for three years, looking more like me than I do, and not been able to go to her and tell her. I have watched my son go through all kinds of things at the hands of his father and not been able to protect him. I have been silent all these years in order to hold up my end of a lie. I have made such a mess of things that I don't know where to start repairs," she grimaced, fighting back tears.

"The first thing we are going to do is pray. Lindersyl, God can repair all that's in disrepair, but you have to ask for His forgiveness and for His help."

For the first time in twenty years Lindersyl had told the truth out loud to another living soul. And it felt mighty good. She knew it was God moving in her spirit, disrupting things, breaking down the devil's strongholds, but the devil was also keeping watch over her, and without hesitation, she began to doubt herself.

"God don't want to hear nothing from me! Remember me with the Buddhist altar and the beads!"

"God has no worry over that. Right here, right now, Lindersyl, before you board that plane, give yourself over to the Lord," said Olivus.

Lindersyl was embarrassed. She could hardly go to God after all the tomfoolery and lies. Afterall, she had called God out and told Him that He wasn't handling things to her liking. She had threatened and challenged Him to step up or she was gonna step out and serve a god who would. And in her brazen neurosis, she had.

Olivus took Lindersyl's trembling hands and kissed them.

"I'm scared," she said to Olivus as they kneeled down to the floor next to a row of changing tables. "What if God strikes me down? You know, sends a lightning bolt right down through the bathroom ceiling?"

"God does not hold grudges, Lindersyl; people do. C'mon." he said, helping her into a kneeling position.

"I don't even know if I remember how to do this . . ." she began crying softly.

"Just bow your head and tell God what's in your heart. Ask Him to teach you how to pray."

Grier started for the ladies but saw a tremendous gathering outside of it. She had always been told to avoid spectacles. Whatever was going on in the bathroom had the onlookers in tears. As she got within earshot, she could hear her aunt's voice, crisp and strong, "Father, it was you all along! Lord Jesus tell me what to do and I will do it . . ." Grier turned on her heels and headed back to her seat. She had heard all she needed to know. If Lindersyl Gottlieb had called on God in serious praise and worship, surely whatever she laid claim to would be her victory. "God is good, all the time." Grier whispered, wiping her eyes.

Olivus helped Lindersyl up from the floor and held her as women began filing into the bathroom, patting her back and giving encouraging words.

"De Lord sure gwan to bless you chile. Come now, wash your face clear," an older Jamaican woman spoke, taking Lindersyl by the hand to the face bowls. Olivus followed. When her make-up and hair were squarely in place, Olivus took Lindersyl's hands in his and got back down on the floor. This time he was on one knee, with a ring fixed between his fingers.

"Olivus!" Lindersyl screamed in surprise.

"God said it was time. I love you Lindersyl Gottlieb. Like the four elements of fire, wind, water and earth, so powerful that nothing on this planet can end them, so my love will be for you. Will you do me the honor of becoming my wife," Olivus asked, choked on his own words.

"If God says it's so, then it is so. I will honor you all my days. Yes, I will marry you Olivus Blackstock."

The ladies erupted in cheers and well wishes as Olivus hurried Lindersyl past the crowd to her waiting plane. They paused at the gate long enough for a final kiss and his parting words, "Satan is not happy with you Lindersyl. Be careful not to fall into old habits. When in doubt, baby, fall down on your knees and ask the Lord to intervene."

"I love you."

"And I love you right back, future Mrs. Olivus Blackstock."

You used to mean the world to me,
My eyes were blind—I could not see the truth for all your treachery . . .

All Right Now, Patti Labelle

grier
Virgin Atlantic Airlines, Flight V201
May 18, 2001

Grier performed an impromptu balancing act as she walked swiftly between the seats of the Virgin Atlantic Airlines first class section, slamming the two bright green Louis Vuitton Epi carryalls she carried into anything in their path. She pouted resentfully when her ticket showed her sitting next to her aunt. Whatever little scene Lindersyl was having back in the terminal with Olivus was sure to snowball into the flight from hell. Her aunt had spent most of the previous night drinking and crying and most of this morning vomiting and pretending she was fine. As soon as they were airborne, Grier was certain she'd finish puking her guts out. Too often of late Grier had found herself cleaning up behind her aunt, tossing out empty champagne bottles and washing out the insides of garbage cans after Lindi's spillage wound up there rather than the toilet. Tossing her bags so they scattered the length of the two seats, Grier turned to address one of the flight attendants.

"Is it okay if I change to another seat? I'd like to sit by the window, as would my aunt, who will be boarding shortly."

"Ma'am I'm sorry but this flight is solidly booked in first class, we allow business class to upgrade to first class if it looks like there will only be a few people in first class. We just filled the last of the six remaining seats. Maybe someone will switch with you once they get on board."

"What about business class?"

"Business class is only about forty percent full this morning. You're more than welcome to move; however, we cannot reimburse you any of the money for the switch."

"Can I keep the same meal plan that I chose from up here?" Grier asked, her eyes pleading, for the cilantro-lime chicken tortellini she'd requested.

"I guess I can do that. You can sit wherever you like in the two middle rows—the red or blue seats—and as soon as the flight gets underway, I'll bring all the comforts of first class to your new seat."

"Cheers." she grinned, grabbing her bags up from the seats and exiting the opulence of curtained off seating.

Taking a seat as far to the rear and away from first class as possible, Grier plopped down, tossing the bags under the two empty seats to her left. She'd worn beige cargo pants and a midriff shirt with beige and turquoise stripes, tying her matching cargo jacket around her waist. Rather than interrupt her style, she asked another attendant for a blanket as the goose bumps from the arctic blasts of air circulating through the plane pushed up on her arms.

The captain made his take off announcement and suddenly a wave of panic came over Grier, what if Lindersyl hadn't made it on board . . .

"No, not this trip. If she ain't aboard, her arse is left!" Grier said aloud to herself, before tucking her feet beneath her and drifting off to sleep.

At thirty-four, she was the first real sign that any embers burned at all between her parents. A third-generation Gottlieb, she was passive at best; antagonistic at worst when it came to her family's history. Grier could barely remember her maternal grandfather, but revered him all the same. So much of who she was it had been reported, was due to or greatly resembled him in some way. Grier had been terrified of her grandmother, whom she remembered as a menacing old woman. Faye Gottlieb was more like a picture of a person than an actual person. She sat rigid and still, her eyes cold and distrusting—even with her own family. Once, Grier had tried to hug the woman, sitting upright and plastered to a study chair. Faye had nearly bent the eight-year-old in two trying to remove Grier's arms from around her shoulders. "Are you plotting on me, girl? What's your angle? I don't have any money, I don't have any candy, I don't have anything for you to steal and I don't want your nasty little digits all over my blouse." After that, Grier would walk a mile in the opposite direction to get around her grandmother. Lindersyl told Grier once that her grandmother had never been heard uttering a single kind word, unless it was a lie. As for her mother, Grier considered Lillian a virtual stranger. They didn't care for each other and that was fine by Grier who over the years had assessed her mother as a more decorated version of her grandmother. Easiest to avoid the lot of them. Grier likened her father to a boil that broke out in the same spot every now and again. Even after the pain and swelling had gone, the soreness remained. She had always been uncomfortable around him because when he wasn't flipping out—cursing and screaming at anyone caught in his midst, he was "watching her" with a rather unnatural glare. Grier's younger brother Eisendorff was perhaps, the one bright spot in her life, and he had as many problems as she did.

She'd avoided her parents most of her teen years, thanks in part to boarding schools and colleges and as an adult, while she still sought their approval for her near-every move, she could no longer hide her disdain for them. Phone conversations simply to say 'hello' turned quickly into full-scale arguments, replete with four-letter words. Now against her every desire, her office was sending her back to Connecticut. She had to play the 'corporate game' so she had accepted immediately. On American soil, there was no ignoring her family. The Gottlieb's would not be ignored. They were known for tracking her down and barging in on her unannounced—for her own good, of course. The call to her mother a week ago had ended well enough, though she found herself covered in hives almost as soon as she'd handed the receiver to her aunt.

"Ma'am, please pull your seat up to the full upright position; we're just about ready for take off," a flight attendant called from behind Grier's head.

Grier nodded in the attendant's direction, never opening her eyes and pulled her seat back forward. Beyond all the discomfort she was bound to endure at the hands of her family, Grier most dreaded returning to spaces she once shared with Brice, the former love of her life. A charismatic gynecologist who'd attended medical school with her brother, Brice was what Black women's dreams were made of. A successful, well-adjusted Black man who was financially and mentally secure and who had dreams of a loving wife, 2.5 children and a golden retriever named Rex. For as much as Grier knew about love, she'd certainly say she loved Brice, but she could never get pass the way he looked at her. The way his eyes surveyed her body with a want and a desire that she found ugly and frightening. It was not his eyes looking back at her, but those of her father. She often complained as a pre-teen to her mother that "Daddy's looking at me again", to which her mother simply remarked, "Well, take your little fresh ass to your room and stay there. Think every man and beast wants something from you."

But her father had been fixing his eyes upon her inappropriately and it would take years of sidestepping him to challenge the uneasiness she felt. Not until Brice came along and looked at her with that same longing, did she get it. She'd figured on losing her virginity to Brice once he'd graduated from medical school—that three-year window of growth was time enough to consider sex, but she was unable to quell the apprehension she felt. Brice had been the picture of patience, and after a while she was able to look at him and touch him without recoiling, but then there was that pesky face of his, looking back at her like Johnathan Holland. Alas, she dumped Brice because she felt ashamed around him. She'd confessed her father's obsessive way with her to Brice, but soon felt shame and guilt replace the relief she'd originally felt at sharing her thoughts with another person. Grier felt that she was the reason her parents did not get along. She was the reason there was so much tension and pain in that household. She could not expect to live happily ever after with Brice, knowing she'd ruined everyone else's lives.

Brice was far too good of a man to be pulled into the maelstrom her father's incestuous innuendo had created. Grier still loved Brice—even after being without him for three years, but felt she didn't deserve him. She'd even thought of taking a female lover to rid herself of the forestalling affects of her dad's behavior, but Grier had no interest in women. In addition to not being attracted to them in *that* way, she was repulsed by the neediness of those she'd encountered, recognizing that it aptly resembled her own.

Grier hustled through the plane's cabin to the bathroom after a three-hour nap. Peeking around the curtain that sectioned off first class, she could see her aunt, sleeping soundly—a humungous diamond ring decorating her left hand and bouncing kaleidoscope lights around the first class section of the cabin. She and Olivus had obviously made up. How he, like Arthur, dealt with her aunt was a mystery. Not only were they successful and good-looking, they were also patient and accommodating. Grier's father had always told her that it took a *real man* to see a woman through her own bullshit. When she looked at Olivus, so attentive and understanding, even as her aunt sat drunk or hung over, playing coy or the strumpet, she felt happy for them. That was a relationship that seemed able to withstand anything. For a brief moment Grier had come to think of Olivus as the perfect man. Then she remembered that she had run out on someone much like him. Maybe she'd grown enough in three years to give Brice another try. She owed it to herself to find out when she landed.

Chapter Three
Homecoming

The six-hour ride across the Atlantic had been a great comfort to Lindersyl. Lulled into one long continuum of reading and daydreams by the almost weightless buoyancy of the plane, she could not have asked for a more comfortable flight. After refusing the offer of a pre-flight drink by the cabin hostess, Lindersyl said a prayer and then, wrapping her memory around points of happiness during her childhood, began reading her father's journal.

The annals of a life wrought with mystery and intrigue, love and patience, Micheaux Gottlieb, though long departed, guided Lindersyl into a space of understanding. Lindersyl had inherited the journal from her father and fought her mother—almost quite literally—to gain possession of the six volumes that comprised his life's memoirs. A court order gave her possession of the first five, which spanned 1923-1965, with the final volume, (1966), the last year of his life, still believed to be hidden somewhere among her mother's things—or more likely burned in the fireplace of Gottlieb Grove. Her father had always insisted she and her sister keep private journals so that "the printed truth outlives spoken lies". Though she'd never cracked the cover on a single one, Lindersyl had conveniently thrown the first volume into her hand tote in case she bored of in-flight drinking and carousing. Now on a mission to remain sober and lifted by God's grace, Lindersyl was so very pleased with herself. She was happy she'd decided to return to Gottlieb Grove with Grier and anticipated the moment she could reveal herself to her children. Lindersyl opened the leather bound journal and was hit in the face with spraying lent and dust. The book smelled of wet wood, yet the ink and pages were dry and legible. She read aloud at some points, and at others, driven to tears, scanned her father's penmanship as if dissecting the hidden meaning of hieroglyphics. Her father left nothing to his memory, writing everything from his wife's infidelities to his deep depression following the death of Marcus Garvey. Lindersyl didn't know what type of business her father had with the portly, dark-skinned man who visited their parlor every month. That laughing and ruckus bravado she heard was "menfolks' business" and "grownfolks' talk" so she had been obliged to steer clear. She could hardly have known then that it was Milton Webster and members of the Brotherhood of Sleeping Car Porters, or that her father was a prolific speechwriter and financier of the equal rights movements. Micheaux Gottlieb was a 'Race Man'. In the hand-bound journal of 300 pages, Lindersyl was most fascinated by a series of excerpts titled: The Anguish of Love. One particular passage jolted Lindersyl to attention and made her rethink all that she had ever thought of her mother.

MG, 1923

It's been ten years since I left these shores, and now, following the death of my mentor, I have amassed a small fortune and a reputation rivaled by White businessmen around the globe. My parents and older twin sisters Sylvannah and Linda have passed during my absence and for once in my life, I am truly alone. Lonely and feeling out of sorts from the shock of returning to Jim Crow society, I sought out my best friend and roommate from Rosedale University.

Dent Johnson had moved his family from Tennessee to Shelby Mississippi to be nearer his baby daughter. He had refused to marry the girl he'd "gotten in trouble" senior year, but also refused to abandon them altogether. Dent lived across the road from Annette and their daughter, War Baby, with his parents and their fifteen children, including fifteen-year-old sister, Faye-Essie.

The white paneled house sitting along the corner of Broad Street, was the envy of most in the neighborhood. It was surrounded in the back by a virtual forest of Magnolia and fruit trees. By all appearances, Dent had done pretty well for himself and his family. When I arrived, they were preparing for Faye-Essie's Sweet 16th Barbecue scheduled at the end of the week. Thinking I may be interrupting the flow of the gathering by just showing up and announcing I needed a place to lay low for a few weeks, I changed my mind almost instantly when I saw Faye-Essie. God, had she grown. She had been a child bouncing on my lap and riding my back when last I saw her. Now she was fit and curved and molded into a woman. She still had long, athletic legs and muscular arms, but she also had some femininity to accent them.

Against myself, I stared at her incessantly the first night there as she ripped away at my ears with talk of her life since last we'd seen each other. She talked of the silly boys down the road who pinched and pulled at her like kids, when she felt she was much too mature for their games. I could take the hints wrapped around coyness. I was in love! Me. Mitchell Bates was smitten with a lovely little thing. What a wonderful surprise. God had filled my loneliness and I intended to make it for life.

By the time Faye-Essie had stopped talking up her own little saga in the early hours of the next morning, I had decided to take her with me. She would be a fitting bride. Young, wide-eyed, and unspoiled. She would bear me children and keep me company in my old age with her tales of the everyday, which because they came from her thick, pursed lips, intrigued me. I gave the first grown-up kiss she'd ever had to welcome in her 16th birthday and then sent her to her room to dream of all the things she had giggled about with her girlfriends. I asked her parents' permission to marry and take her away. They had their reservations because of the distance I intended to move, but felt comfortable knowing Faye-Essie would be with a 'good man' who was acquainted with the family. And since her parents kept having children, one less mouth in the house to feed was a blessing.

Flat and country in her mannerisms, but complete in her beauty, I couldn't imagine being without her. I'd known women, foreign, wealthy, and well-bred, but they all paled in comparison to the tight-waisted, Nilla-wafer-eating Faye-Essie. With fourteen brothers and sisters, Faye-Essie had spent most of her time picking wild flowers and trying to make herself a standout, so that she could leave the "baby factory" behind and have a husband of her own. She was a 'school teacher', but only knew so much herself. You know the country teacher only gave lessons to those under the age of six, and stuck to the basics of Bible stories and counting numbers up to 100. She enjoyed simple things and was proud that every child that came up around Shelby had learned to count, read, write their names, and learn about Jesus through her efforts.

I stayed with her and her parents for six weeks, making sure that Faye-Essie really did like me and wasn't still holding some old silly little girl crush. One dance and one kiss at the Annual Strawberry & Blues Social in Clarksdale and there was nothing left to do but marry her. In her red and white, checkered shirt and coveralls, she accepted my ring. At twenty-six, a full ten years her senior, I took my bride, Miss Faye-Essie LeDora Johnson. It was only after the wedding that I told Faye-Essie that we would be moving to Northeast Connecticut, to an all-Black city called Mosse Point.

That was the easy part. Getting my new bride acclimated to her modern surroundings was a trial. First, I got her teeth fixed and straightened so she wouldn't have to cover her mouth every time she laughed. I found that she was scared half to death of the buses and trains that whizzed by her at fast paces on the streets. She would jump, almost into my arms, at the sound of a honking car horn. I bought her pretty, feminine dresses and high-heeled shoes and pretty smelling perfume . . . and even silk stockings. Faye-Essie thought she had died and gone to heaven when we traveled to Paris and she experienced integrated accommodations and polite service from whites, she didn't want to come back to America—and certainly not back to Connecticut. For all the blessings she felt from being out of the South and out from under that certifiable white cruelty she'd known all her life, Faye-Essie was faced for the first time with colored folk who were jealous-hearted, vengeful and equally as cruel as whites. They had money and plenty of it, these colored folks. And where Faye-Essie had come to think of some people as being 'above' and 'beneath' her, she had tried to treat everyone kindly. Our Connecticut coloreds had no such rationale. They were society folk and their station, their "things" were more important to them than anything else. They didn't speak to one another *and caused a scene every time Faye-Essie waved or yelled from the curb her Shelby-esque "How y'all?" I don't mind these folks much at all because they're silly. I've seen money and wealth and it ain't here in Connecticut; it's abroad. What is a five-room house when you've been in one with fifteen? Or what is ten acres when you've seen ancient Roman Cathedrals? They're all a bunch of dumb, stupid idiots—overemphasis intended! They need my services, they have the money to pay for those services and so I deal with them. Barring that, I would just as soon hang out at Tamar's Speakeasy and drink hooch. Faye-Essie is another matter. Her age and immaturity shows to them like an open sore. She breaks my heart with her midnight sobbing when she thinks I am asleep. I fixed her teeth 'cause she wanted them done, not because I didn't see that gaping toothless hole in her mouth when I married her. I never saw anything wrong with her just like she was. But then, I'm just the man who loves her. But these graceless cows are devastating with their loose tongues and Faye-Essie is still just a kid. Her feelings are soft and soggy to the least suggestions that she not good enough. I can't keep her mind off of other people's judgments long enough to do anything of consequence. It's gotten so now that she won't go out without me. She says the women are always making nasty comments or looking at her with accusing eyes.*

New Entry

Today this particularly awful heifer got to Faye-Essie—that Truman Hines' old ugly wife, Maggie. She works for the Christian Women's League that give the dos and don'ts to the new country arrivals to Mosse Point so that they don't embarrass the better bred colored people. She knows damned well that Faye-Essie ain't new to the city, but she handed her a brochure called "You Are Not In The Fields Anymore" that included codes of conduct like: don't smile too broadly, don't come into town with work shoes on your feet, don't fix your hair or do your children's hair out of doors and control your stomach and buttock muscles when walking down the street to avoid being picked up for solicitation. Faye-Essie ran up in this house like something was behind her and I grabbed a shotgun from above the fireplace aiming at the doorway to kill whatever moved through it. Well nothing comes after a while and no one is outside. All I hear is Faye-Essie balling her eyes out. I still think something sinister has happened to her—men can be treacherous out in the streets with a woman walking on her own, so I go in to the bedroom to make her give up the name of the scoundrel. That's when she tells me about that monstrosity of a female form giving her that brochure. I almost grabbed Faye-Essie and whacked her with the butt of that gun across her hindparts, I was so hot from madness. I was relieved, but not too much. I got her a glass of water and calmed her down. I told her I would take care of things. I couldn't whip Faye-Essie for scaring me like that; I could never hit her like I see these men around here do, but I damned sure could pop Maggie in the mouth. I went straight over there to that house with my shotgun still in my hand. And half those dumb, stupid idiots in town followed me because they never seen me upset and because they like commotions. Looking at them mangy nothings traveling behind me, I got more upset, until I didn't even say anything to Truman when I saw him in the front yard. I just beat the hell out of him. Laid that gun on the ground and knocked him around the four corners of his yard for having no control over his household. His wife come running out onto the porch talking about "Stop beating on my husband." I was running up them front steps to knock her block off when the official town idiot Milford Watson says, "Mitch, brother, you can't punch out no lady" and grabbed my arm. I shook him loose, still determined to get her. I grabbed some pinecones and rocks from the ground in front of me and threw them at her until she ran her dumb ass back into the house. I told all of them out there, I'd kill them without hesitation if they ever mishandled my wife again. After that I got my shotgun and went on home. We have only been in this town a few months and no one really knows me. Today, they don't know me, but they know better—and that's good enough for now.

New Entry

I moved Faye-Essie onto the Grove three months ago. I can't get used to the sheer magnitude of the property—especially since we have spent nearly the first half of the year in a little cold water flat until my lawyers could work out the property inheritance. Faye-Essie is fine these days. After that scene with Truman I found Oskar's old girlfriend, Dame Antoinette Riboux, a Black French School marm and enlisted her to help Faye-Essie with a little refinement. Two months later, with all the charm and grace of an aristocrat, Faye dropped the Essie, forgot the Johnson and became Mrs. Micheaux Gottlieb. I thought it was cute—everyone needed to belong and nearing seventeen, Faye was operating like a woman twice her age. I was proud of her. Out of appreciation to Dame Riboux, and to lessen this type of burden on other country Black girls, I opened a finishing school alongside my new brokerage house. The Gottlieb Finishing School for Colored Girls opened in 1926 under the direction of Dame Riboux, though Faye took all the credit for the picture perfect young ladies who graduated the Gottlieb Finishing School. I realized it then, Faye's hesitance about being out in the streets alone, about meeting and socializing with people, and about not being accepted, was gone. But then, so was Faye-Essie. Instead of cowering from beeping automobile horns, Faye was now tooting her own. She looked older and more stern, her lips now formed a single, creased line across her face. No smiles—that was for silly little girls, not refined ladies.

Far removed from the pretty little country girl who used to daydream about me for hours on end, Faye-Essie had become one of the very people she despised. Oh, she socked it to them good, the ones who had given her a hard time. I'm waiting for the day when someone comes to my door to whip on me for something that Faye-Essie did or said. To make matters worse, I only have myself to blame.

How often Faye had given Lindersyl the same nasty-toned instructions as were in that pamphlet. Who would have believed that her mother's nasty, pinched disposition which had caused Lindersyl to despise her mother her entire life, was in fact a reaction to being mishandled? By the time the plane touched down in Mosse Point, Lindersyl felt ready for anything Lillian, Johnathan and Gottlieb Grove threw her way.

Lillian pressed her hands hard against the thigh of her jeans as if smoothing out wrinkles. Her palms were wet with anticipation. Having arrived more than an hour early and rehearsed her welcome, she, now at the moment of Grier and Lindersyl's plane arrival, realized that these were her closest family members, not her husband's business associates. She couldn't welcome them like some tour guide to their own home. Fishing an Altoid from her Bvlgari Sophia bag, Lillian watched impatiently for some semblance of a child she hadn't seen in three years, and a sister she may no longer recognize at all. She'd spent the better part of the morning soaking in a rich avocado mud, trying as she might, to erase—or at least mask—any blemishes she had. Though her sister was hardly as verbally critical of others' appearances as she herself was, Lillian knew she would be eyed and examined closely. By the time she looked herself over in the mirrored reflection of the backdoor's glass in crimson tank, blue jeans and mules, Lillian deemed herself acceptable, if not flawless. She had to be. With Lindersyl at the Grove, in the same house with Johnathan, there was no telling what to expect. Lillian wanted to take the high road, accept things as they were; yet not concede any of her own footing in any way. It had been a long time and Lillian's anxiety had only grown as she listened to Johnathan half the night mumbling and laughing to himself. When she awoke this morning, he was sitting on the floor among a foot-high stack of photos and letters. His face was haggard with emotions, eyes red, t-shirt soaked with his perspiration.

"What're you doing, Johnathan?"

"I'm minding my business would you believe?" he said, cutting his eyes from her back to the photos in his hand.

"Are you so stupid as to believe that she's going to come in here, running and jumping into your arms?" Lillian had replied.

"Lillian, please, just leave me be," he'd said, turning his back to her.

Lillian felt the familiar burning in the pit of her stomach she got whenever Johnathan and Lindersyl threatened to come in contact with each other. Johnathan lived to fight with Lillian, but with Lindersyl occupying his thoughts, he hadn't the energy to spar.

Lillian tucked tail as always and shrank into the background of his life. She had no choice but to receive Lindersyl as friend, sister, and ally until and unless Lindersyl crossed that line. Lindersyl could not help that her brother-in-law was helplessly, hopelessly craving her. But if Lillian found one smidgen of reciprocity in Lindersyl to Johnathan's desire, she wouldn't hesitate to fight for her marriage, literally.

Lillian admitted to herself that she missed Lindersyl. And so long as Johnathan was nowhere to insert himself between them, things would be like old times. Lindersyl was the one person alive that Lillian could not battle and win—not when it came to Johnathan, Eisendorff or Grier. If Lindersyl decided at any time to disrupt Lillian's fantasyland and reclaim her household, all Lillian could do was bow out. Lindersyl had a fighting spirit in her that Lillian never got. Even as children, Lindersyl was known to argue, debate and fight back when she felt at all put upon. Their father had found it delightful, while Faye had done everything imaginable to douse it.

Lillian leaned against the bank of public telephones along the airport wall, instinctively looking down at her shoes and noting their shine and sheen. She could hear her mother's voice saying, "Only whores and miscreants wear scuffed shoes". Faye had insisted their shoes be cleaned inside and out, laces and soles after each wear. And though almost everyone she'd ever met who witnessed her shoe-cleansing ritual labeled it "odd", Lillian had never been able to break the habit.

"Young ladies of exceptional grooming are fit for exceptional grooms." Lillian heard her mother's voice say, and smiled. For as much as Lillian had taken to her mother's micro-mothering, Lindersyl had been the opposite and absolute bane of their mother's existence. Those little torn up shoes their mother found and discarded weekly always found a way back into the house and onto Lindersyl's feet.

"Lindersyl," their mother would shout, pronouncing each syllable as if a separate word. "What have I told you about those trashy shoes?"

"That whores and miscreants wear 'em because they're dirty on the bottom," Lindersyl responded this day with her eyeballs eyeing the ceiling in annoyance.

"They are dirty on the bottom, the top and run over until you're almost walking on a slant, so why have you pulled them from the garbage and back onto your feet?"

"Because *I* like them and they are mine to throw out, not yours," Lindersyl replied with as much sarcasm as her ten-year-old ego could produce.

"Oh, really? Well, if I catch those shoes on your feet again, I'm gonna whip your ass until you are walking with a permanent lean. Now take them off!" Faye demanded.

Lindersyl removed the shoes slowly, twisting her mind around something horrible to say to her mother so that she did not walk away completely beat. The comment came out of her mouth without thinking, and Lindersyl was encouraged by her own cutting abilities.

"Mother, Daddy's shoes are beat to poo-poo and he wears them all the time. Is Daddy a whore or a miscreant?" Lindersyl asked, knowing full well that she was aiming for the beating of her life.

Lillian thought to step between them, but had had enough of her sister's flagrant abuse of house rules. Hell, Lillian considered it poppycock too, all of the rules, but wasn't about to challenge their mother. Lillian braced herself, smiling inwardly, waiting for the beating to commence.

But like a flash of lightning, Lindersyl was yelling for and running to their father. And if she could make it to the gathering of elders in the grove where her father stood, she'd not only avoid a spanking, but also get their mother in a heap of trouble. Micheaux didn't mind stern words, but he refused to have the girls hit. Usually Faye chased Lindersyl until one of them grew tired, but this day, Faye didn't bother. She had a special punishment for Lindersyl that wouldn't be given until her husband was out of town days later. And sure enough, like clockwork, at the stroke of midnight the night Micheaux left town on business Faye marched Lindersyl from the house and out into the night air. She was being banished from the main house and into the carriage house, full of mice and creepy crawlies. Faye had already denied Lindersyl dinner, so the trip, by kerosene lantern in a night slip, caught Lindersyl and Lillian by surprise. Lillian had been brought out to bear witness to what happened to "bad elements". Lillian had watched her sister shivering, yet defiant, even in her punishment, and was torn between reaching out to help her and being pleased that for once Lindersyl was being humbled, repositioned into submission, and thoroughly disciplined.

Lillian didn't care for Lindersyl's attempt at usurping her mother's authority by tattle-telling to their father.

"The next time I tell you to do something, I'll bet you do it!" Faye had yelled, content that she had gotten the last laugh on Lindersyl.

"Not likely." Lindersyl said, with rolled eyes.

Lillian saw her mother grab a hickory stick from the shelf over canning supplies and ran from the carriage house, through the orchard and up to her bedroom. She couldn't save Lindersyl and she no longer wanted to see her suffer. Why couldn't Lindersyl just let their mother win? Lillian could hear that hickory stick echoing all over the grove as it slammed into Lindersyl's flesh, but she never heard her sister cry out. She thought for a moment that Faye had killed Lindersyl and crept from the bed down the kitchen stairwell to the backdoor. Faye was in the backyard with Lindersyl's shoes, holding them over a trash blaze. The fire in her mother's eyes was as hot as the one consuming Lindersyl's shoes. It frightened Lillian to think what her mother might have done to Lindersyl and it was fear enough to force Lillian to side with Lindersyl. Lillian waited until her mother was relaxing in the parlor, with Courvoisier in hand, to sneak back out to the carriage house. Lillian carried blankets, a pair of pajamas, a ham sandwich she'd plucked from a tray of food for her mother's luncheon the following day, and a bottle of milk. She also tucked a small tin of skin salve into her back pocket. When she yanked open the carriage house doors, Lindersyl jumped in fear, wiping her teary face with the backs of her hands.

'Lil, what are you doing in here? She's gonna get you too if she finds out you are in here."

"No she won't. Here," Lillian said, with a wave of the hand. "She's drinking in front of the fire. Put these on so you don't catch cold."

Lindersyl looked with admiration and gratefulness at her sister who had proven her love, with food and supplies.

"Did it hurt?" Lillian asked.

"A little. But I ain't cry until she left. That's why it took so long because she was mad that I wouldn't cry. I don't care! And I'm gonna tell Daddy soon as he come home."

"Lindersyl don't do that. You should've left those shoes in the garbage. You know how she is. And why you ask her if Daddy was a whore or a miscreant?"

They both laughed.

"You knew she was gonna light you up for that, now didn't you?" Lillian asked, still laughing.

"Yeah, I knew!" Lindersyl laughed, chomping down on the ham sandwich covered with lint from Lillian's pocket. Lindersyl picked at lint in her mouth, but then decided to swallow it with the meat and bread.

"Lindersyl, seriously, you had better stop testing Mama like that or one of these days she is going to hurt you real bad." Lillian warned.

"If she hurt me, I'll hurt her worse. Besides, so long as you and Daddy are around, she'd never get away with it."

The irony, Lillian thought, staring at her shoes, forty-five years later, was that if Lindersyl had not been so gullible as to believe that, she might still be married to Johnathan Holland and mothering her own children.

Passengers from the Virgin Atlantic flight had alighted the plane and dashed spiritedly through the terminal, having passed through customs. In a crowd, Lillian knew to look to the feet to find Lindersyl, and sure enough, when the size 7.5 Bruno Magli boots stepped in amongst the others, her sister had officially returned. Then, face-to-face, the Gottlieb sisters stood, both resting on one hip and examining each other from head to toe. With only slight differences, they both looked about the same. Lillian's usual peek behind Lindersyl's ears to check for telltale facelift scars, had been abandoned this morning. There was hope in both their faces that after so many years apart they would behave as their father had instructed in his will: with unchecked love and respect.

"Hey, Lillian," Lindersyl smiled, opening her arms to receive her sister.

"Hey yourself," Lillian smiled back, walking into her sister's embrace.

Lillian rested her head on Lindersyl's shoulder, amazed at how much Lindersyl's face had become a living genealogy chart. She had the perfect combination of their parents' features. The older Lindersyl got, though, the more she looked like their father, Lillian thought, pulling Lindersyl back from her momentarily to look into her face. They both sniffled a bit, but refused to cry openly. This visit would be different, Lillian promised herself. This visit they would remember themselves. Over her sister's shoulder, she spotted Grier, looking so mature, yet younger than her years.

"Can your daughter get a bit of the love going about?" Grier smiled broadly, kissing both her mother's cheeks.

The three headed for Lillian's Benz happy to be in each others' company. Feeling the giddiness of being home again overtake her, Lindersyl began the sisterly chiding for which she and Lillian were famous.

"Ooowee! Lillian, your backside sure got wider," Lindersyl said, turning her head sideways to take in the scope of her sister's hips.

"What?" Lillian grimaced, looking over her shoulder at her own hips.

"No, it looks nice. You've thickened up enough to be considered Black", she said, giving her sister a pat on the butt. "Your butt used to be so flat—especially right after you started losing that pregnancy weight. Ass just fell away from grace . . . but look like you got it back with interest."

"Stop touching me like that in public Lindersyl! You can be so silly sometime," Lillian snapped.

"Don't start, you two," Grier admonished.

"You've got your nerve anyway, looks like you going bowlegged at sixty," Lillian said, ignoring Grier.

"Your mama's sixty! I am fifty-seven and fine, thank you. And how you goin' stand there talking 'bout I'm goin' bowlegged? What kind of sense does that make?"

"Watch it, you're sounding pretty ethnic . . ." Lillian said with a raised index finger.

"I'm sounding like I sound."

"You got some young boyfriend wrapping your old head around the notion that you young and spry," Lillian said, stopping to face Lindersyl.

"Just 'cause your bottom **done** fell out, don't mean mine has. Don't let the smooth taste fool you. And please, do not take your hot flashes out on me."

"Honey I am still in the **prime** of my life. I don't know anything about hot flashes and they don't know me."

"That's why your breasts all swollen up like that; look like you need milkin'. That ain't nothing but menopause."

"So, all of your new growth is by artificial augmentation, I take it?"

"Oh, I had them lifted, but nothing added, thank you," Lindersyl smiled, vogueing with her hands pushing her breasts together.

"You poor, old fool. That young buck got you hallucinating. He must be a killer diller honey!" Lillian laughed.

"Girl, he *is* the ying to my yang, the champagne to my caviar—"

"The long-handled scratcher . . . to your nasty little itch!" Lillian laughed, forgetting Grier was there.

"Okay, that is quite enough, *Ladies*! Can we make the remainder of this journey in quiet," Grier snapped.

Lindersyl and Lillian snickered at Grier's distaste for their manner.

At least they weren't fighting.

Chapter Four
A Family Affair

Welcome to your life
There's no turning back . . .

Everybody Wants To Rule The World, Tears For Fears

johnathan
Gottlieb Grove, East Garden Study
May 18, 2001

"She's laid up with half of the men I know. Ain't got the common sense God gave a field mouse and she ain't got no claim to this house or nothing in it! I just don't see why she's got to stay here," Johnathan yelled into the receiver.

For most of the morning Johnathan had sat running his hands across his reddened eyes with worry. Talking incessantly to anyone who'd listen, he'd begun complaining about the planned arrival of his sister-in-law almost as soon as the sun had appeared in the sky. No one was particularly interested, especially not Janie, one of a dozen or so girlfriends he'd taken over the years. He knew she wasn't listening, but he couldn't help but vent.

"Johnathan, I grew up with Lindersyl, I've never had a problem with her. Maybe you just have that 'in-laws' syndrome where you feel foolish admitting that you like her craziness," Janie blurted out, regretting each syllable instantly.

"You just don't know her ways. I used to live in a house with her years ago, me and Lillian did. She's a tack, plain and simple and I don't want her on this property, let alone sleeping in this house."

"Well, babe, I suggest you get over it because if I'm not mistaken, that is her people's house, not yours!" said Janie, extinguishing the conversation and Johnathan's rage in a single phrase.

Johnathan hung up the phone and moved to put a t-shirt on over his bare chest. Janie wasn't worth shit outside of the bedroom. He should have known better than to call her in the first place. Johnathan could hear a car moving up the driveway. Surely it wasn't them already.

When Eisen pulled into the driveway of his parents' home, the fear was real and painful. In fact, had his sister not called to announce she had landed at Mosse Point Airport, he would have made himself scarce for months. No matter how many times Eisen tried to convince himself otherwise the moment he and his father came into each others' space, Eisen was merely the shadow of the man he thought. Eisendorff would not defend himself against his father. His backbone slipped and his shoulders defied his 6'2" stature, slumping him forward. Ironically, he was as much like his father as his father himself—from the clothes he liked to the kinds of women he attracted.

Eisendorff found himself saddled for life with the infamous Terrie with whom he'd fathered a child, just as his father had chosen Lillian as his beast of burden. At least Eisen had the good sense not to marry Terrie. His mother was, as his father referred, "suitable for display"—refined mannerisms and flawless beauty, but little else. A man could only take so much of that before he had to go for the guts and glory of a woman. And a woman who enjoyed her womanhood, was a treasure indeed. Maybe that's why his father always had girlfriends—to counteract and balance out Lillian. Eisen was happy to see his mother's car missing—he had no stomach for her high-drama. Lillian seemed to belabor the fact that she was a woman. She was one of those rare "fragile" women who still believed in sitting, behaving and conducting affairs a certain way. Her pristine manner, normally tolerable, became unbearable around her sister, who despite being taught the same etiquette was still staging a rebellion against it. With her away from the house, Eisen could handle his father's wrath, minus her screams to "leash the savages". She always said that to keep people from fighting, along with "If you colored people don't learn to leash the savage in you, you will destroy my house and still not solve a thing."

Johnathan heard the rev of Eisen's Jag in the driveway and hurriedly put away the old photos and keepsakes that had occupied most of his time that morning. He didn't want to deal with Eisen, but just telling him to go away wouldn't do. That boy always had something to say back to him. Johnathan loved Eisen a great deal; he just couldn't accept any signs of weakness in him. Of course, Eisen resented him for it and always tried to hold his ground. He felt Eisen was plotting on him, hoping to edge him into a heart attack or stroke. Today was simply not a good day.

"Hey Johnathan," Eisen called up to the doorway where his father stood.

"Hey yourself," Johnathan said flatly.

"Uh, I brought this tea around to you. Something came up last night." Eisen half smiled, reaching the trembling paper bag out to his father.

Johnathan grabbed the bag and reached around with his fist balled up. "I oughta knock you into the middle of next year!" he hollered.

"C'mon man!", Eisen yelled, pushing his father back off of him.

He was relieved that his father's punch had fallen shy of his face. Eisen recognized that the old man was troubled far beyond Goldenseal tea and decided to walk away. He did not have to be in his father's house—his aunt and sister would keep until later. Eisen would just ignore his father, and try maintaining a strict diet away from Gottlieb Grove.

But as Eisendorff headed back to the carport path, his father rammed him hard in the back. Eisen caught himself in time to miss the pavement, but was met with a right hook to the mouth. The grass was wet from a fresh watering and some spots, which had been over-watered created muddy patches. As Eisen rolled into the wet grass and felt the cold dampness of mud on his trousers, he began to cry. Crying like he'd always done. Cowering in the grass to escape his father's rage, he tried to block his head from Johnathan's punches, which rained down on Eisen like sledgehammers. Here he was a successful psychotherapist, and the most emotionally unstable person he knew faced him in the mirror each day. He couldn't fight his father like a stranger and with an intent to harm, so he had no choice but to take it.

"You little sissy! Always were afraid to take a punch like a man?" Johnathan taunted him.

Fighting words.

Eisen grabbed Johnathan by the legs and clipped him onto the lawn. He became a mad man, grunting aloud. When he was able to maneuver on top of his father, he gave as good as he'd gotten. The first punch stung his knuckles, turning them into fireballs of pain. Johnathan looked hurt from the one punch, but Eisen figured the opportunity to whip him may never come again, so he held him down and choked him, submerging the back of his head in mud. Then, like something from the World Wrestling Federation, Eisendorff jumped off of his father, ran back to the side of the house, and counted off from five. When he made it to one, he got a running start and jumped to land right in his father's gut. His motion was deliberate and on point, until he stepped off the pavement and into the grass. That's where the traction of concrete gave way and he slid into the mud, landing his full weight on Johnathan's leg. Johnathan let out a horrendous yelp, but seemed to gain more of an agitation, than wounding from it.

The two were still tangling around in the grass when Lillian pulled up to the carport with Lindersyl and Grier.

"Not more of this . . ." Lindi sighed, covering her face.

Johnathan and Eisendorff never stopped their tussling about to look up. They meant to have this out until the very end. The two "wrestle-maniacs" huffed and puffed, out of breath, but too pig headed to admit they wanted to stop. Lillian didn't want to know what they were fighting about, as she rightly guessed it was much to do with nothing.

"When one of them hurts the other well enough, they'll stop," Lillian said dismissively, waving her hand in the air.

Both Grier and Lindi knew from experience that jumping in between Johnathan and Eisendorff was a 'no-no', so they did their best to ignore the battle being waged and headed into the house. Lindi was sorry to see them attacking one another, but delighted that Johnathan looked to be getting the worst of it. Maybe now he'd stop picking fights with his son.

"You had enough old man?" Eisen called out to his father, who he had in a headlock, spinning around in an awkward circle.

"I'ma kick your ass!"

"Yeah? You and what Army? Talkin' all that mess on the answering machine, but it looks like you were selling wolf tickets."

"Let go of my head 'fore you rip it off!"

"Why? Does this hurt?" Eisen grinned, yoking his father's head tighter.

"Hell yeah it hurts. Now let go!

The mood turned playful as Johnathan realized he couldn't possibly win this fight.

"You promise not to hit me if I let you go?" Eisen sang out.

"Eisen, I ain't playin' no more. Let go!" Johnathan screeched, his face flushed with humiliation.

"I ain't playin' no more. Let go . . . . sound like a little sissy, Johnathan," Eisen mocked.

"Let go!"

"Say you're sorry for cursing at me and punching me in my face."

"Hell no!"

"Fine!" Eisen said, tightening his grip again.

"Okay! Okay, I'm sorry," Johnathan conceded.

The two broke apart and hit the grass in exhaustion. Johnathan was laughing, only because he didn't want to cry in front of the boy. The pain was enough to convince Johnathan, sight unseen, that his leg was broken and hanging by the skin. If Eisen knew he could do this to him, hell, he'd drop by the house everyday to whip him. Better to grin and bear it. Make him think he just got lucky.

"Hey boy, when your mama pull up? I didn't see 'em come in," Johnathan said in between labored breaths, noticing for the first time that his wife's navy Benz was pulled up alongside them.

"I 'on't know. I was too busy whippin' your ass, Pops."

"Stop that foolishness."

"I got your foolishness right here—"

The two were interrupted from their rematch by the sounds of laughter. The kind of sweet laughter that was unblemished and untainted. It was the kind of laughing women did in singular company and could throw their heads back and crow. Lindersyl's home!

When Johnathan went to stand up, the pain in his leg shot up to his earlobes and then down to his toes. Oh, the tears were coming; it was broken.

"You all right?" Eisen asked, noticing his father's pinched expression.

"Yeah, just need to walk on it a little," he said.

Eisen went over and helped his father hobble into the house. With mud caked to their faces, clothes and shoes, they looked like they had been making mud pies when the oven exploded. Lillian, Grier and Lindersyl sat around the den before a table of Earl Grey tea and chocolate amaretto biscotti. The ladies were enjoying themselves when, as if sensing them in the doorway, the laughter stopped. Lillian didn't bother to turn around. She sucked hard on her teeth and yelled at the top of her lungs, "Johnathan and Eisendorff, you just couldn't leash the savage, could you? Well, if there's a single drop of mud on that carpet or my floors, there's gonna be hell to pay!"

Eisen and Johnathan looked at each other and started sniggling like little girls.

"Awh, woman, shut your mouth. We'll get it up. 'Sides, I got one of my favorite faces in the whole world staring back at me." he said limping over to Grier, who simply sat and motioned her 'hello' with a nod. He tossed his muddied wallet, keys and cellular phone onto the coffee table, causing the three women to wince in unison.

"What kind of greeting is that for your father?" Johnathan bellowed, pulling her up from her seat and giving her a bear hug.

"Daddy!" she shouted, pushing back away from his mud-soiled clothes.

He didn't want to let her go though and eventually her squirming gave way to the childish giggles he recognized. As soon as he'd kissed her on the forehead and released her, she became angry with herself. She couldn't stay upset with him. She loved her daddy no matter what.

"And who is that fine sister over there?" Johnathan forced a whistle from his lips, both turned on and annoyed by Lindersyl's presence.

"Hey Jumper! How you?" Lindi smiled, her mother tongued Southern accent peeking through. Gliding her tiny body against his, she didn't mind the mud.

Johnathan looked over at Lillian who was eyeing the number display of his vibrating phone and then back at Lindi before releasing his embrace. Lindersyl still smelled of white tea perfume and Big Red chewing gum. She was the woman of a thousand fantasies and a thousand and one nightmares. But as much as he loved her, he also hated her. "You still fucking anything moving?" he whispered, "Come stepping up in here with some nigger's bite marks all over your neck! Some shit never changes."

Lindersyl pulled back from him with a curious look.

Lillian looked again at the display of Johnathan's cellular phone, which had been ringing off and on continuously for four minutes. Tossing Johnathan a careworn look, to which he responded, "That's my phone and it ain't bothering you, so don't bother it", Lillian simply sighed. Not even for company's sake would he neglect his appetite for strange women. The call was no doubt from the nineteen-year-old, Lillian decided.

"C'mere girl!" Eisen finally said to his sister, "I just knew you was gonna stay ugly like you was when we were little. That water over in London must have an ugly fading agent in it."

"Asshole!" Grier giggled, jumping into her brother's arms.

"You know old Brice still ringing every doorbell in town looking for you?" he whispered in her ear, as they walked to the kitchen door.

"Screw Brice!" she shouted.

"Grier!" Lindi admonished.

"Sorry."

"What Eisendorff, you too big to greet me properly? You better bring your little self to me," Lindersyl smiled. Eisen looked just like his father did thirty years ago, only more arrogant. He watched his aunt's smile turn to shock as he reached her. Her head barely reached his armpit. "How's my baby?" she asked, stretching up to embrace him.

"I'm doing well Auntie Lindi . . ." he fought back tears. He wanted to make a joke out of it, but holding Lindi was holding the only family he had. He closed his eyes and cried aloud. Eisen had known since he was a small child that his parents didn't love him. But he could always count on Lindi. She'd have hugs and kisses and kind words whenever she came to visit. Lindi was his fairy godmother . . . his guardian angel and he loved her with an indescribable intensity.

When he opened his eyes again, Grier and Johnathan were also crying. Lillian had left the room.

When darkness comes and pain is all around
Like a bridge over troubled water, I will lay me down . . .

Bridge over Troubled Waters, Aretha Franklin

harry jean-jacques veda
Gottlieb Grove, Poolhouse
May 18, 2001

Harry Veda pushed himself forward on the couch and pounded his fist into the palm of his hand.

"Go to the body Evander!" he yelled at the television screen. His burgundy silk pajama top was unbuttoned, exposing a rug of gray chest hair. Harry was both bored and annoyed by the rematch bout between Evander Holyfield and Mike Tyson, which seemed more like television hoopla than a real bout. He was about to lose dearly on a bet that said the match would end inside the first round, so his interest was waning quickly. Besides, Lillian would be around soon. He leaned back on the couch, closing his eyes and tucking his hands behind his head. As soon as he'd seen that fox Lindersyl and Lillian's pickney drive up, his spirits lifted. Lillian had been dropping in only at his request these days, trying on the eve of her thirty-fifth wedding anniversary to salvage what residue there was of her marriage, yet he'd tidied up the bedroom in anticipation of her arrival. The linen had been changed and sprayed with linen potpourri, everything had been dusted and wiped down, except of course for his corner of shame, a three by four section of the bedroom where his degrees, musical instruments, compositions and cricket balls sat gathering dust. He slept with his back to it, trying with all he had to forget he ever had a life and goals before Lillian. Harry was taking it all in stride. He had to where Lillian was concerned. He loved her, but Ole Lil' was a bit of a numbskull when it came to keeping up appearances. And being married to a man meant for her sister, who never wanted her from the jump, was a part of the ultimate façade. Harry knew his place. It was the same place he'd had since he started working for the Gottlieb family in '62: *Love Lillian with great passion when she came to him, and from a strict distance otherwise.* For twenty-nine of the thirty-four years she'd been married, Harry had been there to patch up her ego, nurse her bumps and bruises, and cushion her fledgling pride. He couldn't bother to ask questions about the nature of Lillian's relationship with Johnathan. He knew what he knew. Most of all, he knew his place.

Harry worried none about Johnathan, who seemed most pleased when his wife was in the poolhouse and out from under him. Years ago, frustrated, Lillian had moved into the poolhouse with Harry to Johnathan's indifference. Like a fool Harry had redecorated and made space for his love, only to have Lil move back in with Johnathan when it became apparent that he could care less. Of course that was early on in her marriage, whereas now, Johnathan and Lillian frolicked about the grounds hand in hand for public display and then retired, each to their separate corners to brood. Johnathan was so happy that someone else had taken over his husbandly duties, that he occasionally solicited Harry's help when Lillian was 'acting out of sorts'. "Veda, can you take her out to dinner or something? One of the girls called the house today and gave her an earful", or more often he'd simply announce to Harry that Lillian was "having one of her 'sick headaches'", which indicated she was pressing Johnathan for some form of intimacy he didn't care to reciprocate. Harry was no fool. He understood Lillian's brand of love. Inasmuch as she did love him, she loved being Mrs. Johnathan Holland even more. And for this reason, Harry would not allow Lillian to forget that her entire existence was built around a lie, or that her only solace was in his arms.

Harry's father had often warned him of designing women. But twenty-nine years ago when he came to Gottlieb Grove and set eyes on Lillian, she seemed harmless enough. There he was walking around with a brand new PhD in hand but so fascinated by this young lass that he could think of doing nothing but cutting grass and cleaning a swimming pool to keep near her. Of course she was Johnathan's sister-in-law then, and she loved Harry as much as he loved her. But Lillian's mother was having none of that. Faye had turned Lillian dead against him when she saw how much they cared for each other.

"You're nothing but help. Nigger help that don't speak the language. You fit nicely into the background of this place, foreign nigger. The background includes the grove, the poolhouse, the carriage house and your quarters. It does not include my daughter. She needs someone worthy. And you are not he," she'd told Harry.

Why it was assumed that he did not speak English just because he was from another country baffled him. He spoke English, French and Patois. Harry thought to tell Mrs. Gottlieb a thing or two especially given her own humble beginnings in the Mississippi Delta, but Lillian begged him not to, promising that one day they would get married and leave the Grove. But Lillian was much more like her mother than was evident early on. And when Lindersyl showed up at the Grove with a man and children in tow, the same man Lillian had dismissed as 'unworthy', she couldn't resist. Johnathan Holland had been groomed and remade into a picture of a Black woman's nigger heaven: Hair conked, gold tooth removed, cufflinked and monogrammed, and with a high earning job at her daddy's company. Harry figured Johnathan an opportunist, but when he returned to the Grove the following summer, Lillian, his Lillian was Johnathan's wife and the very children who had once been Lindersyl's, Lillian now claimed as her own. Harry never got a complete understanding of how Johnathan and Lillian came to be wed, only Faye Gottlieb had made it so.

Harry wrote home to his father, *"Mwen pa ka manje. [I cannot eat]. Mwen pa ka domi. [I cannot sleep]. Tout ko mwen cho [My whole body is hot]. Mwen toudi [I'm dizzy]. My heart is broken in a million pieces because of Lillian. She has taken another man as her husband. If God is kind, He will send her back to me."*

Harry thought God had answered him when Lillian came to him a few nights after her return and climbed into bed with him. Later he knew for sure that Satan had answered him instead. That the best thing he could have done was heeded his father's warning and left the Grove to pursue his life with a proper job and a proper wife and family. But more than wanting to do things right, he wanted to do them with Lillian. Ole Lil. To her credit, Lillian had maintained her relationship with him, even when there were consequences. And the consequences had been many and great. Harry always wanted children, but he only wanted them with Lillian; so children were out of the question so long as she remained married. Besides, Lillian did not care well for children—especially Eisendorff and Grier. Occasionally she cuddled the kids of friends and distant family, but, a child's crying always overshadowed their novelty for her. They posed too great a distraction to her gaining Johnathan's favor. Surely he couldn't fully appreciate her if she were constantly looking after crying, hungry and filthy kids. Harry couldn't imagine her having children with him. Where would they live? In the poolhouse with him? Never! Their relationship was sick enough without kids.

Harry likened Lillian to a fickle cat chasing a ball of yarn; she never failed to return Johnathan's fleeting, barbaric displays of affection. With Lindersyl back home, the truth would smack Lillian in the face like a harsh and unrelenting wind. The only woman Johnathan Holland ever loved was her sister, Lindersyl. And he loved her *totally*, the way Harry loved Lillian.

When Harry heard the front door slam shut, he immediately went to the bar and poured a glass of tomato juice. Lillian would want something stronger, but Harry had no stomach for her when she drank. Harry stood at a distance as Lillian walked to the bar, picked up the glass and swallowed a few mouthfuls before turning to him. She looked dispirited and he knew he couldn't talk to her just yet. She'd only start crying and the only thing he detested more than a drunk woman was a sobbing one. Harry pushed his bare chest forward when Lillian pulled herself up onto a barstool next to him. He welcomed her head against his chest, her fingers twisting through the tangles of white curls.

"You wanna talk?" he asked.

She shook her head 'no'.

"Well, Duchess, take your juice on into the bedroom and lie down. You look to need a little nap."

"I can't; I need to get back. There is no way she is running me from my own home and she just walked in the door.

"Just try to enjoy your sister and forget about Johnathan," Harry reasoned.

"You are all I have in this world," she said, embracing him tightly. "Promise you'll never leave me . . ."

"Now Duchess, how can a man survive without his heart?" he replied, kissing her lightly on the forehead.

Harry smiled inwardly. He knew his place. And though it looked to most like a living hell, Harry had the benefit of occasional sprayings from heaven.

Make me weak and you can make me cry
See me coming and you can pass me by . . .

Nothing Can Ever Change This Love, Sam Cooke

lindersyl and johnathan
Gottlieb Grove, Master Suite Pt. 1
May 18, 2001

Johnathan bent this head down and stared blankly into the pages of Walter Mosley's *Black Betty*. The Easy Rawlins mystery, which had just days ago intrigued him beyond words, seemed listless and dull with Lindersyl and Grier in the house. Lindersyl was somewhere trying to avoid an argument with Lillian, while Grier and Eisendorff sat idling by the pool. Grier had tied her loose white linen blouse into a knot at the waist, leaving the cuffs unbuttoned. She wore a white tank under it that fought to restrain the imprint of her nipples behind it. She was perfect. She wore crotch-high denim shorts that revealed only the most beautiful legs Johnathan had ever seen. Lindersyl's used to look like that, but the pregnancies had made the backs of hers look like blue-lined road maps, varicose-veining locations up and down her frame. Grier had her back to him, laughing loudly at something Eisendorff was saying. Eisen was terribly animated, yet she remained poised in gesture, despite her ruckus. So perfect. Johnathan squeezed his eyelids shut tightly, trying to force his thoughts from his child. Johnathan thought of Grier as a small child, fragile and precious the way his doctor had advised him to whenever those 'other' thoughts crept in. Most times when she was little, before the madness started, Grier just wanted to be held by Daddy and fed by Mother for contentment. She was unspoiled and beautiful—the perfect example of love done right. Johnathan had seen love done wrong so often that loving Lindersyl and Grier, then Eisendorff seemed impossible. His own family was a family within a family—an uncle who had fathered daughters, only to father his daughters, sons and daughters. Johnathan's father detested it, but had done the same. Mothers and aunts had turned their heads, their backs and their hearts from confusion, pain, shame and embarrassment. Some of the women had run away with other men, leaving their children and grandchildren to fend for themselves. Johnathan's mother was one of those who'd left. After all, Claudine Holland was only thirteen when she had him and by all accounts shared the same father as he did. Some say Claudine surfaced in Detroit, others, say Chicago. She did not write, visit or wire and Johnathan's grandmother—now his mother, plopped him down amongst the other genetic hybrids her husband and their children produced. The children and the children's children all lived together, strangely happy, though at times strained by scorn, guilt and mockery. What did Jolie expect her kids to do besides lay still, sit still and keep quiet? No one spoke about what went on in their home within their family. There was really nothing to say, except "That's a damned shame that man can't leave his own girls be." There were seven girls and one boy, each girl eventually was forced-upon by her father; four of the seven, Claudine, Ruby, Sugar Baby, and Doll, had kids for their father, the others, Twin Baby, Etta and Mimi, were bitten, but not poisoned. They left either as soon as, or shortly after being violated. Some church people in the area knew and helped the girls leave, got them bus tickets or drove them as far as Memphis, but no one wanted to call the law and that would be the only way to stop it. That, or kill him. Mostly though, those who were borne into the Holland home, stayed there. By the time Johnathan was dropped, he had three other cousins / siblings to play with. Johnathan didn't understand completely what was meant when a neighbor called him a "bastard and damnation before God", but knew it wasn't good. By the time Johnathan began college, the children of the children were producing and still by the same beast.

Johnathan's father, Eisendorff, had been born Elliott Graham, but had changed it after a bar fight ended with him killing a man and being charged with manslaughter. Justice in a small Southern town for a Black man was contingent upon white authority taking the initiative. The hole in the wall where the murder had taken place was situated in a field dividing Bolivar County from its neighbors. The sheriff was more concerned with corn liquor production than debating who should send one no account nigger to prison for killing another no account nigger. Still, Elliott thought it best to move down the road a few hundred paces to another county. There he took the first name of a Russian industrial cleanser he'd seen at a gas station Eiskendour and the sir name of the man he'd killed, Holland. No one was certain where Elliott came from, who his people were or his intent—and most figured it best not to ask. Elliott showed up on a Wednesday, started flirting heavily with a local farm girl of fourteen and had asked her mother for her hand by Friday. Jolie's people were happy to get rid of the starry-eyed teen who spent more time daydreaming than tending to the animals. Jolie's mother was a widow and the five hundred dollars she was given for Jolie made parting with her eldest less a dilemma. People thought Elliott had money, but all he had was what he'd robbed off of others. Elliott was faithful for years, happy that the law had not bothered to arrest him or that Brady Holland's folk hadn't come to kill him. He liked the young girl well enough, less for anything than her youth. No one had 'known' her and that was more important than how she looked, cooked or cleaned. By all measure, Elliott counted Jolie a good wife; still on occasion he whipped her, smacked her face a few times or kicked her, just so that she wouldn't get too beside herself thinking she was important. Only white women could afford the luxury of being coddled and looked after. Besides, Elliott was drunk with power; he had held life and death in his hands and let the pulse and heartbeat of Brady Holland slip right away. He could have stopped beating Brady when his breath grew weak, but found it tantalizing, and liberating to slowly drive a man's spirit from his body. He did it with his own hands, his fists pounding into Brady's flesh over and over again. When the dying man's blood and saliva mixed with Elliott's sweat, he relished the way the fluids soothed his burning knuckles and took from the sensation the adrenaline needed to finish the job. The fight had been over a ten-cent whistle Elliott tried to take off of Brady. When he went to defend his dime-store property, his life was taken instead. Elliott took Brady's last name as a reminder that he could open the power of life and death at will. When Elliott smacked Jolie, he felt pleased that he could restrain himself, knocking a tooth loose, but not breaking her jaw. He didn't want to kill her—just to make her fearful. As soon as she flinched or whimpered, Elliott knew she was afraid and her fear was what made him the ruler of his home, it was what made him a man.

By the time their first child, Claudine, was twelve Jolie had turned cold and indifferent, even to the whippings. If he smacked her, she just looked at him with dagger eyes as if to ask, "Is that it?" She didn't cry anymore, and she certainly didn't flinch. Jolie only waited for him to die. She thought it would be soon, but it was slow to happen. She had been grinding glass and occasionally mixing it with the hotcake batter and the stew for years. It had to be ground ultra fine to keep Elliott from crunching on it, but that also meant that it would take the glass that much longer to cut his intestines to shreds and bleed him out. So she waited. What Jolie didn't know was that Elliott had been the victim before of female hostility and he knew the signs of a poisoned plate. Elliott saw Jolie watching his fork, eyeing his bites and chews with anticipatory breaths, hopeful that he would keel over soon. He'd fed his first plate of glass-seasoned stew to a stray dog that meandered into their yard once or twice a week. Over the course of the weekend Elliott fed every plate of food Jolie set before him to the dog. By Monday morning the dog was passing more blood than stool and died before nightfall. Elliott stopped beating Jolie after that; because she was now as evil as he was. She was prepared to kill and to watch him die a little at a time with only concern for what to wear to his funeral. He would not be able to let his guard slip again with her, so he ate at the jook while he smoke and drank, then came home just sober enough to dodge whatever weapon she may have lying in wait. By the time of the dog's death, Elliott and Jolie had four children, all girls. Claudine was beginning to look just like her mother had when they'd met. Her breasts were like little rosebuds, forcing Elliott to look at them to remember her mother's before she'd had children yanking and stretching them out of shape. Claudine was a good girl, obedient and quiet like her mother used to be. Elliott had seen the boys looking at her and Claudine disdainfully pushing them aside. She wanted nothing to do with their nasty-talk and grabbing. She was still pure, though ripe and her disdain would eventually turn to a blush and then to a scorch. Elliott thought to put an end to all foolishness at once. First he caught the two boys always following Claudine out in the fields and took a cowhide to them. He beat them ferociously and with all the might he had, being sure to stop short of killing them. Elliott told them that they had better not tell who'd done it to them and they had better stay away from his daughter. Satisfied that no young boy would come within an inch of Claudine, Elliott then got it into his head that she deserved the genuine love and affections of her father, not some wild boys getting their kicks at her expense. When Elliott laid down next to Claudine that first time, it was to protect her from those mannish boys. He would have none of them defile her. That's what he told himself, though he knew damned well it was a lie. Claudine did as her father said, though the girl sensed it was wrong. Elliott thought to himself how wonderful and beautiful Claudine's obedience was. When he finished with her, he told her to clean herself up and not to mention it to anyone. He had already decided to take Claudine for his own and leave Jolie to spoil and seethe until she died. It wasn't a year before Claudine was pregnant and Elliott took stock of his actions, not because he was ashamed or feeling guilty, but because others would not understand. Jolie would not understand, but he didn't care about her. He did care about Jolie's brothers and uncles finding out though.

Claudine was kept indoors, her mother plotting day and night to kill Elliott, but having neither the heart nor the courage to follow through with each plan she hatched. Claudine's belly was big and she needed her mother's support, of which there was none. And when Claudine's labor began, to drive home her mother's noninvolvement, Jolie sent for a midwife and then left to stay at her sister's place. Jolie would not deal with this until she absolutely had to. Elliott was at the jook eating dinner and drinking rotgut, leaving Claudine and the midwife to tend to things by themselves. Claudine delivered Johnathan on the dirt floor of the living room with the childish giggles of her sisters running and playing outside as background music. Claudine bared the pain of labor as she had her father's violation, in silence. And when the midwife handed Johnathan to her, she turned her head and uttered the first words she'd say during the whole ordeal, "Take it outside and feed it to the dogs."

The midwife thought the girl had gone mad, but noted the anger in her eyes. Claudine repeated again, this time with more agitation, "Take it outside and feed it to the dogs!"

The midwife backed out of the door and sat in the cool evening breeze with the baby wrapped in a torn sheet. Claudine's parents were nowhere to be found and the other kids were running around the yard like lunatics; shoeless, hair standing on edge and as muddy as pigs. The baby was quiet while the midwife thought what to do next. As if sensing the presence of another person, the baby started to wail, causing the midwife to look out over the landscape. "Thank God, here come your granddaddy," she said, pulling the sheet back to look at the baby's wrinkled face. And there it was, like a neon arrow, flashing in Elliott's direction reading, "*I am this baby's daddy*". The midwife sat frozen, afraid to say much to the man everyone in town considered a sociopath. If she had known clear that he would be there without Ms. Jolie, she would never have come to the house.

Elliott walked up to the midwife and asked, "What it is?"

"A boy," she said with fixed non-emotion.

"Finally . . . a boy of my own," Elliott said, confirming her assessment and too drunk to know he'd said it.

"The girl ain't doing too well, Sir, so I'm taking her to the hospital in Memphis. They need to keep her from bleeding so bad, maybe stitch her up," the midwife said, racing back into the house to swaddle Claudine's lower half and get her into the back of her buggy.

"Yeah, take her," Elliott said, looking at the disheveled, heaving body of his daughter. "You can take her wherever you want, just leave my boy right here with me!"

Johnathan never recalled seeing his mother. The photos of her in the house began to bleed into all the other similar faces in photos that made up the family within a family. Johnathan knew only the rumors about his father and could get nothing out of Jolie one way or the other. Finally, one day when her nerve got the better of her, Jolie put a gun to Elliott's head while he sat on a bar stool at the jook and pulled the trigger. Everyone knew what she had been up against and the same law that let Elliott take Brady Holland's life, allowed Jolie to take Elliott's.

Johnathan had heard it was a spiritual curse that his father had been under, lusting after his own daughters, so when the same thoughts entered Johnathan's mind, he had to run, quick, fast and in a hurry to the nearest therapist and try to fix it. He'd never told a living soul, outside of his therapist what was in his thoughts. Johnathan kept telling himself that it was because Grier looked so much like Lindersyl that it made her desirable. He did everything from beat Grier senseless to sending her away to boarding schools to make the thoughts go away. And even when he really had nothing but a father's love for her, the Devil had convinced Johnathan that it was all or nothing. That he was cursed, just like his father, so he may as well do as his father had done. Grier had only been home four hours and already, Johnathan wanted her gone.

At least there was Lindersyl.

Johnathan put *Black Betty* down and carried Lindersyl's luggage up to the master bedroom suite, masking the hobble of his walk. Eisendorff had done a real number on his leg and while his ego and machismo dictated that he do it for the ladies, he'd just as soon they carry their own cases upstairs. Each step required that he grit his teeth and balance his weight against a banister that was more for decoration than support. He could feel the aging wood bend under his pressure and prayed that he wouldn't embarrass himself in front of Lindersyl by breaking the rail and falling down. He looked over his shoulder at Lindersyl who followed him, deep in conversation with Eisendorff. She laughed at something Eisen said and though facing Eisendorff, she averted her eyes to meet Johnathan's. Johnathan immediately straightened his back and released the banister, stepping up through the pain until he reached the top landing. Eisendorff pushed open the doors of the master bedroom and inhaled the smell of freshly laid carpet. It looked different from the last time Eisen had seen it, but he couldn't note, beyond the carpeting, what was different.

Johnathan saw the ring on Lindersyl's finger and didn't like it one damned bit. He wasn't sure if it were some kind of womanly decoy to keep him at bay or the real thing. Either way, he was vexed.
"Lindersyl, now I heard you got a man and everything, but house rules are house rules and we both know how you are. No screwing in here! You feel the need to throw caution to the wind, I suggest you throw it at your own place. Got it?" Johnathan said.
Eisendorff felt flushed with anger and embarrassment. "Man, why would you say something like that to her? That was just plain rude Johnathan *and* uncalled for."
Lindersyl interceded, "Eisendorff, baby, it's okay."

"Yeah, Eisendorff, it's okay. What are you getting yourself all worked up over? Lindersyl knows that I was just fooling," Johnathan said to Eisen, then turning to Lindersyl asked, "Right?"

"Of course," she said to Johnathan. "As for the house rules, Johnathan, I left my screw buddy in Ladbroke, and we both know there is *nothing* here that compares."

It was Johnathan's turn to sigh.

Lindersyl noticed that most of the things in the master bedroom lacked Lillian's touch—that femininity that suggested that a woman was about somewhere and shared the space. This must be Johnathan's room she thought to herself. To prove it, Lindersyl went to the wardrobe and flung the doors open. Only Johnathan's things. They were definitely in separate bedrooms. This made Lindersyl happy, though she tried not to act like it. Eisendorff announced that he was going to get Grier's things and bring them up, causing Lindersyl's right eye to jump. She didn't want to be alone with Johnathan so soon.

"Eisendorff, be careful with Grier's luggage now. I know you built yourself up like Hercules, but that girl's stuff weighs a ton. I don't want you to hurt yourself," she admonished.

Eisen smiled and gave her a kiss on the cheek. It had been a long time since anyone had worried over him like that. "Yes, ma'am."

When Johnathan saw Eisen turn onto the landing, he crossed the room to Lindersyl and stood as close as he could without being obvious. He didn't know whether to grab her and kiss her or smack the hell out of her. He looked at her with a knowing look, which she refused to acknowledge or return.

"Lindersyl, I've missed you."

"I doubt that."

"I have and if you would bother answering your phone, you'd know it."

"Johnathan, you need to stop calling me."

"Why? Because you got some woman's child up in your house pretending to be me?"

"I don't need to pretend anything! You need to stop believing your own hype. Olivus and I are happy, in-love and getting married."

"You ain't marrying nobody. Lindersyl," he said moving in closer to her and grabbing her arm so she could not move away. "Don't make me kill that nigger. Now, I put up with that big mountain you married years ago because you were going through something and you needed somebody, but I'm not about to let that happen again—"

Grier came flying into the room at top speed with Eisendorff fast on her heels. "Daddy, tell Eisendorff to cut it out!" she screamed.

Johnathan gave a half-smile, imagining this to have been a common scene among them had he and Lindersyl reared their own children together. He looked at their reflections in the mirror above the bureau, the four of them, parents and their children. "Boy, let your sister alone," he said softly.

Lindersyl placed her arms around Johnathan's waist to steady him against Grier and Eisendorff's horseplay, but she had felt it too. It was that obscure moment when time seemed to have transported them into a realm that erased the lies and showed them 'what could have been'.

"Alright guys!" Lillian called from the doorway, her eyes darting between her sister and her husband. "Lunch is almost ready."

Lindersyl and Johnathan both felt deflated.

Lillian took Johnathan's hand and pulled him to her. "Why don't you help me set the table?" she asked, kissing his hand.

"Yeah, all right," he responded, walking slowly from the room and watching Lindersyl and his children get smaller and smaller behind him.

Lindersyl gave Eisendorff a wet willy causing him to dart out of the path of her wet index finger before she stuck in his other ear. She had to stay focused on her children, because Johnathan had a way of pulling her back into his web of sordidness without warning. It had taken only minutes for that soft bravado and familiar swagger to make her swain. He was still as cool as cucumber to her, and she had to remind herself how giving Johnathan an inch meant forfeiting something dear.

"Aunt Lindersyl, are you listening to me?" Eisendorff asked, having asked his question three times.

"No, baby, I must have been daydreaming. I'm sorry. What did you say?"

"Never mind. What were you daydreaming about?"

"Just this family I used to know that lived near here."

Johnathan was taken aback when he saw the impromptu lunch spread Lillian had managed to pull together in the fifteen minutes since she'd returned from the poolhouse. *Yes, he was clocking her moves as well.* Poor thing: she needed to know someone cared. Johnathan smiled inwardly, glad it was Harry taking care of her snivels instead of him. In addition to Waldorf chicken salad and fresh fruit, Lillian had tossed Asian sesame oil over a pot of cooling noodles and beef stir fry to round off the table delights. While the food had him, Johnathan was already fed-up with Lillian. She'd walked out when it got too hot for her; then walked back in and interrupted when things between he and Lindersyl had begun to warm. He eyed her suspiciously, leaning against the refrigerator with his arms folded against his chest, as she moved from the kitchen to the entertainment room with serving trays. She'd said she needed help setting the table, but it was already set.

The foolishness had already begun.

Johnathan started to say something real ignorant, but decided not to bother. He was amazed by the way the sunlight filtered into the entertainment room with an array of colors, making a rainbow against the far wall. He generally had no taste for God, but thought to himself, how miraculous the hand of God must be to make something so beautiful by happenstance. Johnathan's spirits had lifted and he tried to remember the last time he had danced. He wanted to dance and maybe even sing a bit if the mood struck him right. Johnathan pulled a handful of compact discs from the rack next to the stereo system and started piling them into the six CD trays.

"It's been a long time since I heard this," he said wistfully as Nancy Wilson began singing *When October Goes.*

Lillian looked at Johnathan with great amusement from the doorway. It had been years since she'd seen him 'cut a rug'. Once upon a time, he'd been a smooth glide across dance floors. Lindersyl and the children had slithered in behind her, and also watched Johnathan's grooves and pivots. Grier jumped in to dance with her father when the Jackson 5 erupted from the speakers. In kind, Eisendorff grabbed Lindersyl and escorted her to the middle of the room. Lillian was annoyed enough that they were dancing about without her, basically making her earlier interruption for not. But the fact that they were also ignoring her culinary efforts really took the cake. Harry had told her to focus on her sister, but how could she with Johnathan always under foot. And with the children also there to disturb her efforts, Lillian was so annoyed with Johnathan's attempts at paternal devotion, that being with her sister was sidebar to everything. Lillian decided she should have just stayed at the poolhouse. When Sam Cooke began crooning *Nothing Can Change This Love,* Johnathan cut-in on Eisen and took Lindersyl in arm. Lillian saw no reason to stick around when her sister's head took cushion on Johnathan's chest.

Johnathan sang every word of *Nothing Can Change This Love* in Lindersyl's ear as if it were his own, loving decree to her. The children, who he'd forgotten about, were busy eating and filling in the backdrop of Johnathan's perfect reunion. Lindersyl felt good in his arms and the two of them moved as one. They had danced this song so often over the years that they both forgot themselves. The children were too busy engaging each other to witness Johnathan kiss Lindersyl full on the mouth. They never saw Lindersyl pull away from Johnathan abruptly and smack his face, or the two of them run in two different directions from the room. Tears were flowing all over the Grove except the entertainment room, where a love story of Shakespearean proportion had just unfolded before an inattentive audience.

Breathe into me, oh Lord, day by day,
So that my heart is pure before You always, always . . .

Breathe Into Me Oh Lord, Fred Hammond & Radicals For Christ

arthur collier
Office of Arthur Collier
Chipping Norton, Oxfordshire
May 18, 2001

Arthur Collier hadn't slept more than four hours a night since he'd come across Lindersyl's 'niece". That child's face, her innocence, had disturbed him in ways he couldn't describe. Arthur had made a conscious, prayerful effort to avoid any thought of Lindersyl; particularly those of a carnal nature after mistakenly showing up unannounced at Ladbroke to see if Chasen had moved in. Arthur had thought Lindersyl's age, if not her mind would catch up to her. They spoke rarely and then, it concerned Chasen. They saw each other on even rarer occasions, so it seemed harmless enough to ride up to her door and knock a few weeks ago. Instead of being met at the door by the occupants, Arthur had encountered his ex-wife with some guy in the backseat of a car in an open garage. She had the gall and lack of shame to detach herself from this person, walk up to him "full in the nude" and start carrying on a conversation. He was disgusted as much by her actions as this young man's obvious lack of control over her. Then too, Arthur reasoned, he should have called first. Arthur had only just gotten Lindersyl's naked body from his mind when Grier introduced herself to him at service. He knew he should have left her alone, but a man can sometimes delight in his own sin. How perverse he felt eating with Grier and imagining how it could have been had Lindersyl been that ladylike and civil with him. In his heart he pretended just that. When he got home and realized how he'd saturated himself in Grier's attention and wallowed in her interest, he vowed to steer clear of her. Remembering Grier's promise to sit with him in service, Arthur had faked illness to avoid her. How could he tell her the truth, that he saw her as the unflawed version of his ex-wife. By now Grier was on a plane over the Atlantic or back at home with her family in Connecticut, so his concern had drifted from her to his son, Chasen, whom he still had yet to locate.

Despite being a grown man, not being able to locate Chasen was a sign of danger. The boy had no money and nothing to barter with outside of his own body—and Chasen was much like his mother in that regard. He would find a way of "getting over" even if it meant using unscrupulous means. Arthur had been there to cut Chasen's umbilical chord and considered him to be his own wayward child. Seeing Grier had cracked Arthur's resolve not to deal with Chasen irrespective of his 'lifestyle', and his church's dictates for parents of gay and lesbian children. He also knew what local British legislation said of homosexuality, but God had spoken to Arthur all his life and had never told him to abandon Chasen. Until such time, Arthur would love and protect his son.

This morning unlike the precious few, Arthur decided to catch an impromptu snooze to get himself together. His office was full of people set to interrupt his beauty rest, so he'd cleverly dimmed the lights and made a palate for himself beneath his desk with a trench coat. There were afternoon meetings to discuss growing tensions between Tehranian backers of his tanker imports and those controlling London harbor ports. Generally Arthur was the voice of reason and rationale, but without sleep, the weeklong meetings had brought out the absolute worst in him. He'd been screeching, yelling and tossing in an occasional poorly dispersed expletive, to everyone's horror. Arthur made up his mind that without sleep, today's meeting would be the undoing of someone. He had to get some sleep. Still, lying balled up in the fetal position watching feet parade by his door, Arthur couldn't rest. He had no idea where Chasen was and feared that without a legitimate means of support or a roof over his head, it would be no time before Chasen was in trouble. His mind ran a hundred miles an hour contemplating what would happen if Chasen had actually found Grier or Lindersyl before they left and gone with them to the States. That boy would surely die if he got caught up in Lindersyl and Lillian's mess. Arthur had to find him.

Arthur's stomach let loose a fierce grumbling that was audible enough to cause the person standing on the opposite side of his desk, pushing his papers aside, to come around to his side and investigate. So many people had come in, seen he was not visibly there, and gone on. Who in the world was this?

"Deacon Collier, what are you doing down there on the floor? Are you ill?" the brown wedges asked.

When peeking his head around the corner of the desk, Arthur saw that the brown wedges belonged to the widow Mrs. Macon. Arthur groaned to himself realizing he'd have to make quick maneuvers to refasten his pants, (which were marking ridges in his flesh as his expanding girth grew), straighten his shirt and wipe the slobber from the side of his face without Mrs. Macon seeing it. She was a lovely lady, but too aggressive for his taste. Lindersyl had been far more aggressive than the widow, but Lindersyl was not serving God, so her overall baseness didn't bother him as much. Aggressive pursuit in the widow just looked unappealing to Arthur, and the best he could do was side-step her until she realized that. What business she had showing up on his job unannounced had him curious. That she had spied the papers on his desk before she realized he was in the office, irritated him. Squirming to zip and button his pants while still lying flat, Arthur called out to Mrs. Macon to have a seat in the waiting area.

"Deacon Collier, you haven't answered my question. Why are you on that floor in the first place? What exactly are you doing up under there?" she asked.

"Mrs. Macon, a woman's tongue is often her ruin. Would you *please* wait for me in the reception area?" Arthur said sternly.

The widow gave a shocked huff under her breath before uttering, "Sure, I will wait out in the reception area."

Arthur waited until her wedged footsteps grew faint to get up from the floor. There were three hundred people in and out of the building and it would take the widow Mrs. Macon to track him down, pants unfastened, beneath his desk! By the time Arthur made it up from the floor and adjusted the rest of his clothes, he was greatly annoyed, convinced that had he stayed down there on the floor just a bit longer, sleep would have come. He walked out slowly, eyeing the widow in her Sunday best on a Thursday afternoon.

"Mrs. Macon, what can I do for you?" he asked, extending his hand to her.

She noted the cool, impersonal tone he gave her and didn't appreciate it one bit. She had already made up her mind months ago that Arthur would be her new husband. She was tired of being *the widow*. Few people even knew her given name. How do you call a woman "the widow Mrs. Macon" when one portion of the name created pity and the other invoked her dead husband, as if he still had claim to her? The name made her off-limits, unavailable and unattractive to men. Adeline Holstrom decided that she had been the widow long enough. She had been pretentious and coy; softly aggressive because she thought that was the kind of woman Arthur liked. The stories she had heard about his first wife . . . Adeline looked up the side of Arthur Collier's head. She had wanted him for so long, and so blindly, that now, being in his space, outside of church and spiritual pretense, she didn't know that she cared much for him at all. Arthur knew that she like him and yet he had refused to give her a single indication that he liked her back. Beyond general niceties, Arthur had not been particularly caring towards her either. How foolish she felt when she thought on it. She was determined in the face of reality to lay the conditions of her visit across the entire Deacon board, rather than on her own concern over his health.

"Deacon Collier, I apologize for troubling you at work. The Deacon board said you weren't feeling too well so they sent me over with this card and tin of biscuits," she said, fishing the green tin of McVities Fruit Shortcake from her oversized handbag. She spoke without looking directly in his face and released the box and card as soon as he had grip of them.

Arthur realized he may have been too abrupt with her and tried to make recompense. "Sister Macon, that was awfully generous—"

"The Church prides itself on looking after its members. We hope you're feeling better soon," she said, turning and walking spiritedly to the elevator.

"Wait, Mrs. Macon. May I offer you some tea or something? There's no need to run off."

"Actually, there is every reason to do so," she said, slipping through the closing doors of an elevator.

Arthur didn't know what exactly, but something bad had just happened. Too tired and worried about Chasen and Grier, to think on the widow, Arthur pushed his door closed, unfastened his pants, and crawled back under the desk. If he felt up to it, he'd look for Chasen tomorrow.

It hadn't escaped the widow that the onset of Arthur's cavalier behavior towards her had started with the arrival of his "niece". She had watched him with that young girl, looking like an old fool, and given him the benefit of the doubt. Every man, especially an aging one wants to be thought of as attractive by a young girl. But now, having been dismissed from his office and banished to the waiting area while he fastened his clothes, she had no intention of sticking with him. There were too many other sanctified fish in that church pond to keep him on her reel. What was he doing under his desk with his pants unfastened anyway? Nasty thing! She couldn't wait to get back to the church and tell it.

Slowly, surely I walk away from self-serving, undeserving, constantly hurting me love . . .

Slowly, Surely, Jill Scott

grier & eisendorff
Gottlieb Grove
Eisendorff's Old Room
May 18, 2001

Many of the secret passageways and hidden stairwells of Gottlieb Grove had been closed off once Lillian and Johnathan took possession of the main house. Initially developed to aid the Southern plantation and convict leasing runaway, the rooms had been built within existing rooms so as not to disturb the balance of existing space. When visitors saw the upstairs they often commented that they thought the rooms would be bigger or looked a lot bigger from the outside. Lillian and Johnathan, who were always on the brink of being called child abusers, could hardly afford to have Eisendorff or Grier lock themselves off behind one of those walls and wind up dead as doornails in the pursuit of adventure. Eisendorff's old room, formerly his Aunt Lindersyl's, had the only remaining hidden space—a small side room behind an imposter wall, masked as an ornate bookshelf. The shelves had always been full of books, usually dusty volumes of Paradise Lost and Mosse Pointe Judicial Codes of Ethics, even when it became Eisen's room. He had assumed that the books belonged to his aunt or grandfather and never touched them. "There's a whole world behind those covers," his aunt had said years ago.

A funny thing happened after lunch and a few hours of dancing, when the horseplay between Eisendorff and Grier resumed. The chase started in the living room and moved out into the orchard and then back into the house and ended in Eisendorff's room. They both moved with the chase techniques of their youth, though their speed had slowed tremendously with age. Grier utilized her natural ability to stop on a dime, causing her brother to torpedo pass her and into the bookcase. Along with the books falling to the floor, the shelves shifted to one side, revealing another room.

"What the—?" Eisen exclaimed.

"Oh, my God Eisendorff. What did you do?"

"What do you mean, 'what did I do'? I just hit the case."

"What's in there?" Grier asked, craning her neck from a safe distance across the room.

"Let's see. Wait, has this been here all along?" Eisen asked, afraid to move in one direction or the other.

It took a few seconds for their eyes to adjust to the poor light and dust. They both sneezed and coughed a bit in the interim, looking from one side of the space to the other in amazement. It smelled of wet paper and mothballs. The room, about half the size of the outer bedroom had a bed, tea table set, and antique roll top desk and chair. On the hardwood floors were stacks of old papers and news clippings. The walls were painted a pale yellow with bright yellow and red flower borders and lined with foreign posters from France, Germany and Liberia. Grier looked at Eisendorff, frightened by the discovery. "You didn't know this was here? It has to have been here since we were little."

Eisendorff didn't answer her right away. He was too busy examining things. There was a ceiling window—like an astronomer's lookout that allowed natural light into the room. On the far wall was a light that blew out as soon as Eisendorff flipped the switch on the power. It was dim, but they would adjust to it. "Nope," Eisendorff said slowly, rolling up the cover of the desk and pushing the loose pages of handwritten notes about. "This looks like Lillian's handwriting."

"Wait a minute," Grier said, moving into the outer room and locking the door. "I don't want anyone to interrupt this adventure," she laughed, eyes dancing.

The pages had been torn from an oversized journal of roughly three hundred pages and were signed with the letter 'L'. They both became excited at the thought of finding secrets and tell-alls of their mother, whose habits neither knew with certainty. The two grabbed handfuls of written pages and small boxes and moved to the floor directly underneath the sky window. Eisen began reading aloud, with Grier reading silently next to him.

Diary Excerpt: June 7, 1963

America and the American South are two very different and distinct places, and 1963 has brought about a sense of eminent change cradled by mass white hysteria. My first-born, Grier is just about a month old and the bloody bludgeoning of Negroes has heightened as we demand our equal rights. Even though it's been going on for centuries, only now does it seem to make the national headlines and newscasts. The reckless abandon and evil through which many of these genteel white folks kill and maim, rape and destroy, has made me wonder if starting a family now was the right thing to do. I fear the world I have brought this child forth into and worry that one day it will swallow her whole in the name of sport or fun.

Johnathan has been working to get Colored people to register and vote at the polls just like the white folks do. But he seems to grow more taxed and sullen each day. Colored folk know their rights, but they also know their place. And standing alongside some redneck that spits in your face and drags you out into the cold and quiet of night to lynch you, is certainly no way to gain equality or acceptance. The stakes are simply too high. The cost of freedom, is death. Johnathan only came to realizing this fact last night after he'd stared death in the face and was able to walk away unscathed. It was really cool out last night for it to be June, but Johnathan came trembling into the house, sweating profusely and talking out of his head.

He'd been gone for three days, going up and down Highway 61, near Clarksdale trying to get people registered, when he and his group ran into a major fork in the road, also known as Southern Justice.

Seems the highway patrol had gotten word that an uppity group of niggers were running through their fair county, spreading melee and pandemonium to the 'decent colored'. Accused of trying to take away what white people had, the group was doomed from the onset. Among Johnathan's colleagues were an eleven-year-old boy and one of a growing number of women activists, Miss LeRoi Fowler. Well, it didn't take long for the supposed indigence of these Negroes to grow sour on the patrolmen, who in turn called their deputy and a few other young white boys out to the side of the road. The whole group was beat mercilessly. Johnathan, who received the first blow with an aluminum flashlight, was knocked out cold. When he came to, he was in jail. The local NAACP, made up of mostly area college students and a few professionals from up New York, posted bond and were able to send most of the group back to Jackson in one piece. Tattered, bruised, and disheveled, but still in one piece.

Two of the group, Johnathan's friends Richard Shaw and Miss LeRoi withstood severe beatings and torture. Richard's private parts were set afire and although he survived into the night, this morning, he was dead. Miss LeRoi had permanent damage inflicted on her kidneys and one of her eyes. Johnathan doesn't want to admit it yet, but he's scared. He wants out of Mississippi not so much for himself, but for Grier and me. He wants to fight and he's looking for one everywhere we go. It's in his body language and stammering. Johnathan tried talking last night about what he saw, but he was one throbbing muscle of anguish. I stroked his head and calmed him, covering his chilled body with a throw cover. He told me to expect a knock or call that said he was dead any day, because this was simply one fight he was not going to back down from. This afternoon, he went to the grocer and argued with one of the whites standing out in front of it. Just stood there toe to toe with this pale-faced gas attendant insisting he address him as 'sir'. The man thought it was a joke, but when Johnathan's tone took on a threatening edge, the man bowed out gracefully. I fear for Johnathan's life if he continues on this way. Many of the Colored onlookers told the whites that Johnathan was a sickly man and was out of his mind. But crazy or not, these white folks ain't going to let no 'big buck' intimidate them. Far as they're concerned, Johnathan's next move would be violating their white women.

"I will not have my daughter growing up as I did. Bowing and scraping and yes-sir and no-sir, and can I get your bigoted ass something else? If it costs me my life, I'm willing to give it," he told me.

I knew it was too soon, but this morning, I came to Johnathan simply to comfort him and we made love almost till daybreak. I told him the doctor had warned me from getting pregnant again too soon, but he assured me it was never too soon for us.

Grier started screaming about eight so we got cleaned up and played with her for a while. Grier is a good baby and she's very responsive to Johnathan. And he's such a good Daddy. He even takes her onto the campus sometimes. I think he wants to show her off to the fellas; let them see what a good daddy he is. My mother and sister believe he's using Grier as a means of getting other women. Y'know, a baby is a natural magnet for women. But every woman on that campus knows whose child that is.... Mine and Johnathan's and they know I'd claw their damned eyes out if I ever find they've been trying to keep time with Johnathan.

The woman I need to watch out for though is not some little strumpet on campus; it's my own sister. I see the way she looks at him when she doesn't think that anyone else is watching. How she fawns over him, hanging off his every word and finding a reason to place her hands on him. If she laughs and he's nearby, she falls over onto his shoulder or dances her hands across his chest or shoulders.

When Johnathan and I are happy and playful with each other and she's around, she starts to sulk and whine about every little thing. But when we are upset with each other, she is always right there, reinforcing my negative thoughts or trying to get me to believe things she's heard he was doing. She seems to forget that she and I came from the same parents. We were brought up in the same household and around the same influences. I was there when mama taught her how to get a man's attention, because she was telling me along with her. I've had encounters with women who've tried to sleep with Johnathan behind my back, because he'd tell me. My "talks" would always suffice to end whatever notion the ladies may have had about Johnathan. But how would Johnathan react if my sister really were trying to get it on with him? Would he have the strength to resist her or even to tell me all about it? So far he hasn't said anything and that worries me most. He won't see her coming until he's already caught.

L

Eisendorff and Grier looked at each other astonished. "Eisendorff, Aunt Lindersyl really was after Daddy. Go find an extension cord. We're going to be here all night if we have to, to get to the bottom of this," Grier said to Eisendorff, more upset and confused than she had ever been in her life.

But I don't know how to leave you, and I'll never let you fall
And I don't know how you do it, making love out of nothing at all . . .

Making love out of nothing at all, Air Supply

lindersyl and johnathan
Gottlieb Grove, Master Suite Pt. 2
May 19, 2001

Lindersyl watched her sister's ascent into Harry Veda's bedroom from the master suite of the main house. Like a bad soap opera, Lillian remained, obvious and predictable when it came to men. Lindersyl did envy the way Lillian had managed to keep her husband and her lover in such close proximity, though. Johnathan in the main house; her lover employed as the pool man and living in the poolhouse for the past twenty-nine years. Free and clear of animosity, anger or jealousy, both relationships seemed to have flourished under the seemingly dire circumstances.

The large balcony of washed stone and African statues gave Lindersyl the vantage point, even in the dark of the midnight hour, of seeing directly into the poolhouse without anyone in the poolhouse being able to see her. Two cast iron loungers with solid gold embroidered patterns and tassel were in a far corner next to a matching hors devours table. The tangelo tree her father had planted on the eve of Lillian and Johnathan's wedding was still spouting its fruit just off their balcony. If Lindersyl leaned out slightly, she could just grab a few of the new crop.

Sitting along the cobblestone railing, Lindersyl forced her attention back to her sister and a now disrobed Harry. He had a beautiful body. Six-pack abs, toned and tight everywhere else, but Harry was strictly not her type. Perhaps it was because he had his shit too together for her comfort. Or maybe it was because she pitied him for sniffing behind her sister's sorry behind for half of his life. She'd offered herself to him once when she and Lillian had a rowel, but Harry had quickly reduced her to the depraved and devious woman she was. "For the life of me, I cannot see what beauty men find in you," he'd told her. He refused to be a part of either sister's plot to ruin the other. Lindersyl had been so ashamed, that for years she had steered as clear of him as possible. In time they did become friends.

Lindersyl volleyed her attention back and forth between Harry, who was rubbing Lillian's back with shea butter and the expression on Lillian's face, as she lay topless across the bed, her silk peignoir gathered about her waist. Watching his technique, his shiatsu motion down Lillian's spine, caused Lindersyl to tense. Lillian had married Johnathan out of spite and kept him out of habit. Harry was creating such a tender pleasure for Lillian that the familiar flash of jealousy and resentment Lindersyl had for her sister surfaced without warning. If she loved either how could she torture them like this? "Better still," Lindersyl asked aloud and ashamed, "why is it any of my damned business? This should not bother me. Why is this bothering me?

My sister's mess—and pleasures—are her own. Lindersyl . . . let it go!" she admonished herself. Yet, she watched on. When Lillian penned Harry to the bed to engage him in a playful wrestling match, Lindersyl's brow furrowed in an angry display of bitterness.

Johnathan stared up to the pool house window from inside the gazebo. There Lillian was again with that girlish giggling echoing across the grounds. Foolish old bat! "Oh, Harry . . ." was all Johnathan would be able to hear from the master suite. Tonight Lillian and Harry would keep Lindersyl awake though instead of him, as he'd generously relinquished his bedroom to her. Already it seemed to bother Lindersyl. Johnathan tossed back another gin and tonic waiting for Lindersyl to step out onto the balcony again. His own guilty pleasure. When the moonlight danced across Lindersyl's face, it was as if something mystical were taking place. He watched her expressions change, noting every facial muscle's, protraction and extension. Let Lindersyl fret enough over her sister's malaise, it would serve him all the better. Soon enough the moonlight would show her tears like silver streamers and her beauty would be that much greater. Johnathan became aroused at the thought of Lindersyl's tears. Years ago when he first saw how beautiful she became when grieved, he did all he could to keep her crying.

Lindersyl felt a slight tingling in the pit of her stomach and rested her hand across her belly button as if to calm it. She looked at the door and knew without question that he was on the other side of the door. She walked over on the balls of her feet and strained to listen through the door for any signs of his breathing. He was definitely there and Lindersyl reached to turn the lock in one swift move.

Johnathan leaned heavily against the wall next to the master suite, his heart beating in his ears like sonic booms. He reached out for the doorknob several times before gripping the handle. In an instant he heard the door latch click. Johnathan pulled at his shirt collar, praying under his breath. Pulling down on the handle, his breath caught up with him and he pushed his weight against it, opening it.

Lindersyl could hear Johnathan's heavy footsteps coming from behind her and shifted her position to appear as though she were looking about the grounds, away from the poolhouse. Surely he knew of his wife's whereabouts, but there was no reason to rub his face in it. "Got everything you need?" he asked.

"I think I can manage. Thanks for asking," she half smiled, looking down at Johnathan's hand which he'd rested against the small of her back.

"Gottlieb Grove hasn't changed much since I was last here," she replied. Turning her face away from his incessant gaze, she continued. "I like the new hedge designs. And, that tangelo tree is still doing her thing," she said.

Johnathan couldn't bother to answer Lindersyl with her standing so close. He simply mumbled in his throat to acknowledge her statements. His heart palpitated in a rhythm he was unaccustomed to and recognizing it, he began taking long, deep breaths. How was it that she could still do this to him? He walked over and sat on the corner of the bed, mind going fifty miles an hour. Johnathan felt ashamed and yet anxious, because surely, even at this stage of going nowhere fast, if there were any chance of winning Lindersyl's affections, he was going to try.

A few minutes passed in silence before Johnathan decided to go for broke. He stood and straightened the creases in his pants, inching up to her until he stood directly behind her. He inhaled her sweet aroma with deep drags. When dared by the voice in his head, he lifted her hair from her shoulders, exposing her neck and shoulders and brushed his lips across her neck. She didn't pull away from him. She wanted him as well, Johnathan reasoned, before spinning her around to face him.

"Kiss me Lindersyl," he whispered.

Before she could answer him, he'd attached his lips to her bottom lip. He sucked hard and awkwardly like a mannish schoolboy with his eyes closed and an unsteady pace.

"Jumper! Jumper!" Lindersyl protested, wrestling herself free of his grip and pushing his face off of hers with both hands.

"You don't want me?" he asked, his heart in the brink of implosion.

"Jumper . . ."

"You can't tell me that you don't want me! I know you do. I know it!"

"Jumper, please—"

"I love you."

"I know you do . . ."

"You think I'm a crazy old fool . . ."

"You know better than that. I enjoy having you near me, but Jumper, I can't do this anymore. Not to us. Not to Lillian."

"I hate her!"

"You don't mean that. Come here," she said pulling him near.

"I hate her . . . I hate her."

"Why did you marry her?" Lindi asked heatedly, her passions waned. "You had everything; your woman, your kids, your whole future straight in front of you. And you chucked it aside. For what! For what? Jumper, for once I'm not asking that to end an argument. I am asking because I want an answer."

Johnathan sat back and folded his arms across his chest, studying Lindersyl's every movement. God, she was beautiful. He watched her unbutton her jacket and toss her hair over one shoulder. She rested her left hand on the sliding door and he wondered if this musician she lived with felt about her the way he did. He had no answer for her, though she stood waiting. The room suddenly seemed darker and less enchanting to Johnathan. If only he could make love to her, she would know just how sorry he was for whatever it was he'd done to upset her. In all the women he'd known, it was Lindersyl he sought. Anastasia, Betty, Janie—even Lillian, in some way reminded Johnathan of the woman he could not shake. She had a command over him and no matter how he cursed her, Lindersyl knew he could do little without her say.

He covered her hand on the glass door with his own.

"I love you. That's it. Hopelessly, Feebly, Painfully. I love you," he said.

"Johnathan, please . . ." Lindi sighed, turning to him, wet faced and sniffling.

"Don't cry. This doesn't have to go any further. I'm sorry," he handed her Kleenex from the nightstand.

Lindersyl laughed in spite of herself.

"Look, let's talk later Jumper. I've been here all of six hours and already I'm in tears. This is just a bit much for me right now," she said.

"You're right. I'm sorry . . . I just g-g-get so carried a-a-away wh-when-"

"I know, Jumper, I love you too," she smiled, cupping his face in her palms, flattered that she still brought out the stutter in him.

Lindersyl leaned forward and kissed Johnathan lightly on the lips. He intercepted it easily, parting his lips slightly. Of soft innocence and long-awaited satisfaction, the kiss was tender and passion-filled. At the moment of separation, they were drawn instantly back together. This time the kiss was more heated and marked by strong agitation and emotion. Johnathan's tongue explored the once-familiar territory of Lindersyl's mouth, while his hands kneaded her rounded bottom in his palms.

Lindersyl pressed hard against Johnathan with her crotch, meeting his erect penis against her thigh. She moved her fingers up and down

Johnathan's spine, scratching at the material and clawing into his skin. She slid her tongue into his ear, causing him to teeter on his feet. Undeterred, he maneuvered Lindersyl backward to the leather sectional at the rear of the bedroom.

"Jumper, we can't."

"We won't. I promise."

Hesitation removed, the two resumed their snogging session. Lindersyl lifted her pant leg and pushed her knees into the leather, straddling Johnathan's frame at the waist. She pushed the tip of her nose along his neckline. His crotch was hot against hers, forcing her to take sense of herself.

"Jumper, really, that's enough," she said breathlessly, her blouse in a tangled ball below her shoulders.

"Okay . . . okay baby," he said, removing his hands from her waist. "Just one more kiss before I go to my room."

Lindersyl smiled broadly, knowing that this one more kiss game was going to put them one step closer to making love. Johnathan playfully bounced her on his lap, smacking her bottom and kissing her chin each time her body swung down. Perceiving his heightening excitement by the third bounce, Lindersyl weighted herself to him and bent her body into his. She wrapped her arms tightly around his neck, stroking his nape with her index fingers. "God, help me" she whispered to herself. Johnathan closed his eyes, resting his head on hers and his hands on her hips.

A sudden knock on the door as it was being pushed open found Johnathan standing, kissing Lindersyl's hand good night and Lindersyl, giving him a gracious nod in return. After years of sneaking, they'd become experts at detecting intrusion and near-revelation of their relationship.

"Aunt Lindi, we wanted to say good night to you before it got too late," Eisendorff said, tugging Grier's pajama sleeve to propel her forward. "Johnathan, I'm going to stay here tonight in my old room if you don't mind."

Johnathan gave an annoyed toss of the hand suggesting he could care less where Eisendorff slept. Grier and Eisen passed out their customary kisses and filed out of the room.

"So, you're sure you don't need anything else before I turn in," Johnathan voiced out of breath and louder than normal so as to appear nothing more than cordial with Lindersyl.

"No. I think I've just about all I need . . ." Lindersyl whispered, winking as he closed the door behind him.

Nervously biting her bottom lip, Lindersyl picked up her jacket from the floor and grabbed the used Kleenex sticking out from the corner of the sofa. She could feel sweat running down her back and legs and thought briefly to Johnathan's lips against her neck. As she turned to toss the tissue into the trash pail, she met Lillian's angry face staring back at her from the pool house. To Lindersyl's horror, Lillian had found a blind spot in both houses from which to surveillance her lover and her husband. Once she was sure Lindersyl had seen her, Lillian turned, yanking the curtains closed, her silhouette bending to kiss a sleeping Harry good night.

"Thank you Father for your intervention," Lindersyl prayed aloud, before phoning Olivus.

It takes a special kind of fool to stand out in the rain, somewhere in between nothing left to lose and nothing to be gained . . .

The Kind of Fool Love Makes, Kenny Rogers

lillian and lindersyl
Gottlieb Grove
May 19, 2001

Home fries and bacon could be heard popping in the frying pan in the Gottlieb kitchen. Johnathan, in the spirit of family, had thrown on an apron and commenced to "burning". A relentless lover of Southern cuisine, he'd larded and buttered, jellied and fried until the whole house smelled like Big Mama's House. His entire family was underfoot, minus one. Lillian had gone down to the pool house the night before and stayed over. It was a welcomed disappearance though for Johnathan, who rarely got the chance to be alone with his kids or Lindersyl. Years ago while in college, he, Lillian and Lindersyl had shared a house together and he'd forgotten that full house sound.

Johnathan turned wistful when he heard Eisen and Grier laughing and goofing around on the floor up above him. He wanted so much to join them. They were too young to remember when he used to join them. He felt only slightly ashamed by his behavior the night before. In fact, he was still silently pissed that the kids had disturbed them. It's like they knew when to peak around a corner, open a door, foil his plans. He could still feel Lindersyl's lips against his, her arms wrapped tightly around his neck. He touched his fingers to his lips and closed his eyes. Today's plan: feed the kids and get them out of his house. Then it would be Lindersyl alone. He would try again and this time he would not fail.

Despite tossing and turning most of the night, Lindi was up at 6:30, belly dancing by 7 and sprawled back out in bed by 8. Lindersyl smiled nervously at her own reflection in the ceiling-to-floor mirror of the master bedroom suite. God really did answer prayers. That was the good news. The bad news was that if He responded so well to her prayers, He was also aware of her not-so-saintly behavior with Johnathan and the lingering desire for him that forced her to sleep with a pillow between her knees the night before.

She retied the silk ribbon in the front of her nightgown. She was happy now that she had taken to lifting a few weights to tighten her arms and shoulders, which looked perfectly divine in her spaghetti stringed slip gown. It was early afternoon in London and Olivus should have been leaving to unlock the doors to the club for set-up. He would no doubt be tired, but she just had to hear his voice. She dialed direct from the house phone, sprawling her body across the width of the bed. She was starving, but didn't want to risk running into Johnathan without the kids or Lillian being present, so she pressed her belly against the mattress beneath her, forcing the tiny gas bubbles to escape her throat.

Olivus picked up on the first ring. His voice, deep and rich "My Lindersyl," he answered.

She always fancied the way the Brits took possession of a person, making them "theirs". She smiled and responded, "My Olivus."

He chuckled a bit before turning serious. "I miss you crazy, Lindersyl."

"Me too. You sound tired."

"I'm okay. Had a scuffle at the club to deal with earlier. I don't want you to worry about it though."

"You all right?"

"Oh, it wasn't me. I got what I wanted and ain't got no need to box anymore."

Lindersyl smiled again. The flatterer!

"So why it bother you so much?" she asked, stifling another belch.

"Some damned fool bloke come in there with another man. Right off I don't like that kind of patronage, but I couldn't very well tell the door not to let them in. Anyhow, this man's wife out with the girls, she sees him hugged up on some man. The worse part is I knew one of the cats."

"Oh, no. That's not good," Lindersyl replied, turning over onto her back, annoyed that she could barely hear Olivus for the rumbling of her stomach.

"Worse still, you know the guy too."

"How's that then?"

"Chasen."

"Oh, by all things true and divine! Well, was Chasen the guy with the girlfriend or the one with the boyfriend?" she asked, knowing full well, but needing to ask.

"Which one you think? And Lindersyl, he was in there trying to catfight with a woman, throwing those sissy punches," Olivus said, disgusted even at repeating it.

"Oh, that poor thing. He got his ass whipped didn't he?"

"You know he did."

"Why didn't you help him?" she said, half-laughing.

"I wasn't trying to mess with that guy. No disrespect, but he's got a funky way about him that I only dealt with that couple of days he stayed with us for your sake," he said flatly.

"I know. And I appreciated it."

"Well, I love you, so that mean I have to deal with your crazy ass folk."

"True."

"Speaking of which, how you making out?"
"Okay I guess. Can I be honest without getting you upset?"
"Yeah."
"I had a tense moment with Johnathan last night. We kissed."
"Did you enjoy it?"
"Enjoy it?"
"The kissing, Lindersyl. Honestly."
"Physically, I guess I was excited, but it was wrong. The fantasy, the memory is far more than the real thing. We're not kids anymore. Johnathan smelled of tobacco, cognac and the past. Emotionally, I felt sick, like I was cheating on you. Anyway, today I'm moving into my old house on the other side of the tracks, so there'll be no more of that."

"Good. Keep that sick feeling. I don't want to have to kill that nigger. I'm praying for us. And anyone who gets in the way of God's plan for us will be dealt with," Olivus said.

Lindersyl sat silently for a moment. Last night Johnathan had threatened to kill Olivus, and now Olivus was making the same threat against Johnathan. Olivus never used street language and his inflection was sinister like he really intended to hurt Johnathan if he had to. This was turning volatile. Foolishly, Lindersyl was as turned on by Olivus' machismo as she was shocked by it.

"Olivus, where are you?"
"I just walked into the living room. Why?"
"What are you wearing?"
"Wool trousers, the gray ones with—Oh, Lindersyl, no, ma'am. Keep it on cool until I can put my hands on you, baby."
"Olivus!"
"I'ma make a lady out of you yet! None of that funny business over the phone, Internet or uplink."
"Olivus!"
"Lindersyl, God is trying to deal with us. He's putting something in my head for us. If you cannot control your urges, you are going to end up with your body in some strange bed with someone other than me. And I am not standing for that mess. You hear me, future-Mrs. Olivus Blackstock? Every time you feel the need to be fresh, start praying."

"I hear," Lindersyl sighed. She'd never considered celibacy an alternative to anything! But Olivus Blackstock was worth it. She found herself excited by the thought of finally being married to someone she loved and who loved her.

"Are you convinced of my love?" he asked, interrupting her thoughts.

"I am."

"Then please, let me love you right, with respect and adoration."

"I understand. Olivus, I love you and I am so glad that I didn't do anything last night I would have regretted."

"You'll be fine."

"I know. Look here, Olivus, go on and get the club opened. I'll call you from my place later."

"All right, babe. I love you. Be good for me."

"Me too, and I will."

Lindersyl held the phone a while after Olivus hung up thinking of Olivus' way with words. Be good for him. In the receiver she could hear voices from downstairs.

"Hello?" she called into the receiver, before she heard it disconnect.

When Lillian awoke, she knew instantly where she was. The sleep had been that peaceful. She didn't feel any kinks or knots in her neck or back and the sandalwood incense Harry liked to burn was cheering in a fragrant 'good morning'. Harry was lying across the bed with his head on her thigh reading the morning paper. He was an early riser, a throwback to his childhood in Petion-Ville, Haiti, where the workday started at the crack of dawn. At the age of five he'd been indoctrinated into the brutally tiring world of fishing and fielding in Port au Prince, about an hours walk from the hilly Petion-Ville. Since Lillian had known him, she'd wake to find him either doing sit-ups on the deck or flipping through the business section of the newspaper. She loved to lie in bed and listen to him mumble his "Uhhhms" and "Ohhhhs" over the stock pages.

Lillian reached over and touched Harry on the cheek. He had recently shaven and the balmy skin under her fingers made her want to slide her face across his. Harry patted her thigh to acknowledge her and then returned to the paper.

"Almost done," he whispered.

"Take your time." she smiled, knowing 'almost done' meant it would be another half hour or so before he put the paper down. Johnathan would never bring in the morning with her like this, she thought.

Lillian and Harry's romp the night before had placed Lillian for the first time ever on the opposite side of the bed. It had been calculating on Lillian's part, the thought being that if Lindersyl were still watching, to give her an eyeful. But waking on that side this morning, she saw the room from a totally different vantage point. Lillian looked around the room and stopped her gaze on Harry's degrees hanging in a deserted corner of the wall. The papers were browning and the signatures fading. She could just make out the PhD year of conferment, May 1963. On the floor, littered beneath it was a compas instrument case. The dust atop it looked to be an inch thick. She turned her body to free it from the weight of Harry's head and yanked the covers back. She tapped her bare feet across hardwood floors to stand in front of the instrument box. Uncharacteristically, she took to the floor, squatting first, then sitting akimbo. At the sound of the case latches popping open Harry took note for the first time that Lillian was no longer beneath him.

"Duchess, what you doing?"

"Nothing. Read your paper."

"Duchess, don't fool with that please," he said uncharacteristically forceful.

Lillian stopped short of opening the lid, looking over her shoulder to a grimacing Harry. He rarely spoke to her in such sharp tones. His demeanor was surly and the gaze he gave over tiny reading spectacles convinced her to drop the issue. He used to play the compas for her when she was young. Now he didn't even want her near his most valued things.

Her feelings were quick to bruise. She rolled her eyes at him and got up from the floor. If she wanted this, she could go back to the main house. In fact, feeling the tears well up, she decided to do just that. She gathered her robe around her shoulders and searched beneath the bed for her slippers.

"Where you going, Duchess?"

"Don't question me."

"Awh, come on Leelee Ann. You being awfully sensitive aren't you? I just don't want you messing around with my compas," he said, jumping from the bed and blocking the doorway.

Lillian looked at him with unconcerned eyes. She shrugged her shoulders and slid her feet into her slippers.

"So I won't touch your compas. I got it," she said, pushing him aside to clear the doorway.

"Leelee Ann, I'm not dealing with this foolishness! Your sister is here less than a day and you're blowing my mood. Now you know better than to be in that area of the room anyway."

"I know better? Need I remind you that this is my house? I can go in it wherever I damned well feel," she said, deciding to hurt his feelings the way she felt he'd done hers.

"Don't start that Duchess! Not this morning."

"I'll start whatever I want"

"You know what? Fine! Go the hell on back to the house Leelee Ann. Give Lindersyl and Johnathan my regards."

Playing dirty huh? Lillian decided to offer the ultimate blow, "You may need to start looking for another job. I think you may be past it!" she said, running from the room.

"I'll show you who's past it," he yelled, grabbing her on the stairwell and yanking her back to the top landing. "You leave this house and I'm packing this shit and leaving for good. I'm sick of this! Sick of it you hear me? Now get your ass back in bed Leelee Ann and don't make me say it again."

When he turned her loose, Lillian picked up her slippers from the stairs and walked back into the bedroom. Harry followed behind her, watching over her as she returned to bed, pulling the covers slowly up to her waist. She wouldn't look at him, only at her palms. Harry sat down on the bed next to her and ran his finger down her cheek.

"You want croissants or toast?"

"Croissants," she looked at him full in the eye.

"I'm not your husband, but I'm also not a toy Leelee Ann. Just because I play the fool for you don't make me a fool. You try that again Duchess, and despite how much I care for you, I will leave this place and never come back."

"Okay."

"Now, what made you go meddling in that stuff?"

"Just wondered why you never played for me anymore," she said sheepishly.

"The compas is a passion. So is philosophy and learning. But then Lillian, so are you. A man my age cannot afford an expanse of passions; only one. I have you," he said, kissing her forehead and walking from the room.

He gave up his life—his career for me, Lillian thought. And after what she'd seen the night before of Johnathan and her sister, her marriage was over anyway. Maybe it was time she gave serious contemplation to making herself a worthy passion of Mr. Harry Veda.

Harry took a sawed-off machete and broke the shell of a coconut. He hit it far harder than necessary, spilling the content all over the countertop. He simply mumbled to himself and turned his attention to the oranges and grapefruit, squeezing them with all his strength until the skins rippled.

If Harry were younger, he would cry. But at sixty-one he had grown weary of his own tears. A stronger man would leave Lillian. A man with a weaker constitution would have whipped the flesh from her bone. In her old age, Lillian was not becoming kinder, milder, or meeker. She was becoming the splitting likeness of her mother in form, disposition and action. The truth was that he was beginning to feel trapped and unfulfilled, not to mention unappreciated. Surely Lillian wasn't meaning to rub his face in the poo by asking him about the compas. That compas and those degrees sat at the farthest end of the room, with no lighting or signs of life near it. Every time he touched that compas and started writing scores, he hated what he'd become. And every time he felt his muscles tighten or ache from doing manual labor, then saw her laughing and shopping and entertaining, he became angered. The anger had come on gradually—maybe four or five years ago. Sometimes, he hated Lillian too.

"She better eat this damned food and let me be, 'cause today, my love is empty," Harry said to himself, walking the stair to the bedroom with tray in hand.

Lillian was out of bed when Harry returned to the bedroom. She was sitting on the edge of a recliner, giving the oddest look.

"Leelee Ann."

"Harry, I've been unfair to you for a long time. I think it's time for me to demonstrate my commitment to you the way you have to me. I am on my way to the Big House—"

"Leelee Ann! Damn it!"

"Harry," she said, taking the tray from him and taking hold of his hands. "I'm going to the Big House to ask Johnathan for a divorce. Will you marry me?"

Johnathan swallowed hard, forcing a painkiller down his throat. His leg was still hurting like the dickens, but he didn't want to appear weak in front of Lindersyl. She'd walked into the kitchen in a blazing red dressing gown, a kimono sort of silky thing that had Johnathan's full attention. She wore her hair in a loose upswing that allowed pieces of it to fall to her shoulders. He turned his head under the light and then again with the beam of the sun cutting through the window to note the changing appearance of her body's curves beneath it. And though he could hear the kids talking non-stop to Lindersyl, he hadn't a clue what was being said.

"Jumper, you not joining us?" Lindersyl asked, tossing him a curious look.

"Naw, doctor said I had to lay off the fried foods or else. I had some grapefruit and papaya salad with my toast, thank you. That'll hold me until lunch," he said trying desperately to mask his latent desire for her.

A drizzle of syrup ran from Lindersyl's fork and balanced awkwardly on her lower lip. Johnathan moved from his leaning position across the chopping block with napkin in hand to dab at her, undaunted by the presence of his kids. As he reached Lindersyl's side, he noticed a purple bruising at her collarbone and stopped dead in his tracks. It was a passion mark. He hadn't done that! Had it been there last night? Maybe some other man had been there last night . . . But who? That Haitian was the most likely. Could he be clever enough to have both his wife and Lindersyl running behind him? Johnathan walked back to the chopping block, having a mental tug of war with his emotions, and resumed leaning.

Eisendorff pushed back from the table in total disgust. In addition to the bacon and home fries, his father had prepared pancakes, cheese eggs, heavily buttered toast, chorizo (a Mexican sausage stuffed with fried onions, garlic, chilies and spices) and grits. Unfortunately, it had been years since Eisendorff had indulged and his stomach was turning flips as the grease made its way through his system. He watched his aunt loosen her frock to release the pressure in her stomach, and laughed.

"Did you in didn't he?" he laughed, poking at her stomach.

"Nothing left but to pass out," she said.

Eisen didn't like the way his father watched his aunt, but having taken in his aunt's earlier phone conversation, there was obviously far more to their relationship than he'd been aware. He was having a rough time looking Lindersyl in the face, having read how she'd tried to seduce his father from under his mother years ago. Eisendorff looked at Lindersyl and thought how cold-hearted she'd have to be to snatch her sister's man, however willing his idiot father was. The journal pages had been divided evenly between him and Grier and as soon as it was polite to do so, Eisendorff was excusing himself from the table to resume reading. While his father watched like a hawk from atop the chopping block, his aunt had peered up periodically with an apprehensive smile.

When Grier interrupted her father's gaze to compliment his cooking skills, he nearly bit her head off. "You could eat like that all the time if you weren't off doing God knows what overseas!"

"She eats just fine in London. Don't you, Love?" Lindersyl interceded.

Grier didn't answer, but looked up and smiled in her aunt's direction.

"Lindersyl, where you off to today? Walkin' the strip?" Johnathan asked, dripping of sarcasm, annoyed that she was officially beneath his skin again.

Lindersyl took a deep breath and sighed. She placed no stock in Johnathan's cussedness, but preferred he'd not act silly in front of the kids. "Lil and I are gonna do a bit of shopping," she answered, then with her own brand of venom added, "Where is she anyway? I didn't hear her come in last night".

"Pool house." Johnathan smiled, unmarked.

"That still going on then?" Grier asked.

"Well, have a look for yourself. The wanton woman returns," he chuckled, pointing out the window to Lillian, making her way across the lawn in a negligee and slippers.

"That damned Lillian!" Lindi mumbled.

When Lillian made it to the kitchen door, she looked surprised that everyone was up. She took a few deep breaths to get up her nerve before stepping inside.

"Lil, what are you doin' outside dressed like that?" Johnathan protested.

"You know exactly what I've been doing; don't play with me Johnathan. Matter of fact, I need to speak with you, alone."

"Why? You gonna tell me that you're pregnant by the pool man?" Johnathan spat.

"Fine, show your ass Johnathan. I guess it can be said in front of family; you'll find out soon enough anyway. I want a divorce. I've called Wade McLinch to represent me. I'll file; we'll say something like irreconcilable differences," she blurted out.

"I don't care if you get the entire bar association of Mosse Point to represent you; the answer is 'no'. I will *never* sign divorce papers! And get your ass upstairs and put some clothes on."

Lindersyl was both perplexed and saddened by Johnathan's refusal. Hadn't his marriage to Lillian been the only thing standing in the way of *their* happiness? Even though she wasn't exactly clear how she felt about him, she felt rejected, tossed aside.

"Johnathan, I thought you wanted out of your marriage. You've been claiming it to be a hindrance to you from the start." Lindersyl interjected.

"Lindersyl, stay out of this!" Johnathan yelled.

"Why? Think maybe I'll say something sensible to you? You don't want her, but you don't want to let her go. Are you afraid that you'll end up alone and broken-hearted? Or maybe you'll end up with someone like me?" Lindi shrieked, her voice changing to a high-pitched yell.

Eisen left the room with his hands covering his ears.

"Don't you mock me Lindersyl Gottlieb in my own goddamned house! I will not have it! I'm not signing no divorce papers and I ain't hearin' no more 'bout this shit!" Johnathan yelled, sprinting passed them to the carport. Without another word, he was in his car and gone.

The sisters looked at each other with suspicion. Lindersyl wondered if the divorce request was her sister's reaction to seeing Johnathan with her the night before.

In a tense show of support, the sister's embraced. They wept silently, both of them terrified of getting exactly what they'd always wanted, and inadvertently giving the other an ounce of happiness.

*But paradise is here, it's time to stop your crying,
The future is this moment and not some place out there . . .*

Paradise Is Here, Tina Turner

grier and brice
Residence of: Lindersyl Gottlieb
North Mosse Point Connecticut
May 19, 2001

The old Mustang handled well once Grier got used to the automatic transmission. She fussed for a moment with the radio stations before mashing the CD button. Her attention was diverted as an approaching car headed straight for her. She and the other driver both leaned on their horns. Before the collision should shape further, Grier realized she was driving on the wrong side of the road and swerved. She apologized profusely, with her heart in her throat, to the other driver whose middle finger seemed frozen prostrate.

"Geewillickers!" she shouted just as Kenny Rogers came blaring from the sound system. Her aunt thought the country-crossover artist walked on water and was rarely without the singer's music at her side. Grier would never admit it to Lindersyl, but she liked him too. And as she tried to calm herself from her near-collision, Grier found herself delighted by the country singer's voice and made the rest of the seven-mile drive with ease.

Lindersyl's house was going to be a welcomed change to the nonsense going on at the Grove. Her mother and a divorce, indeed! Grier grimaced at the thought, rounding the corner of Lindi's block. Her aunt's home was a modest two-story cottage she'd transformed into a loft. The first level was one big wide-open space with the kitchen, living room, dining room and study all visible. On the second level were two full bedrooms—master's and mistress' suites. The landscaping was tended to bi-weekly and everything was in pristine condition though no one had occupied the house in years. The front door was flanked on either side by little pygmy-looking statues her aunt had sent back from Harare one year. As a kid, Grier had thought they came to life at the stroke of midnight and terrorized people. As an adult she could still feel their deep-set mahogany eyes following her. She stood frozen at the front door, readying herself to run pass them.

"Get a grip!" she laughed aloud at herself.

Grier stepped into the foyer of Moroccan tile and terra cotta walls and then down five stairs into the vestibule. A Hungarian excavator and his researcher wife had built the house in the mid-1960s. It had taken nearly four years to build and was to be a place of retirement for the two, only they died in a plane crash having never set a foot inside. Lindersyl was the first and only person to live there and even she was only there two years before fleeing to England.

Grier supposed that's what she so enjoyed about the place; it was still new after forty years. There was a hollowness to the house that made everything she touched 'hers'. Grier chose the bedroom closest the stairwell as her own, throwing her clothes from the suitcases onto the bed. She would sort and hang them later. She felt agitated, the way she always did just before her period each month. Her lower extremities were moist and warm and she was ashamed and unnerved by it. Why was this happening? Surely it was hormonal, but why?

Grier pulled off her jeans and Oxford University sweatshirt, leaving them in the middle of the floor. Her flesh said, go ahead, touch yourself. Orgasm yourself to death. But her mind, her spirit said 'Don't go there Grier, you'll only feel worse afterward. She debated in her mind for several minutes before becoming frustrated and peeling off her undergarments. Grier turned on the shower and smiled, "not today Grier. Not today."

The thought of giving into her hormones was only as appealing as it was arresting. She always felt guilty as the sensation subsided. Afterward she prayed for clarity. God said fornicating was wrong. But could you fornicate with yourself? Something that felt so good had to be bad. Medical communities around the globe said masturbation was natural, normal. But they also said that pornography and strip clubs were harmless outlets of sexuality. Johnathan and Lillian had hardly directed her in the ways of positive sexual expression. They were as dysfunctional as her aunt. She could still remember her mother begging her father to make love to her and her father summoning Mr. Veda, the pool attendant to oblige her. It was sick, but Mr. Veda seemed honestly to adore her mother. Whenever she saw Mr. Veda with her mother he was gentle in word and deed. He always ran his hand softly down her mother's back, stroking her like a cat when talking to her about the ridiculous duties needing to be performed around the pool. Grier imagined him to be a gentleman in all regards. Mr. Veda made love, she surmised, and probably had no notion of the likes of screwing, banging or shagging. She imagined her Brice would have been the same.

Grier was as afraid of becoming desperate as she was of sex itself. She'd watched her mother sacrifice everything to be devoted. Mrs. Johnathan Holland, and for what? It was a devotion her father saw as a weakness. He'd laugh at her mother for it. And her mother would simply pick herself up off the floor, push her hair back into place and compose her thoughts. Next time she would dress sexier. Next time she would put on some irresistible fragrance. Next time she would make sure he wouldn't leave for the other woman's house. But when each 'next time' came, not only would Johnathan leave, but he'd also taunt her on his way out the door. It had never stopped and Grier couldn't bear to think of herself heading in the same direction.

Grier positioned the showerhead so that cool water ran directly into her face. Did God want her to avoid Brice to keep her pure and honest? What was the difference between laying alone and laying with someone else?

Would God have given her this want, this desire if He had no means of her satisfying it? Grier turned the mid-wall jets on and allowed the force to push against the center of her back. Grier thought of her aunt and Olivus on the kitchen aisle. Repulsive. Animal. Basic. Something to rise above. Cro-Magnon instinct. But also, exciting. Could she seek spiritual counsel for something so . . . so . . . worldly? She pushed the soap button and closed her eyes as the dispenser shot a jasmine-scented body wash over her shoulders. She always likened this part of the shower spa to the Jetsons cartoon or going through a car wash. This shower did everything except scrub your back and towel you off. She lathered quickly, then rinsed. She had a thought. Call Brice and talk to him. God did not bring forth weak children. If she were truly a child of God, she would be able to see what she needed to see. Brice would reveal himself to her as Godsend or a wicked man. She would fast. She would pray. She would not touch her own body to satisfy any sexual urges. That was for her husband to do. And until she could call her husband by name, it was forbidden territory.

Grier toweled dry and threw on an oversized t-shirt. One thing she'd missed while in London was America's mindless television programming. She microwaved a bag of popcorn flipping the channels by remote from the kitchen.

"Geewillickers! What's happened to Joan Rivers' face?" she exclaimed, noting that the nipping and lifting had the former A-list comedian's face in suspended animation. She flipped again, tossing a handful of popcorn into her mouth. She spit it back out into her hand. She gave herself a quizzical look in the microwave glass door. "If it was too hot for your hand, twit . . ."

She grabbed napkins and headed for the couch. Some new wiseguy Mafioso show was on HBO. Pass! She couldn't stand the way Italian Americans were portrayed as these ignorant ruffians who spoke not a word of Italian beyond utilizing a few food-related words. All she needed was to hear one more *moolie nigger* comment and she'd explode, particularly since her experience with real, living Italians in Tuscany proved them darker than she and hopelessly in awe of Black women.

After an hour of flipping channels Grier found herself glued to PBS British comedy night. She was hacking with laughter at the antics of the menacing trio of geriatrics on Last of the Summer Wine, when she remembered the journal pages she had. Grier pulled out her reading glasses and started with the stack she had chosen from the pile in Eisendorff's hands. The very first thing that she saw when she flipped over the page, were the words: *My sister slept with my husband.*

February 10, 1966

    My sister slept with my husband. Johnathan claimed it was by trickery, but I don't believe it was at all. He'd become a bit too cordial with her over the past few months, and long before I made it to Connecticut, I knew they'd betrayed me. It had started innocently enough with her showing him around Connecticut and slowly progressed to her rubbing his temple and shoulders, taking every possible opportunity to hee and haw in his face. She couldn't rest knowing that I had a husband and family all my own. But for better or worse, I love my sister. Johnathan only admitted the affair once I confronted him and after years of convincing me he'd never lie or cheat me, I may never be able to forgive him.

    "You want her, don't you," I asked.

    "No."

    His answer came too quickly and with forced non-emotion.

    "You've had her," I stated blankly, knowing the answer by the way his eyes studied the printed pages beneath him. He was eating breakfast and using the morning edition as a shield to my interrogating tone. But it was no use. The truth was wrestling, bouncing back and forth between his lips and his eyes. His lips moved to explain and his eyes tightened in mocked torment. His head shook from side to side and he breathed out as if the weight of his crime were finally being lifted from his aching body, relieving the pressure, but also exposing the open wound to the elements.

    "I don't know what happened. One minute she was lying in bed next to me joking and laughing at nothing in particular, and the next, she was touching me. I thought I was dreaming because everything seemed so hazy, but then I woke up next to her."

    I didn't say another word, but proceeded up the stairs to the nursery where I pulled Eisendorff and Grier's clothes into a small suitcase I'd pushed under his crib. I could see this coming on for months and had chosen to ignore it, but now there was nothing to do, but go on with my life. My heart was brinking the moment of implosion, straddling the threshold of bursting into a million, zillion little pieces, but somehow I still had my faculties about me. I was hurt, humiliated and frustrated. After bearing him two children and giving my all to him, listening to my family bad-mouth him and feeling evil stares on me for even associating with a man of such lowly character, I had been proven wrong. I had been lying to myself for years. "The Man With No Name" is what people in Connecticut had called Johnathan. He had no money, no class and little direction. But I didn't care, because he had heart and spirit and he loved me. He was my man and he could have my name if he wanted. How foolish I had been.

Eisendorff napped quietly on his stomach, thumb tucked securely between his tiny lips. I looked down at him and wanted so badly to cry, to grab him up and explain that I had tried my best to give him the things he deserved, but was still condemning him to a life as a fatherless son. I stroked down a few stubborn strands of his thick black hair and turned to finish packing our bags. I didn't have the time to fold and sort things as I'd wanted and the more that I thought of the deception I'd been handed, the quicker my pace became. I ended up yanking the two remaining drawers of clothes from the dressers and dumping the content into the case. By this time a two-and-a-half-year-old Grier came peeking into the room to witness the commotion. Her eyes were bright and curious and the snaggle-toothed grin she normally wore was replaced by a miniature version of my own distressed glare. She stood in the doorway looking at me and me at her.

"C'mere Sweetie," I finally said, causing her to run into my arms crying. I tried to comfort her as much as possible, but it was no use, as my own nervous aggravation was coming through. I wrapped her coat around her shoulders, over footed pajamas and placed her back down on the floor, before covering Eisendorff with two blankets to beat back the February wind. With two bags and the children weighting me, I struggled down the stairwell and out the front door.

Johnathan, I suppose, had been too ashamed to try and continue our conversation, figuring we'd pick it up later. Even the racket I'd made clearing my things hadn't jostled him from the study. But as I got Grier and Eisen situated in the car and returned from the driveway to retrieve a few things of my own from the master bedroom, Johnathan came tearing out of the house.

"What're you doing?" he yelled, grabbing my pant hoop and jerking me backward. I wanted to punch and scratch and kick him the way I'd imagined I would if ever I found he was unfaithful. But that somehow didn't seem right. I ignored him; freeing myself, pushing my things into the trunk and slamming it shut. His tears were real and hysterical and slobber trickled down his face onto his dress shirt. On his knees he begged me to stay, but I couldn't. I suddenly feared going back into the house, as the children, sensing the conflict had begun crying in the back seat. My sister, who had been silently taking in the whole scene from a safe distance, appeared in the doorway. She didn't look pleased by her handiwork and I sensed that perhaps she and Johnathan both really felt remorseful. I looked hard at her bent posture and convinced myself not to feel any pity for her. My children were my only concern. I pushed past Johnathan, who grabbed my leg as I started by him. All I could hear was Grier crying "Daddy, don't cry . . . don't cry" as I kneed him in the chest hard, and continued up the stairs two at a time.

I watched from the bedroom window as Johnathan placed Grier, who'd run from the car to console him, into the arms of my sister, and darted into the house. Grier's shrieking got louder and my sister, unable to stand the sound, placed Grier back into the car and locked the doors.

"You bitch!" *I heard Johnathan yell from the bottom of the stairwell, only slightly above the sound of breaking glass. They were in the study. I was torn between intervening and allowing her to fall to her fate. My head felt like an elephant was sitting atop it, and my thoughts jumped about, zigzagging wildly. I had to get to my children; they were all I had left. I walked out to the car and coaxed Grier to calm down. Her little face had turned red and her anxiety was causing her to gag. I spoke in a loud, uneasy tone, trying to fade out the sounds of my sister's screaming.* "You are the big sister now Grier, remember? You have to look after your brother and keep him from crying for just a little while longer. Mommy has to go get Auntie L."

I couldn't leave my sister. Besides, Johnathan had no right taking his frustrations out on her, as theirs had been a collaborative effort . . . a joint venture. Grier agreed to stay in the car and I started the engine to warm them from the frigid air. She immediately started talking to Eisendorff in a hushed voice, easing his squirming.

I was prepared to bring my sister out of what was our family home, at all costs. Johnathan had never put a finger on me in any but a loving way, but I could tell from the continued grappling I heard, that she was getting it pretty good. Just as I made it to the front steps, she appeared at the patio doors. Visibly shaken, her eyes were wet from crying and her clothes were ripped. Johnathan came up from behind her slowly, methodically like an animal stalking prey. His eyes darted from left to right in a deranged, hypnotized manner. I jumped in the car and leaned over to unlock the passenger side door. "Get in the car" *I yelled to my sister. She slid in without looking back or at me. She scooted down in the seat until only the very top of her hair was visible.*

Johnathan walked up to the front of the car and slammed his hands down on the hood.

"You can't leave me. I love you."

"Oh, was that before or after you fucked my sister?"

As if noticing her for the first time, Johnathan turned to my sister and began yelling and pulling on the door.

"Tell her! Tell her what you did to me!"

He kicked the fender a few times rapidly, causing the car to rock violently.

My sister said nothing, but then she didn't have to. I opened my door and got out to face him.

"She has nothing to do with you and me. I trusted you and you betrayed me. All the while I kept asking 'Is anything going on between the two of you?' and 'What's happening to us?'. You had nothing to say. You made me think it was me. You made me believe I was failing you as a wife. How could you?" I finally broke, tears streaming down my cheeks.

Johnathan reached for me, but I moved aside. He stammered and tried unsuccessfully to catch his thoughts up with his words. Frustrated, he simply fell silent.

"Stay away from me and my children, Johnathan. I'm going to my uncle's place to think about this whole thing and I don't want you coming around there. If I catch you there, I swear I'll turn my father loose on you."

"I can't live without you," he bellowed.

I turned and got into the car. I wanted him to suffer, but I couldn't bear to watch him flounder about, latching out for any remnant of our failed relationship. Johnathan saw that I had made up my mind and his eyes took a dramatic turn into darkness. His face pinched into a strained little knot, causing his features to become virtually indistinguishable. He fiddled with his pants pocket, mumbling to himself first, then insisting aloud, "I will not live without you."

Johnathan placed a small nickel-plated revolver against his chest.

"Oh shit! Johnathan, no!" I screamed, jumping from the car, reaching him just as his body barreled to the ground.

But it was too late; Johnathan squeezed one bullet from the gun into his chest. I will never forget the sound his body made when it hit the ground. He was listless in my arms, staring up at me. Dead weight was the first thing I thought. The skies opened up and the light drizzle that had fallen off and on all morning, gave way to an ice cold shower. The rain diluted his blood before it could seep into the concrete cracks, creating a pink stream of misery to drain along the slope. The children's screaming sounded so distant that were it not for my looking directly at them, I would have sworn it was coming from a million miles away. I don't remember how we got from the house to the hospital or the minute-to-minute happenings from that moment on. Next thing I recall was waking up in my mother's parlor with the children asleep on either side of me. I tried to raise my head, but couldn't. I was fully clothed, dressed in a black dress and pumps. The kids were also dressed in black. I pushed my upper body up on my elbows, unfocused and dazed. There were people all around me, milling about and speaking in muffled whispers. Quietly dismal, they were mourning. In a state of shock and panic, I forced myself to ponder where I was and how I had gotten there. The events of days' passed flooded back and I felt *light-headed and nauseated. Johnathan was dead. He'd killed himself. I looked at my children, now fatherless for real with no possibility of Johnathan and me reconciling. They would grow up knowing their mother had pushed their father to suicide. I had killed him. I felt my chest tighten and reclined back on the sofa again. If I had stayed, Johnathan would be alive. So what if he had slept with my sister? It meant so little now knowing he was gone. My eyes felt sore and even without a mirror, I knew they were red and swollen.*

My mother's brother, my uncle Fritar, seeing I was up, though not quite about, stepped into the parlor. He was about the same height and weight as my father and always wore a smoking jacket no matter what the occasion. Usually they were red or green, but today it was black. His face looked drained, but he smiled with his pipe fitted tightly between his teeth.

"How you holding up?"

"Is he really dead?" I asked, my throat dry and pasty.

"Fraid so my dear. But now, we all got to take that journey at some point and well, he lived a good long life. Beautiful wife and family. And he was so proud of you girls. Yep, you and your sister sure made your daddy's life worth living."

"Daddy?"

"Yes sir, he sure went away from this Earthly house without a care in the world. Got to see his two grandbabies get borned and everything. Old Micheaux, I hear, willed you girls everything; didn't leave your mama nothing," he said, exhaling pipe smoke from his nose and mouth at the same time. It was a habit of his I used to marvel at as a child, but watching him do it now while speaking of my beloved father, felt like mockery.

"My daddy's dead?" I whispered in disbelief.

"You'll be alright girl. Least Johnathan's still on this planet to help ya. Damned careless not to empty a gun before cleaning it. Seem kinda awkward to me, but I'm sure he'll know better next time. Would've been a shame to lose your Daddy and husband in one weekend."

My eyes lost focus of the burly man before me and my body seemed to curl up with his pipe smoke and dance above myself. My thoughts became fragmented and frayed until I could no longer recognize my own speech. That's when the room began spinning and everything went black again.

May 29, 1966

My father was dead. That beautiful, proud warrior had succumbed to a heart attack at the age of sixty-nine. No one was home when his chest tightened and the thumping chambers suddenly clenched like a fist and refused to reopen. All of the wonderful things he'd done for me, the lessons he'd taught, my battles he'd fought for me, the loving supportive arms he'd wrapped around me, were gone. I walked through days at a time with nothing at all on my mind. White space, like a lit blank projection screen filled my vision, until I was unable to distinguish faces, sounds or circumstance. Were it not for my children, I would have swallowed the sedatives given me by Dr. Driscol one at a time until the pain and anguish, the white light, had diminished. I needed my daddy, but my kids needed me. Beyond the exhaustion dealing with my daddy's death presented, was the realization that I still had to deal with Johnathan and my sister.

The deception, the failed suicide, and the guilt of both incidents left everyone worse for wear. Even my children, as young as they are, appear traumatized by the events that have unfolded over the last month. They now cling to their father with great anxiety. Grier is afraid to leave the safety of my arms and Eisendorff cries uncontrollably at the least disturbance. That gunshot going off continues to echo in my head, so it makes sense that it would terrify innocent minds.

While concentrating on the kids, I agreed to allow my sister back into the house. There was no place for her to be. Having turned to our mother for a place to stay a few days earlier, both were begging me to give her refuge back in our home shortly thereafter. There was really no reason to fault her or turn my back on her. After all, I'd taken Johnathan in, bullet-wounded and weak, so it was only fair to take her in as well. Quiet and hidden from sight during her grief, my sister remained out of my reach for nearly three weeks. I employed a nurse to handle Johnathan and went about busying myself—rearranging furniture, skimming a few of Daddy's Negro-related books he'd willed me, and tending to the children.

I was only beginning to feel myself again today, checking my appearance in the hall mirror and seeing the dark, maddening circles under my eyes, gone, when my sister dropped yet another bombshell. Wrapping a terry towel around my newly washed hair, I watched her approach me from behind, in the window reflection, her walk a confident swagger. It was a sure sign of trouble, like a broom whisking across my feet and disappearing before I could spit on it.

"Please come to the parlor and sit with me," she smiled. "We must talk and it is pressing".

"What are your issues?" I asked, folding my arms across my chest and leaning against Johnathan's oak liquor cabinet.

"I wanted to let you know that I love Johnathan and always will . . . and that we are expecting a child,"

"You're expecting a child? What does that mean?" I asked her, determined to make her take back the lie she told and examine the severity of her claim.

"I am pregnant and Johnathan is the father. I've already told him and, though he wants me to go to Mama Luce and get rid of it. I'm sure that once the child is born, he will love it as he does Grier and Eisendorff,"

I walked to the door, pushing her aside. "I want to hear nothing of this. What you and Johnathan do about your bastard offspring is of no concern to me. It does not affect me in any way at all, so do as you like," I told her. It was more than a possibility that she was pregnant and that Johnathan was the father, but why was she telling me this and with that fucking smirk on her face and while we both were in the process of mourning our father's death? I had no room for her tomfoolery in my life and attempted to exit the room.

That's when things turned ugly.

She spat behind me, laughing that the battle had finally been won for Johnathan's affections, and I was out.

"I got a piece of your rock. Now, what?" she laughed. "You know most people here think that he and the children are mine anyway, and now with our own child, you are clearly the outsider in this equation. You don't fit in here anymore anyway. Gottlieb Grove is not big enough for the two of us, and after speaking with Mama about this last night, she feels as I do, that there simply is no room for you here."

She had planned this the whole time I was away. She had my man and my kids and she intended to keep them. I had trusted her, naïve as I was, to look after my family. She had betrayed me. Yet it was not her fault, but mine. Warnings from my mother to leave that "no count Delta nigger alone" had turned slowly into her convincing me that the children should be turned over to her and Daddy or to my sister to care for while I completed my course study. It looked bad on the family that after all my upbringing I was nothing more than a loose woman with two illegitimate children.

Still later, those words turned to "those kids need some semblance of you in their lives and your sister is the closest thing to you". Everyone seemed to know that I was slowly relinquishing my relationship with Johnathan, undermining my love, belittling my passion, denying my desire and admitting falsely that I was not good enough for him. I had given him over to my sister, because in my heart I had come to believe that he could rule the world, were it not for me. Johnathan was the diamond in the rough that comes along every now and again and that our family couldn't afford to allow some other woman to acquire. If Johnathan loved me enough, he would confess his double-dealing and walk away from the Grove with me and our children. But as my father suspected, and I later realized, Johnathan wanted to be 'somebody' more than he wanted me. That's how I know God has either forsaken me or is punishing me. How could He have let my life come to this?

Up until this moment, I had learned to push my insecurities and heartache to the back of my head. I had been a willing participant in my own undoing and I had no one to blame but myself. With my sister's glib admittance, the white light I had fought to suppress returned. I shut my eyes tightly and tried to pray my way through the immediate shock. But there was her voice, taunting me, sneering at me. My sister's face was so close to mine that the spit from her angered words tagged my cheek.

Her open palm grasped my entire face, pushing it back.

"Say something, I dare you!" she yelled. "What are you gonna do? Cry? Daddy ain't here to help your ass now!"

When I hooked her by the neck I didn't fade out of anything. I was conscious, in my right faculties and aware of every movement I made. I would have to pray about this afterwards, I decided. I proceeded to beat her ass until I had exhausted every bit of despair, frustration and hurt from my body. I blackened her eyes, hoping to remove that sly, 'what-are-you-gonna-do-about-that?' look from them. I put knots all over her body, pounding my fists into her flesh and allowing the absorbed shock of impact to linger, my knuckles still submerged in her skin, before striking her again. The silent torture I found myself engaged in was broken by the deafening sound she forced from her body after a while. It was the kind of savage cry animals made just before their eyes walled back into their heads and they gave up the ghost.

Yet, even as she grabbed her stomach and doubled over, her smirk displaced by horror, I would not believe her pain. There was no compassion for a dethroned drama queen. I didn't believe for a second that she was hurt or that as soon as I released my grip of her, she wouldn't start fighting dirty.

Then I saw the blood running down her leg.

L

The phone rang, startling Grier an inch off the couch. "Where is the bloody phone?" she asked following the sound as near as she could. She found it sandwiched beneath the cushion of a chaise.

"Hello," she said cleaning popcorn hulls from her dental work.

"So . . . you are home then?"

Grier put her hand to her chest and felt a palm of perspiration. It was Brice. "Hello. Are you still there?" he asked after a lengthy pause.

"Yes. I'm here. How've you been?"

"Lonely."

"Sorry to hear that," Grier replied sheepishly.

"Grier, we need to talk."

"We do. Can you meet me tomorrow for lunch?"

"I'd rather meet you tonight."

"That's not a good idea. Tomorrow, let's say noon at My Thai. Is that place still open?"

"Yeah. Okay then Grier, tomorrow it is. I want you to know that I've missed you."

"I've missed you as well. By the way, how did you know I was here?"

"Your mother called me."

"Damn and blast!"

"I'm glad she did. At least *she* did call . . ."

Grier deserved the lashing she was getting and took it through gritted teeth. "You're right, Brice. I should have told you I was leaving, I just didn't know how. The only thing I could think to do was run."

"Run from what? From whom?"

"From you."

"Why? I would never hurt you. You do love me don't you? You did love me anyway, didn't you?"

"I did and I do. Everything was just really complicated and I needed to think and get away. If I told you to give me space, you would have gotten upset and left me."

"No, I wouldn't have, I would have given you space! Grier I am not going to pretend I'm not still upset about this. But, more than anything I am hurt. If I did anything to cause you to disregard me and my feelings, tell me so I can apologize. If I have not, then explain yourself."

"That's just it, you didn't do anything to harm me. I was . . . afraid. I was feeling boxed in and—"

"Is this about the wedding night?"

". . . Kinda"

"Grier, all men are not your father. All men don't live and breathe sex. And all women are not your mother or your aunt. I told you I would wait for you to be ready and I did. I have."

Grier was relieved only momentarily.

"You've waited for me to be ready—but have you waited to get your own needs met?"

"You're asking if I'm sleeping with someone? No."

"Yeah, right."

"I said 'No'! You are the one I want to spend time with, the woman I want to share my name and bear my children. You don't believe me because you think you're not worth it and I'm telling you that you are. If I never had sex with anyone but you, I'd be okay."

"Brice, I feel ashamed when I think of intimacy. I don't want to, but I do. I need . . . I don't know *what* I need . . ."

"You need a hug?"

Grier laughed at his expression. It was a phrase he often used and it was almost always a fair assessment. "Yes, I suppose I do."

"Then open the door."

Grier whipped her head around to see Brice with flowers in hand at the back door. He looked absolutely scrumptious—better than she remembered. She unlocked the door and noticed her ashy legs staring back at her. She almost slammed him up in the door trying to close it back.

"Wait Brice, my legs are ashy. I wasn't expecting you."

"I know you better open this door woman! I'm not worrying about your little ashy legs. Come on wrap your arms around my neck and tell me how much you missed me again."

Grier laughed thinking of how silly she must look trying to shut the door on him. It was the same kind of fool-heartedness she exhibited whenever he was near. At least this proved that she still loved him. Sometimes she thought she loved Brice too much, and wanting to please him, had ignored her own needs altogether. Grier liked what he liked, felt what he felt, believing that if she disagreed with him in the slightest, he would leave her. Compromising her will to please him on the simplest of issues created a snowballing sense of resentment towards him that she could neither express nor explain. She and Brice Rhyne had hit it off instantly, but she soon found herself competing with her own reputation. It started with Brice telling her that he remembered her as a former Ms. Teen Connecticut, and her drowning him in charm. She'd walked around the entire evening sounding like she was answering a panel of judges. Grier said all the right things, smiling coyly and batting her lashes in between sentences. Brice was in awe; but that meant she had to gloss her teeth with Vaseline and appear awe-inspiring whenever he was around.

Once they'd started dating, she found herself constantly cooking gourmet meals because Eisen had told Brice she was a licensed culinary chef. It was something she'd done as a fluke and had come within two points of failing her final cooking project. Of course, Eisen, who'd become her personal publicist, neglected to tell Brice that tidbit. That she simply didn't have time to prepare meals of any real magnitude or substance except for holidays, was inconsequential. For love, Grier would stay up to ungodly hours to prep food she'd cook later in the week. Brice wanted and expected a hot, three course meal at least three times a week, often calling her at work and telling her what he was in the mood to munch.

Grier felt a droplet of sweat run down her forehead and wiped at it before it entered her eye. She and Brice stood looking at each other, he leaning against the kitchen counter and she against the dishwasher.

He stared at Grier so intensely that she became embarrassed. Finally, Grier adhered to his request, snuggling up to his warmth, her arms swathed around his neck. She took his hand and led him to the couch, grabbing the stacks of pages she'd been reading and tossing them beneath the sofa cushion, "Just some unfinished business I need to address," she said to his questioning face. Brice didn't press it and took a seat next to her, then balled himself up with his head in her lap. She stroked the top of his head which he had shaven clean.

"Brice, I'm so sorry about leaving you. It's like everything I did for you, I did to impress you, but I wasn't sure you even knew the real me."

"Silly girl. I know that your smile is like a thousand first moons and your walk like the calming motion of the sea. Your laugh is music to my soul and your virtue an amazing, amazing thing."

"Brice—"

"No, let me finish," he said, sitting up and cupping her face. "I see women all day long and I see the best and the worst of them and in them. I look at them and the games they play and feel blessed to know that you even exist among such creatures. They ask me a bunch of inappropriate questions about my love life, they rub up against me by *accident* and these females expose themselves to me even when they are fully clothed. I find it all to be sad and abhorrently unladylike. When I asked about your gynecological appointments with Dr. Luce the one time, you referred to your female anatomy as your *feminine being*. I'm at work listening to women refer to their own body parts as coochies, nappy dugouts and the formidable 'p-word'. No matter how physically attractive these women are, I am repulsed by them."

"Really?" Grier asked, looking deep into his eyes.

"Grier, you are a rarity. And let me peace your mind, Eisendorff and I are best buddies, but I'm not in to mindless sex. I told him I wanted a good, clean, wholesome girl and that's when he introduced me to you."

"But it's not as if you're a virgin. How do you manage not having it?"

"Who says I'm not a virgin? You are a victim of your own stereotyping Miss Holland. Perhaps the reason I can respect your virginity is because . . . I'm also protecting my own," Brice said, looking up to meet Grier's gaze.

"What? Brice, I've heard from more than one source that you were a regular playboy in school. You cannot seriously be telling me that you are a virgin."

"The assumption has always been that because I ran with your freak brother—pardon my choice of words—that we were freaks together. I've never answered those curious looks and winks one way or the other.

"Are you telling me that you . . ."

"What I'm telling you is that I don't want to share myself with some woman who has little or no regard for where she places her body. Grier, God put you in my path to be my wife and I will never take any woman to a marital bed who is not my wife."

Grier felt so overwhelmed that she wanted to scream and laugh and cry at the top of her lungs all at the same time. Brice Rhyne, the most eligible bachelor in all the country, might be a virgin. Brice was a virgin? Brice, a virgin . . . just like she was? Brice was a virgin just like she was *and* was in love with her?

Brice didn't want Grier to know that he was as fragile as she was when it came to matters of the heart. They seemed fixed to get back on track, but there were three missing years of her life he needed to know about. He treaded softly.

"So how were things in London? Your aunt still procuring men as love slaves?"

"London's wet and overcast, but fun. And no slaves hidden in the wine cellar, mind you. Aunt Lindersyl has a steady bloke these days."

"Not your Aunt Lindersyl," he said in mocked surprise.

"She's with a nice guy, who is younger than the both of us but that doesn't mean she's slowed down any. The truth is that I don't believe Aunt Lindersyl can control herself much. In fact, Eisendorff and I are convinced that she's been doing a little bit of everything with whomever she chooses, maybe even our Dad."

Brice held his tongue. His suspicions were the same as hers and her brother's. Together Eisen and Brice had witnessed some rather ominous dance moves between Johnathan and Lindersyl one night in undergrad, followed by some heavy wall banging in Johnathan and Lillian's bedroom. Only the next morning they found that Lillian had spent the night in the pool house. Eisen and Brice had deduced that something happened between them, but never mentioned it.

". . . Your aunt can take care of herself. But all of your aunt's frolicking didn't give you any ideas did it?"

"On the contrary, it scared me half to death. She and Olivus go at it like animals in heat. She calls it passion, but it looks more like possession. They seem so out of control that it frightens me."

"You've actually seen them?"

"I think she does it on purpose! Every time I turn around she's bent over the kitchen counter or stairwell banisters. I've come to walk through most rooms with my eyes diverted to keep from alarming myself."

Olivus took her hand, seeing the visible residue of fear on her face just mentioning it. "Grier, I promise, I would not do anything like that to you."

While Brice was in a peaceful place, Grier wanted to address other major concerns with their relationship; a laundry list of likes and dislikes she'd never shared.

"Brice, I hate most of the foods you like. I'm a salad and fruit type of girl, but you like meat and potatoes. I love watching wrestling matches and foreign films and eating those Now & Later taffy candies you can only find in the worst neighborhoods. I also don't like kissing you after you'd eaten that goose liver pate . . ."

"Grier, I love you. The rest, we will work out."

Brice knew that Grier was far from this wonder woman he'd come to know, but he wasn't willing to throw their relationship away based on that. He was determined, no matter what, to make Grier his wife. Brice rested his head on her shoulder and smiled to himself, drifting into a deep sleep with thoughts of the two of them in that same posture, fifty years from now.

*The way I'm needing you, I guess I'll play the fool —
It's my heart, not my mind and it's taking over*

Cruel, Human Nature

harry and eisendorff
Gottlieb Grove, Poolhouse
May 19, 2001

"Just because you whip your daddy's ass don't mean you get to whip mine!" Harry laughed, pushing Eisen down into a patio chair. "I saw you out there yesterday afternoon tossing him around."

Suddenly Eisen wasn't so sure his big march down to the pool house to set Harry straight was such a good idea. He stood on the poolhouse deck, getting up his nerve to knock Harry Veda into the middle of next week. Harry was right, though. It was one thing to trade punches with Johnathan, who would beat him to within an inch of his life. It was quite another to throw his fist up at Harry who would *kill* him. Eisen sat pouting.

Once before, as a teenager, when his mother's affair became obvious, Eisendorff and Harry had come to blows. He'd gone to the poolhouse to defend his mother's honor, only to find she had none to defend. Clad in their skivvies, Lillian and Harry were enjoying a lively shuffle to the Staple Singers' *A Piece of the Action*. It was the first time Eisen had noticed his mother was a woman, with breasts and swaying hips and the ability to be sensual. Her hair was pinned up with little glazed chopsticks and when she rotated her hips to the beat, her white kimono fell against her curves, revealing full, ample thighs. Eisen was as awed as angered that night. A pain began in his chest that intensified and spread to his head and stomach. He clenched his fist, shaking until a spraying of blood burst from his nostrils.

"Eisen! Baby, what's wrong?" Lillian screamed, believing the bleeding had come from another of Johnathan's attacks on him.

But Eisen cringed at the sound of her voice, and he pulled away from the hand she placed against his cheek. He walked over to Harry Veda, who was busy fastening his robe about him, and pushed him as hard as could. Eisen felt like he was moving a block of cement and managed to move Harry only a step.

"Calm down boy," he admonished Eisen, stepping backward from the push. "What you mean by barging into my home?"

Eisen threw as many punches as he could until his body fell limp and exhausted to the floor. Not one of the punches actually hit Harry, who with little effort flipped Eisen about the room like a rag doll.

"You calm enough for me to let you go?" Harry laughed, tossing Eisendorff to the couch.

Lillian was so furious with Eisen that it took a few moments to get her mouth and the syllables they were trying to construct to join. But when she did, she went into Eisen with both feet.

"How dare you!" she began yelling, yanking a brush from the side table and striking him across the back. "I don't know why you bring your simple ass home if all you do when you get here is disorder mine and your father's lives!"

Even Harry was confused by Lillian's words and jumped between them. He asked Lillian to leave, which she did under rancorous protest. After she'd gone, Harry found a cold towel and placed it under Eisen's nose.

"Eisendorff, I think you're pretty brave coming down here to protect your mother, but she don't need protecting from me. I love her and neither you or your crazy Daddy going to change that," Harry said.

And nothing had changed their "romance". But what they'd had then was nothing so intrusive as to destroy his parents' marriage. This thing now—a divorce, called for another attempt at straightening out Mr. Veda.

Harry sat sharpening a pairing knife on the deck with his "old man" glasses teetering on the edge of his nose.

"You come to my door with a lot of huffing in you. You here to do battle young soldier or to share in a drink?" he asked.

The question threw Eisen off. His intention was to say something like "Why are you destroying my family?" and then punch Harry in the face, before running for his life. But seeing Harry there so calm and relaxed, so paternal, he wanted to be his ally; not his enemy.

"Drink." Eisen said.

"What you like? I got some Juna, some soda water and some Heineken," Harry asked, tossing the knife onto the table and making his way to the kitchen.

Eisen had made the mistake of sipping Juna from Harry's unattended cup as a kid believing it to be liquor, instead the sickeningly sweet juice made from gourds had ripped his stomach to shreds. "Beer will do just fine." Eisen called behind Harry.

"So," Harry sighed, handing Eisen a cold bottle and bottle opener. "What gotcha so fired up this morning?" Harry sat right next to Eisen and placed his arm around his shoulder. The closeness made the words "You're tearing up my family asshole" clog up in his throat.

"Why? Why have you proposed to my mother . . . a married woman?"

"I didn't. She, the married woman, proposed to me. We've been companions almost as long as you've been alive. I said 'yes' because maybe it's time to make it legal. Now I don't believe for a second that she'll divorce your father. I'm not stupid. Lillian is going through something with your father that she's gone through before and I am caught in the middle of so long as I am with her . . . And so, I help her pack, watch her walk away, and then, help her unpack and walk back in."

"Has it ever occurred to you that all this time she's been using you to get back at my father? She slips down here to make him jealous, then runs back up there when it suits her. No man should let a woman have that much control over him."

"You're too young to understand the things a man will do for the woman he loves. Not the woman he likes to touch on and be kissy-kissy with all the time. Love is battle and I love Lillian, so boy, I got to do battle," Harry laughed.

"That didn't answer my question."

"You just came and went in this house. Jaunt off to your little military school and to college, but you never paid close enough attention to see what was right in front of you. Your mother practically lives here, in the pool house with me. Come on inside and look around," Harry said, waving Eisendorff into the house.

The two men went down into the living room and then across to the parlor. There were signs of Lillian all around. Her knitting baskets, her house shoes, even her computer.

"Look here," Harry whispered, pointing to a painting over the fireplace. "You see this painting? That's Duchess and me at the Stomping Ground in Cuba, 1970. We were celebrating our fifth anniversary together. Some friends of ours took the photo and for our tenth anniversary Duchess had it painted," he beamed.

Eisen stood biting his lower lip, confused as all hell about what he saw. He walked all around the house, upstairs into the bedroom, bathrooms and nooks. His mother's things were everywhere. This was where she *lived*. Eisendorff also spotted Harry's degrees on a wall in the far corner of the room. This was no migrant day laborer, but an educated man. Harry Veda was an educated man who'd wasted too much of his time with a woman so pretentious and manipulative she didn't appreciate him.

"Since she loves you and Johnathan only loves himself, why didn't my parents get a divorce and the two of you get married?" Eisendorff asked, sounding like a ten-year-old.

"Couldn't. Lillian and Lindersyl made their beds and they have to lie in them."

"What? What's Aunt Lindi got to do with this?" Eisen asked, thinking of the journal pages.

"Soon enough, they'll tell you. Be patient," Harry sighed, embracing Eisen. "We're all grown folks here Eisen, so you want to talk like men, then we talk. But the next time you come to my door looking for a fight, I'm gonna fetch a switch and rip your flesh with it. Hear me?"

'Yes sir," Eisen responded shamefacedly.

Eisen finished his beer in silence and bowed out gracefully. He trekked back up the hill and across the walkway to the main house, trying to figure out what all of these things meant. His mother wanted a divorce, his aunt may have been sexually involved with his father, and the pool guy, who ranked the sanest among the looney tunes, was firmly set to become his stepfather. Eisen went back to his old room and took all the photo books, journal pages, news clippings and mementos his old army bag could hold and crammed them inside. He needed to be quick about it in case Johnathan came back. Johnathan was suspicious enough to make him empty his pockets, so walking out with a full bag of things he hadn't walked in with would set off all kinds of alarms. When he had all he wanted, Eisen carefully pulled the faux bookcase back into place and replaced each book back onto the shelves. Eisen then took the back stairs off the kitchen to his car, still in the port. He didn't bother to say his good-byes to his mother and aunt. Right now, the only thing he wanted to do was figure out the answers to riddles everyone on the Grove—Harry, Johnathan, Lillian and Lindersyl—knew, but weren't willing to share.

Eisendorff drove to his condo and for some reason found himself in the mood to engage Mr. Thornbush. And it wasn't his normal, disrespectful manner either, but a desire to grip up another Johnathan or Harry for being smart enough to hide wisdom and genius behind exaggerated and acceptable forms of coonery. Johnathan did it all the time in business and amongst the ladies; playing stupid and biddable long enough to snag his victims. Harry too, was far more clever than Eisendorff could ever have imagined. He was one of the wisest men Eisendorff had ever met, and yet, for all intent and purpose, Harry Veda appeared to be the town idiot. And while Eisen found Harry's relationship with his mother terribly sinful and more than a bit disgusting, Harry was having his cake and eating it too. Perhaps the sullen Mr. Thornbush, former, Mr. Sammy, was equally as cunning. Eisen carried his duffel bag over his shoulder to the front desk of the condo and rang the service bell. He could see the reflection of Mr. Thornbush straightening his hat and tie in the window alongside the desk. Plastering his most congenial smile across his lips, Mr. Thornbush assessed it a waste of time when he saw that it was only Eisendorff at the counter.

"Yes sir, how may I assist you?"

"Mr. Thornbush, I just wanted to stop by and say good morning and to apologize for my behavior over the years. I thought about what you said last time and you were right . . . so, please accept my apologies." Eisen said, extending his hand to Mr. Thornbush.

Mr. Thornbush looked at Eisendorff with a suspicious glare before taking his hand and answering, "Well I accept your apologies with grace because I know your parents raised you better than that. We all get a little ahead of ourselves sometime, so we just wipe the slate clean. And I am sorry too for saying some of the nasty things I've said."

Eisendorff left Mr. Thornbush at the desk, happy that he was well on his way to being more sensitive to other people's lives. Something about those diary and journal pages he'd read was making him take note of his own behavior, connecting chain links in his life to those of his parents. For once in his life, Eisendorff felt like he belonged to real people and not an image or reputation of them. More than anything, Eisendorff felt tired. When he walked pass the answering machine, he noted the flashing light, but waited until he'd laid back on the sofa with his shoes off to reach behind him and mash the button. There were two messages; the first from the host of his swingers group naming the location of this month's excursion, the second was also from the host, frantically announcing that Terrie was back on the excursion list and had already sent her RSVP. Only a handful of people within their "group" knew that Terrie and Eisendorff had conceived a child together as the result of "said group" and fewer knew that part of the terms of engagement since their baby's birth had been strict compliance with a "no contact" rule.

The baby.

The child could hardly be called a baby anymore. He was either two or about three as close as Eisen could remember. Of course Eisen couldn't be sure of anything concerning the child as he'd never laid eyes on him, though Terrie had kept in contact with his attorney, dropping off photos, firsts and mementos. Eisen wanted nothing to do with the woman or the child. At least he never had before. But something odd was happening to him. He felt ashamed not knowing anything about his son, or the child's mother for that matter. Terrie had simply been a 'playmate'; they were just two swinging swingers who got too carried away to be sensible one night and conceived a child. They didn't even know each others' full names, until issues of paternity came up and then, Eisendorff had insisted that he had shared Terrie with two others that night who could just as easily be the father. Terrie had been as cool as could be though. Terrie Nataiya Thompson or TNT as she was known in group was no poor slag or pocket hooch chasing down wealthy men. Terrie's grandfather had been a textile merchant, sweatshopping and day-laboring Third World citizens for decades into his own global fortune. Terrie's parents, like Eisendorff's hadn't bothered to raise her, but had placed her in the hands of caregivers, hosts and boarding schools. She became a legendary underage party-girl in her teens, a cocaine addict in her twenties and a pouting and bored socialite in her thirties. Terrie had only traded cocaine for sex and as excesses rule her life, it wasn't enough to date a lot or sleep around. Terrie wanted group sex with men who didn't know her, didn't want to know her, and who didn't recognize her outside of the dimly lit caverns they had sex in. Terrie and Eisen had crossed each other twice that Eisen could recall, though Terrie only remembered the once. And when she found that she was pregnant, Terrie was more concerned about how it would affect her caverns excursions than anything else.

According to Cavern rules, no "conditions" were allowed: drugs, STDs or pregnancies. Terrie's family could have cared less; though Eisen cared the least. And when blood tests confirmed his paternity, Eisendorff's attorney and hers agreed to terms of paternity: yearly support checks provided the first day of each new calendar year, a five percent annual increase of support, costs of daycare or nursery school and all medical expenses. Beyond that, no contact was to be had between the two adult parties or the father and the minor child. All correspondence, requests and calls for amendments were to be made through their lawyers. For three years Terrie had been missing in action from the caverns, playing mother. And now, the thought of this woman, a mother, the mother of his child, being involved in the business of the caverns upset Eisendorff. It didn't matter that he hadn't seen his son, had no clue what the kid looked like, or that he could only remember his name, Avery, because it was the same as the enamel whitening solution he used on his teeth each morning. Eisen didn't want his son growing up in a household where his mother did the things Terrie was known for doing.

Eisendorff tossed the idea around of asking that Terrie be barred from the caverns. It was no place for her. He poured a glass of orange juice into a bowl (a bad habit from his childhood) and sat sipping it on the sofa thinking up a way of keeping Terrie out of his "personal" space. The phone rang and he picked it up on the first ring. It was his attorney.

"Yeah, Doc. What's up?" Eisen answered the phone.

"Eisendorff, Terrie's attorney has sent a letter of willful restraint to me asking that in lieu of our directive three years ago to have no contact with each other, you be barred from the Cavern of Luna indefinitely."

"What? She's asking that I be barred from the Caverns! She should be barred! She's the mother for crissake!"

"And you, man, are the father! So as head of a household that you do not head, you are the one standing in dereliction, not Terrie. Or at least that's the way she's playing things out. So long as the child is not in the Caverns or subject to witnessing any such activities that occur inside the Cavern in his home, Terrie is free and clear to do as she pleases. The question is do you want to adhere to the demand, fight it or schedule a meeting with Terrie and her attorney to discuss this?"

Eisen thought for a minute, tapping the duffel bag at his feet with his big toe. He was a hypocrite; ready in one breath to dismiss his mother, father and aunt from his life for whatever their indiscretions, when he should be burned at the stakes himself.

"Doc, tell Terrie's attorney I want to meet with him and Terrie. And oh, I want the child there as well."

Terrie and Eisendorff had come to a compromise of sorts. Temporary as it was, Terrie had agreed to stay away from the caverns, provided Eisen begin visitation with their son Avery. In addition, and for the same "unfit parent" reasoning Eisen had given, Eisen too, was now prohibited from going to The Caverns Of Luna. The phone tag between lawyers had taken less than an hour. And since it was Friday afternoon, Eisendorff's first official weekend of shared custody was set to begin in a matter of hours. He and Terrie would meet at her lawyer's office where he'd sign an amendment to their earlier agreement, have their respective lawyers sign off on it and have it filed before five o'clock.

Terrie signed her name and initialed in the two designated spots on the contract Eisendorff held, without looking directly at the pages. She peered up at Eisendorff glibly, connecting the dots of her son's face with this stranger. She was only slightly embarrassed that she'd never really looked at the father of her child. The lights had always been too dim, and besides, she told herself, the way he felt, the way he made her feel, had been more important than his looks. But looking at him now, Eisendorff Holland wasn't bad at all. In fact, Avery looked very much like him, right down to the gap between his two front teeth. As the attorneys closed the meeting, Terrie touched Eisendorff's arm to get his attention.

"Mr. Holland, your son is in the hallway with Sophia, his nanny. She has a list of his schedules, allergies, and habits," Terrie said formally.

"Terrie, c'mon. What is this Mr. Holland business? That's our son you're talking about."

"Eisendorff, do us both a favor: take the kid and go play daddy; just don't try playing a couple with me."

"What?"

"And I don't appreciate you trying to get me barred from the caverns on account of Avery. I've been enough mother and father to him over the past three years to be able to do what I want without permission from you. You didn't care how he was living, what type of 'influence' he was under or anything until you found out that I was ready to get back to *my* life. You've got a lot of damned nerve."

"Terrie, wait. I didn't make the rules of the game. Women who are mothers have no business in the caverns because you can't be the whore and the matriarch. It's unsightly and a turn-off. Daddy's can do what they please. That's just the way the world is."

"You sound like an absolute idiot, especially since I heard that your mother used to park herself up in there regularly."

Eisen thought better of smacking Terrie in front of their attorneys, who fortunately hadn't heard Terrie's remarks.

"That's a damned lie and you know it! But since you want to play nasty, maybe I'll see about keeping Avery for the long haul and then you can go park yourself up at the caverns."

Eisen walked out into the hallway and retrieved his son. Sophia came as part of the package, though he hardly wanted some stranger staying in his home. Eisen introduced himself to the girl, who looked only about fifteen.

"Hey sweetie, I'm Mr. Holland. How old are you?"

"Nineteen."

"You're a young-looking nineteen. You sure you ain't some twelve-year-old runaway? I'm not trying to get locked up housing you now." Eisendorff said playfully, poking the girl in her arm. She laughed sweetly and told Eisendorff that her age was always in question, so she wore her driver's license around her neck, which she did.

What a breath of fresh air Sophia was. The two of them would get along great.

Avery let out of terrible scream when Eisen lifted him from Sophia's lap.

"Is he sick or something?" he asked.

"No sir, kid's just scream like that sometime."

"Can you make him stop?"

"He will by himself when he gets ready."

"Okay, so why don't I give him back to you until he gets ready," Eisen said, laughing. "So what do we do now?"

"First, I need to go to your home and child-proof it."

"Child proof? Look sweetie, the guns are in the safe, he's too young to play with matches, and the liquor cabinet is locked. What's to child proof?"

"Mr. Holland, you haven't been around a lot of kids have you? You need things like toilet and cabinet latches to keep him from going under the sink and swallowing cleaners or falling into the toilet headfirst and drowning. You need electrical socket covers to keep him from sticking something into the outlets and electrocuting himself, you need . . ."

"Okay, okay, I get it. So what do we do?"

"Since you have a two-seater, I will take the wagon and pick up all the things I think we'll need. You can take Avery with you and get to know him a bit on your own. I have your address and can meet you back at your place in a few hours."

"Hours, huh? Well it seems innocent enough. I have an account at Millner's, you can just get what you need and put it on my account. I'll call them and let them know to expect you."

"Okay, then." Sophia smiled.

Sophia had heard that Avery's daddy was a real ladykiller, but who would have thought it would be Eisendorff Holland? And who would have guessed that she'd be staying in his condo with him, helping to look after his kid? Talk about cushy assignment.

Eisendorff watched Sophia load Avery's car seat into his car before getting into Terrie's Saab station wagon and driving off. Avery looked at Eisendorff and smiled, exposing his gapped teeth, delighting Eisendorff in the process. It had taken all of thirty seconds, but Eisendorff had fallen in love with his son. How clever, and beautiful and bright he was. Looking at the two-page list of dos, don'ts and instructions, Eisendorff hissed and tore it into bits.

"This is *my* boy. I should know him like I know myself."

One day you make me feel that your love is in my hands,
One day you say you'll stay, the next you're changing your plans . . .

Fantasy, George Michael

chasen jacques-antoine collier
The Shark Bar Restaurant, 74th & Amsterdam
New York, New York
May 19, 2001

Chasen stared into the eyes of the drop dead gorgeous waiter refilling his coffee, and smiled. Undeterred by the hustle and bustle of the Shark Bar on a busy Friday afternoon, Chasen scribbled his name and number on a matchbook and pushed it into the server's palm, once he'd returned the smile. The meal of turkey meat loaf and soul rolls had been better than he remembered from a previous visit and the added plus of playing eye tag with the bespectacled waiter had made the trip up Broadway worth it. New York was just a quick stop over en route to Connecticut, where he had a bit of unfinished business with the two Lady Mac Beth wannabes that made up his mother and aunt.

Chasen paid the check and moved with sandwiched augmentation through a crowd that blocked the entire entranceway and continued outside onto Amsterdam. It was an unusually cool afternoon, the kind of weather Chasen liked to spend hours walking aimlessly in. Zipping his leather bomber, Chasen dashed across 72nd street to Broadway for a quick run through the HMV music store. Torn between so many American acts he'd yet to experience and the more conservative brand of music he'd been accustomed to, he had narrowed it down to the new Trina CD and the latest Euro-Jamaican creation Hostage. Better do as the Americans do, Chasen decided, tossing the Hostage disc back into the bin. Besides, he quite fancied the sexual liberation of Trina's lyrics. Stepping back out onto the streets, Chasen couldn't decide whether to hop a cab or walk the forty blocks to his hotel.

With the wind smacking him in the face every step of the way, Chasen decided to walk, dropping Trina into his portable CD player and jamming as he went. He had his father's height, but looked for the better like his mother. Her soft, genteel features: chiseled nose, high cheekbones and soft brown eyes, made him quite the ladies man—when he chose to be. For the most part though, it made him quite the man's man. Chasen had tried, quite successfully, to have productive relationships with women. There had been as many female lovers as male, but Chasen always felt more comfortable in the company of men. Kensington, Michele, Brenda and Ida, were beautiful, exciting women with tremendous appeal and intellect, but he felt something was missing, namely manliness, from all of them. He'd lasted about a year with each of them, except Kensington, who'd lasted almost two years and had damned near convinced him he wasn't gay.

But then he met Ralph Hallowell, and fell head over heels in love. The relationship with Kensington was broken off and he moved to Denmark to live with Ralph. An older man, Ralph, insisted Chase return to school and go on to university, financing his every move. Upon completion of his lessons, Ralph even found a company willing to hire Chasen. Still wild and undisciplined, Chasen made as many enemies as he did friends in his job and eventually gave up the corporate world to become an interior designer.

Something he was quite good at, Chase dove headfirst into renovating and redesigning the vacation homes of many of Denmark's wealthy. Unfortunately as Chase's fortunes grew, so did Ralph's insecurities. Feeling he would be dumped before long, Chase moved his things out of their place while Ralph was away on holiday. Instinctual, given that Ralph brought back a friend with him, a much younger, naïve, replacement. To his diva credit, Chasen had simply shaken the guys hand, wished Ralph well, and gone back to London.

Chasen had spent far too much money on nothing in particular and was penniless and homeless by the time he boarded a Eurotrain to London. Fortunately he had an innate hustler mentality. He'd take care of himself, or find someone else to before he reached Victoria Station. He weighed his options: he could bunk with the Deacon (what he called Arthur Collier), but then he'd have to listen to his fake Daddy's ramblings about God and salvation and his going to hell. With nothing more than a duffel bag on his back, Chasen had ridden the London Underground for half the day, then phoned a married friend, whose wife had no clue he enjoyed men. Chasen and David Bucket had dinner and drinks at Ollie's, pilfering free entry from a doorman who knew he was Lindersyl's relation and the food and drink from Lindersyl's tab.

Chasen saw his aunt's man, Olivus Blackstock, looking as dishy as ever, and started toward him to be sociable. But as always, as soon as Olivus spotted him, he'd tossed him a nod and walked away. Chasen had intended to hit Lindersyl up for a few thousand pounds, if not a place to lay his head for a few weeks, even though he wasn't particular about her. She had always been good to him and if she knew he were doing without, she would help him. Instead, as he went to corner Olivus, David's wife popped up out of nowhere and started screaming in his face. Chasen hated bitches, especially loud ones. This tacky cow had the nerve to push her drugstore, press-on nails into his face and call him a queer. He stole on her quick landing a fist across her eye. Her fake leather hat—an 80s throw back, went flying across the room. While he was being proud of his moxie, she jumped up and beat his ass good. Chasen was good at the hit-and-run variety of fighting and had she stayed on the ground he would have scratched her face up good fashion. But home girl had jumped up and stomped him mushy. Afterwards she grabbed her husband by the hand and yanked him out the door.

Chasen could see Olivus looking down on things from the office tower. That dollup didn't even try and help him. Wasn't no sense in asking Olivus for shit. If he wasn't fistfighting alongside him, he certainly wasn't going to give him any money or lodging.

Chasen got up from the floor with half the club laughing at him and calling him a 'battyboy'. His lip was split, his eye swollen and his side bruised. He'd also peed his pants when one of 'maniac wife's' swift kicks landed too near his kidneys. Chasen admitted to himself, for no more than pride's sake that had this happened to some other bloke, he would have laughed until he cried. He steadied himself along the bar rail and put a drink napkin to his lip.

"Bitches are crazy!" he screamed, grabbing his sports coat and staggering out into the London streets.

One of the doormen tapped his shoulder. "You need to go to hospital?"

"Naw, thanks mate."

"That's what you get hitting a lass. If your mother were here to see this she'd have whipped your hide for sure."

"That asshole Olivus didn't even try to help me."

"Awh man, you weren't supposed to be fighting no girl. What Ollie look like *helping* you to fight a girl? You crazy as hell! Besides, Ollie aching over your mother so bad since she left, he can barely put one foot in front of the other."

"She left him?"

"Not for good, you twit! She's gone with your cousin, Grier, to the States for a few weeks. They left earlier this week."

"Where they staying in the States?"

"At the 'Grove' is all Ollie say."

Sons of guns! They were at Gottlieb Grove, the pair of them. Chasen balanced his wobbling head between his hands and had a moment of eureka! The only people who should be taking care of him were his parents; not his aunt, not her lovesick boyfriend, and not his part-time married lover; but his parents, Johnathan and Lillian Holland.

Chasen pushed his hands deep into the pockets of his overcoat, happy that he'd purchased enough travel vouchers when with Ralph to secure safe passage over the Atlantic. He also thanked his lucky stars that Arthur Collier hadn't changed the combination to the safe in his house. His Wednesday night safecracking coincided with Arthur's Bible study. Chasen swiped a little over five hundred pounds, which made a comfortable two-for-one conversion into American dollars. His knapsack had been replaced with a Louis Vuitton knock-off and his canvas deck shoes for Prada replicas courtesy of Canal Street. No sense alerting the family to his life's downward spiral, he reasoned. Chasen would board the midnight train to Mosse Point, Connecticut, full of soul rolls and resentment. It was a regional Amtrak train that would spin through up-state New York and much of Connecticut before reaching his destination at eight o'clock the next morning. En route, Chasen would fantasize a great reunion, just as he had since boyhood.

Some people live with the fear of a touch and the anger of having been a fool,
They're not willing to listen to anyone, so nobody tells them a lie . . .

Innocent man, Billy Joel

lillian and lindersyl
Gottlieb Grove, Main House, Master Bedroom
May 19, 2001

Lillian and Lindersyl were finally alone with each other and neither particularly wanted to be. Lindersyl was eager to get a sense of Lillian's true reaction to seeing her with Johnathan the night before. With Lillian's divorce announcement, shopping would serve as a buffer and discussing Johnathan would be less volatile. They may actually have a bit of fun in the process.

Lindersyl sat on the floor of the master suite twittling a pencil between her fingers and trying to remember where her last train of thought had gone. Her age was definitely catching up with her. Of late, thoughts left her mind before she'd collected them enough to act on them. Frustrated, she tugged at her tennis dress, which was a size too small and straining against the fullness of her stomach. She cursed Johnathan silently for cooking all that mess knowing she didn't have sense enough to abstain. Lindersyl thought of putting on a girdle and then remembered that that had been her original loss thought. She popped her lips in disgust acknowledging that she could hardly put a girdle on up under a tennis dress. She gave herself a once over with her stomach muscles pulled in tightly. "It's not that bad. Yeah, this will do fine," she convinced herself.

Lindersyl took advantage of Lillian's closet rummaging to check out their mother's gem chifferobe. It was loaded to the gills with every imaginable kind of jewelry, to which Lindersyl felt she could lay rightful claim. She eased open the doors first and then the drawers of the unit to avoid alerting Lillian. Faye-Essie sure had good taste in fine gems. Of course the Bvlgari was locked up in the safe, so Lindersyl would have to settle for the everyday until she could remember the combination. For now, Lindersyl was happy to play "dress up" from her earlobes to finger tips in her mother's antique jewels.

Lillian hesitated leaving the walk-in closet. Oh, how she hated to have to reign in her sister as old as they were, but it had to be done. Lindersyl had gone up to change into her mall-strolling gear, only she looked more in line to stroll the red light district. It was one of those infamous tennis dresses, the spandex kind with slits on either side. Lillian peaked around the corner and noted the curve of Lindersyl's legs. She could carry it off, but should be too ashamed to try. Their mother had always said Lindersyl was trifling. Lillian glimpsed her sister stooping and stretching to rifle through their mother's gem chifferobe. She closed her eyes tightly, distressed that Lindersyl's tennis panties were too small to cover the lower half of her big hips, turning them into the sort of things worn by lap dancers and hookers. Those babies of Lindersyl's had ulcered her legs into varicose vein maps, with red and blue lines running from the back of her knee up her thighs. Lillian thought of mentioning their unsightliness to Lindersyl to get her changed into something more suitable. But as if by mental telepathy, Lindersyl saw her own reflection in the mirror, extending her gams out to view them from behind. She frowned, then pulled a small compact from her handbag and began applying facial foundation to her marred tapestry. When she was done, the scars had been brilliantly masked. Lillian didn't want to fight so she held her tongue, boiling just beneath the surface.

"My poor sister done lost her mind . . . Ain't got the sense God gave a mole. Hips just out there like some little young dumb girl," Lillian said under her breath, stepping from the closet in jeans and a pink silk camisole top.

She startled Lindersyl who was stuffing a pair of Tiffany & Co. earrings into her bra.

"Put them back Lindersyl," she stated flatly, stepping into her pink satin heels.

Lindersyl tossed one earring back into an open drawer and then dug into her cleavage for the other one, which had slipped down a bit farther. She looked over at Lillian who gave her an admonishing look before snatching the recovered earring from Lindersyl's hand.

"I would thank you to stay out of these drawers!"

"Okay—okay," Lindersyl conceded, holding her hands up over her head in mock surrender, exposing her buttocks in the process.

Lillian twisted her face in disgust. "You're not wearing that are you?"

"Sure am," Lindersyl smiled, grabbing her bag from the bed and looping her arm through one strap.

"Now, Lindi, that dress is entirely too short," Lillian frowned, yanking the back of it down. "I can see your big butt sticking out with you standing upright and still. Imagine what it will look like once you start that little shake dance you call a walk or Heaven forbid, you need to bend to pick up something?"

"That's the point Lil! It's a tennis dress and it's supposed to fit like this."

"The operative Lindersyl is that is supposed to *fit* and that does not. It would be bad enough if you were on a tennis court, but it's extreme for the mall," Lillian insisted.

"Lil, am I driving or you?" Lindi asked, walking to the door.

"Does that mean this conversation is ended?"

"Sure does."

"I'm driving."

"Well, you look great Lil baby. Love the shoes," she laughed, pinching Lillian's cheek. "Stop pouting!"

"Lindi stop giving me reason to pout! And keep your hands off of my face; there's no telling *where* they've been."

Lillian and Lindersyl walked out to the driveway giggling at nothing in particular. Harry was on the terrace clearing away dishes in gray sweats that hinted to a favorable build beneath. Lindi paused to check his profile.

"Just as fine as ever! I used to think your taste was all in your mouth, Lillian."

Lillian stopped and looked back at her sister. She wanted to tell Lindersyl to keep her distance from Harry. It was bad enough to have Johnathan hypnotized by her street charm. Lillian's stomach muscles tightened and she forced a half smile to her lips.

"He's alright," Lillian shrugged.

"Bullocks! He's more than all right! He has to be for you to waltz into the kitchen this morning, half-naked and demand Johnathan give you a divorce."

"It's just time," she said, tugging Lindi by the arm and pulling her towards the car.

Lindersyl realized too late she'd stepped on Lillian's feelings. Lillian's face was tight and her posture was withdrawn. Lindersyl should have let it be known that she found favor in Harry, but it was the same surface interest she had for most every man she met. Lillian probably had it in her head now that Lindersyl was out to take Harry from her. Lindersyl made an attempt at diffusing the situation.

"Lil, Harry is a good guy and you're a lucky woman. I hope he treats you right."

"Johnathan he's not! I got a winner in Harry, honey," she said, looking her sister up and down.

"Oooh," Lindersyl moved back in mocked surprised, "Well, you created that drama with Johnathan, so don't blame anyone for it but yourself. Johnathan was not always like this," Lindersyl retorted.

"And you're insinuating I made him this way?"

"I *know* you did because I watched you do it!" Lindersyl said forcefully, pointing a finger at Lillian from the passenger side of the car.

"Will you never let the past rest? Lindi, don't you think I wake every morning regretting what happened?"

"Honestly, no I don't. I think you wake up every morning thrilled as hell to still carry Johnathan's name, but sorry you've ruined so many others to keep it. I used to believe you deserved to be mishandled by him. Now, Lil, I try not to think of you and Johnathan at all," Lindersyl said, rolling her eyes.

Lillian jumped into the driver's seat and released the automatic door lock button.

"Johnathan and I had kids to raise, Lindi-"

"Don't you dare! I had children and a man that I gave up to keep this goddamned precious family name from being shamed! You and mama talking about how 'the Gottlieb girls were the pride of Mosse Point and had to lead by example'. You all taunted me about how much humiliation I'd cause everyone by coming home pregnant with no husband. I've grown bitter and jealous of you over the years Lil, because you *took him*. You told me he wasn't good enough for me, then flipped him until you'd convinced me that I was no longer good enough for him. No matter how sick and twisted Johnathan has become or how much Eisen, Grier and Chasen hate you, you've got a husband and family I will never have!" Lindi said, slamming the door shut.

Lillian didn't know what to say to Lindi; so she said nothing. She'd never considered how Lindi felt always hearing about the kids, when she had been denied the opportunity to rear them.

Lillian moved the car out onto the service road leading to the main thoroughfare and drove slowly along it to avoid pelts of gravel the road maintenance had left. She'd had to replace the glass once already when a pebble hit the windshield and cracked it clear across.

Lindi was turned facing the passenger seat window. She was crying but it felt good to get that off of her chest. Her emotions were running on high and she would give anything for a bottle of champagne right now. She felt like she was going through withdrawals, but because she'd promised Olivus that she would abstain unless in a party atmosphere and then keep it to a two-drink maximum, she would have to suffer her fate sober.

Lindersyl could feel those Daily Bread scriptures Olivus had given her to read each morning breaking through what was about to turn into something very unpleasant. Her melancholy had to be broken if she was to deal with her sister. Lillian was all the family she had, so there was no need beating her over the head about things neither could change, especially since Lindersyl considered their mother to be the real blame.

"Lil, you ever miss Faye?"

"Sometimes. You?" Lillian answered, glad that the silence had ended.

"Not really"

"Ever regret not coming to the funeral?"

"Not really. Hell, I see you got the gossip bench. That was my only reason for wanting to come in the first place." Lindi laughed.

"Honey, Grier pitched a natural bitch about that gossip bench. I had to listen to 'you took grandma's gossip bench and she said it was mine' for damn-near two months. When she realized that I was not going to give it to her no matter how much sniveling she did, she tried to get all spooky on me. She tells me one day, 'Grandma gonna come haunt this seat until you give it to me.' I told her that if that old bat found her way back from hell's gates, I'd personally call on the Devil to retrieve her."

They both laughed.

"Grier told me all about the funeral; said it was nice," Lindersyl said.

"Nice if you call Johnathan getting tanked and jerking off in the bathroom during the service and Eisen fainting when that gas bubble escaped from mama and made her body sit up in the coffin. Girl, the paramedics weren't sure Eisen was gonna come back to us; took three of those ammonia thingies to bring him back around."

"Lillian, Johnathan might need to see a doctor," Lindersyl said, testing the water. She wanted to know how Lillian felt about Johnathan refusing to divorce her.

"We all *know* what's wrong with him."

"Yeah, well some illnesses cannot be helped." Lindi half smiled.

"Why don't you go to him?"

"Listen to you. How am I supposed to go to your husband Lillian when just my being here around the two of you causes friction between the two of us? I can handle Johnathan, but can you handle seeing me with him?"

"Sure. I have Harry."

"And you've had Harry all along Lil. Stop trying to shit a shitter. I know you want to protect me and I appreciate you trying to bring me some level of happiness, but don't divorce Johnathan because you think it will make it better for me."

"I want Harry, Lindi."

"Why, because I'm here? Because you saw the man you married when Johnathan was in my arms last night? Would you have asked for a divorce today if he hadn't shown up to bed me last night?"

"Probably not," Lillian said, studying the leather on the steering wheel, "But last night, I finally made up my mind."

"Oh, just! . . . . Look Lil, you marry Harry because you love him and intend to move off of Gottlieb soil and share in his life. That means no looking back. No going to the club or the spa or the tennis matches, because when you walk away, I inherit all that you leave behind. Mr. Veda has no connections to the things that you are most familiar with and while you may continue to enjoy the richness of your spoils, it will be as a guest. Our guest. Mine and Johnathan's. An outsider, looking in. Now, can you honestly look me in the face and tell me that you can handle that?"

Lillian turned to face Lindi as they stopped for a red light. Her body language, her eyes and her curled lips said 'hell no', but she shrugged and whispered, "I'm sure I could".

"Yeah, right Lil. Like I said, some illnesses, like the one Johnathan and I have, cannot be helped. But maybe it's time he went to see a trained professional. He still throwing tantrums and acting crazy?"

"Not too often. Only when you refuse to talk to him, or when that man of yours answers the line and he can't hear your voice."

"Olivus and I are forcing him to cope. He's been calling the house constantly, listening to the answering machine message and then hanging up before the beep. Finally, I had Olivus erase my voice from the machine message, so now, all Johnathan gets to hear is Olivus when he calls. Soon he'll stop. Y'know, sometimes I wish Faye could have been around to see the mess she made of our lives."

"Mama loved you Lindi, she just had trouble showing it."

"Funny, she never had any trouble showing you."

"We are not about to have the 'mama loved you more than me' conversation. Daddy loved you more than me; mother loved me more than you. But more Lindi, does not equate to not at all."

"Mama seemed to go out of her way to make me suffer. Daddy never tried to hurt you Lil the way Mama hurt me and I wanted to love her Lillian and I tried; but I couldn't. Can you imagine what it was like growing up and as far back as you can remember, hating your own mother?"

"Hate is a strong word Lindersyl. There were times I didn't like the things Mama did, but I've never hated her."

"You've hated me."

"Mama never took from me Lindi. You did."

"Eye for an eye Lil. Besides, I tried to give Chasen back, but you didn't want him, remember?" Lindi whispered.

"Did your vengeance solve anything? And don't go throwing Chasen in my face. Why are we talking about this?," Lillian sighed, slowing the car to a crawl.

"Because I want my sister back! I'm tired of fighting with you. I want you to trust me and for me to be able to trust you. You only wanted Chasen here on the Grove to spite Johnathan and when you realized it would end your relationship with Harry, you changed your mind—again! It wasn't fair to get Chasen caught up in your mess because, Lillian you asked for him four years after you'd left him with us and then changed your mind three times before I could get him a passport. The last time I had to tell you 'no'."

"You didn't mind getting Grier and Eisendorff caught up in yours!"

"If you had left us alone, there would have been no mess for them to get caught up in, now would there?"

"Lindersyl, as always you have a rather limited and self-serving view of your life. You were never fit to parent. Neither of you were. At least with me the children had the proper example around them."

"You've told those lies so long you've come to believe them. Love, you spending your days as Johnathan's trophy wife, your nights as the poolman's playground, and your free time ignoring the children, does not a proper example make!"

"That's not fair! I did the best I could!"

"Face it, we all did what best served our own individual needs!"

Lillian paused a moment, then looked at Lindersyl, "So what do we do now?"

"Tell the truth?" Lindersyl whispered.

"You must have gone mad! How do we explain this to the kids?"

"Well, Lillian, we've got to do something. Eisen's afraid of his Dad, he all but ignores you, and he deifies me. You know he's still involved with that freaky sex group? And Grier, did you know she's still a virgin? I mean, I held on a long time as a girl, but I don't think I could've held that pecan until I was in my thirties!"

"Your pecan was too busy trying to jump out and roll down the street!" Lillian laughed.

"Very funny. Seriously Lillian, being with Grier the last three years has nearly pushed me over the edge. I've wanted so much to tell her."

"You know you can't do that. It would disrupt our entire lives. All that we are . . ."

"Lillian, I said I wanted to, but how would I even begin? Everything would be such a mess."

"Speaking of messes, when was the last time you heard from Chasen?"

"Hmmm," Lindi, grimaced, making mental calculations before she spoke. "I'd say it's been about a year since I've seen him, but I spoke with him a few weeks ago. He sounds fine."

"He say anything about me?"

"Nothing you want to hear." Lindi said flatly, turning her attention back to the tree-lined roadside.

"Lindersyl, you do know that I'm sorry about what happened with Johnathan?"

Lindersyl looked at Lillian, searching for something in her face that would lay oath to her words. There was nothing. Lillian was a good actress, but her performances were always less-than-stellar with Lindersyl as an audience. All Lindersyl could see was her sister, gingerly saddling the fence between Johnathan and Harry, content to mosey them both along until their final breaths.

The two rode for a few minutes in silence. With himself in mind when purchasing the Mercedes for Lillian, Johnathan had equipped it with a massive stereo system. Lindersyl reached into the sterling CD rack and thumbed through the selection.

"Me Against the World, huh? When did you start listening to Tupac Shakur?"

"Lindersyl, that's Harry's. Every time he drives, I have to listen to that thumpidy, thumpidy, thump," Lillian shook her head.

Every time he drives? Lindersyl thought. Their sisterly bond hadn't even allowed *her* behind the wheel of Lillian's prized Mercedes, but Harry was driving it enough that he had his own personal musical selections on hand. The CD was already in the player, along with the Commodores' Greatest Hits and The Dancehall Queen soundtrack. Lindi programmed the player for Tupac and leaned against the headrest.

They both laughed.

"I know exactly what you're thinking, Lillian," Lindersyl said. "If Faye could see us now, she'd clutch her pearls!"

"Then yank them off and whip our asses all over the grounds of the Grove yelling, 'This *is not* a suitable example'!"

They both stopped laughing simultaneously and bit at their bottom lips.

Have you asked why you seem to fall in love and out again?
Do you ever really love or just pretend?

Stop, Look & Listen, The Stylistics

johnathan
Residence of Anastasia Harcourt
Utopia Gardens Apartments
May 19, 2001

"J, things like this happen all the time. Don't worry about it; we'll try again in a couple of hours," Anastasia half smiled, rubbing Johnathan's stomach.

Johnathan turned away in disgust. In all his sixty-two years, the 'this' Anastasia referred to, had never happened to him. It had worked fine this morning . . . and last night. Maybe all the bullshit Lillian was trying to drop on him about wanting a divorce, was messing with his head more than he'd realized. But why? He had wanted to divorce Lillian the morning after they got married. He disliked most things about her; except those comforting things that over the course of thirty-four years a man gets used to having. Lillian was sensitive. She hosted parties well. She got along well with his business clients' and associates' wives. She tried to love him, in spite of him. But those were not things he necessarily valued. As a couple he and his wife had once been functional, but after the first few months of marriage, they grew increasingly dysfunctional. And that's the way they had stayed. He never should have married Lillian, so he should be elated that she wanted to move on. Johnathan told himself he was. But since he couldn't do *it*, there had to be something deep down inside of him that didn't want to let Lillian go. What would he do without her? Where would he go? How would he make a living? Who would care for him? Everything that he had done in his life had been tied up in being married to Lillian. He certainly couldn't count on Lindersyl who was walking around talking about she was engaged to some 'baby boy'. And the dust on the floor knew he couldn't count on the silly broads he "dated" to care for him. Many of them were as shallow and self-serving as he was. They didn't fix meals for him, they didn't care if he were ailing, and they definitely would not go out on a limb for him if it meant inconveniencing themselves in the least. Divorce was out of the question. And how could Lindersyl side with Lillian? For as much as he loved Lindi, he knew that if it ever came to it, she would side with her sister every time.

"Johnathan . . ." Anastasia called.
"What!"
"Did someone wake up on the wrong side of the bed this morning?" Anastasia asked in her 5-year-old voice.
"Stace, I don't want to talk right now. Just let me lie here in peace, please," Johnathan said in a roar, rolling over onto his stomach and burying his head in a pillow.

"Well forgive me for living! I said it was alright that you couldn't get-"

"Could you just . . . . just . . . . be quiet or something!" he stammered.

"You not my damned father! How you come up in *my* house trippin'? As a matter of fact, why don't you get your sorry, broke dick ass up out of my bed and go home? I mean, since you can't stand the sound of my voice, you may as well break!" she screeched.

Anastasia Harcourt was a nineteen-year-old college sophomore, with shit for brains and a deep-seated father fetish. Johnathan was a colleague of one of her professors and when they happened upon one another at a university function, they wasted no time getting to know each other. Anastasia offered nothing to Johnathan in the way of emotional stability or even intellectual comfort. She was simply a good lay. Occasionally she'd throw her little tantrums and he'd get to stroking her back in order to calm her down, and before you knew it, it was back to 'big daddy this' and 'big daddy that'. What she needed was Jesus, but Johnathan's selfishness wouldn't allow him to care for her beyond their bedroom antics. Just a few months ago she'd needed to make repairs on her car, cutting into her rent money. When she came to him, it was for the money, but Johnathan Holland wasn't giving up anything but advice to any woman who didn't have a strong enough hold on him. Johnathan suggested she work a few extra shifts at her part-time salesgirl job in order to make the double rent she'd owe when the next month came around. End of story. Johnathan needed to be needed, but Anastasia was right; he was not her father and wouldn't pay for her company.

Johnathan lifted himself up from the bed and reached for his pants with one hand and his watch with the other. The first thing he needed to do was talk to Lindersyl and apologize. If she was upset with him, then the whole world seemed to be.

"Oh, so you just gonna get your things and leave?" Anastasia yelled. Slamming the bedroom door closed and heading into the kitchen, she yelled again, "Fine then!"

Johnathan hurriedly pulled his pants up and pulled his jacket on over his unbuttoned shirt. He looked about the scarcely furnished bedroom and winced. Everything looked like used hotel furniture and had that plastic, cheap smell to it. How he ever spent as much time in this place as he did was a testament to his lustful nature. Anastasia was beginning to be too much trouble. She didn't want to listen, she always had something smart to say, and now she was putting him out. If he wanted that kind of grief, he would walk down to Lillian's room and jump in bed with her at night. Johnathan grabbed his car keys from the kitchen countertop and Anastasia grunted her disbelief.

"Just leave motherfucker! I'm sick of your ass anyway," she yelled

"I'm going as quickly as I can, Stace. Just calm down."

Anastasia had a mouth like a drunken sailor and temper to match. They'd had incidents in the past where her neighbors had called the police to bring their yelling to an end.

"No, you calm the hell down! You come over here crying like a bitch first thing this morning, talking 'bout your wife wants a divorce. Then you lay up in the bed all day half-sleep and daydreaming calling out for some bitch named Lindersyl!"

"What?" Johnathan asked, stopping dead in his tracks. He felt flushed. Had he really called out for Lindi?

"You ain't deaf! You want this trick Lindersyl so bad, why don't you go lay up in her damned bed?"

Johnathan turned to go, embarrassed he'd opened himself up to this type of thing. He needed to see Lindersyl alone, right away, but was halted by the palm of Anastasia's hand hitting him against the back of his head. He spun around quickly and full of shock. First she'd thrown Lindersyl in his face, now she was smushing him in the back of his head. Johnathan's patience was worn clean through, but he reasoned as he grabbed her that he was too old to go to jail so he couldn't hit her back.

"Do you know I will snap your fucking neck in two?" Johnathan whispered, grabbing Anastasia by the neck and forcing her feet from the floor, pinning her against the door. "Don't you ever mention Lindersyl's name again. Do you hear me?"

Johnathan put pressure against her windpipe when he thought of her hitting him. He only loosened his grip when her eyes began to bulge. Johnathan held her there, her shoulders gripped by his hands until he was satisfied that she understood that 'no hitting was allowed', then released her to the floor, where she collapsed.

"Pack up my things. I'll send a messenger over tomorrow to pick them up," he said closing the door behind him.

Anastasia pulled herself together just enough to clean and wash her face and put her clothes on. Her neck hurt, but wasn't bruised. One thing was for certain now that Johnathan had tripped on her; she wasn't getting any money from him—not even a few of those crisp $50 bills she lifted from the middle of the wad while he slept. She had to go to work to make a living and hated even the thought. It wasn't that she was lazy or anything, but Anastasia didn't deal well with other people. She'd been brought up the only girl of seven kids to working-class parents. She had been spoiled and coddled to a point where she always had one hand out. Working in the Haiko Boutique, Anastasia saw all the rich, socialite women sashaying from spa treatments to brunch to boutiques all day long. She was younger and prettier than they were, so she deserved as much, if not more. Anastasia figured she'd hit pay dirt with Johnathan, only he was a cantankerous old fart most of the time. And he wouldn't freely part with his money for anything.

Her brother Anthony had told her after running into them out on the town that there was a major difference between an old man and an older man. It wasn't age, but disposition. Anastasia had waved Anthony off, understanding what he meant too late. Johnathan was not an older man, but an *old* man.

Anastasia had met Johnathan at a university function her political science teacher was hosting. She thought Johnathan was handsome and very distinguished looking. When she made a pass at him, he'd accepted it willingly and raised the stakes by taking her to dinner after the function. He asked if he could spend the night, and though she was reluctant, one kiss was all it took to change her mind.

Anastasia had fallen in love with Johnathan's manner. He wasn't a boy, but a man. He knew what he wanted and would ask, demand or take to get it. He was good-natured and fun most times, gentle and attentive as well. She didn't like that he was married, but had gotten too involved too soon before knowing. Once she found out, she chose to ignore it. What real harm could it cause? Then Johnathan started bringing his wife into her home. Lillian would call there for him, show up at the door, come by her class and disrupt things on a whim. Now on top of everything else, there was this other woman; this Lindersyl chick, all caught up in his thoughts. It was too much. All Anastasia, wanted from Johnathan at this stage in their relationship was for him and his faded glory to be gone.

Total acceptance is all you'd get
Knowing this you would never regret finding yourself homeward bound . . .

Make Me The Woman You Go Home To, Gladys Knight & the Pips

johnathan, lillian & lindersyl
Metroplex Shopping Mall,
South Mosse Point, Connecticut
May 19, 2001

Lindersyl's hands were half the size of Johnathan's and felt like the fit of a parent's to a child's when Johnathan took hold of them. He was apologizing to her for his belligerent outburst after Lillian's divorce request and now stood, gently caressing the back of her hand, admiring the way the pale violet polish on her nails perfectly matched her dress. Touching her skin was like licking a 9-volt battery, sending little electrical currents through his body. But tonight Johnathan could not afford to make a single mistake. He wanted Lindersyl and he knew she wanted him too. She had become more than the object of his desire; she was an obsession. He did not trust himself in her company alone, as he feared he would ravage her body like a ferocious tropical storm, banging against a tiny coastal village. There would be nowhere for her to hide and no way for him to mask his guilt afterwards. But when Johnathan opened his eyes, he found himself peering at reality. He had only dreamed Lindersyl into his arms. He was alone in his office with his head tilted at an odd and uncomfortable angle with slobber running down his chin.

Holland-Bennett, Johnathan's inherited brokerage house had been without him for most of the year, but once he'd left Anastasia's, he decided to run home, change and head into the office. Old man Gottlieb had graciously passed his holdings of the brokerage to him, but the company pretty much ran itself. With an aged Merris Bennett, Micheaux's original partner, still rolling his way into the office everyday at five-thirty and putting in a full twelve hours, Johnathan did little more than babysit the eighty-nine-year-old. Between Merris and his sons, Holland-Bennett (formerly Bates & Bennett) kept Johnathan's pockets lined and showing up was more out of courtesy. Still coming in always took a mental build up.

Johnathan's secretary looked as if she'd seen a ghost when he walked in mumbling to himself. He looked at her startled expression and shook his head.

"You still trying to reach Denzel Washington on the Internet?" he laughed. He pushed back the double mahogany doors that lead to his office, giving her a tsk-tsk. Connie looked over the top of her glasses and exhaled hard. If he didn't fire her for this, he never would. Even though he'd asked her to stop harassing celebrities on the net, he had never caught her red-handed at her dirty deeds. Quickly she gathered up his mail and messages, pulling her skirt's band around enough to make its thigh high split fall directly down her right leg, and followed behind him. Maybe if he gave her the once-over and liked what he saw enough, he wouldn't toss her out.

"Hey boss, here are the messages, faxes and e-mails. Uhm, is there any reason that you're here today? 'Cause I don't have anything scheduled in the way of appointments or meeting," Connie asked nervously.

"Connie, I work here."

"Lillian's driving you crazy, huh?" she asked with a knowing smile.

"Oh," he laughed aloud, "how well you know me! I wanted to stop in and see you and . . . yes, Lillian is driving me up a wall."

"Well do you need me for anything?" she grinned, shifting her weight to expose her hosed thigh.

"Not really," he smiled back, examining her extended gam.

"Anastasia?"

"Nope," he whispered, with his eyes dancing a bit before looking away.

Connie knew what that meant and turned serious. "Well, your correspondences have all been signed and sent out and I'll be out here if you need me to send out for lunch later."

"Look, do what you would normally do if I weren't here. Y'know dance on the desks, play solitaire and gossip about how mean my wife is to everyone," he smiled, giving her a kiss on the cheek. "Good to see you Connie."

"Yea, good to have you in the office," she half-smiled. Walking to the door, she turned, "Oh, give my regards to Lindersyl."

The foot traffic at Metroplex was light for a Friday afternoon. Usually the government workers came across from the Defense and Finance offices for lunch, but it was virtually empty when Lindersyl and Lillian started their walk through. They marched into Nordstrom and immediately began picking up clothes.

"Lil, what you been up to lately?"

"Not much. I was thinking of doing a 35th wedding anniversary thing for Johnathan and me, until this morning, of course. Other than that, I've been keeping pretty busy—y'know sorority meetings and oh, I've been reading this book by J. California Cooper," Lillian responded, handing Lindersyl a crème-colored linen jacket.

"Nice. I always like her work. You feeling okay?" Lindi shook her head 'no' to the jacket, handing it back to Lillian.

"As well as can be expected. I can't seem to get much sleep in the Big House and don't have too much appetite lately."

"Think you're sick?"

"Nope. Just getting old. Ready to stop the rat race. What about you?"

"I'm doing pretty good. Bored a little from not going into the office everyday. I think Grier showed up just in time. She gives me someone to focus my energy and attention on."

"Prepositions, Lindi! It's like talking to a toddler with you. Anyway, she's a lot like you used to be."

Lindersyl ignored her sister's criticism of her English. "Yeah. That's the funny thing about it, she's got so much of my ways in her, but she's got Johnathan's temperament. And she will set you straight in a heartbeat," Lindersyl laughed, pushing the dressing room door open with her foot, and tossing the armful of clothes onto the floor. She and Lillian always took the handicapped stalls so they could try on clothes together.

"How did Daddy say it, 'That's yall's baby.'"

Lindersyl looked wistful at the thought. No one ever really spoke of Grier and Eisendorff in that manner anymore. It was nice to hear them acknowledged as her very own. "She's turned into a beautiful woman seems like overnight."

"Johnathan and I are really proud of her. We thought she'd get to England and be begging to come home, but she didn't. She's definitely got your iron wills about her," said Lillian, picking the clothes up from the floor and hanging each garment up by color.

"Eisen looks good."

"Just like his Daddy. And he still doesn't have a taste for me—just like his Daddy," Lillian said, hurt that Eisendorff got along so much better with her sister.

"Don't say that."

The ladies redressed in silence.

"So . . . does it still feel the same?" Lillian asked as she sat down on a bench inside the dressing room. She looked at her sister, radiant in red sequin.

"What?"

"You and Johnathan. Does it still feel like it did all those years ago?"

"No . . ." Lindersyl thought a moment, searching for words that could shed light on their situation. She saw it was futile and said nothing more.

"But you still love him?" Lillian pressed.

"Of course I do Lillian. He was my husband and he *is* the father of my children. Had this situation between him and the family not happened, I believe we would still be married today."

Lillian looked upside Lindi's head. She wanted to say something crass. Instead she responded, "You're probably right."

They sat in silence a moment.

"You don't think Johnathan would have cheated on you?" Lillian asked, secretly trying to bait Lindersyl.

"I'd like to say 'no', but then he did cheat on me with you."

"Touche."

"How are things between you, this morning notwithstanding?"

"Mostly we live alone, together. He has intimate relations with his other women and I with Harry. We meet in the kitchen for breakfast and the dining room for dinner. I cook. If he shows, we eat; if he doesn't, Harry and I eat. We retire to separate bedrooms, then start the process over the next morning."

"Sounds rather contrived. Any signs of life?" Lindersyl asked, curious as to whether she and Johnathan were still in a marital way.

"Every now and again we attempt the impossible—a few days ago included. Let us just say that he could put me off sex altogether."

"Really?"

"I know it's shocking for you, but remember, I'm only the stand-in. Trust me, his version with me leaves a whole lot to be desired."

Lindersyl unzipped the red sequined evening gown and decided to dig a bit deeper. "What, if you don't mind me asking, is the problem?"

"I'm not you," Lillian conceded, knowing it was the one thing Lindersyl wanted to hear more than anything in the world. "There's nothing wrong with his equipment, just his delivery. I guess it still gets my goat that I can't satisfy him."

"And it still gets my goat that you would even try to," Lindersyl said, stopping in mid-motion with the gown halfway down her hips. "Remember Lil, you are only the stand-in."

Lillian swallowed hard then lowered her voice, "I guess I could never turn the act off as well as I'd planned."

"Do you mean to tell me you've got feelings for my husband Lillian?" Lindersyl asked more to be nasty than to know.

Lillian chose her words carefully and forced them from her lips with her back to Lindersyl. "Don't be ridiculous Lindersyl! There are times though, when out of nothing but curiosity we kind of bump into each other. I guess what I was asking . . . was when he held you last night, did it feel like it did when we were back in Mississippi? Was it the same for you as when the love was young and exciting?"

It was Lindersyl's turn to spare her sister's feelings. "You are a hopeless romantic Lillian. I felt something comfortable and familiar, but it wasn't the same. His hands trembled against my body and when he bounced me on his knee, it wasn't the furniture creaking, but our joints. You can never go back completely," said Lindersyl.

Lillian turned away from her reflection in a black silk jersey dress to face Lindersyl. "Maybe not, but you two sure looked like old times."

Lillian noted that she was envious and bitter just like old times. She turned Harry over in her head a few times and all but convinced herself that she didn't want to divorce Johnathan after all.

The two redressed in silence and headed for the second floor of the Metroplex. There were six floors in all, each with four wings. Lillian's mood was turning truculent and she placed it on her sister's choice in clothing, when it was really about Johnathan. Lillian covered her eyes with her hands, but peeked through her fingers. With every step she took, her sister's tennis dress rose a little higher. Lillian was embarrassed by the reactions of every warm-blooded man in the mall, but even more disturbed by Lindersyl's lack of embarrassment. Lillian hated that Lindersyl could still *serve up unsweetened lemonade*—that's what their mother called it. Lindersyl was so etched in the minds of men, even as a child, that her looks, her manner could charm them into doing whatever she wanted. Once Lillian had hidden the sugar Lindersyl was to use in a batch of backyard lemonade sells. Lillian had waited with baited breath and devilish anticipation as the customers took swigs of the tart drink. But the rapturous delight of devilment did not come. To Lillian's horror, Lindersyl had convinced the neighbors that she'd used no sugar in order to aid their health. "Too much sugar leads to tooth decay," she'd smiled. They'd beamed back at her dropping their shiny nickels in her palms. It looked to Lillian as if Lindersyl was still sweetening the brew with little more than her charm. Lindersyl had also learned to play eye-tag with men the way their mother once had. Vixen. Vamp-appeal. It was too, too much for Lillian, who'd never quite gotten the point or the hang of it. One thing was for sure, if Lindersyl gave her number to one more strange man, Lillian would step in and force her back onto the straight and narrow.

The one annoying thing about older siblings, Lindersyl thought, was that they always believed their younger brothers and sisters were ripe for reprimand. Lillian couldn't enjoy the day for trying to babysit her. Lindersyl knew that her tennis dress was over the top, but she felt like being a bit reckless. She was hardly prime for the taking by some smooth-talker who'd force her onto the streets turning tricks. Besides, she wanted to know if she still had *it*. After only an hour at the mall, Lindersyl reaffirmed that she did indeed still have *it*. Lindersyl also noted that Lillian was not pleased with her and kept cutting her eyes on her or stepping behind her to block on-lookers from her exposed derriere. Lillian used to be fun. Of course she could hardly be expected to be a bowl of flowers when she'd have to decide whether to plan a 35th anniversary party or a new wedding. Lindersyl understood Lillian's anxiety, but she had no sympathy for her.

The sisters were heading for Saks when a young man in fireman's gear approached them.

"I've been following you for half an hour. What's your name?" he asked Lindersyl.

"Why you wanna know?" Lindersyl smiled.

Lillian instantly became annoyed and stepped in between them, facing Lindersyl. "He probably wants to know because he can see that fire shooting out of your backside!"

Lindersyl furrowed her brow at Lillian, hushing her. Looking up into the startling gray eyes of the fireman, Lindersyl leaned in close. "I wouldn't mind trying your hat on sometime."

"Yeah, I could just imagine you in it . . ."

"Look Sweetie, she's old enough to be your grandmother and not interested in your 'little boy' banter," Lillian interceded again.

"Lillian!"

Lillian yanked Lindersyl's arm, pulling her away from the fireman. "Whatever you're selling young man, we don't want."

Lindersyl was led away peaceably only to keep from making a scene in front of Mr. Gray-Eyed Fireman. As they stepped onto the down escalator Lindersyl yanked her arm free, pointing a manicured finger in Lillian's face.

"What gives? You monitoring my behavior now? I am your little sister Lillian, but I am not a damned child! Don't do that again!" Lindersyl said, before walking down the escalator two steps at a time.

Lillian moved slightly slower behind her not sure that she wanted to catch up with Lindersyl. Lillian was careful about the company she kept, and here she was walking a mall, being seen by half the city with someone who couldn't keep their butt cheeks under wraps. Lillian wanted to know her sister's intentions with Johnathan and about this mysterious young guy she was shacked up with, so she decided to diffuse the situation as quickly as possible.

"Lindersyl, please, don't walk off like that. You can be so sensitive!"

"Leave me alone!" Lindersyl shot back over her shoulder.

"You can't deal with people being honest with you about your lack of feminine discipline. What you choose to do across the Atlantic is between you and that little boy toy of yours, but you will not carry out with me in the streets like some loose woman!"

"I'm fifty-seven-damned-years-old and I'm grown. I don't need your permission or anyone else's to live my life my way. And who are you to tell me about feminine discipline?"

"Shhh! Why must you get so loud? You're acting like you don't have any home training. This crap is so like you."

"You're a pompous old bitch Lillian and I'm sick of you!" Lindi shouted, taking the final two steps of the escalator with her shopping bags sailing behind her speed.

Lindersyl stood in a line that wrapped around the Starbucks interior and out the side door with her arms folded and two shopping bags in each hand. Without champagne, a massive headache had come and gone, then reappeared twice since Lindersyl had arrived in Connecticut. Maybe she was going through withdrawals. She fidgeted uneasily, resting her weight on one leg and then the other. Hopefully a green tea frappucino would alleviate the throbbing she felt in her head. That damned Lillian. This headache was most likely due to her stressing. First she admits she is having feelings for Johnathan then tries to push some antiquated "feminine discipline" on her.

The line inched forward a few steps, allowing Lindi the opportunity to rest against the metal doorframe.

"Lindi?" Lillian called out to her sister who stood just a few feet away. Lindersyl didn't answer. She was too annoyed to speak. Instead she began praying under her breath. "Father, please don't let me kill her."

Lillian walked over and put an arm on Lindi's shoulder, "Lindersyl, coffee's on me!" she smiled, placing one of her bags about Lindi's dress to hide her exhibition.

Lindersyl was just about to smack Lillian across the face when the vibrating beeper she'd tucked into her waistband, began its jiggling dance.

It was Johnathan.

"Lil, hold these," Lindi said, handing the shopping bags to her and rummaging a small pay-as-you-go cell phone she'd purchased at the airport, from her shoulder bag. The mobiles from London didn't work in the States, so she was back to the beep and ring method. Only Eisendorff and Grier had the number, and now, it looked as though Johnathan had it too. Lindersyl quickly punched in the number on display, recognizing it as Johnathan's office line. His voice was tired and raspy when he answered. She couldn't help but think the sound was rather enticing.

"Hey Jumper," she smiled.

Lillian, upon hearing it was Johnathan, tossed the bags Lindersyl had given her onto the ground, causing at least one fragile item to shatter upon impact with the floor. Lindersyl paid her sister's excited display no attention, but distinctly recalled hearing Lillian sneer something to the effect that Lindersyl could walk her "whorish ass home" as she stormed off.

"How's your day going?" Johnathan asked.

"Pretty good. That plate of food you made this morning, believe it or not, has just about worn off."

"You feeling a little peckish?"

"A little. I'm standing in line at Starbucks now. I figured a frappucino and a scone would set me fine until dinner."

"I haven't seen you in seven whole hours and we really need to talk. Why don't you come over to the office and I'll take you to lunch?"

"Sounds tempting, but Lillian and I just exchanged a few words and she's stomped off somewhere. I should try to find her. Then too, if she's left the mall, I have no way of getting out of here."

"Of course you do. I'll send a car for you."

Lindersyl didn't really want to be alone with Johnathan. The magic, as it were, was gone. Their time had passed and now the only thing even remotely interesting about Johnathan to Lindersyl was that she could use him against Lillian. How dare her sister tell her that she had no feminine discipline! Lindersyl would see how much feminine discipline Lillian had when she no longer had Johnathan or Gottlieb Grove to call home.

"Okay, Jumper, I'm in. Where you trying to eat? If it's not McDonald's I may need to change my clothes."

"Lindersyl, are you walking around showing off your goodies?"

"No. I'm wearing a tennis dress."

"That's a 'yes'! You know I don't like you walking around like that," Johnathan frowned, then thought better of arguing with her added, "Is Italian okay?"

"Great. Give me an hour to pick out something and send the car to the Neiman Marcus upper level lot."

"You love me?"

"I'll see you soon," Lindi smiled, ending the call.

Johnathan's favorite color was passion fruit purple; a deep, rich violet color that he said reminded him of Mississippi sunsets. So as soon as Lindersyl spotted the double-breasted suit in the display of Haiko Boutique in that exact tone, she knew it was the one. The women's department was infamous for having only one size of each item in stock and with a suit of this caliber—wide legged, high-waist pants and a tasseled cuff jacket—Lindersyl wasn't surprised to find only two in the entire store. One was a size four petite; the other, a twelve. The salesgirl, a knock 'em dead sister who stood about four inches above her in flat shoes, assured Lindersyl the size twelve trousers would flatter the broader width of her hips without making her look like the side of a house. The girl looked familiar—maybe one of Grier's old friends or something. Even though Lindersyl utterly despised salespeople, she took instantly to the nameless assistant. The girl, about twenty, laughed without much effort and had a habit of tossing her hazel streaked bangs back around her left eye every few seconds, even when they weren't out of place. Lindersyl liked the way she handled things, showing off her dimpled smile and referring to Lindersyl, who was old enough to be her mother, as 'Honey'.

And though the salesgirl hardly looked old enough to have a detailed eye for fashion, she had picked the perfect ensemble. Lindi had to admit, checking her reflection in the store's mirrors, that she did look rather appetizing. The suit fit like a glove with an extreme dip of the suits' lapel, which exposed much of her cleavage and a good portion of her breasts. Johnathan needed no encouragement, she told herself, frowning. All the encouragement he would need would come from her showing up in the first place. Besides, she wanted to put a stinging on him that would keep Lillian feeling like crap the rest of her visit.

Anastasia, recognized the woman in her dressing lounge as the same sister she'd seen traipsing through the mall with a slew of bags when she'd run in late for work. She was only about ten minutes late, but she could not afford to jeopardize her job in any way and made a point of doting on the woman as much as possible. At Haiko, Anastasia's job was simple—serve as a personal shopping assistant to the rich dames who were dropping four or five grand at a time. Despite a dismal salary, she was allowed commissions and (if no one was looking) generous tipping. The chick in the dressing lounge looked about forty, but was probably a few years older. Had that "taken care of" look about her. Then too, any woman her age who could rock a tennis outfit like she was, had to be used to taking care of herself. Anastasia took a swing around the lingerie floor while her charge was in the fitting room to pick up a few items to compliment her suit and greatly enlarge her own commission. When she made it back to the dressing lounge, Anastasia had snagged a crème and purply striped bodice, a pair of black banana-heeled Maude Frizon's and a Vivienne Westwood catsuit.

Lindersyl watched her attendant circumnavigate the sales floor, picking up items and holding them against the lighting. She had already given the salesgirl her shoe size and measurements and was in awe at the young girl's selections. She still couldn't shake the feeling that she'd seen her somewhere before. "What an awfully pretty girl . . . and bright. It'd be a shame to let her go to waste. Maybe Eisendorff would appreciate getting to know a girl with such a gracious personality," she mumbled to herself. Then again, Lindersyl thought, squinting as Anastasia walked toward her, this girl had a belly poof, however slight, that suggested she might be pregnant. Lindersyl wanted to ask her about her dating situation, to play matchmaker but given that she hadn't even caught the girl's name, felt it best to mind her own business. She was sure the young lady had said it, but wrapped in her own world, she'd not heard it and then was too embarrassed to ask her to repeat it. And while she constantly flicked those bangs, the salesgirl would not touch the hair fallen over her shoulder, covering her nametag.

"All right now, Honey, here are a few items that should compliment your suit. I'll give you some time to go through them and try them on. Anything you don't want, just leave in the dressing room," Anastasia beamed.

"Oh, no, I don't have time to try on anything else. I tell you what, I trust your judgment, ring me and wrap me!"

"Are you sure?"

"Certain. If you'll ring me up, I'll step into the dressing room and retrieve my tennis gear. If you don't mind, I'll wear the suit and shoes out," Lindersyl said, handing Anastasia her Visa card, before walking back to the dressing lounge.

Anastasia looked down at the platinum Visa card and almost lost her legs from beneath her. There, in raised lettering was spelled out LINDERSYL GOTTLIEB and beneath it OLIVUS BLACKSTOCK. The name Gottlieb, Anastasia recognized as Johnathan's wife's maiden name. Lindersyl was no doubt some relation to his wife, maybe a sister. More disturbing was the name Lindersyl. It was an odd name and it was the same one she and Johnathan had fought about earlier. This was the woman Johnathan had called out to in his sleep and looking her over, Anastasia understood why. Unfortunately, there was no way for her to compete with Lindersyl Gottlieb.

"So did my credit card explode, or can I manage a few more runs?" Lindersyl laughed.

"Honey, you're good to go for at least another three thousand miles!" Anastasia laughed back, tossing her hair behind her shoulder.

Lindi looked up into Anastasia's face while signing the charge slip and wondered if maybe she should give Eisendorff's number to her. Lindi was still laughing when she eyed Anastasia's nametag and read it aloud.

"Anastasia?"

"Yes. Anastasia Harcourt", she answered handing Lindersyl back her card.

Anastasia Harcourt looked familiar because she was one of Johnathan's lovers. Lindersyl had seen a picture of her in Johnathan's wallet. Young and totally fresh to the world, Anastasia was the kind of girl Johnathan would ruin before she enjoyed her womanhood good.

Lindersyl could not contain her surprise, but attempted to hide it behind a half smile.

"Thanks for shopping at Haiko, Ms. Gottlieb or do you prefer . . . Mrs. Blackstock?" Anastasia asked, dragging out the question.

Lindersyl stopped laughing. "Ms. Gottlieb will do just fine. Thank you so much for your help Anastasia. You've shown me things today I could hardly have imagined were possible," Lindersyl smiled, pushing a fifty into Anastasia's palms along with an old business card with her townhouse address and telephone number on it. Lindersyl felt sick and saddened. "If you ever need anything, please call me."

Johnathan sat on the edge of his desk, rubbing his thumbs across the mouth of a brandy sifter. He was remembering Lindersyl years ago. Always in tight-fitting flowered dresses and barefoot. Seemed she'd rather jump from a moving car than put her shoes on. She'd come a long way since then, often telling him that the country girl no longer existed. But just beneath the surface, Johnathan surmised, Lindi longed for 'Nilla wafers topped with cheddar cheese and fields she could run barefoot through. She'd deny it until the day she died, but Johnathan could hear the past in her laughter. It was a past that had fleeted by too soon and against his will. He would have it back though. At all costs, he would have it back.

The walk from Haiko to Neiman's seemed like the "last mile" a prisoner took on his way to execution. Lindersyl looked around for Lillian's hurt eyes in every face she saw, but couldn't find them. She needed something to shame her from what she was about to do. She could have prayed. She should have prayed, but that would mean that she would have to abandon delighting in Lillian's misery. So, Lindersyl decided not to pray and kept looking for Lillian's face. When she reached the parking entrance to Neiman's, Johnathan's car was right there waiting. The driver, leaning against the hood of the car with his arms akimbo, questioned with his eyes whether she was his intended pick-up. She nodded in the affirmative and handed him her bags. Once inside the driver introduced himself and informed her of all of the features and amenities the car offered.

"Dear, this is not my first time in this car. In fact, if I'm not mistaken, it belonged to my mother," Lindersyl smirked, rubbing her hands briskly across her thighs. She was agitated. She had come face to face with the lovely Anastasia. How could Johnathan use such a nice girl? Was that child pregnant as she suspected? And how could she use Olivus' credit card to buy clothes to entice another man? She was disgusted by her own behavior, but where to stop?

"Pardon me," the deflated driver called back over his shoulder.

"I'm sorry, I don't mean to be rude . . . Is the bar still stocked?"

"Yes, ma'am. Mr. Holland arranged for a few bottles of Bollinger in the cooler. He said it was your favorite. And, no apology needed."

". . . Ah, Bollinger! I suppose one glass won't hurt." Lindersyl smiled, holding the bottle to her cheek mixing the ice chill of the glass with her tears.

One glass quickly turned to two and two to four. After an hour of circling the city, both bottles were empty. Without warning, Lindersyl suddenly announced to the driver that he needed to pull over and get out. She wanted to drive herself and she wanted to be alone.

"Ma'am I can't do that. You've been drinking."

"I can't do that—you've been drinking", Lindersyl mocked, "I have had two bottles of champagne. I don't lose my faculties and coordination until . . . maybe the fourth. Now, get out!"

"I will take you where you want to go, but I will not let you drive," he repeated.

"Fine. Take me to the reservoir. I want to see water on the top slam into the water down below," she said, raising the tinted glass between them.

"What about Mr. Holland? He's still waiting for you and he won't like me not showing up or at least calling him," the driver warned.

"Let him eat cake! Mr. Holland is a ward of the Gottlieb family, dear. This is my Mama's car and he's working for my Daddy's company and living in my friggin' house! He don't tell me what to do or when to do it or why to do it either. I am the master of all I survey . . ."

"Okay, okay," the driver said.

"And don't you call him either!"

"Whatever you say ma'am. Whatever you say."

The driver made his way off the expressway only an exit down from Holland-Bennett and headed for the Agave Reservoir.

This was not at all what Lindersyl had had in mind. She had meant to throw a little suggestive banter Johnathan's way, and then enjoy a hot meal with him. Be the fabulously gorgeous woman of his dreams. Tease him a bit and give him a reason to smile. Torture him for choosing money and power over love. She had not meant to feel anything—good or bad. She had always loved Johnathan, but not the way Lillian or Anastasia or any of his minions of lovers did. They needed Johnathan more than they wanted him and he wore their desperation proudly, like badges of honor. Lindersyl was not offended or angry by these women, but had no stomach for coming face to face with his conquests.

"I am the one he loves! Each of his little strumpets is a specially chopped down puzzle piece, bent and twisted and taped into place to resemble me!" Lindersyl shouted.

Just then, Lindersyl caught sight of herself in the mirrored glass in front of her and wondered aloud through almost a fifth of peach vodka why any man in his right mind would want anything that resembled her. Especially when they could have a supple, gorgeous young thing like Anastasia.

*What's the sense in sharing this one and only life,
ending up just another lost and lonely wife?*

Young Hearts, Run Free, Candi Staten

lillian
Metroplex Mall,
South Mosse Point, Connecticut
May 19, 2001

Lillian refused to cry and blinked rapidly to hold back tears. She walked the food court with no clear destination in mind. Lillian had lived haphazardly under the notion that unpleasant things she ignored long enough, would simply go away. Chasen was one of those 'things'. He was her only child, but even the thought of him made her sick to her stomach. She could care less about his sexual preference; it was her own sexual sordidness that was manifest in Chasen and caused her to retch. He had been a handsome baby, when she dared to peek at him those first few weeks after he was born. She'd tried not to love him because she'd fall in love with him and then be strapped with never seeing Johnathan (and perhaps, Harry) again. Lillian considered claiming Johnathan the father, but given the child's features—decidedly Harry's—it would be an obvious lie. She could hardly explain to Harry her hidden pregnancy so that he'd think it was okay. No, it had been simpler to give the child she didn't want to someone who did—even if it were Lindersyl and that silly Arthur Collier. Lillian had not seen a more hen-pecked man, just whipped and wrangled by her sister's decisions. Still the child was better with them than anywhere near her. And Lillian rarely considered Chasen at all, unless and until Lindersyl brought him up. Anyway, now that she and Harry were going to get married, her life would be carefree and void of hazard. Hazards she seemed unable to maneuver around since she and Johnathan got together. Johnathan had stopped pretending to love her but rather than ignore her, tortured her with that special 'I love you like a sister affection' that no woman in love wants. Johnathan felt no fire, no passion and no sparks for her, just a waning sense of loyalty, the way a man protects an overworked nag from the glue factory. And like that nag, Lillian had always felt she was on borrowed time; that the least little screw up and Johnathan would have her out on the streets so fast, she wouldn't have time to land on her feet. In the beginning the kids needed tending to, Johnathan's demands were growing and he needed a functioning, supportive mate. But the kids didn't want her around and Johnathan simply tolerated her.

When the kids needed to be disciplined, Johnathan warned her in front of them that she had no place putting a hand on them and that for every lick she passed out to them, she was going to get two from him. Johnathan wasn't violent per se, but she knew he meant what he said and wasn't about to test him. By the time the kids were old enough to go to school, they had learned to shower her with a subtle form of disrespect and indifference. She'd say one thing; they'd say another—often the polar opposite. She didn't want either child around, but they made Johnathan happy, and Lillian wanted Johnathan to be happy. They weren't hers and were a constant reminder of Lindersyl and Johnathan's relationship. The resentment ran in both directions though. At six and four years old, Grier and Eisen treated her with such cold direct resentment she often wondered why she wasted her time trying. Lillian had constant daydreams of tying Grier and Eisendorff to train tracks or pushing them over cliffs, but knew her problem was not with them, but with their father. Johnathan undermined anything she did and since the likelihood of Johnathan getting her pregnant was miniscule, Lillian decided to focus her attention on her club status, her favorite charities, and her sorority.

Once the kids reached their teens Johnathan began losing his grip on reality. Lindersyl was married and happy and he was 'stuck' with Lillian. He wanted to be left to wallow and ache, and when forced into family space, Johnathan lashed out, most often on Grier. Lillian was so fed up by then, that she was detached from Johnathan's yelling and hitting and the children's crying and moaning. She didn't care if Johnathan killed the kids and himself, so long as it didn't interfere with her personal agenda. The Gottliebs and Hollands were too famed and familiar about town for Johnathan to divorce her without scandal, so her objective had been achieved. Johnathan could not leave her. And the fact that he was with her and not Lindersyl proved his love of position and notoriety above all else.

Lillian had enough trouble keeping tabs on Johnathan's philandering to suddenly announce she had mothered this child under everyone's noses, but oblivious to them. It didn't matter what her family had achieved, only that there was a man who loved her enough to marry and commit his life to her. Lillian's mother had always made that clear. The most successful woman in the world was a failure without a man. "A girl's father provides for her because it is his duty and there is no value in that for her. When a man chooses to take care of her, as her husband, it makes her true value apparent," Faye used to say. And not just any old piece of a man would do. Lillian was Mrs. Johnathan Holland and that counted for a lot.

Kids didn't matter in her mother's final analysis, though Lillian had used them to stabilize turmoil in her marriage. Lillian never hurt Eisendorff or Grier, but here they were all grown up and angry, telling their shrinks about how horrible a mother she had been. They never told how horrible they were to her. And Eisendorff, a psychiatrist himself, sitting, rubbing his hands together and surveying all the petty little problems his patients brought to him, but still unable to disagree with his father for fear of getting his feet knocked from beneath him. Everyone wanted to blame her; it's Lillian's fault! It's my wife's fault! It's my mother's fault! It's my sister's fault! She'd done the best she could and it was never good enough. Lillian wanted her youth back, and in nix of that would settle for the pretense of being loved and adored by her husband. So what if Johnathan didn't love her and had been forced by Faye to marry her? It was nice when Johnathan pretended. Those moments didn't come often, but when they did, it offered hope to her old heart and flourishes to her walk. But one mention of Lindersyl and it all went to pot. It sickened Lillian to have to endure such romantic rubbish when *she* should have been the one he wanted. After all, Lillian had been there for him through it all. Not that that counted for anything. Lillian could only get pats on the head from the same man who wanted to affect Lindersyl. He wanted Lindersyl to feel the wind against her back and think of his breath blowing against her skin, for her to hear a certain song and think wistfully back to his embrace and rhythmic dance. He wanted her to feel faint and achy all over, longing for him at the most inappropriate moments, in a room full of people, on a crowded train, as she ran her morning jog, and most importantly, when she was twisted and contorted around any other man's body.

And from what Lillian had witnessed yesterday, nothing had changed. When Johnathan walked in, his eyes immediately searched out Lindi. He'd grabbed at his trousers and shirt, covered in mud and was on his way to stuttering when he realized there were others present. To calm himself, he went to Grier, embracing her and tempering his breathing at the same time. But as soon as he approached Lindersyl, he began wringing his hands quickly the way he always did when he was nervous or anxious. His breathing was deep and relaxed, though a tiny bead of perspiration slid down from his hairline to his brow. Lindersyl, too, had started this little rocking motion with her legs, crossing and uncrossing them, while biting her bottom lip. She looked at the linen table napkin on her lap and tried to distance herself and somehow alleviate the sexual impasse she faced. Lindi stood and walked into Johnathan, wrapping her arms about his neck.

Lillian wasn't stupid. She'd caught the exchange many times before. They were talking, communicating to one another without a solitary utterance, through their motions. Johnathan's mustache nudged Lindi's cheek, she shuddered, but didn't pull away. Her fingertips dropped slightly to Johnathan's collar and ever so gently brushed against the back of his ear. Johnathan turned his neck into her touch and in response gave her hip a light, but urgent squeeze. This was their foreplay and had been known to go on for hours, but the game ended when Lillian intruded by stomping her heel into Johnathan's foot. As Lindi turned her attention to Eisendorff, Johnathan had given Lillian the nastiest look he could muster and even displayed a muddy fist to her. Staying around would only make it worse, Lillian decided, and took her leave of them down at Harry's. Coming back, then leaving again—she was yo-yoing for the affections of her own husband.

Having toured the food court for more than half an hour, Lillian finally caught a whiff of fresh baked bread at Auntie Anne's. Instantly she leaned into a temptation for pretzels with as much grease and butter as she figured her system could take. The onset of menopause made her crave for all the wrong kinds of food and while Auntie Anne's was a definite "don't", it would fill her loneliness immediately, if only temporarily.

The heat from the wax paper the steaming piece of bread rested in was intense, and Lillian did her best to balance it from one hand to the other all the way to the far end of the food court. She picked a seat high in the eatery to get a good view of the shopping crowd. Tossing her bags in the corner of the empty seat next to her, Lillian plopped herself down and blew her bangs up off her forehead with a gusty sigh. Miserable, Lillian tried to work out how a day of shopping with her sister had turned into her eating fast food alone in the food court and Lindersyl somewhere loving Johnathan.

"How could she stand in my face and talk trash to my man on the phone like I wasn't even there?" Lillian asked aloud. The gall and nerve it took! She had a good mind to take back her divorce request and go ahead with the 35th anniversary party plans.

A group of teenagers rushing through the outside doors signaled the approaching four o'clock hour. Lillian gave a look of annoyance, before moving her handbag beneath the table. In recent years Lillian's mall hideaway had also become the hangout of choice for a group of upper class, yet crudely teenagery high schoolers. She eyed the first group of kids, all about eighteen, and admired their taste in clothing. Designer couture mixed with hip-hop and lots of braids, on both the boys and girls. "Very ethnic," Lillian thought. Would she have dared to braid her hair as a teenager? Never. Looked too much like a field of cotton or wheat. Much too ethnic for her taste, but still rather attractive on this new generation. If they weren't so prone to random acts of violence and gratuitous sex, Lillian thought, they'd be quite nice people.

One of the boys, with dreaded hair, caught her looking at him, and out of shear madness, Lillian winked. She half-expected to get cursed out or even laughed out of the mall, so she maneuvered her body about so as to no longer face them. Better still, she reasoned, the time had come to leave well enough alone. "I'm picking up school children!" she smirked, disgusted at herself. Lillian passed the group of teens quickly, glancing over at the group in time to intercept the Dred's wink back at her, simultaneously bringing about the complete holocaust of her reckless abandon.

Sit there and count the raindrops falling on you
It's time you knew, all you can count on are the raindrops that fall on little boy blues . . .

Little [boy] Blues, Diana Ross

eisendorff
Offices of: Johnathan Holland
Holland-Bennett Brokerage House,
Mosse Point Connecticut
May 19, 2001

Eisendorff had been too hasty in snatching Avery up from Terrie. It had taken a few hours for the transformation to take hold, but the quietly curious little angel he'd lovingly toted about and doted on had turned into a kicking, screaming little hellion. Eisendorff couldn't stand to hear a child cry—only he didn't know how to make Avery stop. In desperation, Eisen called his parents' home. It was unnatural for the child to cry this way. And each time Eisen thought Avery would stop, he only got louder. He wasn't surprised to find Lillian back at home when he called the house. He was along the side of the road with Avery locked inside the car to keep from strangling him.

"Lillian, I'm babysitting and can't get this kid to stop screaming. What should I do?"

After a prolonged silence, Lillian finally responded, "I've had quite enough screaming to contend with today, so whatever you do, don't bring it here," she said before attempting to hang up the phone.

Eisendorff removed the phone from his ear and looked at the receiver in amazement. "Look, I just need to know what to do. Where is Aunt Lindi then?"

"Where indeed? She's at your father's office no doubt. Why don't you and your charge go check in over there."

"You're a real pip you know that! Why can't you try acting civilized towards me even once? Every time I really need help you turn your back-" Eisen yelled at the dial tone.

Eisen understood now how so many children became abused. It had little to do with the children, but a lot to do with the impatience of the parent. In a war of the wills, Avery had Eisen beat by a mile. As a trained professional, he knew that whipping his ass was not the way to get him to calm down, but their time together was reaching a rather volatile stage. Avery screamed and cried all the way across town, and as Eisen exited the expressway, he fought an urge to pull over and take a strap to him.

To top it off, Eisen's pants had been freshly pissed when he misinterpreted Avery's saying 'bottle' for what was in fact the word 'puddle' or 'pottie'. Eisen rubbed the top of his head, contemplating spanking Avery. Maybe he should give him something to cry about then at least they would both feel miserable together.

Sophia was still out getting supplies and he had neglected to get her mobile number, leaving him strictly in charge of Avery. Avery reeked of urine and there were crumbs all over the Jaguar. The kid never did take the nap his mother claimed he needed and his novelty had worn off. Avery kicked at the back of the passenger seat, causing Eisen to grind his teeth.

"That's Corinthian leather you misfit!" Eisen yelled, pulling over abruptly and walking to the backdoor.

Avery paused, taking in his father's tirade, fearful of the suddenly opened door. Eisen had made up his mind to swat Avery's bottom, but lost his heart when he saw the fear in Avery's eyes.

"C'mon buddy. I need you to stop crying. You're driving me bonkers," Eisen whispered, wiping Avery's face. Avery was soothed momentarily by the coddling and was placed back into his carseat. Eisen made the twelve-mile ride to Holland-Bennett in twenty minutes. Avery's tantrum had ended, but he continued to whimper and groan.

Johnathan's car was parked out front, a good sign.

The last thing Eisendorff wanted to do was go to Holland-Bennett, but if Lindi was there, then that was where they had to be. As if sensing the tension, Avery began screaming as they moved into the parking lot. Eisen nearly destroyed the car seat in his frustrated attempt at pulling Avery out. Dangling by one arm from his father's grip, Avery paused hollering long enough to give Eisen the sharpest 'you must be out of your damned mind carrying me like this' look. Eisen pulled him up into his arms and the screaming resumed. Please let Lindi be here, Eisen prayed underbreath. Lindi always knew how to handle children. Even strange kids on the streets took to her. She'd stoop down low and meet them eye to eye and ask in a very congenial, expectant manner, "What are you going through, love?" And when she found out what it was, no matter how trivial, she always played it up big to make the child feel like it was, in fact, a big deal and that she had a way of making it better.

Eisen breezed through security and onto the elevator thinking of the time he'd run away to drown out Avery. He was twelve and on holiday break from school when Lillian had got behind him about something he couldn't quite remember. Johnathan hadn't made it home from a business trip and he packed his duffle and announced to Lillian he was leaving. She'd told him to be sure to write. Eisendorff ended up sleeping in the park for two days. When the frigid air got to him, he called the only other phone number he knew and it required an overseas operator.

Lillian never bothered to call the police. She said if Eisen wanted to go, then the best thing for him to do, was to go. Grier had not taken the journey from prep with Eisen, so Johnathan was already pretty pissed when he got home to that news. But when he found out Eisen had walked out and Lillian hadn't gone after him, Johnathan was livid. No one knew where to start looking and for reputations' sake, they weren't about to call the police.

Eisendorff got a hold of Lindersyl, who told him how to get into her cottage across town and where to find the keys to the door she kept hidden under a flowerpot. Later she had a neighbor check in on Eisendorff, who'd hit her cash reserve and ordered pizza. Lindersyl had been only slightly relieved though and took a Concorde from London. By the time Eisen awoke the next morning, Lindersyl was right there lying next to him in bed.

Eisendorff smiled at the memory, stepping from the elevator. "Aunt Lindersyl always had a way of making things better."

The smell of Italian food hit Eisen in the face as soon as he walked into the inner offices. As always, the Bennett side of the office was abuzz with the Securities and Exchange Commission filings and dismissals hanging on every movement. But activity on Johnathan's side of the floor was minimal. Johnathan's secretary Connie was nowhere to be found, which was not uncommon. Connie was known to extend herself to Johnathan on occasion, so Eisen thought to knock before entering Johnathan's office. He put Avery down at the door before turning the handle.

Avery pulled a piece of garlic bread from the serving cart and chewed wildly on it. He was as quiet as a mouse. 'You forgot to feed him you idiot!' Eisen laughed at himself. With Avery quiet, he could clean himself up and get along home; after all, he had no desire to see Johnathan. Eisen pushed the double doors open and surveyed the office. Johnathan's desk was a mess; papers flung about and on the floor, the mini blinds in a tangled, jumbled twist, and one of the two chairs for visitors overturned on its side. Eisen moved slowly through the office to the lounge area, where the sofa, television and living quarters were. He could make out Johnathan's shirtless body cradling a large picture frame and rocking back and forth on the floor.

Avery squealed behind Eisen, alerting a weary Johnathan from his slight funk. Johnathan took his time focusing, and smiled to greet Eisen, before realizing where he was and what he was doing. Looking totally drawn, Johnathan stared off again before finally asking, "Eisen, what are you doing here?"

Johnathan got his faculties about him slowly and didn't bother to redress, but stood, scratching his chest and stretching. "Boy, don't you hear me speaking to you? Get on over here and sit down," Johnathan called out.

Eisen walked to the sofa and plopped himself down. He continued to eye Johnathan suspiciously, avoiding looking directly at the photo of his Aunt Lindersyl his father had stuck to his chest.

"What are you doing?" Eisen asked.

"Nothing to warrant your concern," Johnathan said flatly.

"Why can't we have a civil conversation without it turning into an argument? You're sitting in here like some bum in an alleyway and I wanna know what's going on? Now I'm asking you what is wrong with you?" Eisen raised his voice, turning to face a surprised Johnathan.

The sound of his father's angered voice distressed Avery, whose bread supply was almost out. The toddler wobbled into the room, crying for a familiar face to comfort him. What he found was his father and grandfather locked in hostile stares. Seeing Johnathan as the least offending figure of the two, Avery outstretched his arms to him. "Up . . . up . . ." he whimpered.

Johnathan bent and picked up the relieved baby and gave him a gentle embrace.

"Who let you out of their sights, little one?" he asked, in a surprising show of paternalism, carrying Avery over to the door with bare feet tapping the carpeted floors. Johnathan looked out for a frantic parent. There was none.

"Johnathan, he's with me." Eisen mumbled.

Johnathan pulled Avery back from him and gave the child the once over, before giving Eisen a dower smile.

"What are you looking at me like that for?" Eisen asked.

"So you somebody's baby daddy?" Johnathan asked with a hearty grin.

"Give me my son."

"Okay, okay. Well, what's my grandson's name?" Johnathan asked, setting the child down on the sofa.

"Avery. Now, back to my question, what are you doing in here half-dressed and staring at your sister-in-law's picture?"

"Stay out of grown folks business."

"Grown folks business got you acting like this?"

"Just life my boy. It ain't fair."

"No, what's not fair is you and Lillian and Lindersyl keeping secrets. What's not fair is walking in on your father and your aunt humping the kitchen floors clean when you're fourteen years old and pretending you didn't see it. What's not fair is having your father's foot accidentally crawl up your pants leg when you're seventeen, instead of his intended victim. What's not fair is watching your father peaking through a damned keyhole at your aunt while she's taking a shower, having all my friends also see it, and trying to explain that what they saw was a figment of our collective imaginations! My whole life has been an exercise in covering up my shame and embarrassment of you. I'll be damned if I'll stand in your filthy presence a single second longer. And you stay away from my aunt!" Eisen huffed, topping the stairs in a single motion.

Eisendorff was so upset he could hear his heart beating in his ears. He had to calm himself, but didn't feel he could. He was so tired of getting the runaround about 'grown folks' business that he wanted to scream, to run his Jaguar head on into a brick wall. He didn't want to think about his father and aunt. It would be the perfect finish to a miserable day. His head was pounding and to top it off, he still reeked of piss and graham crackers. Eisen's heart sank when he looked into the rearview mirror at Avery's empty car seat. Seemed in his haste to make a stand, Eisendorff had driven from Holland-Bennett and forgotten something—or better, someone. Avery.

Unwrap yourself from around my finger
Hold me too tight, or left to linger . . .

Too Much, The Spice Girls

lindersyl, eisendorff and avery
Agave Reservoir
Mosse Point Connecticut
May 19, 2001

Eisendorff could have shit a brick when in route to the reservoir to hang with Avery, he'd found his aunt drunk as a skunk and perched atop the roof of his father's car. The driver, a dourly little guy, had placed his head between his legs and sat bent out of the driver's seat.

Upon seeing Eisendorff approach with Avery, Lindersyl did a weak job of composing herself and slid down the side of the car to the graveled road.

"Heeeeyyy baby," she said, leaning over to kiss Eisen's cheek.

Eisendorff sidestepped her kiss and went straight for the driver.

"Man, you can leave. Go on home, I'll take her back to the house. What happened?"

"She's been in the back of the car crying for hours about some female shit, man. I don't know what's wrong, but it has something to do with your dad. That's where we were heading—to his office—and she started drinking and made me detour here. I couldn't let her drive and I couldn't leave her like that. She's coming off of her high now, but she's still messed up! I've been trying to get her down from the roof for an hour," he moaned.

"Here," Eisendorff sighed, handing the driver a roll of bills. "Keep this to yourself.

Lindersyl pouted but remained silent as Eisendorff yanked her by the arm over to his car. They both watched while the limo driver kicked up dirt pulling off and away from them. Because she often heard things when drunk, Lindersyl took no notice at first to the sound of a small child coming from Eisendorff's car. When she peered in and spotted Avery, she as much thought he'd start talking Japanese, as he'd fly away. Just another figment of her imagination.

"Who are you? The tooth fairy?" Lindi, smiled, peering in to the backseat at Avery.

"Look." Avery pointed behind her head. "Daddy."

"Daddy?" Lindersyl did an unsteady pivot to turn and face Eisendorff.

"Eisendorff, this your baby?"

"Get in the car and keep your mouth shut. I don't want to hear anything from you for the rest of this drive home."

"Eisendorff, come here. Please."

Eisen moved slowly towards her as if not sure of his footing, with Avery's car seat in his hand. Stepping alongside her, he pushed his hands deep into his trouser pockets and frowned.

"How long have you and Johnathan been . . ."

"What are you talking about?"

"Please, on top of everything else, don't lie to me. I just left Holland-Bennett"

Eisen leaned his head onto her shoulders, without taking his hands from his pockets and sobbed aloud. "Why?"

Cupping his chin in her palms, Lindi searched for something in his face that might suggest he could understand. "I loved him so much . . ."

"And what?"

"And sometimes when you love someone as much as I loved your father, nothing else matters as much as loving them," her voice cracked.

"Nothing else, like your sister?" Eisendorff squenched his face.

"Nothing at all."

"And you have the nerve to admit it?"

". . . I have the nerve to be it! The truth is staring at you Eisendorff. Besides, I didn't go to him today."

"Did it ever occur to you that he was out to use you?"

"Oh, no. If anything, I've used him. I'm not saying it was right. But I do have the ability to separate myself from him. I can be around him and not feel out of sorts. Your father has never gotten to that point," Lindersyl paused, smirking at her own power. "Look at him when I come near: He sweats in a freezing room, he chokes on his words and stammers over the simplest thoughts. His mind is full of millions of things and yet too marred by possibilities to execute a single one. That's how I know he's still very much in love with me."

"You're drunk! If he were in love with you, he'd be married to you, "Eisen said, slamming the car seat into the trunk.

"He *was* married to me!"

Eisendorff thought for a second it was the alcohol, but surmised that it could all make sense. The journals had been signed 'L'. Maybe those were Lindersyl's and not Lillian's words.

But that couldn't be.

"How?" Eisen asked, allowing the word to tumble from his lips freely.

"The license was changed to Lillian's name"

"What about . . ."

"Eisendorff, it may sound cold now, but trust that the emotions behind it were exhausted fifteen-plus years ago. I couldn't afford to lose my marriage to Arthur or disrupt Lillian's home out of greed, so I took what I could when I could, and we've been relatively happy for thirty something years. The Gottlieb girls have to lead by example! Lead by example!"

"Why the secrets and the dishonesty?"

"Try discretion, not dishonesty. Discretion is the mother of true happiness. And while we're on the subject of secrets, what's this about this child calling you 'daddy'?"

"He is my son."

"Eisendorff, I took one look at him and knew he was yours. The question is why you didn't let anyone know that you were a father?"

"I'm still trying to get used to the idea of it myself. This is the first time I've had him to myself since he was born; just didn't know what I was supposed to do with a kid?"

"Do you think you do now?"

"No."

"Good, that's the first essential element to being a successful parent. Know that you don't know everything. I still don't know what the hell I'm doing!"

"His name is Avery and wow, get this, he's allergic to bananas?"

"No! Just like his dad, huh? I remember the first time Lillian fed you a banana and you swelled up so bad, I thought for sure she'd killed you. The neighbors had to keep me from going upside her damned head that night. She should have known better."

"How could she? Johnathan's not allergic to them and neither is she."

"But I am!"

"You?"

". . . Well sometimes allergies run in families and they skip and jump around a lot. She should have just known better than to feed you something like that without first checking, that's all," Lindersyl said, taking a seat inside the car, her head pounding.

"You always seem to make things better—even now. How come you and Lillian are so different?" Eisen whispered, seating himself behind the wheel and reaching out to hold Lindi's hands.

Avery, who'd been perched between the gearbox and the inside storage space, climbed over the seats and sprawled his body across Lindi's lap. She patted his back gently and giggled as he let off a tiny belch. "You can't compare us; it's not fair."

"She didn't want me or Grier."

"Lillian doesn't do motherhood very well. Never got used to the idea of sharing Johnathan with children, I guess. At any rate, she did what she could under the circumstances," Lindersyl said, rubbing her temples.

"What circumstances? The two of you had identical circumstances and you were a great mother to Chasen."

"Hardly. You say Lillian was awful to you and Grier and that I was great to Chasen, only if you ask Chasen, I can assure you, he'd say I was a serious pain in his ass and that Lillian did a fine job with you and your sister."

"Where is Chasen these days?"

"Who knows, probably floating around the atmosphere tripped out on something."

"That's a horrible thing to say."

"Maybe. But you try doing all you can for Avery and ten years from now there's a good chance he's gonna piss it back into your face, saying Billy's dad was at every Little League game, took Billy camping twice a year and taught him how to do algebra and because you weren't there as much as you could have been, you were a terrible dad . . . . blah . . . blah . . . . blah!"

"What are you saying?"

"That you kids have to give us a break sometimes. To you everything your father does is pathological and sadistic and depraved. That's because he's your father. Your father sleeps with a lot of women and you get really upset behind it, but I hear you're the orgy king, yet that's okay. Why the double standard? I bet if he were one of your friends, you'd bang your knuckles against his and think it was right smart, huh?"

"He's my father!"

"He's a man!"

"He's my father though!"

"Granted, Eisendorff, but he was a *man* long before he was your father. *And* you need to respect him as both."

"No disrespect Auntie, but do you know the crap I put up with because he's my father?"

"Eisendorff, your father has not always been a stable man and you know this. But what you don't know is that he was a very brave and respectable man, who lost control of his faculties and had to rebuild himself from scratch. Between Lillian and me, we drove Johnathan to a breaking point and beyond. He made it back to the top and people around the world respect him, yet in his own household, his children call him out like a stranger. Do you know how much it hurts him to hear you call him 'Johnathan' instead of 'Dad'?"

"He never acts hurt."

"You were just a baby when he tried to kill himself. Shot himself right in the chest in front of me and Lillian and you and Grier."

"What?" Eisen feigned surprise, though he had read it in the journal.

"I don't really want to get into all of that Eisen. But you're a psychiatrist, Dear. Analyze your father the way you would if he were your patient. Two children he last saw as children, now grown up and harboring ill will towards him for not being a good father. He was barely a functioning human. I can remember when he sat and stared at walls from sun up to sun down."

"He was abusive and downright mean. He owes us!"

"He sent you to military school so that you wouldn't see the condition he was in and so he wouldn't wind up killing you. How many times did you have to see him whip Grier's ass or bounce Lillian off the walls to know he was having problems? Johnathan wanted you to one day be able to respect him. Your father loves you very much and every time he hugs you or slaps your back, or gives you a call at an inconvenient time to ask for something inconsequential, he's asking your forgiveness. He's asking to be a part of your life; that you not run through the course of your day without thinking of him and wanting to be there for him."

"Then why does it hurt so bad every time he reaches out to me?"

"Because the nine-year-old in you won't allow the 34-year-old man you are to forgive him. You see how Johnathan still treats you like a child? Until the adult Eisendorff steps in and without physical violence, asserts that he is a man, Johnathan will always treat you that way."

Eisendorff sat nodding his head as if her words were slowly sinking in.

"I love you Auntie."

"I love you too, but I need to get my drunk ass somewhere and lie down. Please don't tell your sister about this," she laughed hard, turning to hug Eisendorff with Avery sandwiched between them. "Can you drop me at the Grove? I need to get some rest."

"Sure," he laughed, pinching her cheek.

Eisendorff moved to strap Avery back into the storage area, when he began to make a mental connection. He turned around quickly to his aunt.

"Wait a minute, if you got married and had two kids during the time you were living on Northside Drive with my parents—" he began, but Lindi could not hear him over her own snoring.

*Don't get too close when you dance, cause I don't wanna hear from my friends,
You've been out on the town, with her in your arms . . .*

Make No Mistake She's Mine, Kenny Rogers & Ronnie Milsap

johnathan, lillian & harry
Gottlieb Grove, Home Theater
May 20, 2001

Lindersyl had stood him up.

Johnathan pushed down sharply on the brakes of his Town Car causing the front end to dip. He apologized to a man in the crosswalk he'd almost hit with a wave of his hand, then cursed under his breath. His head was spinning, and while he thought he was very much in control of his faculties, he'd already run two stop signs and a red light, just a few blocks from his office. He felt depressed and dejected and guilty for feeling depressed and dejected. He had no right to feel anything but shame. What he was, was selfish. He had just been told he was a grandfather and had met his own flesh and blood, but had been so privately incensed that he was not sitting or, better, lying against Lindersyl's bosom, that he completely ignored Avery after Eisendorff abandoned him. Johnathan had simply waited for Eisendorff to return from Tantrum Island to retrieve his offspring, then tossed the kid over to him and used the elevator key to lock the both of them off the floor.

Lindersyl had stood him up.

She'd taken his car and stood him up. In Lindersyl's arms, Johnathan felt powerful, yet humbled and needy. She made him hunger for love from a place within him he did not often journey and when he did make that sojourn, so close to her, he often retreated quickly out of fear. Lindersyl was perfection to Johnathan. She was all the things a woman was supposed to be and all the things a man wanted in a woman, which were two very distinct things in his mind.

He'd called her twice since she'd agreed to meet with him, but there was no answer in the limousine. His boyish anxiety had turned to full-blown anger when nightfall came and went. Why had she stood him up?

His worry that something had happened to her was eased by the driver's check-in, saying Lindersyl had refused to come. Why had she left him waiting? It was like she'd been groomed all her life to love him. And when she showed favor to anyone or anything else, it often made Johnathan jealous. Especially where men were concerned. He didn't mind so much her having a boyfriend or two, because he, after all was married, and to her sister no less. But Lindi loved with all that she was and the thought of another man holding and kissing her made him very angry. Angry to the point of destruction.

For years after she'd walked away from him, he'd destroyed Lindersyl's image among her Connecticut friends. He called her loose and whorish to business associates who considered her a worthy ally. When Lindi couldn't get work in Connecticut and he was convinced she'd finally settle in and become his full-time stay-at-home mistress, she suddenly disappeared. As brazen as she was, he figured she was off somewhere trying to fend for herself and counting the days down till she could successfully re-enter their relationship, with her tail tucked between her legs and willing to do as he said. But Lindersyl was not Lillian by any stretch of the imagination. She had sat too long at her father's feet to walk away from her birthright over a husband she could no longer claim as her own. Johnathan never figured Lindersyl would cross the Atlantic to England and completely out of his deceptive web, launch her own public relations firm. She was among her daddy's peers and they restored her faith not only in herself, but also in her abilities to survive on her own. The company she simply called Micheaux handled American entertainers and scholars abroad, usually writers and black musicians and the occasional film studio on location in London. In addition, many European-born blacks, took one look at her grinning tawny face on the society pages of Hello and Match magazines and walked through fire to get under her representation. One of their own would be looking out for them, and Lindersyl worked that to her financial advantage in no time.

For two years, Lindersyl's whereabouts remained a mystery to Johnathan, who'd become fearfully obsessive about finding her. One morning, over a bowl of bran, Johnathan happened upon a Wall Street Journal article about a very wealthy, very beautiful African-American public relations woman taking Europe by storm. And there, looking as gorgeous and determined as ever, sitting atop the Micheaux entranceway granite stone, was Lindersyl. Weeks went by with Johnathan calling and wiring her offices for any semblance or possibility that Lindersyl still loved him, but to no avail. Finally in utter desperation, her confident gaze from the photo eating at him, Johnathan packed a garment bag one morning and boarded a plane for London. He'd planned his operation to the second. He would waltz in, grab her by the waist and wind her up, throw that grand piano he called a smile at her, and allow his charm to work that seemingly tough demeanor back into the wife and lover he'd once had. Johnathan figured she would try to fight it for a day or two, but ultimately be powerless to do anything but obey him.

When he arrived at Micheaux the same afternoon, he was distressed to find that security made up most of Lindersyl's staff. And once they found that "Johnathan Holland" was nowhere to be found on her list of "TO SEE" visitors, he was asked to not only leave the building, but also to refrain from loitering in the lobby, the courtyard or the car park. No one would give him any information about where she lived, or whom she socialized with or even what kind of car she drove. After a week of dodging security officers at the main entrance, Johnathan found his way into the office's rear emergency doors; snaking and scrambling his way up the fire emergency stairs. Fortunately for him the security was a lot more relaxed on the fourth floor, which housed the executive suites. Peeking from the stairwell door, Johnathan adjusted his clothes and stepped confidently into the frantic-paced reception area.

Micheaux was Hollywood glam meets English countryside. Hard wood floors, with alternative wall treatments. Most of the paintings were by new and unknown artists, while the furniture was by classic English designers, most of whom were dead. A small group of businessmen were being instructed on how to reach the board of directors' offices when Johnathan approached the giant mahogany desk. He listened intently as a navy jacketed escort moved from behind the desk to escort them to a Mrs. Collier, who seemed to be in charge of Lindersyl's business affairs. Perhaps catching up with Mrs. Collier, he would be able to find Lindersyl, Johnathan reasoned. Bleeding into the group of about twelve, Johnathan boarded the elevator, smiling and laughing along with the other men at a joke he hadn't quite heard. The elevator contained a gold embroidered bench with tiny gold tassels hanging down from its burgundy fabric. The escort pushed the PH button for the penthouse, which comprised the fifth and sixth floors and took a seat alongside Johnathan.

"Mate, you look nervous, but there's no need. Mrs. Collier is a really lovely lady as long as you guys got your figures right. She's pretty appetizing to look at too, just don't let the husband catch you looking," the guard spoke in a hushed tone.

"Really? What about Lindersyl Gottlieb? I hear she's even more appetizing to look at."

"I hope you all are better auditors than you are researchers, man! Lindersyl Gottlieb is Mrs. Collier. I know that auditors are supposed to keep their eyes on the money, but the least you could have done was followed the money trail. Lindersyl Gottlieb married that haughty-taughty oil twit Arthur Collier a few years ago. If there's any scheming and stealing, he's to blame. Bet on it," he whispered, narrowing his eyebrows for emphasis.

Nonsense, Johnathan thought as he stepped from the elevator, no longer shielding himself with the others. Lindi would never have just run off and married without telling her family and even if she had, she couldn't possibly be happy without him. The scent of Bvlgari slapped him across the nose and he smiled a toothy grin. His woman was within his reach and all of the sick and depraved things he'd done to force her back to him, now seemed trivial. Surely she would forgive him.

The ten or so people in the office zoomed by them without even acknowledging their presence. Like worker bees doing all they could to preserve the life of their queen, he and the others moved in mocked slow motion in comparison. The escort, who stood about an inch taller than Johnathan and wore his hair in a close military cut, stopped at a big crescent moon shaped desk that lead into a smaller lounge area. Two four-foot crystal vases on either side of the desk with gigantic exotic flowers spilling from them, sat in the center of the room. There was a full wall of glass behind the reception desk with frosted ceiling to floor blinds. Greeting the young man behind the reception desk, the escort announced the arrival of the auditing team, while Johnathan took notice of the exquisite detailing of the desk.

"This man is not with our team," a stout, red-faced Brit announced sternly as the rest of the group disappeared behind the glass doors.

"Oh, I'm sorry. I'm Johnathan Holland. I'm Lindersyl's . . . brother-in-law and she gave me an open invitation to visit whenever I was over from the States," Johnathan stammered.

"I knew you looked familiar," a tall blond smiled, tilting her head to one side to take him in. "I recognize you from the picture of you and your wife in Mrs. Collier's office. It's good to meet you."

Johnathan accepted her extended hand, nodding his greeting.

"Well, I'm sorry, but your timing couldn't be worse. Mrs. Collier is gonna be bogged down with the auditors most of the evening. You might want to try her tomorrow."

"Could you just step in and let her know that I'm out here?" Johnathan asked in desperation.

"Usually she doesn't like to be disturbed when it comes to going over financial reports, but since you've come so far to see her, I'll risk it," the girl said.

"Thanks a bunch," Johnathan forced the air from his lungs and sighed in relief.

"I'm sorry, what's your name?"

"Johnathan . . . . tell her Jumper is here"

"Jumper?" she repeated, walking to Lindersyl's office behind her.

"Yes."

"Tell him to leave the address to the place he's staying and I'll get back with him by tomorrow afternoon. I can't stop what I'm doing to see him; make my apologies," Lindersyl could be heard saying.

Her voice cut through Johnathan like a knife and he winced at the thought of her not tearing herself from her work to at least come out and say 'hello'.

"Lindi! It's Johnathan!" he shouted pass the receptionist.

"Close the door," Lindersyl yawned.

Johnathan didn't wait to face the receptionist, but instead tossed a business card with the King's Cross Hotel name and his room number on it onto the desk. A light rain began to fall over London as Johnathan exited the building that chilled the afternoon. He shoved his hands deep into his pockets and turned his face up to the sky. He cried the entire way back to his hotel, where once inside, he sat in his wet clothes alternating between downing scotch and banging his head against the walls. Just when he'd given up all hope, Johnathan got a knock on his hotel room door. It was Lindersyl. Lindi had come to him the next afternoon, shortly after Johnathan had recovered from a liquor-induced black out. She was smaller than she'd been, but had more muscle tone and she wore a beaded black Yves Saint Laurent gown. Her fur draped over one shoulder, Lindi smiled, invited herself in and undressed. They made love for hours until she left for an awards ceremony. Lindersyl made it clear to Johnathan that it bothered her to cheat on Arthur, but not enough to turn him away. She told him that they would always be lovers and friends, but that he no longer had control over anything. It was her ball, her court and her game. If he wanted in, he played by her rules. And so, Johnathan had played the game (and the fool) from then on, though he no longer understood why.

Lindersyl had stood him up.

Johnathan maneuvered through the unlit room with a tea glass full of bourbon, splashing its contents onto the rug. Walking into a coffee-colored suede recliner and ottoman, he slowly turned and backed into it, bringing his hips down slowly. Johnathan ran his hand down the length of his thigh. He was horny, again. His father always said he had no self-discipline. He felt depraved at his age entertaining thoughts of solo flight with Lindersyl and a host of other women littered across town, and quickly turned his attention back to his drink.

The house was unusually quiet. He hadn't noticed at first because of the funk he was in, but now found it odd and suspect that Lillian hadn't come to him yet. Even when she was at the poolhouse, Lillian knew enough to get her ass to the main house, pronto when she saw him pull up.

The quiet distracted him enough to power up the television with the remote tucked into the side of the chair and begin surfing channels. His eyelids were just lowering on the second half of the Facts of Life episode where "Tootie" gets stranded in New York City, when the quiet of the house once again startled him. The hairs literally stood up on the back of his neck. Where in the hell was Lillian? It was almost ten o'clock and there was no dinner on the table! No courtesy call to ask if or when he wanted his nightly foot rub! Nothing!

Bracing his weight against the armrests, Johnathan lifted his body up from the seat and trudged into the kitchen. Not a peep. Then to the dining room, up the den, into Lillian's room. Nothing! Back in the dining room, from the corner of his eye he caught a quick, exaggerated movement out the south window.

Johnathan's eyes adjusted to the darkness and followed the sprinting figure across the back lawn. It was Lillian. Johnathan moved into the outdoors a few feet behind her and continued to survey her actions. She was dressed in a short black nightgown and black satin mules. Her pace was quick, but not quick enough to outpace Johnathan, who covered her mouth with one hand and snatched her up by the waist with the other. He dragged her back into the house and slammed the kitchen door.

"What the hell are you doing?" she yelled.

"Woman, have you lost your damned mind, running around the grounds like this?"

"Which is crazier, me running around the grounds like this or you grabbing me like a damned lunatic?"

Johnathan ran his eyes across her and then stared her blankly in the face.

"Well?" she demanded.

"Sorry. Why didn't you let me know you were home? And are you on strike now? No dinner? No massage?"

Lillian leaned hard on one hip and sighed in disbelief.

"That's not my responsibility anymore. Where is Lindersyl? Is she giving head, but no hot meals these days?"

"You've got such a nasty mouth sometimes!" Johnathan said, honestly shocked.

"Look, did you need me for something, Johnathan, or did you just drop in to tell me how much fun you had screwing my sister this afternoon?"

"Stop acting like you don't know the score Lillian! How you gonna treat me like this?"

"How's that?"

"Don't be mean Lil. You know it ain't right, you got me sitting down here like some lap dog and didn't even acknowledge me. No hug, no kiss, no nothing."

"Johnathan, when did you start starving for my loving? Harry is waiting for me," she said, pushing past him.

"I don't give a fuck about that nigger waiting over in *my* poolhouse for *my* wife! Upstairs Lillian, right now," Johnathan snapped, directing her attention to the stairwell leading upstairs.

"I'm not making love to you! I gotta man and you ain't him!"

"You better get your ass up them stairs and do what I say if you know what's good for you woman!"

"You are out of your flipping mind if you think I'm sleeping with you. I'm an engaged woman!" she taunted. "Why would I want you when I've got Harry? Did Lindersyl drop you for one of those young studs she was giving her number out to at the mall?"

Johnathan's blood boiled in his veins. He didn't know whether to strike Lillian or run from the room. Either way, she wasn't going to the poolhouse tonight. Tonight she was going to do what her sister had not. Johnathan grabbed Lillian by the arm yanking her to him.

Unfazed, Lillian tore her arm away, "Johnathan, go to bed!"

"Lillian, don't make me take it from you, and you know I *will* take what I want."

"Some things you are simply not meant to have," Harry's voice came in over Johnathan's shoulder. "Lillian, go on down to the poolhouse."

"Harry, please, this is between-"

"Lillian, I'm not going to ask you again," Harry said flatly, moving to her side of the room and patting her backside as she walked out pass him.

"Man you must have a deathwish, coming into my house, uninvited, and talking this shit to me."

"You talk big talk, but you have no control over anything, including your wife."

"Motherfucker please! You've been fucking her so you think you got some claim to her?" Johnathan shouted. It was then that Johnathan realized that the silence that had disturbed him earlier was a muffled silence, a deliberate one that hid the fact that his wife was making love to her lover in his bed right above him most of the night, while he was downstairs watching Kim Fields' ass trapped in New York. Harry Veda had taken up the role of master of the house. The veins on Johnathan's neck shot out like torpedoes. This arrogant little piece of a man was making time with his wife and knew that where Lillian was concerned, Johnathan really had no control over what she did. But to take his wife in the house with him in it, the man had to be crazy! Johnathan had lost Lindersyl first and now he was losing Lillian . . . to the pool man. The bastard standing toe-to-toe with him and announcing he'd taken over his home. And with no Lindersyl or Lillian, it occurred to Johnathan that he had no place to go. He'd be homeless or like some aged loner, living in a retirement community alongside the deposed and abandoned. Without a second thought, Johnathan pounded his fist into Harry's jaw.

It was the only punch Johnathan was able to throw. Out of shape and left at a handicap by Eisendorff's assault the day before, Harry proceeded to wipe up the floor with Johnathan, breaking most of the dishes in the breakfront and those on the kitchen surfaces. By the time Harry found himself too exhausted to fight on, Johnathan's bloody body sat propped atop a mound of broken glass.

Lillian staggered in, covering her mouth in shock.

"Oh God!" she screamed.

"It's okay Lillian, I whipped his ass good! We should call the paramedics even though I think I just knocked him out."

"You animal! You're a goddamned animal! I said to let me handle it, but no, you had to come in here and hurt him," Lillian screamed at Harry, flailing her arms about to keep him from grabbing hold of her.

"Wait a minute, this man was about to rape you!"

"He's my husband!" Lillian shouted, pushing Harry away.

Harry backed away from Lillian, her eyes ablaze with emotion. He looked at her as if seeing her for the first time. After promising to be at his side the rest of her life just minutes before, she was now draped over her soon-to-be ex. Harry had saved her from his crazed grasp . . . The knight was supposed to get the love and adoration of the woman he loved after slaying the evil dragon . . .

Harry stumbled his way out the door, contemplating whipping Lillian too. The fickle cow. He walked, stunned, back to the poolhouse. Harry decided not to worry about Lillian for now. He was pleased that the whipping he'd wanted to give Johnathan for years had finally come. His magnified bathroom mirror revealed the source of the aching he felt on the left side of his face: a swollen, fist-shaped bruise that was turning a deeper shade of purple by the minute. Patching the other smaller scratches and scrapes, Harry replayed the events over and over in his head. Finally, after about twenty minutes, he called for an ambulance. He'd finished off a cigar and glass of cognac by the time the paramedics arrived and watched from his deck as the medical team carried Johnathan out. He watched a hysterical Lillian clutching and grabbing at a barely conscious Johnathan and repeating over and over at the top of her lungs, 'I love you Johnathan'. As the ambulance pulled away, Harry began packing his clothes. He didn't intend to be there when the police arrived.

It could all be so simple, but you'd rather make it hard,
loving you is like a battle and we both end up with scars . . .

Ex-Factor, Lauryn Hill

lillian & johnathan
Hospital Room of: Johnathan Holland
Mercer Hospital, SW Mosse Point, Connecticut
May 20, 2001

L illian leaned her torso over onto Johnathan's, pushing her chin deep into his neck. The full-sized hospital bed they shared was just big enough to accommodate the two of them comfortably and for purely selfish reasons, Lillian was quite pleased with their closeness. It had taken her a while to get to that level of comfort, but as her hysteria over Harry's roguish behavior waned, she realized, rather sheepishly, like a schoolgirl whose charm had caused a fistfight, that Johnathan did love her. He had fought for her honor and what's more, he'd done so with Lindersyl in town to witness it. The points she was racking up through her bedside attentiveness were bound to have Lindersyl spending the remainder of her stay across town in her own place. Once before, for her sanity, though Lillian liked to believe it was for love, Johnathan had asked Lindersyl to pack up and leave their home. Though under tremendously different circumstances, if for no other reason than his not wanting her to see him with blackened eyes and a bandaged head, he would not want her at Gottlieb Grove upon his return. The ride from Gottlieb Grove in the back of the ambulance had given Lillian no time to consider Harry and how he would react to her once she returned, but then, such was their relationship. Harry was her lover; Johnathan her husband.

"I could hardly have stayed at the house with Harry with the ambulance there," she reasoned.

Surely Harry would understand that for the sake of the public, despite their engagement, she had to comfort and support her husband. Because Johnathan had been unconscious all the way to the hospital, Lillian hadn't had to explain to anyone what happened. Rolling it over in her mind she decided that a burglary story would work. It would be easy enough to say she was away from the property and upon her return, found her husband lying unconscious on the kitchen floor. Harry would back her story.

Johnathan's left side was bandaged and the pain from what x-rays revealed to be two fractured ribs caused him to shoot up sharply in the bed and yell out. Lillian pushed the red attendant button and dabbed a handkerchief at his sweat-filled hairline. "Darling, I'm here. You'll be all right," she whispered.

"Lindersyl, I love you. Don't leave me," he whispered back.

I never dreamed you'd leave in summer,
I thought you'd go then come back home . . .

Never Dreamed You'd Leave In Summer, Stevie Wonder

harry
Gottlieb Grove, Pool House
May 20, 2001

Gottlieb Grove was peaceful and quiet with everyone gone. No screaming Johnathan, no crying Lillian, no whining Eisendorff or Grier. It was moments like this one; calm and soothing that made leaving it so difficult for Harry. All packed and ready to head home to Petion-Ville Haiti, Harry had paused long enough to smoke a joint that was almost as old as he was. It was a fool idea to even try with his poor lung capacity, but hell, all caution was being thrown to the wind. Harry lit the browning paper edge, tossing his head back by reflex when a firecracker pop came from it, then a puff of smoke. He was having trouble getting Lillian's screaming voice from his mind. She'd called him an *animal*. She'd chosen the man who was to be her ex-husband over him at the most crucial moment in their relationship.

"I give the girl everything a man s'pose to, she still treat me like a fool! No more! Harry Veda is no woman's fool . . . no more anyway!" he spoke aloud to himself.

"She got you talking to yourself again, eh?" Lindersyl laughed.

"Lawd woman, you want to kill me, huh? I thought I got some bad seed—I'm hearing things, voices . . ." he smiled. "Where'd you come from?"

"Sorry Veda! I hadn't had a chance to swing by and give you a bit of love from across the waters since I've been here. Eisendorff just dropped me outside the gate. How're things?"

"C'mere girl," Harry laughed, blowing the exhaust of marijuana smoke from his nostrils and mouth at the same time and reaching for her. He gave her a big bear hug and held her back from his arms to get a good look at her. "That Englishman feedin' ya fanny! Thickening up like a good 'oman ought to after all these years." What he wanted to say was that he could see how her family was worrying her, that he understood her pain and misery, despite her smiling face, and that he wished there was something concrete he could do about her circumstances. But as always, that seemed too much to offer.

"Sod off!" she replied, feigning anger.

"Guess I can't say you resting your hand on your imagination no more. Dem is more than imagination I see!" he laughed.

"Veda, enough small talk. What's wrong? Lillian stressing you again?" she asked, noting his pinched expression.

"You don't know the half of it."

"You wanna talk about it?"

"Long story."

"Looks like you've already started sorting it out," she said pointing to his packed bags behind the doorway. "You've meant too much to me to walk out without saying goodbye Harry Veda."

"I can't talk about this now. I intended to call you 'ventually."

"You are one of the few 'men-friends' that I have Harry. I love you like a brother, and if I can help in any way . . ." she said, taking the dangling joint from his lip and taking a deep drag. "don't walk away without it."

She coughed out much of what she'd inhaled and with eyes watering, cleared her throat.

"Damn girl! You never were good at getting high. You've wasted more of my stuff over the years than I care to think about. Sit down over there. Only reason I put up with you is cause you know how to roll 'em extra tight like I like 'em."

"I'll roll, you talk," she said, still coughing.

Harry took his time running down the events of the evening. He admitted to following Lillian into Johnathan's bedroom around three in the afternoon and goofing off around the confounds for most of the evening. He told her it made him feel intoxicated, getting Lillian in Johnathan's bed. A kind of comeuppance for him having her all the time. He'd paused when addressing Johnathan's threat of 'taking' Lillian, fearing Lindersyl's reaction. They'd spent time getting high on more than one occasion and Lindi was prone to what he termed 'over-emotionalizing while under the influence'. Particularly if sad or angry, Lindi could pitch a bitch and it would be hours before she calmed down. But once he'd said his peace, searching her face for the onset of trauma, there was nothing.

"Veda, you know how sometimes when you love someone so much you tend to ignore and forgive and forgive and ignore so much that after a while, that's all you seem to be doing?"

"What?"

"You know like when it's real love or you're really in love?"

"What?"

"Can you not hear me motherfucker or do you not understand? Don't keep saying 'what' like that"

Harry laughed aloud. He suddenly remembered why he'd stopped getting high with Lindi years ago. Bad enough were the crying, yelling, screaming episodes brought on by sadness or anger, worse were the philosophical rantings. Most of which were quite substantial; though it usually took three to four hours for her to get her point out.

"Go on Lindi! Nevermind me, I know whatcha mean."

"Good Veda, 'cause I don't want nobody else to know, but I'm tired. I've been living my life and trying to give people the impression that my life is 'peachy keen', but really it ain't shit!"

"That's not true, Queen!"

"You call me Queen. Ha! I'm a whore in queen's clothing then, but I damned sure ain't nobody's queen!"

"Lindersyl Gottlieb don't start the nonsense! You are as foolish as you let yourself be. I am as foolish as I let myself. But what better thing to be a fool over than love? I saw you stifle yourself when I say that Johnathan, that no count nigger be at the hospital. You wanted to jump up and run to him, tell him that you love him and you need him and you want him well. But in your heart you know that he's no good for you. You know that I put him in that hospital ward for trying to rape your own sister, and yet your heart want to skip a beat and your eyes want to cry. Mind yourself Lindi. Don't listen to your foolish heart no more. I told you that thirty years ago, you told me that twenty years ago, and today, here we are telling it to each other all over again."

"How do you stop loving someone Veda?"

"You gotta walk away cause the only way out is through the door. I don't intend to be here to pick up no more pieces Lindersyl. I mean too much to me. The same way your heart sank when I told you I whipped that man you love, mine sank when I have your sister cuss me afterwards. I'm a man and I got my pride."

"Lillian smushed your pride years ago. She and Johnathan are two of a kind. I've made every possible excuse for his behavior over the years even when I knew there really were no excuses. I used to love a man who helped destroy my family and who can hold me and tell me he loves me one minute and then dangle himself in front of my sister in the next. I love a man who made me suffer and long for our children, children he wouldn't allow me to see unless I first saw him. My pride is smushed too Veda, but my feelings are only just beginning to make sense."

"You can't punish him forever Lindersyl."

"What then?"

"Tell the truth. All of it this time and to all the right people."

"What about—?"

"What about nobody! What about you?"

"Veda, I just don't know . . ."

"You and Lillian are too much alike for me to stand you sometimes. Maybe you should go."

"What's that supposed to mean?"

"It means that you sit here and cry for deliverance and you get it, then you turn around and don't want it. Olivus is a good man. He's much too good for you!"

"What?"

"So now you can't hear me? Your sister can cut off my balls and put them in a display case, and you cry for me. But when you do it to this poor bastard Olivus, it is okay?"

"I love Olivus!"

"More than Johnathan?"

"As much as."

"Then give him a chance to love you outside of Johnathan's shadow."

Lindersyl smashed out her roach and started rolling another joint. She studied Harry's creamy skin and cocked her head to one side.

"Uh-oh, I know what that look is all about. You can't help but to turn that thing on Lindersyl, but you need to stop it."

"Stop what?"

"I used to t'ink I picked the wrong sister."

"And?" Lindersyl smiled broadly, knowing full well Harry didn't take her seriously.

"Now I know I picked the wrong family!" he shouted, then realizing his guffaw, added, "No offense."

They both laughed.

"Promise me you won't leave."

"I have to leave Gottlieb Grove."

"Fine, then stay at my place across town. Just don't leave the city altogether."

"What I look like staying in your home? You must be looking for a fight. Besides, Lindi, this is where I work, I will have to report in even if I don't stay here."

"Yeah, right! Get another job why don't you? Besides, when was the last time you actually cleaned the damned pool?"

"Oh," he said quietly, adding up the months to just over three years.

Lindersyl made it to the kitchen sink before the vomit reached her mouth. She'd forgotten how sickening and yet delightful the hurl of intoxication could be. She'd also forgotten about the three bottles of Bollinger she'd polished off at the reservoir. Harry handed her a warm towel and glass of ginger kola to ease her over the nausea. She looked at him and shook her head.

"Gonna toss some more of those cookies, Lindi?"

"Naw, that's about all she wrote."

"Good then, no more cannabis for Lindersyl," he smiled. "Why don't you go on up to bed. I hate to think of you alone over at the main house. I got some old sweats you can throw on to keep you from wrinkling that pretty suit."

Lindersyl knew it was not a sexual proposition, but she couldn't help but feel flattered. Harry Veda was a good man. In all the years he and her sister had been together, Harry had not once, to her knowledge cheated. Lindersyl respected him more than she could describe because she knew what a pain in the ass Lillian could be. How could a man love a woman as much as Harry loved Lillian and not be able to express that love outside of a fourteen-foot high brick wall that stretched almost a mile?

A gorgeous and respectful man, Harry had been hired by her father shortly before his death, to tend the newly resurfaced outdoor pool. Thirty-three years and ten pounds ago, Harry walked onto the Grove with a kind of innate wisdom that made him look and sound older. Lindersyl had simply exchanged pleasantries with Harry, who she regarded as just a guy, who eyed at her fanny like all the rest . . . until the day Johnathan shot himself in the chest in the driveway of Gottlieb Grove. It was Harry who'd jumped into action, carrying and pushing Johnathan's twisted body into the back of the car. Amidst hers and Lillian's screaming, Harry had gotten them to the hospital, overseen Johnathan's registration and tended to Grier and Eisendorff. As neither she nor Lillian could assess the events that took place following the shooting, they only had Harry's recollection to properly puzzle the pieces together.

Harry was the only person who knew all the secrets she and Lillian hid. He knew because he watched them unfold before his eyes like a sick, dime store novel. He thought that both Lindersyl and Lillian were sad and pitiful for loving so selfishly. Of course that was before he fell in love with Lillian and found himself stranded among the casualties. Still, even in his admonishing tone, Harry never judged them. He gave warnings, he 'tsk-tsked' them when they refused to heed his warnings, yet he always followed suit with Kleenex, soft words and reassuring gazes from knowing eyes. For that, Lindersyl was grateful. He didn't flatter her and kiss her ass because he feared her family. He didn't care about money or how others perceived him. The only crushing thing Harry had ever said to her came the day of her father's funeral. Incensed by Lindersyl and Lillian's decision to remain at Gottlieb Grove with Johnathan, Harry had read her the riot act, and she, too ashamed at hearing the truth to answer, had pretended not to comprehend him.

Now, limp and draped across his bed, Lindersyl searched for the memories that went along with the words that kept echoing in her head. She settled his Down comforter out of its staunch tuck and over her chest.

"Celebrate your daddy's death! You have no one to run to now who will glorify your pouting, reward your whining or support your fabrications. Poor little girl, what will you do?"

"Lindi, you all right in here?" Harry called from the doorway.
"Yep, come on in and talk to me."
"You sure?"
"Course I'm sure."
"You got something on your mind?"
"Guess I'm sobering up. Veda, do you think I'm crazy?"
"No more than most."
"Thanks a lot!"
"You know what I mean. Everybody's got their fair share of problems."
"What's going to become of Lillian and me? I can't be around her unless I'm drinking or high. She seems to bring out the worst in me. I miss the old days . . . what we once were."
"You're still high or you're lying to yourself! You two haven't had good old days since you were girls. Long as I've known you, you two have been fighting," Harry corrected.
"But we should be able to. If I say I'm okay and she says she's okay, we should be able to get along. That is unless one or the both of us is lying," said Lindersyl.
"You need to see a professional?"
"Naw. Tried it once. This bitch tells me, after about eighty hours on the couch, 'you are very unique. Black people don't have these kinds of problems. A real sista wouldn't share a man with another woman. And she certainly wouldn't share him with her own sister if she was trifling enough to share him at all."
"She actually said that?" Harry asked, kneeled at the foot of the bed with his elbows resting on the edge of the mattress.
"Yeah, I guess she figured since I was not a 'normal' *sistah*, I wouldn't put my foot up her ass!"
"You didn't?"
"I plead 'no contest' and Arthur paid the settlement."
Harry joined Lindersyl sitting on the edge of the bed and turned so that they both stared face up at glistening white stars lighting up the pitch darkness

through the sky roof. He wrapped one arm around her shoulder and pointed out. Harry recognized Lindersyl's blubbering and put a halt to it at once.

"*'Ti chen gen fos devan kay met li'*. A little dog is really brave in front of his master's house. Lillian will never leave. She loves me, but she hasn't the courage to stray far away from Johnathan's yard. And to answer your question, no, you're not crazy, Lindi. You just figured out that not everything in life is worth fighting for," he smiled.

*I'm just a little girl in low-cut clothes who hides behind a face, but really knows
That beauty buys what a child gets for free . . .*

Little Girl, Patti LaBelle

grier
Residence of: Brice Rhyne
North Mosse Point Connecticut
May 20, 2001

Lindersyl was the only sinner in her houses, so when Brice got the bright idea to spend the night, Grier promptly packed an overnight bag and rode across town with him to his place. They had no intentions of setting off skyrockets, but neither wanted to appear to be in violation of Lindersyl's house rules. Brice threw his right leg over Grier's and pushed his body closer to hers, thinking of how he was as afraid of offending her people now as he had been years ago. As had been the ritual before their split, Grier had tossed on woolen pajamas and climbed into bed alongside him wrapping her loving arms around his shoulders to ease him into sleep.

They snuggled a while and talked about where their relationship should go. Their conversation turned to her family and a look of distress ran across Grier's face. Brice recognized too late that talking about her family was a bad move.

"Well, I guess I neglected to fill you in on the latest drama at the Holland residence. My mother spent the night in the poolhouse with her lover last night and this morning, while we were eating breakfast, came back to the house to ask my father for a divorce."

"What? And I know Johnathan hit the roof."

"You know what you know, baby. Johnathan was fit to be tied."

"So what happened?"

"I don't know; I left."

"Tell me, what was your aunt doing during all of this?"

"Eating waffles."

"Did she say anything?"

"Why? You still on that kick about my aunt and my father?" Grier asked. "It's only natural that my mother would be slightly jealous of my aunt when my dad gets along better with her sister, but I wouldn't call it unnatural."

"But then your take on what's natural is-" Brice stopped short.

"What? Is your smug ass trying to analyze me and my family, when your family won't even talk to you?"

"That's real mature Grier, throwing stones."

"You threw the first one!"

"No, I was simply stating what I thought was the truth."

"So, you think I'm twisted? Huh? That I'm crazy or some shit?"

"That's not what I said. You're twisting my words. And stop cursing."

"Well that's what crazy people do, Brice! They twist words! I'm going home!" she shouted, tossing the covers back and swinging her legs off the edge of the bed.

"Grier, I didn't mean it like that."

"How exactly then was I supposed to take those cracks on my family, with my not so natural take on the world?"

"Please, get back in bed," Brice insisted, pulling her backwards with his hands around her waist.

Grier sat with her arms folded across her chest and her lips pointed in anger. How dare Brice. Insulate bastard. Just because he had his shit together, didn't mean he got to look down his nose on the rest of the world struggling around him.

"Grier, I'm very sorry for taking liberties in speaking about your family. I am not sitting in judgment of them or trying to. Nor do I think that anything is wrong with you. I spoke out of turn and I apologize," Brice spoke in a slow and soothing tone.

"Fine."

"Do you accept my apology?"

"Sure."

Brice knew he was forgiven, but as was Grier's manner, she had to sulk a few more minutes before they could resume socially.

"I'm gonna go make us some Tazo tea. Got some Passion . . ." he whispered, giving her a playful nudge and kissing her exposed shoulder.

She nudged him back to show her mended feelings were near repair.

Grier and Brice sat drinking tea and discussing her years in London for most of the night. Just listening to the sound of her voice echo off his walls made Brice excited. He placed the palm of his hand against her chest and felt a chill run through him as the vibration worked its way up his fingertips.

"Brice, what's wrong?"

"Nothing that a cold shower and a National Geographic won't cure."

"I'm sorry."

"Don't be. I'm just very, very, very excited to have you back here with me."

"How excited are you?" Grier bit her bottom lip, running her hand down the length of his thigh.

"Yeah, about that excited. C'mon Grier, cut it out, for real. We'll have plenty of time for that when you are Mrs. Brice Ryhne," he sighed, pushing her hand away.

Brice drug himself up from the table and slid his feet across the hard wood floors to the bathroom. Grier looked hurt, but she was gonna have to realize that it was as difficult for him as it was for her. The only remedy for them was marriage.

Grier studied her pouting face in the mirrored wall across from the bed and began rationalizing her next move. She wanted desperately to show her affection towards Brice, but how? Besides, she hadn't seen him in years. There was no telling that this was even the same man she'd left three years ago. This was not the way a grown woman was supposed to behave. Go in the bathroom and give him some? / Some of what? How? / Stay in bed and wait it out? / He ain't gonna put up with this good girl mess too much longer? / If he loves me he will wait? / Not forever he won't. / Well, he's not that bad off, he is taking a cold shower. When he gets back, we'll cuddle and go to sleep. / No, he's gonna take care of things himself in the bathroom then come back in here wondering what the hell you're doing lying next to him / He loves me. / Does he?

Grier pushed her feet into the heeled satin slippers she'd left under Brice's bed three years ago and walked hesitantly to the bathroom door. The door was unlocked and she walked in undetected by Brice. Grier owed him something for waiting for three years. She slid the shower door open and peeked her head in amidst the cool dampness, stepping out of her shoes and under the shower's head. She stood behind Brice aroused by the water running down his back adding a glistening affect to his skin beneath the lights. Even though she believed they should wait for the wedding night for the "big event", there was no reason not to try a few other things.

Brice's skin felt prickly and iced, but his erection was fighting back. His member would not be manipulated so easily. He was about to start talking to it, begging it to please behave on Grier's first night back, when he felt the soft, but rigid flesh of Grier's nipples against his back. He didn't want to turn around. He couldn't. Turning around meant possibly losing the fantasy or scaring Grier away. Brice Rhyne felt sheepish and silly. He should have admitted years ago that he was a virgin. But how would that have played out? He didn't know what to do anymore than Grier did, but if he could just get her out of the shower with him, he may be able to save face.

"Grier . . ."

"Don't talk, Brice. Let me give you this much." Grier whispered, kissing his shoulder blades and running her hands up and down his thighs. Grier intended to act out one of the scenes she'd witnessed between Olivus and her aunt, but as soon as Brice turned to face her and she caught sight of an actual, bonifide, true-to-form penis, the bile hastened from her stomach to her mouth. Grier threw up all over Brice and the shower floor. They looked at each other compassionately, both secretly relieved.

*Just give me what you can of yourself, that's all I need,
I'll keep it confidential, in secret . . .*

Confidential, Tina Turner

arthur and chasen
Residence of: Arthur Collier
Shepherd's Bush, London
May 20, 2001

"Every able knee shall bend, every head shall bow and every soul will say Amen! Lord, I come to you today as humble as I know how, your merciful and obedient servant. I ask in Jesus' name, whose blood spilled and gave me the authority to ask you to remove the unnatural and abominable manner of my son's ways. Chasen knows not what he is doing and is trapped in a hellish underworld of lust and fornication, beset on all sides by the devil and demons. Please release him from the bondage of sin and immorality. In Jesus name, I pray unto you. Amen."

Arthur Collier grabbed the edge of his nightstand with one hand and leaned on it to help him up from his bent position. He was starting this day the way he had every day since he found that his son, Chasen was gay. Since the child was about nine, he had seen, but chosen to ignore, his son's seemingly feminine manner and the way he'd clung to his mother. His wanting to follow Lindersyl everywhere she went and she not making it better, by allowing him, made them look more the mother and daughter than mother and son. She was a Buddhist. A sinner herself, a heathen, but Arthur had loved her in spite of it. To all the members of Full Gospel, of which he had been a deacon since age twenty-six, Arthur was sleeping with the enemy. And when they married in a civil service at the registrar's office, rather than the church, everyone thought Arthur had lost his way. The sanctified sisters who saw him sitting in the pews alone every Sunday made it a point to bring to his attention whenever possible that Lindersyl would not change. Arthur was a very handsome man, with a strong work ethic and a true sense of civic responsibility; a fine catch for almost any single woman in the congregation. But there he sat every Sunday and at Wednesday night prayer services, alone.

Arthur knew when he married Lindersyl that he was a mere substitute, a stand-in for her sister's husband, Johnathan, but even that didn't steer him away. Arthur passed Lindersyl one day on the street and sat idling in traffic trying to figure out how such a beautiful woman could look so miserable. He didn't hesitate to leave his car sitting in the middle of a busy street and make a mad dash into the park to ask her out. She accepted.

She'd kissed him passionately the night of their first date, with her eyes shut tightly and her mind somewhere else. A quiet, even bashful lover, Arthur refused to have sex with her, but did agree to stay the night with her. He claimed it was to enjoy her company, but secretly he hoped she would try to seduce him. He was ever so eager, just quietly so. Over the next two weeks, he showered her with a kind of "puppy dog devotion" that seemed to open her up.

Arthur had his own company to worry about but he found time everyday to spend with Lindersyl. His family owned the biggest oil conglomerate in the Eastern world and while he'd rather spend his days riding horses, business never stopped long enough to enjoy the richness of his spoils. Born to a Saudi mother and West African father, Arthur had been educated both in the Middle East and England, but in matters of the heart was strictly "Latin". Lindersyl seemed aloof and haphazard about love, like she couldn't bother to fall head over heels or get bogged down in the contriteness of romance. It was a turn-on to Arthur, though it went staunchly against his religious upbringing to have a woman act so 'mannish'. As a result, he turned on the old-world charm. He made it a point never to show up at her door empty-handed: flowers, wine, her favorite dessert, and perfumes. Arthur allowed her to give her love without protest and he very gently gave what he could in return. She was not sex-crazed as he'd suspected, but brokenhearted. More than anything Lindersyl knew that Arthur would accept and love her no matter what. Still he was shocked to hear Lindersyl accept his marriage proposal a few short months later.

Things had gone along fine for them for quite a few years, when her brother-in-law showed up in London. She was secretive about whatever took place during his visit, but Arthur knew enough to be jealous. Lindersyl was easy to get along with so long as you didn't cramp her space or try to impose yourself upon her. She was kept under manners though by Arthur: there was always a hot meal waiting for him, even when she'd been out working all day, she enjoyed pampering him with antique cars (a hobby of his) and hot oil rubs twice a week. She provided sex on demand and never complained about it. Arthur respected her for being honest and discreet, because for all that she did for him, he would have had no clue she was double-timing him until she came forward and said so.

Even with Johnathan always underfoot, Arthur's marriage to Lindersyl was a happy one. Aside from their differences in religion and her being a night owl and he an early riser, they were very similar. Their marriage reached a breaking point though when it was discovered that Lindersyl could have no more children. They were both reaching into their late thirties and Arthur was desperate for an heir. She'd explained her mothering a few kids; the exact number Arthur never got out of her. Something had rendered Lindersyl barren years earlier though she'd only just found out and the thought of not being able to rear children suddenly took its toll on her. She became distant and mean-spirited, refusing to leave the house for weeks at a time. Finally she was diagnosed "clinically depressed" and given the option of going on medication or being institutionalized. Lindersyl actually refused both; but Arthur had assured her doctor that she would take the prescribed anti-depressants and regain her composure in no time.

When her weight began to plummet from not eating, Arthur, as a last resort, called her family in Connecticut. Her sister, Lillian, despite the things Lindi had said of her seemed genuinely concerned and without prodding, hopped a Concorde to London. Arriving the next day, a very stunning and slightly pregnant Lillian, swung into action.

"Lindi, what are you doing cowering in this bed like the world owes you something?"

"Lillian?" Lindi answered, peaking her head out from beneath the covers. "What are you doing here?"

"Arthur called me. Come out from under those covers, Lindersyl girl," she smiled.

Lindi pulled the covers back. She fell over the covers and into Lillian's arms, releasing her anguish onto her sister's shoulders.

"They say I can't have . . . have-"

"I know, I know. Stop crying, Lindi," Lillian coaxed, rounding Lindi shoulders back. "Your life goes on with or without children. So you can't have any more kids? You gotta loving man out there who loves you and a whole bunch of other people who need you."

"What about what I need Lillian? It would be one thing if I had my own children to look after-"

"Don't turn what you're going through into something else—especially not that," Lillian said in a forced whisper.

Lillian explained her own pregnancy dilemma. Pregnant with a child she could not let Johnathan know existed. It was Harry's baby. It was Harry's. And if he knew it, he'd want his child. But that would effectively end her relationship with Johnathan. Lillian told her sister that since she was keeping her distance from him, Lillian thought she'd have Johnathan to herself. Only Johnathan had taken other lovers, consequently positioning Lillian at the bottom of a tower of young, beautiful women to whom he was devoting his time. A baby? From where? He would barely look at her, let alone touch her. Johnathan would have known right off that it was someone else's child. Lillian decided to stay the rest of the year. "You're in need of a baby, and I've one too many," Lillian told Lindersyl without the need for further elaboration. As her pregnancy became evident, Lindi took on the role of adviser, doting on her sister's every craving and whim. The child, a boy, created quite an emotional stir for Lillian, who reportedly took one look at him in the delivery room and turned away. She told Arthur that she didn't feel responsible enough to care for a child after being out of practice so many years and wanted him to agree to take the child. Arthur understood there had to have been another reason or cluster of reasons, but that remained between Lindersyl and Lillian. Lillian refused to even name the child and so Arthur and Lindersyl named him Chasen Xaviar Collier, after Arthur's father and uncle. Since Lindersyl had remained in hiding for so long, it was quite fitting that she should return to public view claiming to have been off having a child. None of Arthur's church friends had seen Lindersyl inside the church until the christening, and had no idea they weren't the child's parents.

Lillian returned to the States a few months after Chasen's birth, giving herself a chance to lose her baby pounds and collect her alibi. This was the one period during which Johnathan had had contact with neither Lindersyl nor Lillian and Lillian felt sure he would be in the mood to cozy up to her upon her return. Especially so, once he heard the news that Lindersyl had just given birth to a beautiful baby son, for Arthur.

Chasen had been reared in a loving two-parent home; of which neither parent present was really his own. The child was so happy and loveable and had brought so much happiness into their home, that Arthur found himself constantly torn between the lies he lived and the truth. He felt he couldn't tell the truth because he saw how having a child around added even more glorious dimensions to Lindersyl's personality. Almost from the day Lillian offered to give Chasen to Lindersyl, she'd crawled out of her depressed funk and sadness. Arthur could not afford to take that away from Lindersyl and risk losing her to another run of depression. The one stipulation Arthur had made to her keeping the child was that Chasen be brought up as a Christian. Lindersyl agreed, actually driving Chasen to the church and giving him a gentle pat on the toosh, before seeing him up the front stairs. She never went in, but would return after services to retrieve Chasen and allow Arthur to continue with the church's affairs, uninterrupted.

Arthur and Lindersyl's divorce was a messy one. There were thirteen years of lies and fabrications to deal with, not to mention a son, whose cute little swagger had turned more suspect than adoring. Angry at the world, Chasen took to moping about the house most of the time, listening to a Walkman and finding new and exciting ways of enraging his father. Once it was coloring his hair green. Another time it was getting his ear pierced. All to which Lindersyl had little to say. "It's your body Chasen, you can do what you please with it. Just be sure to consider how ridiculous you will look when you're fifty! That aside, *please*, clean up your room before your clothing takes root," she'd once replied. Arthur had attacked her behind it, asking if she was sure she wanted to be a mother. Later, he intimated that she'd had such rotten luck with kids because she wasn't fit to parent. Why did he say that?

The argument had begun there and had ended in their divorce thirteen months later. It was a bitter divorce because over the years Arthur's temperament had come to parody his wife's. He gave as good as he got and resorted to cursing her out whenever the mood struck.

"Just 'cause I'm in the church now, don't mean that I always was. You got me fucked up. But don't let the smooth taste fool you; you will pay for leaving me," he told her.

Lindersyl filed for sole custody of Chasen and to retaliate, Arthur sat down and told Chasen of his true parentage. That Lillian and Johnathan were his parents and that he'd been given to him and Lindersyl because she couldn't have any more kids. It was a terribly inhumane thing to do and Arthur paid the price for it when Chasen attempted suicide the next morning. Arthur's attorney also found it necessary to bring up Lindi's bout with depression, her on-going relationship with her brother-in-law and the manner in which Chasen had been given to her, as reasons she should be denied any custody or visitation of Chasen. She and her family were pathological. The divorce was finalized and Arthur won his custody battle, celebrating his victory at Chasen's bedside in the Sheffield Group Hospital for Boys. Chasen was not well and would not be for some time. Lindersyl had thought it best to sever all ties to Chasen and Arthur and worked to that end night and day. Arthur didn't celebrate long though. He missed his wife and had no idea what to do with a rebellious teenager, who was absolutely no blood relation to him.

Upon returning home from the boys' hospital, Chasen was hell on wheels, refusing to respect Arthur as anything more than an unwilling guardian. Arthur was not his father, his family or his friend. Chasen's real family was in America, having a great time without him, and as clear as he could see, it was all Arthur's fault. Chasen, at fourteen, refused to go to school, work or church. Chasen's one seeming source of comfort and enjoyment, aside from plotting against his mother and her sister, was the company of a schoolyard mate called Danker. Arthur ignored what he thought to be a curious and unnatural bond between them—overly affectionate and decidedly secretive—Arthur went to great lengths to keep them separated. Chasen threatened Arthur with bodily harm if he tried to kick him out, and the fear of his threats went a long way. Exactly four years long, during which time Chasen admitted and began acting on his homosexual urges. Finally, Danker's parents sent him to live with relatives in the States and Chasen returned to a slightly warped level of normalcy. Meanwhile, Arthur tried to gain some sense of himself. He'd said and done things to get back at Lindersyl which he'd have never thought himself capable. He had harbored such hurt and anger over her affair with Johnathan and her seeming aloofness with him, that a "silly disagreement" had turned him into a nasty and maniacal man.

For all that he'd done to see him clear into heaven's gates, Arthur had failed. Chasen had not only turned to homosexuality as his chosen lifestyle, but had walked away from the church. He said he didn't believe in anything or anyone because there was no one who and nothing that believed in him.

"If there is a God why is there starving and suffering and hatred and greed? If there is a God, why has he left you, his faithful servant, alone and empty?" Chasen had smirked at him one night just before his nineteenth birthday.

Arthur gave Chasen his birthday licks early, jumping on him full throttle and putting him out of the house for his blasphemy. He had never raised a hand to Chasen before and his brutality scared him as much as it did the boy. Calling for a police escort, Chasen was physically removed from the house and put out onto the streets of downtown London. God had taken care of Chasen his whole life and yet the boy didn't recognize it at all. It was for Chasen's own good that he go out into the world and see what a horrid and cruel place it was, and learn, without reserve, Whom it was that would continue to bring him along.

It was the right thing to do Arthur reassured himself for the millionth time. It had been nearly six years since he'd knocked Chasen about and tossed him to the streets, yet Arthur worried after him as if it were yesterday. He had no idea of Chasen's whereabouts, but felt confident that he would be all right provided he found his way back to the Lord . . . and didn't head to the States to find Lillian and Lindersyl.

My heart and I have been a fool, I know,
I guess it's time to close the door . . .

Don't Wanna Cry, Big Maybelle

lillian
Gottlieb Grove, Driveway
May 20, 2001

On rare occasions the gods played terrible tricks on Lillian, and tonight, riding home in a taxi in the rain, she was convinced that this was one of those moments. She'd peeled her dignity up from the floor of Johnathan's hospital room and realized about three hours too late, that she had made a costly mistake. Johnathan did not want her. He *still* did not want her. How could she explain herself to Harry when she had no earthly idea what the hell was going on herself? Had she become so desperate for Johnathan's attention with Lindersyl around that she had pushed Harry away for good? When the cops interrogated her about what had happened, she said as clear as day that it was 'the pool attendant' who'd done it. Whenever Johnathan bled, whether it was from nicking himself while shaving, or in a fight of some sort, it always took her back to the time when he'd tried to commit suicide. The sight of his blood always lost its red coloring before her eyes and until she was able to calm down, all shades of red, turned a dull shade of gray. As a result, she'd learned to walk away as soon as any scuffle ensued.

When Johnathan expressed his gratitude for her loving and tending to him by calling her Lindersyl, dazed or not, it was time to reassess the situation.

"Johnathan, it's me, Lillian," she'd said in a stern voice that commanded attention.

His eyes opened slightly and he got a full glimpse of Lillian, still in her nightgown and mules, and gasped.

"Noooo! I want my Lindersyl. Lillian get Lindersyl."

"Baby, you don't know what you're saying. I am here and everything will be all right. I love you, Jumper."

"Where is Lindersyl?" he began crying.

Lillian pushed hard on the nurse's call button and waited impatiently for the nurse to make her way in. A tall Jamaican head nurse raced into the room, looking to attend to whatever the emergency might be.

"Ma'am, is there something wrong?"

"Yes, my husband is delirious! He keeps looking in my face and calling me by my sister's name."

"Well ma'am, his medication has just about worn off. He's not drugged . . ." the nurse said noncommittally.

"Then perhaps the pain is making him delirious!" Lillian said from between clinched teeth.

"Or perhaps he would like to speak with your sister . . ." the nurse countered.

The gaze Lillian gave warned of her low propensity for games and the nurse moved to Johnathan's side to check his heart and blood pressure. Johnathan opened his eyes again as she pushed the cold metal of the stethoscope onto his warm flesh. He moaned.

"Mr. Holland? Can you hear me?"

"Yeah."

"Do you know where you are?"

"At the hospital."

"Do you know why you are here?"

". . . A fight?" then becoming more coherent, "That motherfuckin' Haitian punched me in my face about my own wife!" Johnathan yelled.

The nurse took a startled step backwards, looking to Lillian suspiciously.

"Okay, 'Nurse Cratchett', if you can get him some more drugs to calm him down, it would help," Lillian said, rolling her eyes.

"Him or you? He is just fine. His bruises will need to heal, but there's no reason why he can't go home in the morning. And it looks like he's not as delirious as . . . others," she said with pursed lips.

"Oh, don't you get smart with me! I pay your salary,"

"Save your fighting spirit honey, 'cause you gonna have one serious fight on your hands when this man regains his strength," the nurse laughed exiting the room.

The cab driver, a sixty-something blues fiend, played the same two songs by Big Maybelle over and over again throughout the hour-long drive to Gottlieb Grove. His radio did not work, but his CD player did and he had the blues something awful. With a big rig jackknifed along the expressway rerouting them to back roads, Lillian found herself caged in a seedy stew of her own melancholy. Big Maybelle was the original blues-shouting sister, and the happiest person in the world could turn suicidal if they listened to her long enough.

> *I'll always love you, this I know*

"Would you turn this shit off?" Lillian complained under her breath.

> *But I don't want to cry anymore*

"At least turn the volume down to a decent enough level, jerkweed!", she mumbled, tossing her head from side to side in a dramatic display of displeasure.

If only Harry had picked her up from the hospital . . .

She'd tried to reach him all night, but there was no answer in the pool house. Jumping in the ambulance when the paramedics arrived seemed like a good idea at the time. She had intended to stay with Johnathan until he was released, doting on him as much as possible and proving that she could be counted on when Lindersyl was nowhere to be found. Now knowing that she had no place at Johnathan's side, she also had no choice but to vacate the hospital and return home.

By the time Lillian reached the outer-gates of Gottlieb Grove and punched in the security access code that allowed the cab onto the service road, her eyelids were swollen from crying. Sunlight had begun to peak in over the hills as the six o'clock hour rolled around. She'd been at the hospital all night and was eager to go to bed. Lillian arranged for a private ambulance to pick Johnathan up from the hospital and hoped to make her presence scarce for the next week or so. In fact, she thought as she closed the taxi door behind her, she might as well apologize to Harry and make her peace with him. But from the reflection cascading across the screen door, Lillian could just make out her sister's silhouette molded into the fetal position and cocooned by that of her beloved Harry.

When you can't hear My voice, please trust My plan,
I'm the Lord, I see you, and yes, I understand . . .

I Understand, Smokie Norful

grier
The office of: Grier Holland,
Xytex Corporation
Frances Drive, Mosse Point Connecticut
May 21, 2001

Xytex was the exact same company, no matter which location one happened upon. From the busy pseudo-chic furniture to the door handles and telephones, the Connecticut office looked exactly like the one in London. Courtesy of the owners' deranged and misguided notions of what was 'in' at any given moment, he went about redecorating each of his eleven offices whenever the urge struck. When Grier left the Connecticut office three years ago, she faintly remembered the pale green carpeting and textured wallpaper being stripped, but was never around to see what had become of it. Now upon her return, she saw that it was the same mauve tone of the office she'd just left behind in London. Even her high-back leather swivel was there, waiting to receive her. It was as if she'd simply had her business belongings shuffled into this new location or she'd fallen into a three year slumber and her entire time in London a mere dream. The same faces she'd despised when she left, had greeted her when she returned. "Narrow-nosed ass kissers", Grier mumbled under her breath as she plastered her standard hostess smile across her lips and nodded to acknowledge her office mates. It was moments like this she wished she had a better relationship with her father, so she could waltz right back to the elevators, out the door and back to Gottlieb Grove, where her father would take care of her. Tossing her laptop onto her desk and reassessing her situation, Grier sighed loudly. It was way pass noon and she wasn't expected until the following day, but she felt the need to drop in on her old stomping ground after her fiasco with Brice. She didn't want to think too much of his continued interest in her or the way she'd embarrassed herself in the shower with him.

When she left college she was expected to take a cozy job at Holland-Bennett, same as Eisendorff had. She was the older of the two, but had taken a couple of years off from school to travel. This allowed Eisendorff to enter college after her, but manage to graduate before her. Working in a family business was appealing—her grandfather had started the company—but within days of Grier's graduation, and before her return to Mosse Point, she received a phone call from Eisen that killed her chances of a successful matriculation from college to the family business. He said their father had cursed and humiliated him in an all-office conference and later when he tried to discuss it with him, Johnathan's wrath met him head on. The end result: a broken jaw. Eisendorff didn't need to work at Holland-Bennett, but the world outside was very cold, especially to someone perceived to have had a silver spoon tucked between his lips. Holland-Bennett had Eisen entering an established company as a junior partner, but, as Grier later pointed out, he was a junior partner to a father he could not stand to look in the face. That was all the convincing Grier needed to find her own niche. Fall on her face or not, she had to be responsible for herself.

Grier also found her father's behavior so bizarre that it was uncomfortable being around him without other people being present. His eyes often spoke of something sordid and suggestive; something that as a child she was unable to comprehend, and as an adult she refused to examine too closely. She had known others to look at her in that way, mannish boys . . . Brice. Grier had seen her father look at her aunt that way and on rare occasions, her mother. She felt ashamed that the man who was supposed to love her with a fatherly, protective love, had somehow come to see her as more than his daughter. Johnathan saw her as a woman. He had been the first to notice her slightly curving form and the first to bring up boys and her budding breasts as a teenager, not her mother. Johnathan had insisted on observing a mother-daughter talk Lillian was to have with her, but through which Lillian sat silently, examining a reflected frown line on her forehead in her compact. Johnathan eyed Grier suspiciously as she sat fidgeting in her seat, trying to figure out why she had been sitting with the two of them for half an hour with no one saying anything.

"Some little boy been pulling at your tits?" Johnathan finally scowled, his voice a bull horn of anger and suspicion. "Girls back when I was coming up didn't get tits till much later . . . . thirteen, fourteen."

"I am fourteen!"

Johnathan's face contorted as he mentally counted the years. Once he realized she was right, he crossed one leg over the other and went silent again.

"Have you started menstruating yet?" he'd asked in a coarse and direct way that instantly brought tears to her eyes.

Her sob-filled answer in the affirmative from behind the palms of her hands, shielding her face from her parents, would not protect her from Johnathan's anger. Grier couldn't get pass being asked in such a manner to defend herself or even say something flippant. She looked to her mother constantly for some kind of reassurance, some kind of acknowledgment that her father was in the wrong. But Lillian never put the compact away.

How long ago had it begun? Why hadn't she told him? What else was she keeping from them? The questions came and went without her having the energy to cry and speak. So she cried . . . and cried and then cried some more. But instead of the tears causing the conversation to halt, it had merely prolonged it. Eisendorff, hearing the commotion, and wishing to show off his newfound militant stance, stepped in to aid her. It was one of the hundreds of times he would intervene on her behalf and take her beating for her.

"You should know better than to speak to a young lady like that!" he shouted, folding his arms across his chest and leaning against the breakfront.

"What the hell do you know about it?" Johnathan fumed, standing from the sofa.

"I know what you ought to know, Pops! We were at school and she had the headmistress get me out of class cause she had an upset stomach. Since you were nowhere to be found, and Lillian, here, was off in Europe, I got the call when it happened. Unlike you, I was there and I took care of my sister," Eisendorff managed to say before the palm of Johnathan's hand slapped him across the face.

"Carry your narrow ass upstairs and stay out of this. You ain't nobody's father," Johnathan yelled.

"I got news for you, neither are you, Pops!" Eisendorff yelled behind him.

Grier was hot on Eisendorff's heels, running up the stairs behind him. If she could just make it into the room with him, Eisen would protect her from the beating she knew she was going to get. She had withheld information from her father and in doing so, she had also caused him to realize just how little she needed him. Lillian never took sides in fights with her father, often saying, "I have no opinion at all regarding this matter", before walking away. Grier never heard her exit speech, but noticed as she herself was leaving that Lillian had closed her "frown-line finding" compact and disappeared. At the top of the stairs Grier had just reached Eisendorff's room when her mother's whimpering in the hall bathroom forced her to stop.

"Mommy?" Grier called out, pushing the door open.

Her mother sat on the bathroom tile with her body propped against the bathtub. Lillian's perfect make-up was smeared and her perfect hair fell across her face like a mad woman's.

"Go away Grier. Just go away. Sometimes it is so much better when you kids have someplace other than home to come to—even on winter breaks from school."

Her mother's words hurt, but seeing the condition she was in made her realize how much of what Lillian said came from pain, rather than just being nasty. Over the phone, many times, Lillian spoke to Grier as if she were the biggest headache in the world; unwanted, unloved, and a menace. The tone she heard now was exactly the same. Grier took her mother's hands and helped her up onto the side of the bathtub, before taking a seat on the commode.

Her mother was mean-spirited and non-committed, but she was also human. How many times Grier had sat watching her mother stare out of the kitchen window at the swimming pool, her elbows resting on the sill and her auburn tresses blowing back behind her like a flag. She was so beautiful. Like a portrait of herself, sometimes, nothing on her moved at all, except her eyes, following you from one point of her peripheral to the other. Gentle and surreal in appearance, it was always a mystery to Grier why Lillian didn't love her, didn't want her around, couldn't find time, wouldn't make time. Why was it that no matter how well she did in school, or activities Lillian couldn't be bothered to grunt in her direction, let alone praise her efforts. Eisendorff was more like a father to her and Lindersyl, a distant mother, yet, Grier refused to give up on her mom. She coddled up under her every chance she got, holding her breath and counting the seconds until she was pushed away. Only occasionally, if Lillian were in a really good mood, would she allow Grier to sit with her, or lay her head in her lap, provided, Grier did not speak. Grier called it "keeping mommy's silence company".

"Mommy, what's wrong?"

"You have to ask? Grier why didn't you tell me that you had started your period?"

"You were in Europe."

"Grier, I haven't been there all this time. And if you could call your brother, why couldn't you pick up the goddamned phone and call me? I am supposed to be your mother! I am supposed to be here to help you understand what is going on with your body and why. That is my responsibility. It's like I woke up one morning and everything around me had changed. Eisendorff looks at me and his gaze goes right through me, but then it always did. I figured it was because he was a daddy's boy. But you were always able to come to me and tell me what was bothering you. Maybe some small things you never mentioned, but something as big as this? I . . . well, I just wish I could have shared in that with you," Lillian sobbed.

"Do you? You confuse me so much sometimes. One day you are as mean to me as one person can be to another. The next, you are the mother I remember when I was a little girl, loving and caring and supportive. I just don't know who I'm coming home to sometimes, so to keep my own feelings from being hurt, I push you away. Why didn't you stand up for me downstairs?"

"That was between you and your father. I don't get into things like that, because it's easier on me once you all have gone back. I do have to live with that man! Grier, sweetheart, I've been through a lot in the last few years . . ."

"Like what?" Grier frowned, "You always make it sound like you're fighting some personal war, but you never elaborate. What is the problem?"

"Grown people's stuff."

The look on Grier's face told Lillian, 'grown people's stuff' was not going to get it this time.

"Your father and I separated for almost a year during which time I was with Lindersyl. Being around your aunt and Arthur made me realize for better or worse, Johnathan was my husband and instead of walking away from each other, we needed to work things out. Needless to say I came to that conclusion alone. Your father was not interested in reconciling and when he saw that I had put on a few pounds, he made it clear that he found me terribly unappealing . . ." she said studying her palms.

"Daddy cheating on you, huh?"

"What do you know about such things?" Lillian snickered at Grier's intuition.

Grier didn't laugh.

"Probably," Lillian conceded, "but I can't say for sure."

"I know that daddy is always looking at other women, even when you are standing right there with him. He is not a casual flirter, mom, he's actually on the 'make'".

"Grier!"

"That's what it's called!"

"I am well aware of what it is called, yet I don't believe that such a thing should be heard coming out of the mouth of a fourteen-year-old."

"Sorry. All you and daddy do when me and Eisendorff are home is argue. That's why we don't want to come home, because if we aren't here, you won't fight."

"*Eisendorff and I!* Grier, you really must mind your language skills.

"Sorry."

"Grier, your daddy and I wake up fighting and we go to bed fighting. One night Johnathan was sleep walking and I caught him in the kitchen at the table with his finger pointed defiantly at the toaster, hollering 'Goddamn it Lillian, you gonna do what I say and like it woman!'" Lillian laughed, "It has nothing to do with you or Eisen. Sometimes married people hit a dry patch. Your father and I have hit a dry patch."

Grier spent that night in bed with her mother, talking about boys and love and being in love. It was the first time she'd had a chance to really listen to her mother talk about regular things in a soft, even tone. No yelling, or shouting, just snuggled up together in bed, sharing themselves. Grier realized that her mother was quite likeable. She had a pretty good grasp of things and was very smart. In another time and place, they could have been great friends. But under the circumstances, and with her father being who he was, Lillian would revert back to her old, insecure, angry self, if for no other reason than to hide the hurt. About 3am, while lying in the comfort of her mother's arms, Johnathan released the embrace Lillian had around her and yanked Grier from the bed.

"You been out there pushing your ass up in them little boys' faces haven't you?", he yelled, whacking her across her backside with a wooden Fuller brush.

Grier thought for a moment she was dreaming; then the pain sank in.

"Fucking little slut! Strip down, girl!"

Grier's eyes went wide. She couldn't strip naked in front of her father; even if he was whipping her. Why was he doing this? Why now, after the initial conversation had been over for hours?

"You out there being a little slut! You screwin' girl? Answer me!" Johnathan screamed.

There was no liquor on his breath. There was no break down or build up to Johnathan's madness and there was nowhere for Grier to run. From the corner of her eye, Grier could see Lillian ease from the bed and out of the room. With Lillian out of the way, Johnathan grabbed at the front of her shirt and ripped it clear from her body.

"So you think you're a woman? Come home pregnant, hear?" he yelled.

"Daddy stop it!", Grier yelped, scurrying pass him, covering her bare chest.

"You tell them little nappy-head boys to stop it? Bring your ass here girl."

Crying would not help and no one was going to intervene. When Johnathan pulled at her bloomers to steady her with one had and pounded the brush against her back, Grier knew only she could stop him. She would have only one chance to do it and do it right, and while she had seen men kneed in the groin before, her heart beat loud in her ears as she contemplated disabling her own father. "Lord forgive me," she mumbled. Then with one quick jab into his boxers, Grier ended the trance Johnathan had been in. He went down on his knees, clutching his private parts and bellowing in agony.

"You put your hands on me again like that and I swear, I'll kill you in your sleep," Grier yelled, running from the room.

Johnathan would never have the opportunity to embarrass Grier in the workplace the way he did at home. His unforeseeable fits of rage left everyone on pins and needles. She would not give him that authority, no matter how many obstacles she endured while forging ahead as a young executive. Unfortunately, her keenness to be back in the Connecticut branch of Xytex had dissipated almost from the moment she walked into her office.

Grier's job was to handle the electronic end of its corporate communications, but she handled so many other areas of public relations and administrative tasks, that her title, Director of Integrated Communications Strategies, seemed vacant. Established in the late 1970s, Xytex was an international financial printing operation that was as successful as most of its clientele. As a result, the company's image needed constant overhauling. They were the biggest and brightest, but seemed to always be a step behind. When Grier came on board she had a degree in hand, the reputation of her family as security, and a half-dozen recommendations from her college professors. She was young and gung-ho, wide-eyed and enthusiastic. Though traits Grier knew made her a favored employee with the board of directors, it also made her a nuisance among her peers. Six years of dedicated service brought six promotions and the major hair breakage, thinned stomach lining and nightly anxiety attacks that went with it.

Grier could not cope with work and Brice's unmet sexual needs boomeranging around in her head. She woke one morning and decided she had to go. With the proposal to institute a new electronic media service for Xytex and its clients in the hands of the board of directors that afternoon, Grier found herself packing by week's end. Johnathan and Lillian were none too happy about the move to London, but once she'd contacted Lindersyl and told her of the opportunity, it was pretty much a done deal.

Lindersyl always said that there was nothing wrong with Grier's relationship with her parents that a mind of her own wouldn't cure. Being back in the same office she'd had three years ago was bringing back all of the confusion and uneasiness she'd felt before leaving.

Grier had tried to outrun her problems dumping them on the shores of America in hopes that someone else would have pilfered through them and taken them on for her while she was gone. But the distress was her own, and like a loyal lap dog, it had been right there awaiting her return when she alighted the plane in Mosse Point. Only added to them were her mother's unofficial divorce petition and ongoing affair with Harry Veda, her aunt's peculiar past, perhaps with her own father, and Grier's own reattachment to Brice Rhyne, though she was no closer to satisfying him sexually than she was when she'd left. Leaning her head back against the chair's headrest, Grier bit down on her lip and tried to fight back the tears, as the old familiar gnawing in her stomach began.

You must have been burning candles to make your love so strong;
You must have sprinkled dust all around my bed, you must have had a black cat bone . . .

Voodoo, The Neville Brothers

johnathan & eisendorff
Hospital Room of: Johnathan Holland
Mercer Hospital, SW Mosse Point, Connecticut
May 21, 2001

Lindersyl's pager went off in Eisendorff's pocket just after seven. Sophia had put Avery down for the night and gone to bed herself, when Eisendorff decided to pull Avery from the bed and hold him while he slept. Eisen laughed at the thought of being a father. How ironic that something he'd run so desperately from had turned out to be an unbelievable joy. Avery was snuggled in Eisen's arms sound asleep when the pager began vibrating. Eisendorff knew Johnathan would be trying to reach Lindersyl and he was in just the mood to run interference between them. Eisendorff didn't care what had taken place between them years ago, he didn't want his father anywhere near Lindersyl. He loved her too much to see her hurt. Eisen had taken Lindersyl's pager off of her to eliminate any temptation she had of seeing Johnathan. And would you know? It was Johnathan's cell number showing in the display of the pager. To hell with Johnathan, Eisen thought, let him think Lindersyl was ignoring him. Eisen had settled into his sweats and a t-shirt and was just kicking back to watch an encore performance of For Love of Ivy, when the beeper started again. Finally he turned it off.

A gorgeous and very classy Abbey Lincoln was just about to read Sidney Poitier the riot act, when the phone began ringing. The caller ID said it was Mercer Hospital. Who the hell would be calling him from Mercer?

"Yeah?" he whispered into the receiver, suddenly nervous.

"Dr. Holland?"

"Yeah?"

"This is Dr. Dodge at Mercer Hospital."

"Hey man, what's up? Ain't heard from you in a while."

"I'm pretty good. How about yourself?"

"I'm cool."

"The reason I'm calling is . . . seems your father was brought in a few hours ago, beaten up pretty badly. And before you go getting yourself upset, he'll be all right. He's stabilized, but he's been asking for you and refuses to go the hell to sleep. Visiting hours are over, but ain't nobody getting any sleep until you get here. As a professional courtesy I can let you in to spend the night if you can get here within the next hour."

"Yeah, Dodge, I'm on my way," Eisen whispered.

"Good, the nurses will be happy to hear that," Dr. Dodge said laughing.

"By the way, do you have any clue how it happened or who did it to him?"

"Nope, looked like a barfight or something. Your mom was really upset and kept saying something about she never expected 'him' to do this."

"Thanks a lot Dodge, I owe you one."

Eisendorff replaced the phone to its pad and rubbed the palms of his hands across his head. What was going on? Harry was the likely culprit and it probably had to do with the proposal and divorce request. Why was Johnathan requesting he come to the hospital? As much as he didn't want to deal with his father, Eisendorff's curiosity about the brand of torture Johnathan was enduring piqued. Fragments of his earlier conversation with Lindersyl also tormented Eisendorff. Johnathan could probably shed light on it. Eisen fingered the journal pages sprawled out across the width of the living room table. The answers to all the puzzles and riddles was a quick drive across town to Mercer Hospital.

Nothing can prepare a child, for the sight of a parent confined to a hospital bed. The tubes with varied colored smaller tubes, like tributaries, spilling from Johnathan's body, the flashing space aged machinery and the faint beeping sound of the heart monitor, froze Eisendorff in his tracks. He was crying, hard and loud when his eyes finally reached Johnathan's pasty face. Harry had delivered a beating of massacre proportions upon him. Johnathan looked weak and disoriented, though Dr. Dodge insisted that the beating wasn't the only cause.

"It's the medication that's making him groggy. We has contusions, a fractured right leg and the normal black eye and busted lip. We also found that he was anemic, hence the ashy look of his skin. He's much better than he looks," Dr. Dodge half smiled, patting Eisendorff across the shoulders.

For the life of him, Eisendorff couldn't figure out why he was crying like a baby over a man he couldn't stand. Maybe it was that he looked so helpless. In all his life, Eisendorff had never known Johnathan as anything but strong and confident, determined and steely. But here he was as destructible and fragile as any other man. Eisen took no sordid satisfaction in his father getting his comeuppance and wanted to hold him and rock him in his arms the way he had Avery earlier. He wanted to reassure his dad that he loved him and that every thing would be okay.

"I'll leave you guys alone," Dr. Dodge said, interrupting Eisen's thoughts. "Your mom was here earlier and we put clean linen on the extra bed for her, so you're welcomed to pull the partition back and rest when you feel like it."

"Dodge, thanks for calling man, I appreciate it."

"No prob. By the way, how's your sister?"

"A nut job, same as always, Man, now stop asking, because she still ain't going out with you," Eisen replied, only half-joking.

Eisendorff pulled the hard hospital issue chair closer to the bed. Johnathan was resting, but fitfully.

'Daddy, don't fight the drugs. Let them do what they are supposed to do," Eisen said, taking Johnathan's hand in his. "That's it, relax."

Johnathan's eyes opened slightly and he gave a faint smile. "You came."

"Course I did, Dad. Of course I did."

"I have to tell you what happened . . ."

"No, just rest. We can talk about this some other time. You need to build your strength."

"I've been resting all evening. I'm hungry as hell . . . why they didn't wake me to feed me something?"

"Well let's see," Eisen said moving to the other side of the room, "your tray is still over here on the rack. Looks like you got creamy chicken stuff with some tan lumpy gook and little green slimey things on the side," Eisen laughed.

"Sounds like something your mother made," Johnathan's laughing was heartfelt and strong, but also painful. "Damn!" he yelled grabbing his side.

"Careful, Dad," he warned.

It was the third time since he'd come into the room that Eisendorff had addressed Johnathan as either Dad or Daddy. He could tell that his son had been crying. It meant so much to him that he had bothered to show up at all that Johnathan felt a lump in his throat. When he'd opened his eyes, he could have sworn that it was his mother sitting there. The softness of his words the security and comfort in his voice.

"Listen, Eisendorff, I want to tell you something."

"Dad, I don't need to know what happened tonight, especially if it will upset you."

"It's not so much about tonight, as it is every night of my life. Yeah, tonight, that Harry Veda beat the stuffing out of me . . . but I deserved it. Lillian and I were having it out and I threatened her. He came to her defense; which is more than I would have done had the tables been reversed," Johnathan said, his words trailing off.

"Maybe it is time to let her go Dad. If she loves Mr. Veda, get her out of your system and move on."

"She was never in my system, Eisendorff. Never."

"What?"

"Truth is, if I hadn't been so hell-bent on living *the life*, I would have walked out on her thirty years ago," Johnathan said, wincing as his own excitement caused his head to spin.

"What?," Eisen asked again, certain that the pieces were all about to fit together perfectly.

"You asked me earlier, so now I'm telling you—I love Lindersyl."

"Oh, come on."

"Eisendorff, every time I look at Lindersyl Gottlieb my body loses all natural function—blinking, breathing, swallowing. I've hated her for it, having dominion over my person—despised her every nook and cranny. But hating her, disavowing my love, in no way releases her hold. Thinking of her, whether she is near or far, I feel helpless. It is not her fault. She does not want to hold me captive. It is a blessing, a boost to her feminine charms, but she takes absolutely no glory in causing this kind of despair. An unwilling captor she is for sure," he sighed, reaching for Eisendorff's hand.

"What is it Daddy?"

"I need to apologize to you for not sharing this before now. I didn't feel it was my place. Being here, and this is not some death bed confession, mind you, but being here made me realize that I needed to say this because it could have been."

"Fine Daddy, I'm listening."

Every time Eisendorff said "Daddy" it made Johnathan's heart flutter and he would have to calm his dancing emotions enough to begin again. Since he was a small boy, Eisen seemed to take great pleasure in calling him anything except Dad, Daddy, or Father. He'd instead called him Pops, Johnny or John-o, which he despised. Even after he'd done his best Kunta Kente versus the overseer whupping, yelling "How are you to address me? What is my name?", Eisendorff would not submit. Johnathan would not be his 'Dad' by hook or crook. Yet, here, after all the maltreatment, Eisendorff was finding it in his heart to forgive his father's ignorance.

"I watched Lindersyl for near 'bout a year, walking around campus with her big sister, but never got up nerve enough to speak. Always two steps behind Lillian and hanging on her every word, Lindi was kind of withdrawn. Very strong willed and opinionated, she was, still is, very shy and quick to upsetting. She would never have paid me any attention at all had Lillian not been there. Lillian was a goddess to her. Course Lillian was a goddess to everybody down there. The only Black gal in the state of Mississippi to ride around in a new convertible every year with a mink stole draped across her shoulders. Lillian is still legendary on Rosedale's campus for those badass furs and sling backs. She was Lana Turner and Eartha Kitt—Hollywood, larger than life. Hell the female teachers envied her and the male professors loved her. Lillian didn't want any of the older men who came to court her, though. She had set her sights on my frat brother Vernon

Longmire, and he only wanted what I wanted; her money. Lillian paid me to go out with her to make Longmire jealous—to make him want her. That was my only function.

In that way I was the envy of the campus. I used to love when she'd give me the keys to her '61 convertible and tell me to drive her around the campus a few times so everyone could admire us. I was pleased as punch to drive her around, escort her to her parties, and pop her on the backside every now and then out in public. Lillian didn't require much else. She didn't want me and I didn't want her. She had a great body-even now, I wouldn't kick her out of bed, y'know? Our relationship was taxing, restricting and bothersome for me on many levels, but it was the most carefree union I've ever had. In addition to providing me the necessary business contacts, clothing, transportation, money, weekly barber appointments, and sundries, Lillian allowed me all the outside sexual intimacies I could handle. She was a virgin and intended to stay that way. But everything in Lillian's life had a stringently contrived order, which she and that maniac grandmother of yours created. In time she and Longmire got together and he started driving her around. He was a lady's man though, and so Lillian had to settle for being his 'main squeeze'. She and I continued to keep each other company. Platonic, above-board, company. I was a Greek man and so we partied together, but she was difficult to be around once Longmire got under her skin. Her whole attitude changed. She started finding fault with everything about me—my posture, my clothes, my hair. When she suggested in that not-so-subtle manner of hers that I see a dentist friend of hers who would be ever-so-willing to fill in the gap between my two front teeth as a favor to her, she crossed the lines of our friendship. She knew I needed money—always did. I had family and a whole county of people who put their money together to get me into school. Lillian paid my way so I wouldn't have to go home or hold my hat in my hands to family. We were best buddies, but somehow she got in her head that she needed to make me her personal charity so that I would be "acceptable" to the 'money set'. I went along with Lillian's nonsense, because, quite frankly, I needed the money. She could be intrusive and demanding, but she was paying my way and helping me to establish myself as a man of means in business circles. I wasn't trying to stay in Clarksdale all my life. She was ashamed of who I was and it became evident when she visited my family up in the Delta. She was cordial, but distant and once we made it back to Jackson, we had all but parted ways. As a final parting gesture, we decided to go to a mixer that night on campus. And that is where Lillian introduced me to Lindersyl. Boy, I saw her and instantly, I knew that I was looking at my wife and the mother of my children. She was just so beautiful and graceful and soft-spoken, that I felt like I needed to build myself up to her and make her like me. I mean, your mama's people had money when most Black people didn't have a pot to piss in or a window to throw it out of. The first time I got a chance to talk to her at the party, my tongue tied up on me. It was like I had a mouthful of glue forcing my tongue to a standstill. I blamed it on the liquor I was consuming and to cover my humiliation, I slapped her backside as hard as I could. Her eyes went wild and I figured her cup of punch was about to land in my face. Instead, her eyes welled up with tears. She only said two words, "how disappointing," before turning and walking out.

Once the crowd went back to partying, I went to Lindersyl's dorm and apologized. She pulled my face down to hers, disheartened and serious and clasped my face in her palms. I could feel her breath on my face and I wanted so badly to kiss her that my heart sank when she pointed a delicate finger in my face and said, "You ever try that again, and I'll get my daddy to come down here and rip you another asshole". The next day I showed up at her English class and took her flowers. They were pissy wildflowers I'd picked from behind the football field. Eisendorff, if you could have seen her face when I stepped into that class and handed them to her . . . it was like heaven and earth in that blush. She tilted her head down and smelled them, her nose twinkling under the scent. When she looked up, at me, so pleased and excited by the simplest show of my affection, I knew I would never love another woman as long as I lived. And guess what? I never have. There I was a grassroots organizer, going door to door in neighborhoods spent by dank and despair, convincing people who had everything to lose that their vote was worth the risk. I was proud and amazed at how people listened to "Jolie and Eisen's boy". I was making a difference, but wasn't sure if people were noticing my substance and my character or the fine cars and high-tone pretty girl on my arm. I was trapped between being my own man and being a made man and didn't want to start that same mess all over again with Lindersyl. But they were as different as night and day, Lillian and Lindersyl. Lindersyl had the same money as Lillian, but didn't care for it. Lindersyl knew what I was fighting for and did everything she could to support and encourage me. When Lillian saw that we were actually getting along, she decided that she couldn't live without me and made it her business to stay firmly fixed between me and Lindersyl.

Johnathan took a sip of ice water before returning his gaze to Eisen's searching eyes.

"Lindersyl was different. I didn't desire her with an adolescent desire. I wanted to read her poetry and sing her songs in broken, flat keys. I wanted to go that extra mile as a man to prove that I could answer her every need, but there was no way for me to express this to her. Not, big time Johnathan Holland."

"So what about the other guys and the kids everyone was always talking about?"

"Things are not always what they seem."

"So here come the riddles again. Why does everything relating to our family turn into one of Aesop's fables?"

"I've replaced my past with a truth that isn't. Is there more? There is always more. But it's not for me to tell. I just wanted you to understand that I have loved and been in love with your aunt Lindersyl for more years than you've had life. That will not change, ever. And if she'll have me once Lillian is out of the picture, I want her back and at the Grove."

Johnathan's eyes were *dancing*. Eisendorff wanted to hear more, but knew it wasn't going to happen. Anyway, in Eisendorff's heart, he already knew what needed to be told. He decided to just say it.

"Aunt Lindersyl is my mother isn't she? Me and Grier belong to the two of you."

Johnathan never responded. Just laid there smiling, looking straight through Eisendorff with the most peaceful look. Finally, Johnathan nodded and smiled, resting his head back on the stack of pillows under his neck. Then he drifted into a restful sleep holding tight to Eisendorff's hand.

Chapter Five
chicken don't have no alligator

*Heaven please send to all mankind, understanding and peace of mind,
And if it's not asking too much, please send me someone to love . . .*

Please Send Me Someone to Love, Sade

chasen & lillian
Gottlieb Grove
May 21, 2001
Time standing still . . .

Chasen had watched EMS workers hoist a badly whipped Johnathan and a hysterical Lillian into the back of an awaiting ambulance before creeping his rental car slowly along the path of the service road. Remembering the many side and hidden entrances onto the property and into the house from a single childhood visit, Chasen was able to walk right in from the outdoors, undetected.

He'd taken full run of the house, stepping over broken glassware and chairs in the kitchen, sniffing around Lillian's bedroom for hours and making her walk-in closet his personal playground. The silks, furs and cashmeres and wonderful smelling perfumes were just too much for him. Everything in 'Lillian Land' had a place. Everything was in Lillian's own, meticulously refined order. He took a hot bubble bath in coconut milk and shea butter, while thumbing through a stack of photo albums he'd found in the study. With Lillian's floor length cape of merino wool and white fox wrapped around his naked body, he'd just decided to destroy that order of Lillian's, by tearing her house apart, when the grand dame herself, appeared, getting out of a taxi.

Though he had planned on slapping her face and shaking her violently when their paths crossed, he now wanted to embrace her and inhale deeply that "mother smell". But her perfect hair was out of place and the look on her face was decidedly sour. Still to Chasen, Lillian was the most beautiful woman in the world. He watched her slow stride up to the pool house door, where she paused long enough to take in something disturbing. When she'd turned so she faced Chasen again, her eyes were sinister and brooding. Like his own face earlier, Chasen muttered aloud, "That's *my* momma."

With her movement now a light sprint, Chasen moved equally as quick to restore things to their rightful place before Lillian made it into the house. By the time she walked into the living room, Chasen was alighting the stair with his arms outstretched to greet her.

"Oh, for crying out loud! What are you doing here?" she called out from across the room.

"Well, Mother, can I get a Welcome Home hug or something?"

Lillian moved into and out of Chasen's embrace with one fluid motion before asking again why he'd shown up in Connecticut and more to the point, why he was in her home.

"Ain't this a bitch? How long has it been? And you got nothing but tacit distrust and suspicious eyes all over me."

"Now is not a good time for your tomfoolery Chasen. Not at all. Why are you wearing my things? Do you need something? Money? Tell me where you're staying and I will have a check dropped off to you sometime tomorrow," she said, turning from him and oozing herself down into a chaise.

"Money? I have money. My aunt's money has supported me well over the years. I would like *my mother* though, to spend some time with me, love me, show me she cares."

"*Your mother* is over in the pool house sleeping off her inner whore," Lillian sprung up from her seat suddenly. "Why don't you go over and say 'hello'?"

Without thought or planning, Chasen smacked Lillian hard across the face.

"You are my mother! Say it! Say it!"

The force of his hands shaking her, jostled Lillian to tears. No one around her really loved her except this unwanted bastard child who she couldn't allow herself to love back. Fighting to catch her breath, Lillian looked into Chasen's face and saw those big saucer hazel eyes of Harry Veda's *and* a perfect way of exacting her revenge upon Harry and Lindersyl. Chasen's grip on her, even the baritone of his voice and the way he tilted his head to the side when questioning her as if to ask, 'Do you understand what I'm saying?' was so much like his father, that it overwhelmed Lillian. Eventually Chasen had to grow up to take on Harry's characteristics, but the two men were so much alike that it was startling. Physiology had cemented what proximity and nurturing could not. Forced into her space as he was now, Lillian had no choice but to love, or at least acknowledge Chasen. If nothing else, he would be a loyal subject, an ally as the emotional landscape of the Grove shifted. Her mother had always told Lillian that the only men a woman can trust are her sons. Lillian looked at Chasen, like Eve in the Garden of Eden checking out the fruit of the forbidden tree and saw that it was ripe and good for devouring. She smiled. Lillian allowed herself to fairy tale the situation. *This was hers and Harry's finest creation—an ember of their love.* She pulled Chasen close, annoyed at once that he'd been in her coconut milk and shea butter bath emulsions. She kissed his forehead and then uttered into his ear, "I *am* your mother".

With rocks still tightly locked in his jaws, Harry refused to acknowledge Lillian's presence in the poolhouse doorway. She stood, her arms akimbo, peering apologetically into his face from across the living room, where she'd muttered under her breath at him a few times. He hadn't strained at all to hear her, but could just make out something about her not wanting to disturb him, given he was not alone. By this childish remark, Harry deduced that Lillian was aware that her sister was there. By refusing to respond, he had opened the door for further confrontation, as Lillian's propensity for being ignored was frightfully poor.

"Hey Lindersyl, you want breakfast?" Harry called to a barely coherent Lindersyl, who still lay sprawled out on her back, her head dangling off the foot of his bed.

"Just coffee . . . something strong," she yelled back.

"Lindi, bring your ass down here and face me!" Lillian yelled up to her sister.

There was a brief moment of silence in the house as Lindersyl made her way down the stairs, Harry's sweatpants and jersey swallowing her frame. Chasen stood in the pool house doorway charged with energy as he watched the drama unfold. He watched with anticipation as the woman he'd grown to believe was his mother and his newly-professed mother, prepared to do battle. He'd witnessed Lindersyl's episodes with Arthur in his childhood and could not fathom Lillian as any real match for her; but Miss Lillian was serious about this old broke up looking pool cleaner. So big, bad Lindersyl may truly have a fight on her hands this time, Chasen figured.

Harry pushed the skillet back onto a cool aisle and removed the flame from the burner. He folded his arms across his chest and took a deep breath. Figuring he'd have to dash between the sisters at some point, he silently readied himself as Lillian took sight of Lindersyl. Though he could only make out a silhouette of the other person standing just outside the screen door, he assumed it was Eisendorff and decided to pay him no mind.

"What are you down here making all this noise about Lil?" Lindersyl asked, yanking up the collar of the jersey to cover her exposed shoulder.

"You had to screw him didn't you?"

"What?"

"Don't 'what' me!"

"Lil, I didn't even meet Johnathan yesterday. I went out to the reservoir and got pissy drunk! Girl, you wouldn't believe the mess I made of Johnathan's car. He is gonna—"

"It's not enough to have my husband, you want Harry too?"

"I know you are not accusing me of Harry!" Lindersyl said in utter disbelief, plopping her body down at the dining room table. "Lillian, Harry and I smoked some forty-year-old reefer last night and it was nothing but vomiting and sleeping on my mind after that. We talked about the two of you and your upcoming nuptials most of the night."

"Poppycock! You smell of him all up around your neck," Lillian smirked, walking around Lindersyl, taking quick whiffs of her neck.

"I'm wearing his clothes, you silly cow! Who else am I supposed to smell like? And Lillian, I ain't in the mood for a whole bunch of your foolishness this morning, so don't keep pushing up on me," Lindersyl said, standing and pushing the chair back with a quick kick.

"Or else what?"

"Else I'ma whip your little silly ass!" Lindersyl said, finally annoyed enough to fight.

"Scandalous!" Chasen called from behind his hands.

Lindersyl recognized the voice, but couldn't think of a reason she'd be hearing Chasen's voice. Harry's place was the last place on earth Chasen needed to show himself. Suddenly Lindersyl took note of Lillian's smug expression. "How could you?" she whispered to Lillian, before turning her attention to Chasen. "Chasen? Is that you?" Lindersyl asked, glancing up and then walking over to him.

"It sho is, Miss Want to be Mommy Dearest," Chasen said, moving forward so that he was almost face to face with Lindersyl.

Lindersyl did not begrudge Chasen his romantic entanglements, but had made it clear she would not stomach the flamboyant gender-bender mannerisms. Lindersyl had taken to swatting Chasen with the daily paper whenever he forgot himself, and grabbed Harry's unread Mosse Point Gazette between her hands. She had stiffened the paper taunt in her hand and was just about to pop Chasen across the back when Lillian intervened.

Lillian grabbed Lindersyl by the hair, yanking her backwards. It was clear that Lindersyl and Harry had done nothing to warrant her suspicion and behavior, but Lillian was also bruised by Johnathan calling for her sister at the hospital and was prepared to secretly fight over that as well. Lillian was happy in herself that Chasen had been tossed into the mix: an element of surprise.

Harry could never bring himself to tell Lindersyl how much he hated her son. He'd suspected from the conversations Lillian had had with him that Chasen was a homosexual. Harry's father and grandfather had told him as a kid there was nothing more despicable than a man with women's tendencies. Harry had been warned that if ever he found himself leaning into such perversion, his body would be found at the bottom of a ravine. These were not madmen, but village and town elders, respectable men warning him, so he'd taken it to heart and made no qualms that he would rather see a man dead than gay. Damned 'butt boy', swirling his head around and popping his lips like no chaste and respectable woman would dare. Now here it was the first time they'd meet face-to-face, and Chasen was a troublemaker to top it off.

"Now what?" Chasen asked, with arms flailing about.

Lindersyl gave Chasen an admonishing look that immediately quieted him. His resentment seethed from within him and onto everything in his path. Lindersyl did not want to fight with him.

"C'mon ladies," Harry said, grabbing Lillian tightly by the arm and forcing her up the first few steps to the bedroom. "Lillian, take yourself upstairs and wait for me."

"Don't talk to my mother like that!" Chasen yelled.

"Chasen be quiet!" Lindersyl called over her shoulder.

"Oh, don't even let me get started with you, Miss Girl. How you goin' tell somebody to shut up?" Chasen said with a swerve of the neck.

Lindersyl smacked Chasen across the head with the rolled up newspaper. "You will not address me out of name again, do you understand me? I am still your mother!"

"Oh see, that's where you're wrong, Lindersyl, you are not my mother! She is!" Chasen cried, holding his head.

Harry made it to the stairwell landing, ignoring what he considered a problem between mother and son, when Chasen's diatribe pierced his ears. Was Chasen saying that Lillian was his mother? Had Lillian given birth to him?

Releasing his hold on Lillian, Harry backed down the stair. It was only then that he began to look closely at the young man dressed in light crepe shirt and Chinos. Chasen's dark chocolate complexion and chiseled build alarmed Harry under sharp scrutiny. Chasen was still engaging Lindersyl in a sort of base tit for tat argument, exposing only his profile to Harry. But under the harshness of the rising sun coming through bare windows Harry awakened. With only slight variations of Lillian's features strewn in, Chasen Collier looked like his mirror image. They stood shoulder-to-shoulder and then face-to-face, Harry looking from Lindersyl to Lillian for an explanation.

There was an eerie silence as all the pieces fell into place. Lillian sat frozen on the stair landing with her hands covering her mouth.

"Duchess! What did you do?"

"Harry, baby, let me explain—"

"Duchess, *this* is my son?"

"Harry, I can explain—"

"I asked you a damned question, woman!" Harry yelled, grabbing Lillian by the shoulders and gripping her tighter and tighter until his fingerprints bruised her skin.

Lillian did not answer fast enough, causing Harry to turn and address Lindersyl.

"Lindersyl, this is my son?"

With her eyes cast down, Lindersyl, nodded in the affirmative, at which point, Lillian's sobs, quiet and reserved until then, became racked with emotion and fear. She closed her eyes and held them shut as tightly as she could to avoid meeting with Harry's pain. Like a man devoid of any sensibility, Harry's hands dropped from Lillian's shoulders and he walked emotionlessly over to Chasen. He eyed him suspiciously for a moment, before picking up the bags he'd packed the night before and walking out the front door.

"Harry, Johnathan and I were going to try and make things work that time around. He . . . He had moved back into our bedroom and he wanted to have a second wedding . . . I couldn't ruin that-" Lillian screamed, running behind him and trying to pry one of the suitcases from his hand.

Harry dropped his bags at once, and shouldering Lillian, slammed her to the grass. "A lesser man would kill you right now. I regret the day I ever set eyes on you." Harry whispered, looking deep into Lillian's eyes.

"Daddy!" Chasen called behind Harry, as Lindersyl jumped on Chasen's back to cover his mouth, causing both to tip to the ground.

With his body laid back on Lindersyl's in a cramped pile, Chasen received the cruelest blow of all when Harry turned on a dime and responded, "I would rather Lillian had killed you than to have a faggot call me Daddy!"

I cover my ears, I close my eyes
Still hear your voice and it's telling me lies . . .

Telling Me Lies, Dolly Parton

grier
Home of Brice Rhyne
North Mosse Point, Connecticut
May 22, 2001

Grier kissed Brice on the cheek and crept from bed so as not to wake him.

She had a slight headache that wouldn't go away and thought of a hot steam shower to open her head. Really it was her nerves getting the better of her. Grier had been reading journal entries all night and was so sickened by her aunt's behavior that she felt ill. She'd told Brice it was a personal project she was working on, but offered no details beyond that.

Grier wanted to mull over the diaries and her mother's divorce request. She wanted to make structural connections between her aunt's behavior and what she was reading, but it was too hard on her nerves. Grier wanted answers to questions, left unasked too long, but was also fearful of the answers. She understood more as the hours ticked by why her aunt courted the bottle. Sometimes life seemed too hard left or right, backward or forward, but uncomfortable as hell standing still. If she could just get into the shower and relax ten good minutes, she would wrap her mind around everything and try to make some sense of it. But no sooner had Grier turned the showerheads that the doorbell rang. She redressed, knotting her robe tie and peaked over at Brice, still sleeping. Good. She'd forgotten the lack of space a couple made, and while pleased as punch that he was there, the alone-time she made for herself, could not last long enough.

It was Eisen at the door. How did he know she was at Brice's?

"Why are you here? And why are you here so early? It's 6:30," she asked, annoyed that he seemed relaxed and carefree after her night.

"We need to talk."

"Fine. Want some breakfast?" she relented, knowing relaxation was out the door.

"No, but I would like a drink."

"Once again, it's 6:30 in the morning."

"Yeah, but I need it."

"Fine. Help yourself," she said, pointing to Brice's liquor cabinet sandwiched between a row of bookshelves.

Eisen took a big swig of brandy from a wine glass and then sat down next to Grier on the couch. Holding her hand, he got up again and reached for the brandy sifter. After downing another glass, he turned to her, speaking very soft and low.

"Last night I got a call that Johnathan—Dad was in the hospital. He's fine. He got into a fistfight with Harry Veda and got toppled," Eisen started.

"Well, good for Harry Veda," Grier replied, wondering from where all of the 'Dad' talk was coming.

"Grier, this is no time for sarcasm. Dad and I had a long talk and I guess he thought he was on his deathbed or maybe it was the drugs, but he started confessing his life . . . There's something you should know."

Grier's heart had almost stopped as Eisen took a dramatic pause, searching behind him for the sifter once again.

"Enough with the brandy already! What is it?" she pleaded.

"Grier, Daddy and Aunt Lindersyl have been messing around for years."

"What? Eisen, we already read as much in the journal. Why all the Matlock drama?"

"Seems Lindersyl and Dad were an item before he married Lillian. That's the reason they are constantly fighting like two jealous heifers over his worthless behind. They really are jealous of each other."

"I don't understand. That would mean that Johnathan and Aunt Lindersyl were fooling around back at Rosedale University. How in the hell did Lillian end up with him?"

"Hook and crook."

". . . and Grandma."

"You got it. Anyway, Dad really loves her. He says that when Lillian leaves with Harry Veda, he wants Aunt Lindersyl back. He wants to marry her and put her back at the Grove with him."

"I think I'm going to be sick . . ." Grier said, running from the room to the kitchen.

Eisendorff held her head over the sink, placing a warm dishrag to her forehead. "Grier, there's more."

"Eisen, I don't know if I want to hear this?"

"I gotta get this off my chest, Sis, and you are the only one I can tell."

"Fine. What else?"

"I think we belong to Aunt Lindersyl."

"Belong to her how?"

"I believe she is our mother."

"That's not possible."

"It is the only thing that is possible Grier."

"Look, I don't know where you've gotten this crap, but I don't buy it!"

"I know, it's hard to buy into, but it's the only logical answer. Think about the journal entries being signed with only the letter 'L' and being found in Aunt Lindersyl's old room. And Grier, Dad all but admitted it."

"No! Eisen, I'm not listening to this!" she said, walking swiftly to the front door.

"Grier, please—" Eisen yelled behind her, throwing himself in between the front door and his sister.

"Leave Eisen, now please!" she insisted, pushing Eisendorff out into the early morning chill.

Grier secured the front door, then sprawled out on the floor. She cried until she became flushed and out of breath. How was it possible that the woman whom she'd always revered as her saving grace, her guardian angel, be the cause of her hellish childhood? Knowing how she and Eisendorff had been treated, if Lindersyl were their mother, she would have come and gotten them. But it didn't take long for many of the childhood remembrances Grier had to align themselves with her brother's theory. Her father's ranting and raving about how much she looked and acted like her mother, despite being nothing like Lillian at all.

Lindersyl being her mother would also explain Lillian's hands-off approach to parenting. It explained why whenever there was real trouble with her or Eisendorff, Lindersyl showed up and "handled" things. Now instead of having a Super Aunt who knew all and handled all, she had an absentee, guilt-ridden, half-ass mother, who was too selfish to give up her single lifestyle to care for own children. Perhaps she really was the loose, irresponsible tramp her grandmother had spoken of so vehemently. That must have meant that the stories often told of Lindersyl having two children out of wedlock were accurate. Only these weren't some forlorn, faceless orphans, but she and Eisendorff.

Brice wiped the sleep from his eyes, awakened first by his arm's brush against the chilled sheets on Grier's side of the bed, then by Grier's sobbing. He searched the bedrooms and kitchen, before finding her lying out in the foyer by the door. His mind went first to her parents and their impending divorce.

"Grier, love. What's wrong? Is it your parents?"

Grier looked at him and moved her hands about as if to free the words from her mouth. They wouldn't come. She reached for Brice and he joined her on the floor, holding her. When she began talking, it was in matter-of-fact detail. "Brice, Eisen just left here saying that my Dad is at Mercer hospital and that he's okay, but that he practically admitted that Eisen and I are his and my aunt Lindersyl's children and that he's been in love with my aunt—my mother, since before we were born. Lindersyl is our mother and once our father gets divorced from Lillian, he wants Lindersyl back. He wants her back at the Grove, living with him."

"What? Is that possible?" Brice asked stupefied.

"It is. And the thought that Lindersyl could be my mother is something I can't deal with," she stammered.

"Calm down. Why not? How did she treat you in London?"

"Like a daughter. Very loving and kind. If she didn't have company over, we'd usually sleep in the same bed. She'd ask me about my day and give me advice about work. Then I'd lay in her arms and she'd hum and rub my back until I went to sleep, the way she used to do when I was a . . . little . . . girl."

Bolting from the floor, Grier shouted with confusion, "Wait, that *was* Lindersyl, not mama rocking me to sleep." Getting a mental picture, Grier began screaming at the top of her lungs. Not until she was hoarse and fatigued did Brice move in to hold her. Wrapping his arms around her from behind, he backed the two of them up against the living room wall.

"It's all right Grier; it's all right," he said sternly, rocking her from side to side.

Then as if suddenly remembering something, she pulled at her clothes, "No Daddy! No Daddy! Mommy, get the gun! Oh, no, Daddy's bleeding! Mommy, Daddy shot himself! I can't make Eisen stop screaming! I can't keep my hand over his mouth 'cause he keeps moving from side to side! Auntie L, take Eisen off of me so I can help Mommy wipe up Daddy's blood! Daddy's gotta go to the hospital! That pink stuff inside Daddy's skin is so slimy looking . . . We gotta stuff it back inside his body and catch his blood in that wash bowl so the doctor's can pour it back into his body!"

Brice looked and listened in horror as Grier went on for nearly twenty minutes, talking and moving about as if reliving an event. Finally too tired to continue, Grier had collapsed in his arms. Brice got Grier settled into bed with a shot of Phenobarbital from his bag, before calling every number he could think of to get a hold of Lindersyl. When she arrived hours later, it appeared she'd been through the same cyclone as Grier. Brice administered another dose of Phenobarbital for Lindersyl, leading her to bed alongside Grier.

Even before Grier could open her eyes fully that afternoon, more screaming voices and flashes of scenes from her childhood danced in and out of her mind like color slides. Convinced she was having a full nervous breakdown, Grier reasoned that if she could make it up and out of bed, she would empty every bottle of pills in the house into her system and make a final, peaceful transition from life. Her heavy eyelids opened to Lindersyl's face pushed against her side and she began to cry all over again, though quietly.

"How could you? How could you?" Grier cried, pushing Lindersyl's body off of her own.

"Grier!" Lindersyl managed between slaps to her chest and stomach. Lindersyl restrained Grier's arms down at her side and drew her body into her own.

"Grier, come on, listen to me."

"No! You don't love me and you don't care about me. If you did, you wouldn't have denied me all these years."

"Girl, listen to me," Lindersyl said, grabbing Grier by the shoulders, "I don't know what you've been told, but I love you and Eisendorff as if you were my own. I would give my life for your happiness and security."

"You love us like we were your own? How convenient since we *are* your own! Daddy told Eisendorff everything! We belong to you and Daddy. Why didn't you come and get us? What was so wrong with us that you didn't want us?"

Lindersyl was tired of denying things. She looked at Grier, so panicked and hurt and it broke her heart.

"It wasn't that Grier. I couldn't get you. How can I explain this to you? I need to talk to your father. We need to have this discussion together."

There was a pause that half convinced Lindersyl she was off the hook. Then Grier turned and faced Lindersyl looking as if she would attack her if the next words she uttered were not the gospel.

"Why did Daddy try to kill himself?" Grier managed between yawns.

"What?"

"We were in the car and Daddy had the gun and you were screaming at my mother . . . Auntie L . . . . Auntie L is what I used to call my mother. And Eisendorff was lying across me and he was crying and I couldn't make him stop. Then you and Daddy started arguing and you said 'You fucked my sister!' and then Daddy shot himself in the chest and there was blood all over the ground and we were all screaming at the same time," Grier said without taking a breath, then glancing up at Lindersyl, she asked, "Isn't that what happened?"

"Oh, my word, Grier," Lindersyl moaned, clutching her chest. "That did happen. But you were so small that I doubted that you could remember such a thing. You called me Auntie L, not your mother," Lindersyl yawned and rubbed her eyes.

"No, I'm certain it was you . . . but I want to know why my father tried to kill himself?"

Lindersyl rubbed the palms of her hands together briskly and took a deep breath before answering, "I found out that your . . . that Lillian was pregnant by him—"

"So what? He was her husband."

"It's complicated, Grier. Your father and I were very much in love with each other once. We were supposed to have been married, but just . . . things didn't work out like that. I guess he just always resented the fact that he chose to settle down with the wrong sister," Lindersyl sighed.

"Why did he try to kill himself?"

"Because he saw his power slipping from his hands. He'd lost his family and now he was going to lose everything else. He thought it was better to die."

'I don't understand."

"In their household, Johnathan has the power, but can't stand the sight of your mother. Harry loves her with all his heart, but has no money, no power, and no standing. So despite the fact that our parents ensured that she has more money than she could ever spend in one lifetime, Lillian will never surrender herself completely to Harry. She wants that power in her hands. Johnathan is that power—blind and illegitimate as it is. Lillian made Johnathan into what he is. And without Lillian, even then, Johnathan could only go back to being another educated Black man in a cruel white world".

"Then we are your children?"

Lindersyl turned her head away from Grier.

It was all the answer Grier could stand at that point anyway, so she didn't push. She did want further clarity on something else though before the medicine lulled her back to sleep.

"I want to ask you something and I need you to please, please be honest. Did Daddy try and molest me when I was little?"

"No! What would make you ask that?"

"The way he has dealt with me—cold, then warm. And the way he looks at me sometime."

"The problem was that he wanted to own me and I refused to sit still. Once I'd moved to Ladbroke, Johnathan could not deal with it and his mind sort of twisted on him. Johnathan couldn't take his frustrations out on Lillian because she was never home. That made you the likeliest alternative."

The effects of the Phenobarbital were long lasting and potent. Both ladies continued to struggle through the conversation, bent on getting as much information out on the table as possible.

"But did he want to have sex with me?" Grier pushed, repositioning her body so that her feet fell beneath the duvet.

"No, but he made himself believe that you were me. It was something minor at first, like calling you by my name, incidents, which were thought to be slips of the tongue. While your father is very much in love with me still, it is less about love than control. Knowing that I was taking other lovers, Johnathan felt that he could beat that 'propensity for men' out of you to somehow deal with me. Once it was clear what was going on, the guilt forced him to send you and Eisendorff away to school," Lindersyl said.

"We were so young to be away from home. I just kept feeling like I had done something wrong to be sent away to boarding school at eleven."

"Lillian kept some semblance of normalcy in the home by not having you there. As much as she wanted to protect you kids, she wanted to protect her own footing more. I began to sleep with Johnathan again for two reasons: (1) I enjoyed it, and (2) I found that I could influence his behavior towards you and Eisendorff through acts of affection. The added bonus was that I could continue to kick at the wheels of Lillian's apple cart," Lindersyl smiled slyly.

"You cannot be serious! Why would you even want him after all that?"

"Your father is an amazing man and I've never tired of loving him. In addition, he's actually a very passionate and desirable lover," Lindersyl said with the wave of a hand, laughing as Grier feigned loss of consciousness. "Undo your face, girl. Ain't nothing in this world wrong with good loving. Seriously now, I've been trapped in the past, remembering how sweet and kind and generous Johnathan was. And every time I'm just a little nice to him, that beautiful, brave man returns to me."

"Maybe Daddy doesn't deserve your consideration. What about Olivus?"

"Olivus is a young man, Grier. He ain't gonna keep putting up with my mess. And the mid-life crisis that drove me to him will one day envelope him the same way and he will leave me."

"Puhleeze! Olivus worships you! And so what if he does one day quit you? I give you the same advice you gave me about Brice. 'Love him as best as you can cause in the end, that's all you really can control'."

"I said that?"

"Yeah, I think you were sopping drunk when you said it, but you did say it."

The two embraced warmly, before falling slowly back under the covers, Grier wrapped in Lindersyl.

Brice wiped his eyes dry and pulled and tucked the covers around them. He hardly believed all that Lindersyl had said, especially with regard to being Grier's mother. But at least his woman was back on solid ground. Brice had no feeling for Lindersyl one way or the other, but knew lies and half-truths when he heard them. More convinced than ever that Grier needed protecting, Brice waited until later in the day when Lindersyl had vacated to propose to Grier again.

Comfortable in her role as the soon-to-be, Mrs. Brice Rhyne, Grier had found herself grinning as she cooked dinner and ironed Brice's trousers that night. She was going to be the happiest woman in the world. She was certain that Lindersyl was still hiding things, but had had an epiphany from Lindersyl's very words, "Lilies that fester stink worse than weeds'. If the Gottlieb sisters wanted to fight over her worthless father, so be it. Her job was to love Brice and make him happy, not worry about some decades-old love triangle that was too disgusting to give serious thought. Standing at the kitchen window squeezing oranges into fresh pulpy juice, Grier felt like she could take on the world. As sure as the feeling came, it went suddenly and her chest tightened. It was out of the corner of her eye that Grier spotted her father surveying her through binoculars from across the street in a parked car.

*You'll go out to play this evening to play with fireflies till they're gone,
Then rush to meet your lover and play with real fire till the dawn . . .*

It's Not Supposed To Be That Way, Willie Nelson

harry
Hartford Suites Hotel
July 19, 2001

His life could not possibly be the matted confusion he felt enveloping him, Harry thought aloud, pushing the lunch tray of half-eaten avocado and walnut tuna out of his reach. Two months as a virtual recluse at the Hartford Suites had not done much to resolve his unyielding desire to hurt someone. Unable to reconcile that Lillian, whom he now referred to as "La Mirage", had led him on, and alas, asunder for so many years, he'd had an epiphany. It was time to deal with Harry Veda and reassess everything about himself. Throw out the old and contemplate the new. Just thinking of Lillian made his heart beat wildly. At least, he reasoned, he had finally accepted the fact that he and Lillian were over. It had been one thing to accuse him of Lindersyl; in fact, it was bound to happen eventually, but to hide a child from him was quite another thing. At least Johnathan had not pressed charges against him.

Sometimes in life you had to walk away without fanfare or hoopla. This was one of those times. Harry planned to speak with Lillian as soon as he finished eating to let her know his plans to journey to a destination yet determined. Then he decided that it wasn't Lillian's business where he went. Harry did want an explanation, but feared anything Lillian said would only make him hate her more. Nothing could justify her hiding a pregnancy and his child from him. Nothing. Then there was the image of his love child standing in his path, like the Ghost of Misdeeds Past, showing him clearly how he was also to blame for this mess. Lillian was a married woman; however unhappy and Harry had no business with her from the start. He could lie to himself all he wanted about *being there* for her. The truth was that she was beautiful, vulnerable, and willing. If he'd cared for her deeply enough, he'd have forced her to leave the Grove and be his wife.

"My son. *My* son. And neither bothered to say a word," Harry murmured, shaking his head from side to side, as hot with Lindersyl as he was with Lillian. "That 'oman sit up and confide a bunch of stuff nobody care about, but don't tell me she raising my son."

Harry tried to figure out when Lillian could have become pregnant and how she'd hidden it from everyone. To the best of his recollection, Harry placed it around 1967 when Lillian had been terribly emotional and unhappy. She'd left the main house for her parents' home along the outskirts of the property. Initially, Harry had believed it was the kids who caused her to look so puny and become so despondent. Lillian had refused to see Harry, not returning his calls, the love notes he left in the flowerbed each morning or even meet his side-glances. He couldn't fathom what he'd done to cause such a stony reaction. Lillian had never done the silent treatment thing with him before. And only rarely during that time did he catch her staring at him with an abandoned, worried look from her bedroom window. Even then, she would not acknowledge his waves and smiles. Then one day, she loaded her own bags into her Benz and left. There was not as much as a postcard from Lillian. Harry had languished silently for seven months, sidestepping Johnathan and anyone else on the grounds who remembered that he was still there. Harry had been too overjoyed to see her return later that year to bombard her with questions. All she'd ever said to his searching eyes was "female problems". Twenty-seven years later, he understood "female problems" to mean she'd given birth to Chasen.

Lillian had left eight messages on his answering machine at the pool house after his departure in which she attempted to plead her case.

"*Harry, I never meant to hurt you . . . I thought that if I told you about Chasen, it would ruin us forever. I was afraid and I felt alone. I couldn't tell Johnathan I was pregnant because he would have killed the both of us. Harry, please call me, tell me where you are so that we can sit down and talk about this thing and try to work it out. I know we can get beyond this. I know we can,*" Lillian had pleaded into the phone.

It was all a load of crap! His and Lillian's relationship could only have been enhanced by the birth of their son. Lillian's decision had been about maintaining her relationship with Johnathan and nothing more. She and Johnathan had been sleeping in separate bedrooms for years and there was no possible way for her to be pregnant by him, so she had to either confess the paternity of the child or give him away. And just as Harry had insisted Lillian return Grier and Eisendorff to Lindersyl's care, had he known that Chasen belonged to Lillian, no one would have been allowed to rear him other than his natural parents. To think that a mere five years into their relationship, the son he'd always wanted had been born. He was a father. Perhaps, Harry grimaced, face in hand, he could have given Chasen the proper male role model, eliminating his sexual confusion. Instead, the grown, slinky pansy he'd silently ridiculed was his own flesh and blood, his only offspring.

Harry had never been a man to rest on his laurels. He could not stand not going to work and occupying himself. Fortunately, the two foot pile of applications and resumes he'd sent out for employment had finally paid off a few days earlier when Ridgefield Community College offered him a position as acting co-chair of their Philosophy Department. The campus was two hours from Mosse Point and a hop, skip and jump from New York. He had every intention of living his life as if he'd never known Mosse Point. Grateful he'd finished his studies before falling into the Gottlieb trap, Harry was able to wing his way through his interviews, create employment and salary information that was virtually impossible to corroborate, and slide into his new position.

Decidedly taciturn about the whole affair and those three mental cases at Gottlieb Grove, Harry unfastened his bathrobe and walked bare-butt to the hotel room door when a knock came, distracting him from his thoughts.

Amelia Edney had run through his mind barely once in the forty or so years they'd known one another. A former classmate of his who worked in Hillsdale, Harry had bumped into her in the hotel's lobby a few days before. Retaining much of her exuberant beauty—large brown eyes, high cheekbones and the most delicate disposition—Amelia had listened intently to Harry over drinks and then distracted him from his troubles the next morning with a miniature golf challenge. This being her last night in town, he decided not to ignore his growing interest in her. It could have been to coat his ego or prove he was still attractive and desirable to the opposite sex. More than anything, he wanted to be held and comforted.

"My conference is over tomorrow afternoon and I don't wish to pressure you into doing anything but I doubt you'll make the trip out to San Marcos California to pick this little game of ours up again . . ."

"Amelia, you know I've always been attracted to you, but it's just this situation I'm dealing with—I don't know when or where it'll officially be over. I don't want to lead you on."

"Harry, I was talking about picking up our game of miniature golf . . ."

"Cute, Amelia, I'm serious. I can't promise that this will be anything more than tonight."

"It really has been awhile since you played the field, huh? Babycakes, most women aren't looking for a ring after sex anymore," she'd smiled, kissing Harry lightly on the lips. "Harry, I simply want to give you my love before I leave. I want you to accept it: no hidden agendas, no strings attached."

Sensing that much of his life had passed him by and determined not to aid the process any further, Harry had invited Amelia back to his suite once her afternoon session was ended. Tonight he wanted to unwind and celebrate. Harry swung the door open and greeted Amelia with a glass of merlot and a huge smile.

A very patient and agile Amelia rubbed his back and feet, whispered loving sentiments and opened herself up for him to do the same. And for the first time in nearly thirty years, Harry shared his body, without sharing his heart. Amelia touched him with deliberate intensity, moving his hands where she wanted them. Every few minutes she paused and looked at him grinning, "Are you okay?" she'd ask. To which he could only murmur or nod. An hour later he was able to respond with laughter. Harry didn't think of Lillian or Gottlieb Grove once. His dad had told him once that the only way to stop pining over a woman was to find another one to ease you over the hump. Harry reasoned that this must have been what he'd meant.

"How did you do that?" he marveled.

"Harry, get some rest, love. Is it okay for me to stay?"

"Of course it is," he answered in further amazement, pulling her forward to him. "I wouldn't dream of letting you go tonight."

Harry fell into a deep sleep, snoring to beat the band. When he awoke the next morning Amelia was gone. When he read her note, he almost booked a flight for San Marcos.

Your heart is too good to play anyone else's fool, Harry Veda. If ever you need me, you know where I am.—Your friend, Amelia.

Don't need no lessons on God
He knows I'm human, I got weakness . . .

Have a Cry, Kina

johnathan
Gottlieb Grove
July 22, 2001

Lindersyl was nowhere to be found. It had been six weeks and no one had heard from her. Grier was holed up in Lindersyl's house with that nigger Brice, Lillian was underfoot, along with that queer nephew of hers and Harry Veda was gone.

If Lindersyl had left him again, Johnathan had made up his mind to find her and kill her. His head was pounding from prescription withdrawal and the thought of Lindersyl out of his reach was eating him alive.

He had been dismayed by Lillian's presence at the hospital to pick him up—but had taken the ride home in stride. No one else had bothered to show. She was apologetically doting, baby-talking him and asking about which friends of theirs to invite to their anniversary party.

He fixed his mouth to say "Motherfucker" then stopped. He knew where she was coming from and *she knew that he knew* a crash and burn was on its way. For once, he decided to rip the script and stay silent. No sense in getting his pressure up for a nonsensical conversation with his *wife*. The thought of even calling her such made him want to spit.

When Lindersyl didn't show the next day either, Johnathan had camped out at her cottage house with binoculars. He dialed and redialed her pager number, had the operators check the lines for service interruption and then cursed out his own cellular provider for not being able to track Lindersyl's movements like the crime labs did on television.

When Lillian climbed into bed alongside Johnathan suddenly, interrupting his thoughts, he didn't ask her to leave. Maybe this was all he could hope to have after all was said and done; second best. Oddly enough, he felt grateful to Lillian for being there, steadying him so he didn't lose his mind.

"I'm sorry she's not here for you," Lillian whispered. "I know it hurts."

". . . We should probably invite Bob and Connie Dewherst to the party. We haven't seen them in a while," he answered.

Johnathan closed his eyes and smiled. Good ole' Lil was once again riding to his rescue. Time and again, she had proven herself. When he was stuck in Parchman, that sun beating down on him like fire, the humidity so thick that it felt like he was breathing through a woolen sack, Lillian had been the one to sacrifice herself with the nastiest piece of a man known to exist. She did it without batting a lash—made the whores on visiting day sit down and eat those liverwurst sandwiches they'd packed from home. Lord, those days bent and near broke him, Johnathan thought. That's when he knew for sure, with two of his uncles, his father's kin, stuck up in there with him telling him he wasn't shit 'cause his mother was his sister and his father was a murderer, that he needed a new identity far and away from Mississippi. Didn't matter how many people he registered to vote, or how many times he bucked up to white folks, he was a living, breathing curse. Johnathan thought for sure he was going to lose his mind: the sun-up to sun-down work in the broiling sun during the day, and his uncles' taunts at night. But Lillian had come through for him when all Lindersyl could muster were tears. That's when he'd made up his mind that Lillian was the better woman all-around; she was willing to do the things for him no sane, saved woman would. She still was.

My momma would die to see me lose pride
She brought me up right, but Lord, this feeling I just can't fight . . .

Mind, Heart & Soul, Gladys Knight & the Pips

anastasia
Home of: Anastasia Harcourt
Caesar Franco Apartments #3B
July 22, 2001

Three weeks ago Anastasia had taken the eighty-four hundred-dollar cashier's check her father had given her for tuition and cashed it. Having folded and tucked the small stack of hundreds and fifties into a thick, tight wad and stuffed it into her jean pocket, Anastasia had spent the better half of two days pulling cautiously from it and running through shops at Metroplex Mall. It was amazing how even the initial stages of pregnancy had caused her athletic size twelve frame to benchmark out to a sixteen. She had to admit that the subtle change was beautiful on her, though she had no intention of making her pregnancy known to anyone until absolutely necessary. With her tummy a mere poof, the only other area under mommy-to-be renovation was her chest. So far, she'd been able to mask the expansion by trading her halter-tops for short sleeve button-ups. Fortunately, in the unusually brisk weather that Mosse Point was experiencing it wasn't too hard to conceal her condition.

At nineteen, Anastasia had already made up her mind to quit school. She had been on the fast track to success since grade school, but now found the whole rigmarole to be more trouble than it was worth. Fretting over grades, attempting to impress teachers who had their own agendas and finally, stressing over term papers and insignificant historical details for the sake of recounting them as a false measure of her learnedness, was for the birds. She'd had enough of playing the game. Besides, she had found herself desperately lacking the skills necessary to pass the advanced math classes a business / accounting degree requisited. Anastasia's dream of following in her father's footsteps—CPA at 22, owner of the only Black-owned accounting firm in the state of Connecticut by the age of 35—had been thwarted.

Besides her dreams and aspirations had changed so that she could barely stand to look herself in the mirror sometimes. How her poor momma would die if she knew that years of private school, excelled lesson plans, cultural exchange trips and the best childhood money could buy, had culminated in her wanting to become little more than a 'kept woman'. The decision had come before she found that she was pregnant, but it would certainly aid—actually, facilitate her current predicament.

Seeing how Johnathan had been willing to give of his time, if not his money, Anastasia was sure she could become an enchantress to a paying suitor; a lady of leisure. It was on a chance encounter at Metroplex months earlier that she'd recognized Johnathan's wife. Anastasia had been forced against reason to trail her, listening in as first his wife and her friends laughed and giggled with each other, then debated with a furious passion, two other ladies about something inconsequential. Giving face to no one in particular, Johnathan's wife had glam and beauty on display in case anyone glanced over at her in need of a quick infusion. Lillian, as always, looked as if she'd stepped off of the society page; Gucci shades, stately polished nails, perfect make-up, perfect hair, perfect wardrobe, and authoritative posture. Then there was this Lindersyl, she'd met days later. Easily in her late forties, this same woman, whom she found out later was Johnathan's sister-in-law, commanded attention everywhere she went.

Anastasia dabbed the washcloth over her face, collecting the cool droplets running down her cheek. Being pregnant was a lot harder than she had ever expected. How many of her girlfriends had "just done it" and taken it all in stride, was beyond her. If it wasn't fatigue, it was nausea. And in spite of believing that she was a strong Black woman and could do anything she wanted, including making a baby and supporting it herself, Anastasia needed help. She needed to be loved and held and nurtured during this time. For every blithe moment she felt over the seat of creation her womb had become, there were ten moments where she felt overwhelmed and depressed. She looked at her reflection in the mirror and contemplated crying again, but decided it would be no use. She would need the tears later for sure; best to save them for a really trying time. Then Anastasia smiled, remembering how well she'd survived the day before when her usually-concerned, considerate supervisor had reprimanded her for arriving to work two hours late, only to be forced back home an hour later with morning sickness. When she made it home, Anastasia had found herself terminated via answering machine message. Without a second thought, Anastasia had picked up the phone and dialed Planned Parenthood, (#3 on the 'speed dial' after a morning after scare), and attempted to schedule an abortion. By nothing short of God's grace, Anastasia's appointment confirmation was cut short by the first noticeable movements of her baby—a quick fluttering—in her womb. Canceling the appointment in the midst of clarity, Anastasia recognized at once that her child was not an 'it', but either a boy or girl and deserved a chance. Everything had to be considered from the perspective of 'we' from then on. Anastasia had succumbed to her need to inform Johnathan of her condition. Never bothered by calling his home directly or speaking with his wife, Anastasia was terribly put off when no one bothered to answer the phone. It was shortly after nine at night and it was unnatural for Gottlieb Grove to be unmanned. She'd called and left a series of messages over the following ten hours on Johnathan's cell phone. Unfortunately, from that time to this, seven weeks later, Johnathan had been either unavailable or uninterested in speaking with her.

And now, showing ever so slightly, Anastasia was in panic mode as she truly began to contemplate life as a single parent. Her tuition loot had been dwindled down to a measly thousand dollars. Rent was due in three days, along with her health insurance, telephone, cable and Internet service charges, after which, she'd be left with exactly eighteen dollars. Rinsing her mouth out with Listerine, Anastasia gathered her nerve and walked slowly to the kitchen telephone. She would try Johnathan once more by phone; if he didn't answer, she and his unborn child were headed to his front door.

Until the end of time I'll be there for you
You own my heart and mind, I truly adore you . . .

prince

johnathan
Gottlieb Grove
July 22, 2001

"Do you know how much I hate your ass? Do you? Why don't you leave me alone?" Johnathan said, holding Lillian's face so close to his that she could feel the warm moisture of his breath against her cheek. "Now, take this half-burned plate of shit and get outta my room Lillian!"

"He's just a bit cranky," Lillian remarked to Chasen, standing in Johnathan's bedroom doorway, as she removed the tray and headed down to the kitchen. "Did you enjoy your breakfast?"

"Mother?" Chasen called behind her as she swept pass him with the tray.

"Chasen! Don't call me that in this house with Johnathan around. You know better!" she said, pulling him to the side.

"What you doing letting him talk to you like that?"

"Watch your mouth and go on downstairs."

In Harry's absence Chasen had made the pool house his home, but came over everyday to spend time with Lillian. As had been the scene the last six weeks, Lillian had fixed breakfast for Chasen and Johnathan and been met with the same shitty disposition from Johnathan each morning. Boiling under the collar over the humiliation his mother suffered through, Chasen was ready to confront Johnathan.

"Is that faggot in this house again Lillian? I told you he could have the run of the pool house, but he was not to come into our home! Now, ask him to leave."

"No he didn't!" Chasen said under his breath.

"Yes, I did! And if you don't like it, tell your whore ass mother to come over here to this house and retrieve you. I don't know why you ain't at her place no way!" Johnathan said with his head sticking out from his bedroom door. Johnathan hated Chasen with an unchecked passion. Far from being homophobic, Johnathan's distrust of Chasen came from the boy's temperament and the way he rolled his eyes at him. Chasen seemed always to be one step from *reading* Johnathan and it took nasty words and epithets from Johnathan to keep him in line. Johnathan reasoned that if he hurt Chasen's feelings enough, he'd press on or learn to steer clear of him. Then too, it bothered Johnathan that Lindersyl had had this child by another man. Chasen's temperament proved that no other man belonged with her.

"Chasen, you'd better leave. I'll be over to hang out with you a little later," Lillian said, waving him off, without missing a beat. "Jumper, did you want something?"

"Don't call me that shit! Yeah I want to know something. I want to know where that damned sister of yours is and I want to know right now! I know you know where she is . . ."

Seeing Johnathan's mood bracketed by stupidity, Lillian left the tray on the hall mantle. Ignoring his question, she walked swiftly to her bedroom. If she locked the door, he would only break it down, so she pushed it forward, knowing he would be by to bother her in short order.

Johnathan still couldn't find Lindersyl and his dread was turning everything around him into chaos. Whether Lillian was getting married or not, Johnathan had decided to give her the divorce she'd wanted.

Now fully recovered from his injuries, Johnathan was unable to reach anyone other than his two unwanted houseguests to find out what the hell was going on. Eisendorff had taken charge of a family Johnathan didn't even know existed—a girl named Terrie and their son, Avery. Seemed the two, according to Eisendorff's office message, were 'spending time away on personal business'.

With Lindersyl, Grier and Eisendorff out of reach, Johnathan felt hopeless, which meant trouble for all in his path. Johnathan pulled on his boxers and a tank shirt, and then slid his feet into his slippers. Unable to resist driving his unhappiness home, Johnathan walked from his bedroom to Lillian's.

"Lillian!" Johnathan called down the hall.

Lillian was leaned against the wall just inside her bedroom when Johnathan walked in. He saw her, but moved pass her to the bed. Pushing aside a host of frilly, fringed pillows, Johnathan laid across the bed on his stomach, beckoning her forward with a toss of the head.

"Come over here and rub my back . . . please," he half smiled making eye contact.

Johnathan watched with little interest as Lillian tried her best to hide the blush that ran across her face, and lifted her housedress above her knees. She straddled his back and he relaxed slightly, thinking of Lindersyl. He did not protest as she undressed him to the waist and ran her lips lightly between his shoulder blades, before kneading his flesh under her palms. How obvious and tiring this game had become, they both thought, giving simultaneous sighs. Her affections were marked to the highest bidder and he considered asking her to remove herself from his person.

"Lillian, I was by Lindersyl's earlier today to see Grier. She says she hasn't seen Lindersyl in weeks. You have any idea where your sister has run off?"

"Am I my sister's keeper?" she replied stoically, removing her hands from his back.

"Isn't that what Cain said of Abel after he'd killed him?"

"How's this then: I have no clue or interest in my sister's whereabouts."

"She do that to your face?" Johnathan asked, noticing a fading scratch near Lillian's ear.

"Who else?"

"So y'all are fighting again, huh?"

"If you must know, I caught her in Harry's bed. Now, does that get your goat?"

"Depends. Where is Harry?"

"Don't know."

"You think they're together?" Johnathan frowned, turning onto his side to note the back rub's end.

"No. She was at her condo for a few days, but then she went AWOL. Harry packed and left the morning I found her in the poolhouse."

Johnathan pondered the information for a moment, unsure whether to trust Lillian's tint of the truth. "Lillian, we need to have some dialogue about our divorce."

"Oh that! Johnathan, I was just being a bit temperamental because Lindi was getting to me. You know I love you. Now, quit your worrying, there isn't going to be any divorce."

"Lillian, our counsel will be here at the end of the week. There *will* be a divorce. So be prepared to be served in the next few days."

"But Jumper, why? We can work through this the same as we have other issues in the past."

"Don't call me that!"

"Sorry."

"Lillian, I had a talk with Eisendorff while I was at Mercer. I told him about me and Lindersyl and this whole sordid mess."

"What? Why?"

"Lil, I'm tired of the games and the drama. I want her back, and I'm prepared to walk away from everything—you can keep all of this stuff—I just want her back."

Jumping to the floor, Lillian slapped Johnathan hard across his bare back, "To hell with you! Are you blind or just stupid? My sister *does not* want you! She wants to get back at me. Why else would she have slept with Harry? If she wanted you—if she loved you, she'd be here right now taking care of you. But she's not! She only cares about herself. Meanwhile, I am here. *I* am here! After everything you've done to me I sit up in this house with you and you come telling me about a damned divorce! Well, too bad, I ain't letting you go."

Johnathan couldn't think of a way to respond so he growled and ran towards her. "You are going to do as I say, if you know what's good for you. You are going to sign those divorce papers when they come. And I don't believe what you say about Lindersyl and Harry Veda. I don't. You're just trying to keep up problems between me and Lindersyl like always. You'll never change—you know what, I want you out of this house by the end of the month."

Johnathan's eyes were wild with frustration, but Lillian pushed on. Her marriage would depend on how she played the tune of a very familiar song. "This is my family's home. My house!"

"No, this is mine and Lindersyl's—her name is on this house, my name is on this house. You don't have a home unless you count the carriage house down by the stables. Be my guest to stay there."

Johnathan saw that he had trumped Lillian using her own shortsightedness. She simply rolled her eyes at him and murmured, "Johnathan, you will regret this," before walking out. Johnathan listened to Lillian's footsteps moving down the stairwell. Deciding he had won at least one battle in the Technicolor version of the War of the Roses, Johnathan went back to his room and dressed for the day. When the telephone rang, he checked the Caller ID from the upstairs bedroom and recognized Anastasia's number. It was easily the twentieth call in two days. He'd written the relationship off as a loss, but his curiosity was piqued enough to talk. Their last meeting had been anything but pleasant, but convinced of his own magnetism, Johnathan relented. Lillian picked up the receiver from the hall phone and walked into her bedroom with the cordless phone tucked under her armpit. She wished he had the grace to at least go back into his own bedroom.

"Anastasia." she said blankly, waiting for him to decide whether or not to accept the call.

When he stretched out his hand, Lillian removed the phone from her person and handed it to him. But instead of releasing it under his grasp, Lillian held it long enough to move close and whisper in his ear, "If you think my sister is going to put up with this little cat meowing around your nip, we may as well scrap consulting lawyers. You will be back with me inside of a week."

Johnathan gave Lillian a threatening look and snatched the phone to his chest. "Get your ass on out of here before you make me hurt you," he snapped.

"Sure thing, cradle robber!" she hurled at his turned back.

Young, beautiful, supple Anastasia. It had been weeks since he'd heard from her, and against himself, and quite out of response to Lindersyl's dejection of him, he found the dog in him more than willing to chase the cat. Though he'd loved her submissive way, this calling and leaving messages and forcing her way into his space, was strangely desirable.

Johnathan didn't wait for Lillian to clear the door before he began speaking. Perhaps Anastasia was the perfect distraction to his Gottlieb Girl trouble.

"Hey baby. What's going on? You missing your man? I see you've been calling a lot."

"Johnathan, we need to talk."

"Well, talk girl. I'm listening."

"I need to see you. We need to see you."

"We who?"

"Just meet me—can you meet me at my place in an hour?"

"Yeah," Johnathan said hesitantly. "What's on your mind?"

"I'd rather not get into it on the phone. But . . . I got fired and I have no money and I'm afraid I'm gonna be put out and . . . Oh, God, I'm sorry," Anastasia rambled, realizing too late that she was sounding like a five-year-old.

"It's all right. I'm on my way. Put on something sexy for me, hear?"

"Yeah, I'll see what I can manage," she answered.

Johnathan hung up the phone.

"Young girls don't know nothin' about taking care of themselves. Least this one is smart enough to be in school and not some baby-making machine," he smiled to himself, happy that he'd not exhausted all possibilities of 'outside entertainment'.

Chapter Six
Baby-Daddy Wars

*Did you think my life would end that day that you walked out—
When you broke my heart?*

I'm Still Breathing, Toni Braxton

terrie & eisendorff
Gottlieb Grove
July 26, 2001

The guesthouse of Gottlieb Grove had long been torn down. Located at the very southern end of the massive 51-acre property, it had become the showplace of showplaces following Micheaux Gottlieb's death. Faye-Essie's constant restructuring projects fitted Italian marble floors, a formal dining room, and waterside deck of Indiana sandstone onto the property early on. The centerpiece of the estate though, was an indoor pool pavilion with exquisite millwork of Honduran mahogany crafted by a sailboat builder, into the downstairs. As a gift to herself and in celebration of her fiftieth birthday, Faye had a 42-foot koi pond, waterfall and palm garden added. On her sixtieth birthday it was retractable glass doors, and a glass roof that could be opened to the skies, two-lane bowling alley, full wet bar, theater room, and a two-sided stone fireplace. By the time of her death, Faye-Essie's masterpiece was worth more than $6,000,000 and had become the social gathering place for many of Mosse Point's upper-crust functions.

It broke the hearts of most of the society folk in town when the house was simply torn down, it's magnificent structure forever removed from the hearts of those who'd tripped the lights fantastic under its opulence by a vengeful daughter. It had been Faye's two-handed, last gesture leaving the house to Lindersyl in her will. But true to her emotions, if not much else, Lindersyl had arrived at the house two months after her mother's funeral—which she hadn't bothered to attend—and had the "content of consequence" removed to the main house. The furniture, along with glass, asbestos and other inert waste, was extracted over the course of five weeks. Then with a foreman's hardhat and gloves, Lindersyl climbed upon the wrecking trailer and slammed hard into the corner beam of the house, loosening the foundation. She allowed the demolition crew to finish the job. It was reduced to rubble a bit at a time.

Now, trekking across the expansive land before him, Eisendorff had only his memory of placement to set his path. He walked, tripping occasionally over bumps in the gravel, with Avery and Terrie following close behind. He remembered only vaguely the day he came home from college to find his grandma's house gone. The only explanation he'd received then was, "Stay out of grown folks business".

The trio seemed to walk clear across the county en route to Gottlieb Grove's stables. The original plan before they'd begun crossing the Kalahari was to show Avery the family's stables chucked to the brim with former prizewinning thoroughbreds, stallions and two near-ancient Clydesdales. In his absence, Eisendorff found that his son was oddly unfamiliar and fearful of almost everything. Eisendorff decided to keep Sophia on in case of an emergency, but made cooking and cleaning her primary duties. Avery was his job all day, everyday. Loving Avery though, had been so easy for Eisendorff, who now could not imagine living without him. Eisendorff wanted to spend every waking moment with Avery so he asked Terrie to move into his condo. The trio, plus Sophia were attempting to make a go of family life, despite not knowing much about each other. Each morning, Eisendorff made breakfast and dropped Terrie at work before finding some new and wonderful adventure for he and Avery. There had been alphabets and numbers to twenty to learn and, today, animals.

Unfortunately, Eisendorff's relationship with Terrie had not flourished so lovingly under his tutelage. Terrie had been a great lover and she had done a wonderful job with Avery, but Eisen's "happily-ever-after" plans of marrying Terrie and living as a family were aggravated when Terrie announced one night, almost psychically (he had been ring shopping the day before) that she was not interested in marriage. Terrie further aggravated his plans by insisting that her living with him and their child—and even the two of them sleeping together occasionally—was fine by her, but she intended to maintain the same swinging lifestyle that had forged their most harmonious union.

"Eisen, you and me is real cool and all, but you know I could never be committed to you. I need variety and spice in my sex life."

"Life is not only about sex though, Terrie. And are you forgetting that you are not by yourself anymore? You have a son to raise! What kind of a mother screws around with groups of strange people she barely knows?" Eisen had said, furious that she would rather toss a perfectly good marriage proposal to the wayside for the fetish of the group thing.

"Eisendorff, don't you dare stand there and pass judgment on me! For the last three years I have had no choice but to take responsibility for *our* child. And keep in mind that you did not even choose to recognize that I was pregnant or that you had a son until *my* attorney found *yours*. You used to be one of those people you're talking about. Those 'strange' people fed me and your child when he was still in my belly and you wouldn't return my phone calls. They gave me a baby shower, went through labor and delivery with me and made it so that me and Avery were healthy and happy *until* your precious blood test and child support came through. Just because you closed your eyes to the people rubbing up against you in 'group', doesn't mean that everybody else did. I love those people and they love us."

"Terrie, I didn't mean it like that."

"You did! What kind of mother am I? I am the kind of mother who gives a child life when his father says kill him. I am the kind of mother who says I can get through anything—stares from people who see I have no wedding ring; my family's slammed doors and even my child's father ignoring us, for the sake of my son. And marriage should be based on love Eisendorff. You don't love me and I damned sure don't love you."

"I . . . I care."

"You love my body, you love the sexual things I do to you, but you barely even know me. You did not love me when I told you I was pregnant or when I risked my life to have our child. You don't even know my full name, my birthday, my dreams, my aspirations."

Eisendorff's response that he had not asked her to have a child was, well, the wrong response. That conversation ended the way each successive one about their relationship had; in silence. Now, they merely shared the same home and ate breakfast and dinner together to give Avery a sense of family. Though they had shared a bed for two months, they had only attempted to have sex once and then it had been such an emotionally painful experience that they agreed to stop in the middle of it and were too embarrassed to try again. Eisendorff couldn't understand why, though physically aroused by Terrie, they could no longer connect. This was especially disturbing given that sex was what had brought them and kept them together previously. When he pushed up behind her one night in bed, his airtight erection poking her in the butt, Terrie said nothing. She was intent on obliging him, but Eisen found himself stupefied and awkward—where was he to touch her? Where was he to kiss her?

She had gone into their usual kink routine, but this time, as soon as she did that thing that she did—that move that made her famous, he got a sick, prickly feeling. He wanted to look into Terrie's eyes, but he found he could barely raise his head to look her in the face. She gave him a look of annoyed sympathy, so similar to the one she'd given Avery earlier when he insisted on carrying his own dinner plate to the table and dropped it. Eisendorff's arousal died. This was the same woman who had just hours before patiently cleaned up mashed potatoes and meatloaf from the floor, redressed the plate with dinner and instructed Avery on the "more gentlemanly" way of carrying his food to the table. "Tiny steps then look up to see what's there in front of you, then two more tiny steps, until you reach the table."

Avery was so excited when he made it to the table with no spillage that he'd cheered for minutes. Eisen had been equally proud of Terrie's forbearance and understanding. He wanted to make love to her, but, the truth of things was that, he didn't know how.

Since Johnathan had given Eisendorff his first taste of sex along a deserted road with a liquor-breathed prostitute at the age of twelve, he'd never known more than thrust in, thrust out and move it all about. But no one had ever bragged that they had kissed a woman to death or banged the anxiety out of her tense shoulders. Embarrassed that he could not make love, Eisendorff was pleased when Terrie suggested they not engage in any real intimate activity for a while, at least not until they knew each other better.

Everyday Eisendorff grew to love Terrie a little bit more and everyday she seemed deafened a bit more to his claims of love and desire for a family. He was determined to win her over though despite no genuine signs of her relenting.

Every move Avery made was cause to whip out the camcorder and document. Eisen was sure Avery's first visit to the stables would be priceless. So bright and interested in the world around him, Avery had asked all kinds of questions about the horses' anatomy versus his own. At one point he asked to be held up to the eye of one horse to show how big it was in comparison to his own, then touching another horse's hair to compare it to his own. This game went on for a while until the horse began streaming urine and Avery saw where it came from.

"Daddy, that's the horse's penis?"

To which a slightly abashed Eisendorff held his tongue, but shook his head in the affirmative.

"Wow! Daddy his penis is even bigger than yours!"

Terrie and Eisen had a powerful laugh off of that one. "This kid is gonna be the next Paul Mooney!" Eisen kept saying. So many of their moments were priceless. But then, traveling Gottlieb Grove's less traveled roads always made him wistful and nostalgic. Terrie and Eisen took either arm of Avery's and the three ran through the small grove and orchard that used to sit in front of Micheaux and Faye-Essie's home. While Terrie fielded Avery's questions on how the trees came to bear fruit, Eisendorff followed the path to the old carriage house. There was nothing left of the foundation. Ironically, the wine cellar doors were still intact and visible. Like his offspring running around the trees playing, Eisendorff's curiosity took hold.

Aside from two wooden slates giving the lid an "X marks the spot" appearance, the doors had no locks or camouflage from intruders. But then, with all the other security mechanisms active on the property, no one would dare set foot onto this no man's land.

With a bare amount of jousting, the wood slates broke free. When Eisendorff pulled back the doors one at a time and found concrete steps leading down into the cellar, he almost peed his pants. As if stumbling across buried treasure, Eisendorff checked over his shoulders a few times before entering, to make sure no one had followed him.

"Hey Terrie, stay out here. I'm gonna check on something in the cellar. Okay?"

"Sure," she yelled back, eager to entice Avery atop her shoulders to pilfer a few fresh peaches from the branches above their heads.

With any possible distractions stifled temporarily, Eisendorff scurried back to the car for the flashlight he kept in the emergency roadside kit. Then it was off to the great adventures of Gottlieb Grove's Original Manor House. The first thing that opened his senses was the smell of cedar pine. Though it was daylight, the flashlight came in handy as the cellar, away from the doors brought on an eerie form of darkness. With the beam of the light dancing in front of him, Eisendorff could just make out some old paintings and trunks along the side of the wall covered in heavy cloth. As the cellar stretched almost the entire length and width of the house that once stood above it, he feared going too far.

As his eyes marked the darkness, Eisendorff saw the room more clearly. He had been in the cellar before. A place of punishment when his grandmother was fed up with his mannish ways, if Eisen remembered correctly, just behind the stairwell leading into the kitchen was a wicker hamper he used to play in. It smelled of African violets and musk when he was a kid and he was told that it had come straight from Marrakech. Feeling around the edge of the top step, Eisen could feel the familiar ribbed corners of that very basket. The weight of the basket, so heavy and unyielding to his attempts to budge as a child, were now gone. He picked it up by the handles and carried it to the cellar entrance, pausing to enjoy the cool fresh air he'd forgone the previous fifteen minutes. After pulling it to the surface and checking to see where Terrie and Avery were, he smiled at the happy scene of the two of them tickling each other with blades of grass. Eisendorff sat atop the bank of the cellar and opened the lid to the hamper.

Sepia and yellowing images of Lillian, Lindersyl and his grandparents stared back at him. These were the family photos they had set for every season for three generations. He smiled easily at his own youthful image—so much like that of his own son's. Then there were photos of Johnathan and

Grier somewhere else. Still in black and white, the photos gave hint to a rural community far removed from Mosse Point. In one Johnathan stood holding Grier, smiling broadly and looking dapper in conked hair, three-button suit and shades. The water tower in the rear of the photo read Rosedale University. The shadowy figure of a heavy-set woman on the porch was just visible. Apparently she had moved just as the camera's shutter clicked. In the next photo that same heavy-set woman was kissing Johnathan, his hand pressed hard against the side of her face, his eyes shut tightly. In yet another, Johnathan stood behind the woman, his arms wrapped around her as she held Grier. Her face finally discernible, the heavy-set woman was heavy with child and it was Lindersyl. Folded within the stacks of photos were eight or nine journal pages, written in Lindersyl's handwriting. Eisendorff felt compelled to read them despite the growing cramping of his stomach muscles.

Diary Excerpt: June 1965

Johnathan finally went and did it! Those crackers came and got him last night and carried him off. I hoped and prayed that they'd taken him to jail and not to the river. Seems the good folk of Bolivar County didn't take too kindly to him smacking the face of that grocer he's been fighting with off and on for nearly a year. That Mr. Oakley—they call him Mr. Chinaman because his eyes look like Chinese eyes, you know how we do with people—said that Johnathan tried to cheat him out of the money he was due. Johnathan said that Mr. Oakley gave him back the wrong amount of change. They started arguing and Mr. Oakley gets upset and starts calling Johnathan an uppity nigger. He told Johnathan to see how that counting and being a smart ass will get him out of Parchman. Well, Johnathan told Mr. Oakley, that if he was bent on getting him locked up in Parchman, it may as well be for a reason and he smacked the tobacco right out of Mr. Oakley's mouth—spit and all. Mr. Oakley's wife, Fannie, put her palm to her chest and just collapsed to the floor. I guess she figured she had seen it all—a colored man smacking the tobacco out of her husband's mouth. Well, it did serve him right, but now it looks like it's serving all the rest of us wrong. Johnathan waited for Mr. Oakley to call the sheriff; said he wasn't being chased nowhere. But Mr. Oakley acted like it was over because he was scared shitless. But later that night, I guess he had worked his nerve back up. And with his wife witnessing him getting smacked, Mr. Oakley couldn't rest as a man in his own home without exacting something against Johnathan. I got word this morning that Johnathan was being sent to Parchman. The clerk at the sheriff's office said that the judge had seen him last night—actually, "Judge" Marlon Oakley, Mr. Oakley's great uncle, was on the back of the pick-up that came and got Johnathan last night. I know they did it to scare us to death, but they sent that pick-up with the portable electric chair strapped to it to pick Johnathan up. They made Johnathan sit right in that chair and they start to make buzzing sounds like he was frying. Johnathan just looked them all over a few times and laughed. Then he looked over his shoulder to me and said, "Baby, see you in a bit."

One of the boys yelled, "Not if we get to her first."

And Johnathan was up and fighting all over again. I always have liked to see him knocking men about. He is one of those jookhouse fighters who will fight you until you knock him out. As long as he's got even a breath of air in him, he's swinging. And they finally had to clobber him over the head and put him down to make him stop throwing punches. Anyhow, the judge decided that killing Johnathan would do nothing but give me something to brag about and make the other colored men think it was alright to knot up white people. Instead, he put Johnathan on that labor gang at Parchman Prison Farm, on a work detail with a sentence of one to ninety-nine years. They would take their time, if Johnathan let them, and kill him slowly. Break his spirit, then break him physically.

My heart sank when I heard that sentence because Johnathan's family was no stranger to Parchman farm; neither was mine. My mother's brothers and uncles had been given that 1-99 as well for simple offenses like being drunk and disorderly, not being 'civil enough' to white people, or being 'too familiar' with white girls. The rule of thumb is you work until you die and your time is not served fully until they bury you in a Parchman plot. I went into Sunflower County this afternoon to see if I could check in on Johnathan. At least say goodbye. They have plenty of Black trustees, other prisoners who are trusted enough to carry loaded guns and keep watch over the other prisoners. Two of them I recognized as distant relatives. One of them, a cousin, twice removed led me out onto the grounds where the men were just resuming their work detail. Johnathan was among them. I started crying the moment I saw him, and haven't stopped yet. He looked so old, like he'd aged overnight. He was bent to a curve with the shackles cutting into his flesh while he tried to keep pace with the other, shorter, quicker men chained to him. When the chains were loosed, Johnathan fell in line with the others, digging ditches with ten men on his left and ten more on his right. It was over a hundred degrees in the shade and he adjusted his prison issue straw hat to block the sun from his eyes. His lip was busted and one of his eyes was swollen almost shut. It hadn't taken long for them to get to Johnathan and break him. When I heard his deep baritone calling out the chants of the work song, "Don't You Hear My Poor Mama Calling", my knees buckled and I thought that this must have been what Mrs. Oakley felt like when she saw her husband get smacked. One of the other trustees, old dumb ass Scooter Monroe, had grown up with Johnathan in Clarksdale and never did like him. He was getting his jollies watching Johnathan suffer. When he saw the time my cousin was having holding me up, Scooter came over to be nosy. He told me to come back in a few days and he may have a solution for getting Johnathan out. My cousin gave me a look that read: "Gal, not unless you 'den lost your damned mind!". But I made plans to meet Scooter anyway, because I could not bear to think of Johnathan suffering like that.

Diary Excerpt: June 1965

I saw Johnathan today clearing trees with his work detail. His skin is so ashen and he looks real sick. I had on overalls and boots and was able with dumb ass Scooter Monroe's help to get close enough to see him up-close. His teeth are missing and his hair has patches missing too. He moves like his body is hurting however he stands or sits—not that there was much sitting or idle standing going on. Those trustees had those guns trained right on the men; one of them looked to be aiming straight at Johnathan's back, waiting for him to make an offense so that he could shoot him dead. Johnathan was too uppity for his own good the guards had told Scooter, who told me. They said that they were betting to see who could pick him off with one shot. Dumb ass Scooter Monroe then side steps me today and tells me that he would see about getting Johnathan out sooner if I would 'cooperate' with him a little bit. There's not that much cooperating in the world! But it did occur to me that my sister likes those old rough, base-type men—that's what our mother calls them. Men that have the barest necessities to be considered a man: they eat, screw around with women, fight and make a mess everywhere they go. Tomorrow, my sister is coming back with me to Parchman and between the two of us, we're going to do all that we can to get my husband out of that place before it or the gunners kill him.

Diary Excerpt: July 1965

Our plan worked! My sister worked her magic on that dumb ass Scooter Monroe at the Sunday conjugals yesterday. She was in that shed with him for a long time with him just a hollering and baying at the moon. Everyone's attention was on that shed. It was rocking in the field and sounded like a storm was hitting it, splintering it up. While she was in the shed, I got Johnathan changed into something presentable for a visitor: an old woman's frock, wig, Mother Hubbards, *and knitting bag. Before long, people who were supposed to be having their own good conjugal time, stopped and started walking over to the shed.*

White folks love to think Coloreds are sexual savages and those guards were lusted up on what they thought was going on in the shed, so they paid me and Johnathan no mind walking right out the front gates. They didn't even look over their shoulders at us as we got in a waiting car and left. I drove straight to Memphis where Daddy and Mother were waiting. Daddy got the iron cutters for the hand collars that linked the men cuff to cuff. He took Johnathan's old lady costume, along with his convict stripes and burned them in the neighbor's furnace. Daddy got Johnathan bathed, shaved and cut his hair. He then doused him in aloe vera to fight the rashes caused by constant sun, heat and insect exposure.

My sister met up with us at the house later on; everybody looking sideways at her. She cut her eyes to me and smile. "Look like I got you your old man back. Don't forget that you owe me," she whispered in my ear.

I was grateful and knew that that was a debt I had no problem at all returning should the need ever arise. Johnathan has not said a word yet, though. Not a grunt. He's just sitting and looking blankly at all of us around him. We're all headed for Connecticut soon, so I'm ready to praise God that the worst is over.

When Eisendorff began crying, he didn't bother to look over his shoulder. "Lindersyl is my mother. And here is the proof."

*We've come this far by faith, leaning on the Lord
Trusting in His holy word; He's never failed me yet . . .*

We've Come This Far By Faith, Donnie McClurkin

lindersyl
Wynn House Bed & Breakfast
July 22, 2001

Lindersyl touched her hand gently to the side of her face, scrutinizing the swelling in the rearview mirror. The pain shot through her body, causing her to make a mental note not to touch that spot again. She decided that the swelling had gone down, though the pain seemed to be getting worse. Lindersyl was sitting outside her cottage using her father's 1964 Cadillac Florentine coupe as a temporary refuge. She'd found the car at the old main house's garage down by the stables and counted herself blessed that it had cranked up with a violent quake, but still ran well. It had gotten her across town to Brice Rhyne's house, where she'd been summoned to Grier's side.

Lindersyl was still reeling from the news that her children had begun piecing together her fragmented lies and would soon come to know that she was their mother. First Eisendorff confronted her at the reservoir and then Grier remembering Johnathan's suicide attempt signaled that, ready or not, Lindersyl had to tell the truth. And even though this was what she'd said she wanted, Lindersyl also felt guilty and ashamed. So much so that she'd fought her own tranquilizer-induced exhaustion to compose herself and leave before Grier reawakened to ask more questions. But too tired to drive, Lindersyl had managed to maneuver the car only as far as the next corner before she was forced to pull over and park.

The dusty black convertible was the first model to house the new Stereo 8 system and Lindersyl found herself grinning at the sight of an actual 8-track tape jutting out of the dashboard console. She pushed maniacally at the buttons to see if the unlabeled selection in the tray would play. "Old Betsy" had been her father's playground when she was a child. Her dad considered it his own personal space where no wife or children were allowed. Some Saturdays he would wash her to a spitting shine and then sink into her low bench seats, admiring his own reflection in the rearview mirror. He'd turn his music up loud, pull his Dobbs hat down over one eye and recline. Sometimes though, Micheaux could be seen going through a type of confession in Old Betsy. Lindersyl recognized as the music tray shifted to a play mode that she had never seen her father yelling and argumentative inside their home as a child and it had everything to do with him taking asylum in Old Betsy first. She'd watch from her bedroom window her father talking to himself and God, venting his anger or hammering out his issues, before setting foot inside their home.

Lindersyl imitated her father's lean as "We've come this far by faith, leaning on the Lord . . ." came blaring from the speakers. The tears started slowly and Lindersyl could swear she felt her father's and God's presence in that car. She followed her father's lead, asking God 'Why?', 'How?' and 'When?'. She prayed for boldness, courage and His will to be done. When the tears subsided, Lindersyl remembered a place called Wynn House, a Bed and Breakfast about twenty miles outside of Mosse Point run by old friends. She didn't bother to call for directions or ask for reservations. Instead, Lindersyl took each road by memory until she reached the main gates of the property. When she pushed the buzzer outside the gates, the familiar voice of Ivan Wynn responded, "God bless you, good morning."

Lindersyl was taken aback by the greeting and hesitated before saying, "Good morning."

"May I help you?"

"Yes, this is Lindersyl Gottlieb. I'd like to—"

"Hey sister! Come on up the drive. I'll be out to meet you in a few," Ivan responded, releasing the latch mechanism of the gate, causing it to slowly swing open.

Ivan Wynn and his wife Yvonne had not seen or heard from Lindersyl since high school. Yvonne had been a friend of Lindi's years ago, but as her religious convictions turned to fervor, Lindersyl had moved away from her. "I ain't trying to have no Bible-thumper in my business judging me all the time," Lindersyl had commented.

Ivan and Yvonne married shortly after high school, he going into seminary and she, starting their family. Wynn House opened in the late 1970s as a retreat center for local churches, and was later expanded into a full-scale spiritual center and Bed and Breakfast.

Lindersyl turned the car off at the head of the driveway and waited for Old Betsy to stop shaking to open the door. She could see Yvonne standing on the front porch, smiling from ear to ear.

"Come on, give me a hug, girl." Yvonne said, walking down the stairs to the car door.

When Lindersyl embraced Yvonne, something strange happened. She found that the normal routine of touching shoulders and then moving away quickly would not do. She held Yvonne's embrace as if she were holding onto a parent, grateful and comforted by the reciprocity.

"That's right, let it go, honey. You can't carry it by yourself," Yvonne whispered in her ear.

Lindersyl began crying all over again, but this time they were tears of relief.

Wynn House became Lindersyl's home away from home. The Wynns had provided her with a lovely room, facing the garden that had basic comforts, but no luxuries. Televisions, telephones and radios were out of the question. "You've got to eliminate all things that will distract you from hearing God's voice," Yvonne told her. Lindersyl was forced to think only of herself and her children. How would she tell Eisendorff and Grier? Would they accept her with open arms or be rightfully embittered by her deception? Lindersyl didn't want to consider Eisen and Grier's rejection, though it was a tremendous possibility. To fight back the anxiety brought on by trying to figure things out, Lindersyl recited Bible passages and sang the oldest of Old Negro Spirituals, given to her by Ivan. She was allowed one phone call per week and had made a conscious decision to speak only with Olivus. Lindersyl gave him strict instructions not to tell anyone where she was, but to let them know that she was okay. Olivus felt helpless. He wanted to be there with her or, better, to bring her back to Ladbroke Mews. "As soon as you tell your kids, Lindersyl, I want you on the first thing moving, back here. It's really not safe for you there," he'd told her.

Lindersyl promised Olivus that as soon as she was able to secure everything at Gottlieb Grove into its proper place, she would be back. And now, after almost two months of communing with God, Lindersyl was more frightened than ever to step off of hallowed ground and back into the stench and rigor of her own mess.

*You tell me that you love me, but boo, if this is love,
it's a good thing you don't hate me . . .*

Boo, Macy Gray

anastasia
Home clinic of Mariska Barras
July 24, 2001

Anastasia sat in the living room of what the neighborhood elders called a "problem solver". Mariska Barras was the mother of six and grandmother of ten, but her love of children in no way retarded her love of 'correcting the paths of unwanted children'. The epitome of mind transference, Anastasia was more concerned with the horrific yellowing flowered wallpaper, than the task at hand. She had to get rid of this baby and she had to do it now.

"They have no chance of being abused, neglected or killed by impatience if they never make it," Mariska told Anastasia on their first meeting. In this manner, Mariska was truly a problem-solver. For the last $50 she had to her name, Anastasia would allow Mariska to eliminate her turmoil and return to a life of simplicity. The "evil deed", as Anastasia had come to think of it, when she chose to think of it at all, was to take place in a small spare bedroom off Mariska's kitchen and divided from complete view by colorful, jingling beads. The room had just enough space in it for a twin size bed, a footstool and a nightstand.

The little life she had come to love and affectionately call Milo had driven a wedge between her and her parents, and now her and Johnathan. Johnathan had not been prepared at all for her announcement of impending parentage a week previous.

"Fuck that!" he'd raged.

"What?"

"Stace, what you think I'm some stupid ass young knucklehead who don't know shit 'bout the games you bitches play?"

Stunned that his callousness and coldness could stretch to include her and their unborn child, Anastasia looked in disbelief a second longer before mumbling again, "What?"

"Well, cancel that shit! If you are pregnant and it's my baby, you better get rid of it. If you think this is a joke, try me. You need the money—fine! Here's two . . . three hundred. How much it cost to get an abortion?"

"I don't know. I hadn't considered not having our baby . . ."

"**We** don't have a baby! I'm leaving you $500 to get rid of it. And I don't wanna hear shit else about no fucking baby!" he yelled before turning calm. "Now, you going to get undressed or was this a complete waste of my time coming over here?"

Anastasia had snatched the money from the kitchen countertop and run into the bathroom, locking herself inside.

"Fine! Don't call me no more for nothing!" Johnathan had yelled, slamming the front door behind him.

Three-fifty of the five hundred dollars Johnathan had left had gone immediately to paying the rent. Another fifty to buying groceries and household items. Maternity vitamins and travel to and from the free clinic had used up another fifty. Her resolve to have her baby was crudely disintegrated by the time the reality of having a baby—the costs even before the baby arrived, not having any money, feeling as if she had the flu, but not being able to pop aspirin as she had in the past, sank in.

Abortion was probably the right answer, the only realistic solution. The final solution. The free clinic to her dismay would not do it, though.

'Sweetheart, we can provide you with all the pre and post natal care you want, we'll even help you get on WIC or refer you to an adoption agency, but we don't butcher babies."

The doctor's words were bitter and forceful. And only when the maternal side of the doctor crept into the silence, did she approach Anastasia, her yellow clogs banging hard against the stripped wooden floor, and hug her.

"Honey, no matter how difficult things seem now, nothing is worth killing this child over. You've been coming in here and taking care of this child and loving it all this time. I don't need to know your situation; just hang in there. It will get better. Money, a man, your family, none are connected to that baby, but you. The state will help you, I will help you in any way I can—just remember, you have to live with the consequences of your actions," the doctor said sternly, holding Anastasia's shoulders in her hands.

"It's just so hard," Anastasia managed to whisper.

"It's going to get harder. But you've got to fight for that baby inside of you. You've got to protect that angel from everything. Be a warrior for that baby."

Anastasia felt another headache coming on and gathered her things quickly to leave. The doctor added her name to the growing roster of unwed, expectant mothers applying for aid from the state. Anastasia's benefits would kick in instantly, but her maternal instincts would take some time. As she headed out the door, a young girl in a pink sweater and too tight jeans, of about thirteen handed Anastasia a business card and smiled.

"Don't believe shit they say. You came in for an abortion, they wanna give you counseling. You're grown; you know what you want. Fifty bucks, my mom can take care of everything."

Anastasia was as shocked by the girl's tone and edgy language as she was by the prospect of being headhunted for an abortion in a prenatal clinic.

"Okay, this is too weird—even for me."

"My mom's right outside. Sit and talk to her. Can't hurt nothin'," the teen smiled.

Anastasia followed the girl out and around the corner to Addison Park. There, with her grandkids was Mariska. A beautiful woman whose race, age and nationality were undecipherable, Mariska introduced herself and immediately began explaining the benefits of being able to start anew.

By the time she arrived home two hours later, Anastasia had all but decided to keep her baby. Who paid fifty dollars to get rid of a child in someone's spare bedroom? No, she would keep Milo and that was that. Anastasia did another about-face on her decision as soon as she found Johnathan sitting inside her lobby.

Johnathan had taken one look at her and known she was still pregnant. After pushing her to tears, he made one final threat—he'd get rid of her and the child if she didn't have the abortion. He didn't try to come upstairs, didn't ask for sex—just turned and left.

Anastasia had slept nary a wink since Johnathan's visit and knew that he was having some guy follow her. Probably a private investigator, but perhaps a ruffian sent to carry out Johnathan's threat. Too distraught to deal with it, Anastasia had gone to Mariska's the next afternoon and simply drank the concoction of herbs and berries given to her. The "ancient remedy" was supposed to put Anastasia in a mild and restful state, while also causing the lining of her uterus to separate from the wall and expel the child from her body.

Staring at the faded wallpaper and stained furniture as she trembled uncontrollably, Anastasia felt she was in anything but a mild and restful state. With the little room and its content fully visible to her now that Inez, the teen from the day before, had left the beaded curtains open, Anastasia felt herself go lightheaded. When she reached up to grab the wall and balance herself, calling out for Mariska, she instead caught hold of the beads, causing the whole rack to crash to the floor as she did. In her stupor, Anastasia's cries for help seemed only to be audible to her. The sound bounced in her inner ear, until she became so annoyed that she fell silent. For a short time Anastasia lost consciousness. When she felt herself being lifted in the air followed by loud rattling, she thought for a moment she had crossed over to the other side. But when she opened her eyes, she saw the place where the little room was to have been, boarded over with a full-sized poster of the Virgin Mary in front of its entrance. Inez had removed the utensils from the room and concealed all but the handle of something resembling a ladle, under the cushion of the sofa.

"Ma'am do you know your name?" a man in EMS blues asked her.

"Yes. I am Anastasia Harcourt."

Looking to Mariska for confirmation, the EMS guy breathed a sigh of relief when he got a nod from her head.

"Do you know what happened to you Ms. Harcourt?"

Looking to Mariska as the EMS had, Anastasia answered in the negative just as Mariska stepped forward and answered for her.

"My friend was over for a visit and felt a little dizzy. She is a couple of months pregnant and she fainted. Even though pregnant women faint all the time, I thought I should call you just to be safe."

"Good thinking. We're gonna get you taken care of. We'll transport you to Abernathy Medical and have them take a look at you."

"No! I don't have any insurance—I can't afford a hospital bill—"

"Ma'am you have no choice. There may be something terribly wrong with you or your baby. We have to take you in," the EMS guy said.

Suddenly the thought of something being wrong with her baby threw Anastasia into a panic. It didn't matter that she was about to have an abortion; now all she wanted was for everything to be okay. Looking to Mariska for some clarification of what had happened, Anastasia ruffled her brow and frowned. Mariska came to her side and leaned in close to her ear, "Don't worry, I only gave you Raspberry tea because I could see you wanted this baby more than anything else in the world. I put the $50 back in your purse. You fainted from anxiety—nothing more. Now, just relax yourself and do what the doctors say . . . you're going to be a mommy," she smiled, kissing her cheek.

Anastasia had never favored God, figured He had little time or no patience for her stupidity. But here, His hand had touched her and kept her from making a terrible mistake. He did truly look out for fools and babies. Now she had to find out if her anxiety had in any way endangered the life of her child and make it simple and plain to Johnathan Holland that she was having his baby whether he liked it or not.

I feel like praising, praising Him
I feel like praising, praising Him . . .

Hold My Mule, Shirley Caesar

lindersyl & lillian
Saint Peter's Rock African Methodist Episcopal Church
Northeast Mosse Point, Connecticut
June 24, 2001

The Gottlieb family had never been particularly spiritual, but religion was an integral part of their socialization. Thus, Saint Peter's Rock African Methodist Episcopal was the place to see, be seen, know, find out *and* declare all the news and gossip fit for consumption. With her physical wounds healed from her battle with her sister, Lindersyl was left to contemplate how she'd arrived at such a spiritual wasteland, void of any connection with her family. The time at Wynn House had been an epiphany. Lindersyl had spent the time alone on a vegan diet. The no swine, no liquor restrictions had suited her well, returning a healthy glow to her skin. After a three day fast, she'd also sought spiritual guidance from a prophetess the Wynn family had known for more than forty years. Needless to say, when Sara Ross began listening to Lindersyl discuss the Gottliebs, her back grew taller as she stretched her neck in disbelief. Believing she'd found an ally, Lindersyl continued to deliver her tale of an unwelcome welcome home, only to discover Sara's face was not one of support. With a life that had unfolded like a "how to become a saint manual", Sara had not only heard Lindersyl's story before, but had heard it directly from her twenty years previous. After giving Lindersyl a stern lecture that ultimately attacked her unwillingness to go to God in prayer and ask His forgiveness, Sara hugged Lindersyl tightly.

"All God needed was for you to step forward one half of an inch so that He could do the rest. Why don't you want to trust in His word?"

"Look at my life, Sara! I was doing the right thing when God let my sister and my husband take over and destroy my life. How can I trust that God will do what I need Him to do, when it looks like He flat abandoned me?"

"Lindersyl, just because God is on your side does not mean that you will not have problems. When Johnathan and Lillian started their mess, did you pray to God or did you go off and handle things yourself? Why did you keep sleeping with that man long after God told you to leave him alone? More importantly, why don't you love Lillian the way you claim you do?"

The last question confused Lindersyl.

"Sara, are you saying that I don't love my sister?"

"I'm trying to get you to see that the answer to all of these questions is the same. You are still hurt that Lillian took that man from you. You were angry and bitter about it and so you kept sleeping with Johnathan to get back at her—to hurt her, not because you loved him. And you didn't pray about it because God would have opened your eyes to that."

Lindersyl thought for a moment and then jumped up from her seat, "Yeah, you're right! I can't stand her! I've always thought she was oppressive and mean. She spent her life trying to lead mine instead of getting one of her own. And when she felt like it, she reached over and took mine for herself. I hate her and she should be as miserable as I am!" Lindersyl shouted.

"At least now you've said it," Sara said, taking hold and squeezing Lindersyl's hand.

There was something about truth that made Lindersyl light of mind and action. Though totally unexpected, having to deal with Chasen and Lillian confronting Harry, then Eisendorff and Grier confronting her, had given meaning to the disastrous decisions she and Lillian both had made. Lindersyl saw that inasmuch as she had blamed Lillian for taking her family, she had denied Harry the right to raise Chasen. She had as much fault and blame as anyone else—if not more, because turning Johnathan off once and for all would have ended the melodrama before it took root good. Putting things into perspective, Lindersyl lifted God's name in praise and thanks that He had kept the lot of them from killing each other a long time ago.

On the road to recovering her crippled spirituality, Lindersyl dressed carefully and applied only a smidgen of honeysuckle lip-gloss to her lips. Saint Peter's had not looked upon her in more than twenty years, and even her mother's funeral had not brought her back into the sanctuary. There would be the lifelong members eyeing her suspiciously; the men who turned the parish into a meet and greet by gawking at her and of course, the women, who were more comfortable rolling their eyes and mouthing obscenities at her, than letting her alone. Without fail, Eisendorff, Grier, Johnathan and Lillian made eleven a.m. worship service every Sunday. When Grier and Eisendorff were young, Lindersyl had attended, occupying the last seat on the back pew. Admittedly it was because the loud, garish singing the choirs presented as recital rattled her fragile nerves—especially when she'd been boozing. Most parishioners took her backseat presence as a sign of her heathenism. Lindi was also convinced God would strike her with a lightning bolt through the church ceiling at some point for showing up, so she kept a healthy distance from the saints. Irrespective of her disdain for the music or the threat of lighting bolts, this Sunday morning, Lindersyl would be there. Adjusting her hat to tip slightly to the right, Lindersyl thought of the fight she'd had with Lillian, and how easily the right shade of MAC had covered her bruises.

The fistfight between Lillian and Lindersyl had easily been their worst. Lillian had succeeded in etching a myriad of tiny scratches all over Lindersyl's face, bruising her back and side with body punches and severing a track of superfine laser weave from Lindersyl's scalp. Lillian had limped way equally battle scarred: bruised ribs, knife lacerations on her arm, shoulders and across her chest and a host of knots and contusions.

Chasen had been frightened enough to run from the pool house and hide himself when the blood splatter began to hit the walls in waves. Never, in his wildest dreams, could he have imagined these two beautiful, intelligent, sophisticated women so rancorous and volatile. With Harry out of the way, all decorum fell by the wayside and the ladies began street-fighting and shit-talking like old soldiers. The two old girls were too tired to continue and parted easily, Lillian retreating to the main house to be consoled by Chasen, and Lindersyl to no place in particular. Lindersyl walked the grounds for what turned into hours, trying to calm herself. She had tried to kill Lillian with that knife and were it not for Harry's newly shellacked floors, at least one of her attempts to drive that butcher knife through Lillian's chest would have been successful.

When she finally took note of herself, Lindersyl was clear on the other side of the Grove, and was too tired to walk back. Lindersyl was frightened by her own behavior, "I almost killed her . . . I tried to kill her," she kept saying. Lindersyl laid down in the grass and knotted herself up into a ball. She awoke with the sun bearing down on the side of her face about an hour later, with a burning sensation around her ankles. Jumping up, Lindersyl saw that she had positioned her legs atop a red anthill.

"Shit," she yelped, brushing the ants off her skin and stepping into a small pond next to the grass. The cool of the water made her walk into it until she was nearly submerged. Lindersyl let her tears and the muddy silk of the pond mix well before getting out. She walked over to the side of the stables and found Harry's rusted ten-speed leaning against its doors. She hopped on and headed back to the main house, legs stretching to kingdom come and back to fit the 30-year-old bike's peddling. On the ride back, Lindersyl watched Lillian and Chasen leave the house, clutching and clinging to one another. Vexed all over again, Lindersyl went up to her old room to pry open her sealed off inner sanctum. Lindersyl wanted the papers and photos to help her remember what time, drink and distance had caused her to forget. Also, should she need it, there would be proof to support her confessions to Grier and Eisendorff. Oddly enough, the room within a room was not as she'd left it. There were things missing—papers, photos and boxes of mementos. There were also two sets of footprints in the layers of dust on the floor. Surely Lillian wasn't aware of this space. Could she and Chasen have come in there? Not likely, but not impossible either. Lindersyl decided to remove the rest of her things from that room to keep them from being destroyed or used against her. She carried the remaining items out of the house in a bin and loaded them into her father's old car.

Initially Lindersyl had been unable—and quite unwilling to apologize to Lillian, but had grown worried and frustrated when after two weeks Lillian had not made any attempts at reaching out to her.

By the time Lindersyl arrived at the gates of St. Peter's Rock, the rhythmic beat of her heart had picked up considerably. Taking a few moments to reapply her lipstick, Lindersyl spotted Lillian and Johnathan walking arm in arm up the walk. They appeared to be exchanging niceties—smiling broadly, looking—well, looking in love. Before the pangs of jealousy could creep up on her, Lindersyl remembered why she was there. Besides, Johnathan and Lillian often played "in love" for their adoring fans. Hurrying to catch them before they went in, Lindersyl was taken aback, when Lillian eyed her and in a most wicked tone said, "Well if it isn't the whore of Babylon". Johnathan had been desperate to find her and he wanted very much to kiss her wildly at that very moment, but instead he gave a customary snicker to Lillian's comment. When in the next motion, he dropped Lillian's arm and reached for hers, Lindersyl was happy to cock her head to one side and move pass them both into the adytum.

Lillian would not have it! She just wouldn't! After nearly being killed by her crazed sister, and feeling somewhat comforted by the belief that Lindersyl had fallen off the face of the earth, Lindersyl had the nerve and audacity to show up at St. Peter's Rock. The emergency room had called Lindersyl's ritual carvings across her body, "flesh wounds" and wanted Lillian to tell more about who had inflicted them. But Lillian would have no police buffer between she and Lindersyl. Her sister's deeds would not go unpunished, but Lillian had her own brand of punishment and justice to hand down. She allowed herself to be bandaged physically by the nurses and then emotionally by Chasen.

"You are my greatest achievement Chasen. I have loved you so much, but been forced by Lindersyl to give you to her. She has threatened in the past to kill me, this was not the first time. But you saw for yourself that she meant to kill me if I did not do as she said," Lillian told Chasen.

"She is a monster! I cannot believe that she tried to kill you . . ."

"I fought with all that I had in me so that I could be with you. I could not let her kill me when finally, I was going to have my son back."

Lillian was satisfied with Chasen in the pool house, a beautifully obedient child, who would do her bidding in exchange for her attention. Eisendorff was back in his usual funk, Grier was staying across town, and with her sister out of Johnathan's sight, Lillian hoped she'd soon be out of his mind. In fact, with Lindersyl away from things, Lillian figured she could easily manipulate all involved into believing whatever she said about her sister and what took place in the pool house. But now, Lindersyl had turned up at St. Peter's, of all places.

As always the church was packed to the gills and it took nothing more than getting beyond the drama on the parking lot for the anxiety of being in the midst of so many disapproving eyes, to force Lindersyl's legs from under her body. She realized too late that she was about to miss the bench by inches and hit the floor. She was relieved to fall into Eisendorff's arms.

"Mom, I want you to meet someone. This is Terrie Thompson. And you've already met Avery," he said, shifting his position to allow the women room to exchange greetings.

"Mom?" she whispered back, wondering whether to deny or admit it.

"I don't want an explanation. If you aren't ready to admit it yet, it's fine. I love you." Eisendorff said nervously, biting his bottom lip in wait of her response.

"Yes, Mom," she smiled back. Balancing her weight to the tips of her toes and extending herself to embrace him, she kissed his forehead and cheeks. "I love you too and we'll talk after service, I promise."

It was a fight Lillian simply could not win. Though sitting in a pew alongside her husband, his viscerally intense gazes at Lindersyl sitting on the opposite side of the church with *their* family had made Lillian shrink like a hothouse flower. There had never been a time when a song, words of praise or even a spirit-filled message from their pastor—Reverend Milhouse Uttly—had affected her (or anyone in the congregation for that matter). The Spirit, as it were, simply had no place in Lillian's churchgoing. But this day, with Johnathan so obviously and completely out of her grasp, his mask of marital bliss slipped to cover only a very small portion of his face, truth was staring back at Lillian. Johnathan really did want his family back. Did they want him back? Harry had moved on, and Chasen, her one true ally, had slipped out of Gottlieb Grove as easily and without notice as he'd slipped in.

Lillian was strapped and weighed by emotions—anger, fear, disgust, self-loathing and hurt. She saw the results of her own mischief making, her love of destruction, her divisiveness. Her very detestable self, marred and ugly, had become apparent. The choir's very slight version of *I Surrender All*, framed Lillian's mind and her thoughts could go neither forward nor backward. Forced to deal in the moment, Lillian's breathing became deep and protracted. She realized she was crying, sobbing aloud but she could not stop or quiet herself. Emotion wracked her body until it turned into bawling, bending her from one side to the other and causing the sound to bounce off the walls in an eerie, crippling vibration.

Johnathan was useless in subduing her once her arms began to flail.

"Lord, forgive me! Lord, forgive me!" she yelled over the heads of those who tried to hold her down.

An affront to the delicate nature and decorum of St. Peter's Rock, a few of the more upstanding ladies approached and became forceful in restraining her to move her out of the sanctuary. Reverend Uttly hid his face and body behind the pulpit podium.

The commotion from the other side of the church seemed at first to be the crying of a small child. Standing from her seat, Lindersyl could see Johnathan cradling Lillian while trying to fend off the ushers and attendants. Passing Avery to Terrie, Lindersyl ran, with hat flying behind her to the other side of the church. Pushing through the six or seven people who'd gathered at her sister's kicking feet, Lindersyl saw all the fear and anger, hurt and deceit in Lillian's eyes. Her wet face searched out for comfort in a sea of strangers. "Let her go! Let her be!" Lindersyl screamed, shooing away the churchgoers. "Lillian? Lillian."

"Lord, forgive me! Lord forgive me!"

Grabbing Lillian's shoulders and pulling her forward so that they were face to face, Lindersyl shook her. "Come on Lillian. Come on Lil . . . We are Gottlieb Girls, we lead by example . . ."

Lillian's distant eyes drew in on the familiar words.

"Lindersyl!" she yelled, grabbing her sister and holding her tight. "I'm sorry. I'm so sorry!"

"Calm down Lil. It's okay. Remember Lillian, only pretty girls rule the world. And pretty girls don't do *ugly* crying. And you Lillian, are one of the prettiest. That's right, pretty girl. That's right, fix yourself so we can go through the orchard and pick some peaches . . ." Lindersyl coaxed Lillian, who regained enough of her composure to steady herself. Lillian's face lit up as she contemplated running through the family orchard with her sister. Taking Lindersyl's hand, Lillian pulled herself up to sit upright in the pew.

Eisendorff and Grier watched as Lillian bent her legs down and scooted to the edge of the pew. As she stood, Lindersyl embraced her again. "Lillian, God will always forgive you and so will I."

As if the official pardon had been handed to her, Lillian began crying again.

Grier and Eisendorff, with Terrie, Avery and Brice in tow had already moved into the vestibule when Lindersyl and Lillian made it out of the sanctuary. Johnathan was directly behind them, visibly shaken and silent.

"Let's go home," Johnathan finally said. "Everyone, we need to talk."

Chapter Seven
Gottlieb Girls Lead By Example . . .

"We are Gottlieb Girls, of fine stock and breeding, of importance and significance to the global community. We lead by example. We will seek alliances with only those who are of at least our own social standing. We will learn the languages, cultures and orders of far away lands in order to rightfully take our place among the leaders of the world. We will court and marry only from among the best-bred, best-educated and most acceptable families. We will do all that is within our power to preserve the Gottlieb name as a show of reverence to those colored family of ours who came before us and suffered that we might achieve," Lindersyl said, straight-faced and upright, peering down into her sister's face.

Lillian nodded her approval and then the two looked at the stunned faces of Eisendorff, Grier, Brice, Terrie and Johnathan. Both ladies laughed as Grier said under-breath, but audible, "You cannot be serious".

"Our mother was a bit of a stickler for keeping Lindersyl and me in line," Lillian half-smiled, taking a sip of Juniper tea before continuing. Reaching out and taking Lindersyl's hand in hers, she added, "Lindersyl, she felt, was sub-standard and she tormented her regularly. It was always my job to shelter Lindersyl as much as possible. Lindersyl could do nothing to our mother's pleasing. It was always 'not quite' or 'do it again, this time with feeling'. I was our mother's favorite. I towed the line and nursed her madness. Lindersyl refused to go along with the program. She bucked the system and she paid the price. Our mother made her life a living hell and when it was convenient for me, I joined in the mischief against Lindersyl. I played both sides against the middle and pretended to be an ally to both when I was a friend to neither," Lillian whispered.

"It's all in the past." Lindersyl squeezed Lillian's hand.

The sisters looked at one another as if asking simultaneously, "which of us should begin?" Johnathan interceded, clearing his throat. "No matter who tells this story, I will come out looking like a bastard . . ."

"Oh, sit down! This is not about you!" Grier yelled.

"But it is Grier," Lillian countered, then turning to Johnathan, "Johnathan, no one has sole blame in this mess. It is shared through and through. Now, please the sooner we get this out in the open the better we will all feel."

"You have to understand what we were fighting against to understand why we did the things we did. I have dreamed of having this conversation for so many years and now that I am tasked with actually doing it, I'm lost. Eisendorff and Grier, Lillian is not your mother, I am. Grier, I'm sorry I side-stepped you earlier—I guess I just wasn't ready to deal with this," Lindersyl sighed deeply, biting at her bottom lip. "Johnathan and I were married in Round Lake, Mississippi December 8, 1962 when I was four months pregnant with you, Grier. We loved each other very, very much and had dated for more than two years before anything happened . . . Well, no, it wasn't two years before *anything* happened, but two years before I got pregnant—actually—oh, this is me telling the truth," Lindersyl laughed nervously.

"Take your time, Mom," Eisendorff coaxed.

"This old nobody-ass Johnathan Holland was the fire of my soul. He was so country and rugged and I loved him. Ain't that right, Jumper?"

"Sho . . . sho . . . sho . . . yeah, that's right!," Johnathan said dropping his head.

Everyone laughed aloud as the wistful tone and look of Lindersyl and Johnathan began to supplant them back to a place where Johnathan was bashful and Lindersyl spoke in soothing, loving tones.

"Don't laugh at him, now," Lindersyl admonished defensively. "This was my knight in shining armor. Jumper, lift your head up."

"I don't want to," he said, his eyes firmly fixed on his shoes.

Lindersyl moved to his side and rubbed his back gently. "Jumper, ain't nobody goin' fun you for loving me," she said, all airs removed and using her father-tongue.

Johnathan lifted his head to glance her smiling face. "I never should have left you . . ."

"So, Mr. Holland, you divorced Mrs. Collier and married her sister?"

"Not quite," Lillian interjected. "There is no confusing Johnathan's love for my sister. It is a complete and unfettered love. So precious at the time that neither of them paid much attention to the world around them or how their actions could affect them later. Our mother reared us to wait for sex, but Lindersyl and Johnathan decided to test the waters. Mama wasn't going to let her marry him anyway because he had nothing but ambition and promise. And as mother often said, 'neither spent well'. Low and behold, Lindersyl gets pregnant the very first time. Only me and Johnathan knew and we went straight to the justice of the peace. We figured if she was married, Mama and Daddy had no say in her being pregnant. In mid-ceremony, she was only about two months gone, she starts cramping and loses the baby. We never told our folks, because his favorite or not, if Daddy had found out about Lindersyl being pregnant, she would have devastated him. This is around March. By June Lindersyl was pregnant again. This time she goes to about the fifth week before she miscarries again. The doctor said her body wasn't healed enough from the first miscarriage to sustain the pregnancy. I started getting upset with Lindersyl. It was almost like Mama had been right all along about her. That Lindersyl had that trifling Johnson gene in her that made her want to lay up under Johnathan and just have babies. You know your grandmother was one of eighteen kids. She was embarrassed by her parents' fertility and the way they bred. I was trying to lie to the family and cover for Lindersyl, but she kept getting pregnant. Then December rolls around and Lindersyl comes to me with that same crooked, dollipy look on her face. She's pregnant again! This time, I told. I called home and told my mother," Lillian folded her arms, upset all over again.

"Boy, you talking about scared?" Johnathan laughed. "Your grandmother was a beast. The day she met me she set my clothes on fire. I'm talking, struck a match to me while I'm standing there talking to her. Then while I'm dancing around trying to put myself out, she tells me that she knows some white boys that would finish the lynch job."

"Damn. How'd you get out of that?" Eisen asked in amazement.

"Your mama."

"I promised to throw myself in front of a speeding train and end it all if they didn't give their blessings. Daddy wasn't happy, but he said he understood. The next morning we were at the preacher's place."

"Nice ceremony," Johnathan smiled.

"Yeah. I had Grier and Johnathan and we were fine."

"Until the pregnancies started again," Lillian grimaced. "Lindersyl was supposed to have Grier and give her to me to look after while I worked on my Master's. I went to class at night and was to take care of the baby while she was in class during the day. But no sooner had Lindersyl started Fall classes than she was pregnant again. And in between you coming Eisendorff and us leaving for Mosse Point, your mother was pregnant twice more. It seemed the two of them couldn't concentrate on much of anything when they were together. Finally we all decided that it was best for Lindi and Johnathan to part company until she graduated school," Lillian said shaking her finger at Lindersyl.

The listeners looked one to another with blushed expressions.

"I was supposed to be at work; I got me a job at this big Colored law office. And I would leave on my lunch break and go over to the campus and just look through the windows of Lindersyl's classes and watch her learning things. She was so smart and beautiful and I couldn't believe she was mine," Johnathan smiled.

"Sprung!" Eisendorff laughed, pointing at his father.

"Call it what you want. I could not find a way of looking at her for a single moment where she did not stop my breath."

"Look out, Shakespeare!" Brice smiled.

"Their relationship was so beautiful that it brought some long-standing bad feelings out of me! Why had things worked for them and not for me and the guy I wanted? We were reared the same, same parents, same schools, everything. Why did he fall for her like this and not for me? Five pregnancies in three years. I felt inadequate and hurt. I was the older and was supposed to logically get married and have children first. I had been a witness at Lindersyl and Johnathan's first wedding ceremony in early February 1961, and was to sign the document for her when she went into premature labor and miscarried during the service," Lillian paused, looking over at Johnathan and Lindersyl.

"Anyway, I took the unsigned certificate home and folded it up in the family Bible and didn't think too much of it until two years later. You kids were living in Mosse Point with Johnathan and me and he was focused on business under your grandfather's tutelage. Lindersyl was still in Jackson. Your Dad and I had always been close friends, even after he and Lindersyl became involved. Though I'd never taken him but so seriously—I mean, Johnathan didn't fit into our family's day planner of suitors for me, he was slowly transforming into the kind of man I did want for myself. Connecticut businessmen with strong political and economic power got a hold of Johnathan and that Southern accent fell by the wayside, his overalls and dungarees were replaced with silks and cashmeres. I had a desire for him that I couldn't ignore, even when I knew it was improper. All Lindersyl was going to do was keep popping out those babies. That was fine for the South, but ladies didn't show their nature like that. It looked bad to have more than three children in any one family photo. It was obscene! So one day I talked to Mother and she agreed, I should seduce Johnathan—get him drunk—and take him. I did. A few weeks later, I realized that I was pregnant with his child," Lillian dabbed at her eyes.

Lindersyl picked up her story. "It was the middle of Spring—Spring break and I came home to see my husband and my children whom I'd missed more than anything. I only had finals to take and would be back with my family—a college graduate. But from the start, I knew that something was wrong. Hell, I'd been pregnant enough by then to know when an earthworm was about to drop. Lillian had no callers here, so that only left Johnathan as the intended father. Still, I held my tongue and refused to acknowledge what I suspected. Johnathan had changed in a way that was great for business, but terrible for our relationship," Lindersyl sighed, giving Johnathan a chance to jump in.

"The men in the boardrooms all laughed at me. Called me Country Time. Mrs. Faye—"

"Ooh, she hated it when you called her that," Lillian laughed.

"Lord, yes. Your grandmother, pardon me, sent me over to a lady who ran the diction classes at the family charm school, Mrs. Estelle Grison. She cleaned my vocabulary up, taught me to sit and chew food instead of scoffing it down, table manners that I had thought were unnecessary—"

"All the things about you that endeared me to you were gone! When you scoffed my food, I knew my meals answered your hunger. Every time my belly swole with your babies inside me, it quenched *my* desire. When your talk was flat it meant you were comfortable enough with me to be yourself. When you stammered, it meant you were overwhelmed with longing for me. You didn't have to change anything about yourself to please me. That man I met in my own home during Spring break is the one you children, and all the world knows as Johnathan Holland. He has always been and continues to be an unwelcomed stranger in my space," Lindersyl frowned, shifting her body away from Johnathan.

"The entire time I was in Jackson I thought Lillian was making up stuff about your family, Lindi. Can you imagine how I felt when I arrived at Gottlieb Grove and it hit me that she was guilty of bragging, but not lying? I wanted to impress your parents and be the kind of man you deserved. Not some backwoods, country ass nigger with big ideals and nothing to give you but a bunch of goddamned kids! How was I supposed to support us? How? If your mother hadn't got me out of Mississippi and cleaned me up, I'd still be down there fighting peckerwoods or in Parchman, eating fried bologna sandwiches!"

"It's boloney you twit! Who the hell says bologna?" Lindersyl smacked Johnathan across the back of the neck. "Johnathan, you were nothing but a man. And I would have been happy to do nothing but have your babies, bail you out of jail and tend to your wounds. Why can't you get it through your head that I was happy with you not because I didn't know any better, but because I did know better. I knew that you loved me enough to do whatever you had to do to feed us, clothe us and keep a roof over our heads. I never asked you to do any more than love me back, man. You used to stand for something! That's what really hurts, even now, you got so used to having your strings pulled, that you stopped knowing how to act unless someone was orchestrating your moves," Lindersyl rolled her eyes as Johnathan attempted to hold her. "My parents were backwoods country niggers, just like yours.

They had no right to try and force it out of you because they couldn't deal with looking at themselves uncovered."

Lillian began again over their quiet squabbling. "The orchestrating of moves came into play when Lindersyl graduated and returned home to discover I was pregnant. I got in her face and told her and she took the wind out of me. I lost the baby I was carrying, but found solace in their marital problems. Their issues were all the motivation I needed to keep them from returning to their happy state, and take Johnathan from her for good. I tried everything to get pregnant again, but Johnathan wouldn't come near me. I began to torment Lindersyl, along with our mother until she reached a breaking point and tried to leave. There was the infamous suicide attempt . . ."

"What the fuck was I supposed to do? I messed up! You had never so much as raised your voice to me, let alone cursed me. You cursed me out, smacked me, did everything but spit in my damned face. I did not want to live. I had messed up and couldn't fix it. I did not deserve to live. I was going to go shoot Ms. Faye and Lillian, both in the head, for ruining my family. But Lindersyl loved her sister and it would hurt her. I couldn't hurt Lindersyl like that. They had been raised to protect one another no matter what. If I killed Lillian, Lindersyl would never take me back . . . That rain was beating down on my head so hard that it felt like pelts of glass. My babies were in the car crying and Grier, you were trying to get out of the car and stop me from crying. I knew that I could not pull the trigger so long as Lindersyl was looking me in the face, so I waited till she turned slightly, glancing at the kids, and I pulled the trigger. I could hear her screaming, and my blood turned hot in my chest and felt like tar spewing over my other organs. My tongue felt heavy and I couldn't move it to say anything. The rain had light coming through it—it looked like falling stars. Everything went quiet and still and I thought I was dead. At the same time, over in the main house, your grandfather was suffering a heart attack and died. I was in the hospital for weeks and when I was released, I was received into the care of my wife, Lillian Ebersol Gottlieb-Holland," Johnathan trailed off.

"Lindersyl was in no condition to care for herself, let alone her family. She was fainting in and out of consciousness with grief over our father and my mother was insistent she get you kids out of her home. Your grandmother was never fond of children, especially boy babies. Finally Lindersyl left Gottlieb Grove for a boarding house—there were no hotels that would take Blacks back then. You were there for what, Lindi? Three months?" Lillian asked, to Lindersyl's nodded approval. "By then, Johnathan figured she didn't want him anymore, and we began living as a married couple. Because so many people never really knew that I was not your mother, we never corrected them. I still had my copy of their original marriage license with Lindersyl's, Johnathan's and the preacher's signatures. Where Lindersyl's name was to be written out, had been left blank so I simply wrote in my name. We continued our friendship with occasional lapses into the sexual, if not the romantic. But Johnathan and Lindersyl were very much in love with each other—still."

Lindersyl looked at Johnathan, then stared off before speaking. "I couldn't stop thinking that my selfishness, my lack of understanding had almost cost Johnathan his life. I really did feel Johnathan and you kids were better off without me. I stayed on the Grove for a while and Johnathan and I tried to keep things together, but it wasn't the same. You kids were calling me your aunt. I'd lost you."

"The kids you lost were Grier and me?" Eisendorff asked.

"Yes."

"Why didn't you try and fight for us?"

"I did. Grabbed you one day, got you on a plane and to Mississippi. When we got off the police were there waiting."

"I called them," Lillian said. "It was a terrible thing to do, but if Lindersyl left with you two, Johnathan would follow and then I'd be all alone."

"Oh, that's jacked up!" Terrie fumed.

"It really didn't matter after that. I didn't want this new, improved Johnathan and Lillian did. But knowing that my kids were trapped between us tore me up on the inside. Johnathan made us return to the Grove and bought me a place across town as an apology for having us forcibly returned. He would visit me there and I would visit you kids here."

"Why did you leave?" Terrie asked, leaning her chin to her palms.

"How does a woman play the other woman with her own husband? Then one day I got a letter from Bree Babalola, one of your grandfather's friends in Tenerife. She'd heard that I was doing public relations and wanted me to do some work with her in London. I saw Johnathan and you children that weekend like clockwork. I said my goodbyes as though they were meant to last until the next week and just before midnight that Sunday, I was on a transcontinental headed for London."

"Daddy, why didn't you let Mama back into the house with us?"

"Your grandmother was relentless. She had made me and could unmake me. I wanted my family back, but I couldn't go back to being a bum. I was also a fugitive from justice—the state of Mississippi gave me one to ninety-nine, don't forget. Your grandmother threatened to turn me in every chance she got. I had also gotten used to the $20 haircut instead of getting trimmed up in the kitchen with a cereal bowl on my head. I liked the life I was leading—even if it was all a lie." Johnathan answered.

"Lindersyl was considered second best and if Johnathan had to be associated with our family, it had to be with me. I could uphold the family creed. I would keep him on the straight and narrow. I would do more for our heritage than breed." Lillian reasoned.

Lindersyl rolled her eyes at Lillian. "Well you know, they say Mama stayed down at the river . . ."

"Lindersyl! I will not have you repeating that lie! Our mother would never have done that!" Lillian shouted.

"Done what? What do you mean?" Grier asked.

"It means that our mother may have been pregnant with as many kids as her mother, but she'd birth them and then carry them down to the river in a rice sack," Lindersyl said with a smirk, annoyed that Lillian wanted to defend their mother to her.

"Stop it Lindersyl! That's a lie!" Lillian shouted again.

"No it's not. And perhaps the only person blind to her was Daddy. Fluctuating weight problem, indeed!"

"I said stop it Lindersyl!" Lillian said, jumping up from her seat. "Mother did a lot to save Black women from being a bunch of modern-day farm animals. She helped women see there was more to life than being domesticated. Admit it Lindi, had I not stepped in, you and Johnathan would probably have a barnyard of pickneys." Lillian laughed, thinking of Harry by her choice of terms. He always called children 'pickneys'.

"Barnyard? Pickneys? Is that like a pickaninny Lillian? You might need to slow down. But you know what, you're probably right about me having lots and lots of babies. There's nothing wrong with that," Lindersyl said.

Johnathan smiled. "You liked being pregnant too."

"I did. And I loved being a mother."

"So you and Mrs. Holland are not really married then?" Brice asked, still confused.

"Lindersyl and I were divorced on the grounds of abandonment after she left the country. In time, Lillian and I were married by common law."

"Your father and I did continue to see each other on occasion, but being together only made us feel worse when we each returned to our normal, everyday lives—me married to Arthur and Johnathan married to Lillian," Lindersyl half-smiled.

"So is Chasen yours and Daddy's or Daddy's and yours?" Grier asked, pointing from Lindersyl to Lillian, unsure what to call either woman.

There was dead silence for a minute before Lillian spoke up. "I guess since this is the day of reckoning, all of the truth should be told. Chasen is my son."

"What?" Johnathan yelled, jumping from his seat.

"Yes, Chasen is mine."

"I never got you pregnant except for that one time, Lillian. In thirty-five years I ain't never climbed on you—drunk or without a condom—except that one time!"

Grier shook her head in disbelief. She hardly wanted to know her parents' intercourse guidelines. When she looked up, Brice was having a good laugh at her expense.

"I said he was mine, not ours." Lillian whispered.

"Harry Veda? You got a baby with that damned Harry Veda? I'll kill him! How did you hide it from me?" Johnathan fumed.

"Not that you would have noticed."

"Don't play with me Lillian."

"I was in London with Lindersyl. Well, I couldn't bring him here because you would leave me. I couldn't have the poolman's baby! He had no station in this life. I could not possibly bear the scandal!," Lillian said shaking her head. "I had to lead by example because I am a Gottlieb Girl," Lillian's voice cracked under the weight of her emotions.

"But Mr. Veda loves you! Tell him!" Eisendorff barked.

"He did love me. Eisendorff, Mr. Veda is gone—and the reason he left is because Chasen showed up here a couple of weeks ago and he found out. Now Harry is gone, Chasen's gone, presumably back to Europe, and everything is out in the open. So, it looks as though my leadership abilities as a Gottlieb Girl are strangely ill-suited for real time," Lillian said.

"You know what Arthur used to say to me?" Lindersyl asked, causing Johnathan to instantly release her hand. She looked at him surprised.

"Why even bring him up?" he asked.

"Just as jealous as you can be, Jumper. That was my husband and he never had an ill-word to say about you even when I was sneaking off to see you."

"Still."

"Still nothing! Anyway, Arthur used to say 'Gottlieb Girls are no better than any others. Flesh and blood, fragrance and pearls . . .'" then smiling,

Lindersyl added, "Lillian, I love you no matter what. I want you and my children back in my life as my family. It was never really about Johnathan; it was about me feeling like you were better than me, and you trying to dictate my life according to Mama's rules. Lillian, these are rules neither of us could abide by. It's time to face that and move on."

Lindersyl lifted Lillian's hand to her lips and kissed them.

"What do we do now?"
"We pray about it and try to love each other the best we can."

Be still and know your strength is weak
Your proper pose, volumes it speaks . . .

The Wound, Jazzfatnastees

chasen
Gottlieb Grove Attic
July 24, 2001

"Them two bitches!" Chasen screamed at the top of his lungs, removing his ear from the floor planks above the living room. "Arthur was right, Lillian and Lindersyl Gottlieb are evil and I should never have come here."

The wonderful thing about being at Gottlieb Grove surrounded by self-absorbed people was that they did not pay the slightest attention to anything. Chasen had made the soundproof attic space of the main house, which was large enough to be a separate apartment, his home. Making a bee-line each night from the doors of the poolhouse under Lillian's watchful eye, Chasen would enter, take the side exit twenty minutes later and head for the attic through the old servants quarters at the far West of the house. Since the family had done without servants for more than twenty years, no one bothered to even explore that end of the house. Fortunately for him, Chasen had found the keys to the secondary stairwell that led to each floor of the house, from the basement to the attic, and which would allow him to come and go freely under the noses of his family.

He had listened in horror, sneaking down into other parts of the house, first to the theater of unhappiness that both Lillian and Johnathan lived, and then the total breakdown of the family via Lindersyl and Lillian's true confessions. So not only had Lindersyl mothered Grier and Eisendorff, but he, himself, was the love child of Lillian and the "servant" Harry Veda. He believed in romance, but his British upbringing wouldn't allow him to celebrate love between the classes. Servants had no business with those they served.

Once Chasen came full circle at the Grove, the main house seemed to have a certain control over him. He could not simply leave. Despite every indication that he should head for the hills, Chasen felt compelled to not only stay, but also to correct the inhabitants. The Gottliebs had to pay for their sins.

Chasen repeated these thoughts over and over in his mind as he descended the stairs and crossed the West lawn to the rental car he'd had since his arrival.

Chasen allowed his thoughts to drift to much of nothing in particular as he drove the highway from Mosse Point through Ridgefield and down to the outskirts of New York. The draft in the house had given him a chest cold that was causing him to sweat like a man on crack and for the tenth time, he adjusted the air conditioning in the car. Yanking at the collar of his Cambridge University sweatshirt to fan himself, Chasen turned the car onto a narrow and seemingly abandoned street before pulling over. He left the car running and got out, pulling out a cell phone and pushing hard on the numbers.

"Hey, I'm outside," was all he said before disconnecting the call.

A moment later, a tall scrawny white guy with heavy eyelids and a deep scar running from his left temple to his chin opened a side door and waved him in.

"Chase, brother, have things come to this?"

"Danker, you wouldn't believe the shit I've caught myself up in coming to this God forsaken place!"

"God forsaken, huh? If you're mentioning the Lord, must be some shit indeed," Danker mused, moving through a narrow hallway into the front of a small storefront pawnshop.

Danker Simmonite, while reduced to selling illegal firearms and explosives from the backroom of a dinky pawnshop, was once one of the brightest students at the Manchester Academy. But as was his predisposition to violence even as a child, it was not so farfetched that he'd turn to a life of some vice. In fact, it was Danker's fondness for fighting that fostered his friendship with Chasen, who found himself constantly on the receiving end of a pounding. When Danker stepped in to assist him once on a particularly savage melee, Chase struck up an agreement whereby Danker would fight all his ensuing battles for a fee. In time, the long, white gangly Danker had become life-long buddies with the switching, neck-popping Black Chasen.

"So, tell me brother, what exactly are you looking for? I mean, how much damage are you trying to inflict?"

"Enough to level a three story mansion, a colonial poolhouse, and a couple of cars," Chasen said with his back purposefully turned to Danker, shielding his guile-ridden face.

"What the hell is this, World War Bleeding Three? I mean, honestly Chasen, what the blood and stomach pills ya need all that for? Next you'll be asking for C-4 and rocket missiles," Danker fumed, giving way to his British tongue.

"You don't understand—" Chasen began, his voice cracking under hidden sobs.

"This shit isn't for your family, is it?"

Chasen did not answer.

"Chasen! For-fucking-get it! I will not have a hand in this. I know Lindersyl left you at an early age and you probably blame her for a lot of things, man, but she's still your mother!"

"She's not my mother. Her sister, Lillian is my mother and Harry Veda, the pool man is my father."

"No fucking way!"

"Every fucking way! I just found out earlier today and I've been crashing in the servants' quarters. Their sorry asses don't even know I'm still on the property. I want to blow that whole damned house to hell with them in it."

"That's still no reason to kill them. Hell man, just smack the shit out of them or something. Cause a scene on the image-conscious bastards, but don't go killing people. Anyway, I thought you were a lover, not a fighter."

"I thought you were my friend. I thought at least you would understand."

"Oh, don't go pulling that shit on me, man. I kicked plenty of ass for you when we were kids but I've never even considered killing anyone."

"No, your hypocritical ass just sells explosives and illegal guns and shit to motherfuckers who *will* go out and kill."

"Don't take the piss with me."

"If you'd sell it to the average asshole coming in here, why not to me?"

"Because you need a fricking hug already, not a weapon. And if you had come in here and said someone had raped you, tried to kill you or something like that, I'd give you what you need. But not only is this some emotional baggage from your childhood, it's your family you want to kill."

"They are strangers to me, don't you understand that?"

"Look, Chasen, man," Danker smiled, wrapping one arm around Chasen's shoulder, "I can remember when we were kids and every time I turned around you wanted me to stick it to your old man. And every time, you calmed down and realized that the Deacon was just trying to protect you. Why don't you go to your family and confront them? Have it out with them, but don't do this."

Chasen pulled his thoughts together quickly.

"Danker, you been lifting weights? Your arms feel a little fuller than usual."

"Awh, bloody come on," Danker smiled coolly. "Can you tell the difference?"

"Hell yeah. You grown any bigger anywhere else?"

"You slickster you. You offering yourself to me, huh? Well, same rules apply: you can blow me, but I am no damned queer!"

"'Course not Danker, if it's one thing you'll never be, it's queer," Chasen smiled, unzipping Danker's dirty stonewashed jeans.

The traffic headed back towards Mosse Point was one big congested parking lot across all four lanes. "Probably an accident," Chasen said under his breath, fingering the Mauser-Bolo 7.63mm cushioned in the passenger seat and covered by a terry cloth towel. The blocks of plastic explosives and two additional Mausers, a Luger and an HSc, were pushed up under the passenger seat in a cardboard box and wrapped in his sweatshirt. Feeling the cold steel beneath his fingers, Chasen felt an unusual and sensual high. It was the power of life and death . . . and he had it riding shotgun towards a final and permanent solution to his problems.

Deciding that it was too much effort to head back into Mosse Point just then, Chasen pulled the car onto the Southbound ramp and headed for New York.

Smiling broadly, Chasen turned up Randy Crawford's Street Life on the radio and hummed along. After a hot meal and a shower at a hotel somewhere down the road, Chasen figured he'd call back to Danker's and apologize for hitting him over the head with a model ocean liner and taking the things he needed.

Chapter Eight
Coming Full Circle

There's a little piece of heaven, just waiting for you to come home,
Some day, I know you will . . .

A Little Piece of Heaven, The Neville Brothers

grier & brice
Hamer House Condominiums: Home of Brice Rhyne
July 24, 2001

The drive from Gottlieb Grove was made in silence. Brice wasn't sure of what Grier was feeling, but felt so sorry for her. The family had held each other, prayed, cried and passed apologies all around. His primary concern was Grier, but Brice had made a mental note of the light that seemed to go out between her parents—Johnathan and Lindersyl. Some couples only functioned under scrutiny and distress. That removed, they had little to connect them. It was the syndrome cheating husbands and wives went through when they finally divorced, suddenly they didn't find their mistresses or outside men very appealing. Grier seemed to have taken it all in relative stride, but Brice couldn't help wondering if the other shoe was gearing up to drop. Brice had also felt sudden pangs of guilt having not divulged his virginity to Grier once all the confessions started. The time never seemed appropriate, particularly with Eisen sitting there with his sex kitten girlfriend and their kid.

Driving to his house, a small 2-bedroom condo a few short miles from the Grove, Brice contemplated telling Grier, but again chickened out. What if she were still emotionally taxed from her aunt and mother's news? He could hardly dump this on her as well.

As they arrived at his place and parked, Grier continued to stare off, silent. Brice walked around and opened her door. She got out without looking at him. He took hold of her arm, stopping her walk to the front door.

"Grier, are you okay?"

"Yes, I suppose so. Tell me, Brice, are you biding your time, waiting for a convenient moment to break up with me?"

"What? Why would I break up with you?"

"All the way here you've been quiet and you've barely looked in my direction. I figured you wanted to get me away from the Grove before you dumped me."

"Grier, give me some credit. I told you years ago I suspected your father and aunt—your mother, I mean, were getting busy."

"I come from the most dysfunctional family on the planet."

"Hardly. Stop quipping Grier. I love you and soon you will be my wife. So what, your aunt's really your mother, your brother's a freak and your father is a major pain in the ass?" he chided her, poking her in the side.

Grier had to admit it was all a bit laughable were it not so painful.

"In the scheme of things, my love, you are an innocent," Brice smiled, kissing her forehead.

Grier bit her bottom lip, "In every sense of the word, huh?"

"In all the senses that matter."

"Brice, it seems that sex has messed up the lives of everyone around me. I don't know that I want to risk ruining my life by losing my virginity."

Brice opened the front door and allowed her inside first. He'd redecorated areas of the house since she'd left, and Grier gave a frightful gasp to the puke green paint and army green carpet in the spare room they walked to.

"Brice, what have you done in here?"

"I missed you and took my anger out on the room, I'm afraid."

"Oh, you poor dear." Grier laughed.

Brice cornered Grier as she stepped into the room. "Grier, there's something I need to tell you."

"Brice, I can't do anymore heart cleansings today. I just can't, especially if this is something that's going to upset me."

"Please, let me get this out."

Grier held her breath, her mind wandering in those few seconds. *He was gay. No, he was a serial rapist or child predator. She always thought his eyes were beady and too close together. Oh, no, he's on the 'down-low'. He has HIV . . .*

"Brice, what is it?"

"Sit down."

"No. Just tell me already so I can get ready to kill you and plan my getaway before the police arrive."

Suddenly Brice decided her anxiety was not worth the strain. Thinking on his feet, Brice knelt down and took her hand.

"I want us to get married exactly eight weeks from today, September 10."

Grier jumped into Brice's arms. "That's it? Don't you ever scare me like that again. I can't wait until our wedding night. I want it to be so special. I want you to show me how a woman should be loved."

Brice held her tighter. "I will Grier, I will."

You do something to me—something deep inside
I'm hanging on the wire—for a love I'll never find . . .

lindersyl & johnathan
Gottlieb Grove: Master Bedroom Suite
July 25, 2001

It wasn't the same. Lindersyl looked the same to him. She felt the same to him. But she was different. The sweetness was gone, replaced with a rugged edge and knowing disposition. She'd seen the world and known the men in it. She'd been had by more than a few men. She had all the faith in the world in him, but only that he would do as she predicted. She knew him too well for him to play the kinds of games with her mind that he did with the others. Lindersyl had his number and it made his apprehension surface. Maybe Janie and Betty were into him because of the money, Anastasia was into him for the direction and Lillian was with him, well, he'd never really understood why Lillian was with him. But Lindersyl had always been with him out of love—pure and simple. Now that she'd known other men, would he measure up? They were making love because he told himself he was still in love with her, but knew he only wanted her near him to figure out where his manhood stood.

Lindersyl looked at Johnathan shirtless and thought of Olivus' fine-tuning. There was no comparison. She thought of the times she'd slept with Arthur late in their marriage—she'd obliged him out of duty, but hated every moment. To curb him reaching for her, Lindersyl had resorted to playing dead, but Arthur, like most men she'd known, was too busy dealing with his fantasies—eyes shut tight, mind going 100 miles an hour—to know she was not interested. Johnathan presented a similar, but odd challenge. He was still desirable and handsome, but the chemistry was gone. She wanted that familiar, unadulterated closeness, but knew it would not be there. If she could just get it over with . . .

Johnathan ran his index finger down to the small of Lindersyl's back. Her skin was soft beneath his fingers. She was topless, skirting about in her panties. It was a turn-off for Johnathan to see Lindersyl half-bare. She'd always met him under the covers and waited for him to undress her. He'd closed his eyes, but opened them when he felt her breath against his mustache. He watched her lips part to kiss him open on the mouth. He did not want to kiss her back. She moved away from him, then looked him over, peering deep into his eyes before offering that relentlessly guileful smile. It was the look that had fueled a thousand and one dreams, but now felt rehearsed, manipulative. Still his body responded and he became angry and felt stupid.

"How is it possible you can still do this to me?" Johnathan asked, half waiting for her to answer 'black magic'.

Instead of the hurried, laborious frenzy they'd experienced over the years when sneaking, the two kissed slow and deep. There was no light music floating behind them as Johnathan had imagined, no pent up anxiety that someone was just on the verge of finding them out. There was nothing that would allow him to focus his attention away from Lindersyl or finishing quickly. He tensed and pulled away from her.

"Nervous?" she asked.

Johnathan didn't answer, but instead plopped himself down on the bed and threw his body back against the Down comforter. He moved his arms and legs about as if making an angel in the snow. "Come," he half-smiled, beckoning her to join him on the bed. "Let's talk."

Lindersyl slid herself up under his outstretched arm, relieved. They talked of nothing in particular, both attempting to engage the conversation as long as possible.

"Those are our babies running through this house, all grown up," Lindersyl laughed.

"They turned out to be pretty good kids."

"Yeah."

"Did I ever tell you I was sorry about Ana-Leslie?"

"Jumper, don't."

"I am sorry, Lindersyl. I've done some selfish, cruel things in my time, but that took the cake. I loved her too and I grieved for her, but I didn't know how to express that loss to you."

"I know. It was a very empty time for us both I suspect." Lindersyl's thoughts shifted to Anastasia. She was probably feeling empty as well.

Johnathan's touch felt rough to Lindersyl suddenly. Every stroke of his hand caused Lindersyl to stiffen a bit more. She felt her yearning to make love to Johnathan one last time subside completely. She moved away from him and turned her back, but he followed, cradling his body to fit over hers and pushing himself hard against her. He continued talking into her ear. Lindersyl winced at the pleasure she got from the sensation, but easily went back to previous thoughts. Maybe it was that Anastasia reminded her of herself—in love and in trouble.

Lillian pressed her face against the windowpane of the pool house. She could see Johnathan and Lindersyl dancing around the master bedroom of the main house. Surely God would not leave her with nothing, but herself. She was in love with Johnathan Holland, with his evil, sordid self. Lillian knew it with certainty every time Lindersyl and Johnathan got too close to each other in that bedroom. Lillian felt her heart cracking into a million little pieces with every kiss.

"God, it's me Lillian. Please, let him still want me when my sister is through with him."

Lindersyl had wanted so much to have one last, final interlude with Johnathan, but couldn't turn her mind off. She thought of Sara Ross telling her "your body is God's temple; not everything and everyone should have access to it." Convicted and convinced by the Holy Spirit, Lindersyl knew she would never have intimate contact with Johnathan again. She felt overwhelming sadness and was in the process of moving Johnathan's arm from around her waist when his mobile rang. On the fifth ring Johnathan looked at the caller ID and cursed aloud, "bitch", before tossing the still ringing phone atop the pillows. Lindersyl looked Johnathan hard in the face with a disdain she had not felt since she found he had slept with Lillian, and grabbed the phone.

"Hello?" Lindersyl answered the phone.

Johnathan laid back on the bed, his head resting on his hands. Since his body was willing to have Lindersyl (even though his heart wasn't) he would not resist her. A jealous tirade would excite him. He wanted Anastasia gone anyway. If Lindersyl cursed her out, Anastasia would finally get the message and stop calling. Baby or none, Anastasia no longer existed for him.

"Johnathan is here, but I think it is me you wish to speak with, Anastasia," Lindersyl said.

Johnathan sat up on his elbows when he realized that Lindersyl had called Anastasia by name. How did Lindersyl know it was Anastasia and not one of the others? His worry turned to utter panic when Lindersyl got up from the bed and moved to the hallway, still topless. After sitting on the stairwell landing talking and laughing for more than twenty minutes, Johnathan became vexed beyond reason and peaked his head out the door.

"Lindi, what the hell is going on here?"

Lindersyl looked at him, eyes wide and perturbed, and motioned for him with her head to go back into the bedroom.

"No, to hell with that! Give me my damned phone. You want to be best friends with some dumb broad I'm screwing, you do it on your own damned phone," Johnathan swaggered over, his hand out and fingers wiggling.

"I am on the telephone, Jumper. When I am through I will give you your phone back," Lindersyl frowned.

Johnathan reached for the phone anyway, attempting to snatch it from her hands.

"Jumper! You feel like you can disrespect me too, huh? Why don't you smack me and take the phone?"

Frustrated, Johnathan folded his arms and leaned against the wall behind her. Who did Lindersyl think he was, that little young knucklehead she was laying up with? She couldn't run him like that. No one talked to him like that! Then too, she could and there was nothing he could do about it.

"Anastasia, where you staying? How 'bout I come around and scoop you up. We can finish our talk then," Lindersyl hung up the phone and slid it across the carpet to Johnathan.

He had a question in his throat, but knew better than to ask it. In a last ditch effort to salvage their evening together Johnathan scooted up behind her on the landing, his legs lassoing hers. Though she did not move away, Lindersyl was obviously not having. Undeterred, Johnathan kissed delicately at her neck.

"You know Anastasia is pregnant for you," Lindersyl said more as a statement than a question.

"I told her to get rid of it! I don't want no more kids—I can't deal—"

"You told her to have an abortion?"

"Lindersyl, don't take that tone with me. You have no idea what Anastasia and I have been going through."

"I am sure I do, Jumper. Remember me? Why didn't you ask me to abort Grier or Eisendorff? How about Ana-Leslie? Would it have been better to just vacuum her out than have her die?"

"This is not the same kind of situation."

"How so? A pregnant woman expecting your child, I see nothing but similarities."

"I loved you. I wanted our children. Anastasia is j-just someone I sc-sc", Johnathan's words fell into a stammering pattern and he decided to stop in mid-sentence to calm himself, before saying with finality, "Anastasia doesn't count."

"She doesn't count! Just like I didn't count, huh? You think we're both dumb females head over heels in love with you? Just because I love you doesn't mean that I've forgotten your cussedness and cruelty, Johnathan. I blamed Lillian for things I knew you were responsible for because it seemed unnatural for me to love and hate someone at the same time with such ferocious sincerity. And sometimes Johnathan, like right now, I wonder if we all wouldn't have been better off if you'd have laid in that driveway and died in a pool of your own blood," Lindersyl glowered.

Chapter Nine
The Final Blow

*I could see them, all of your lies
But still, I miss you . . .*

Is It A Crime, Sade

The Gottliebs
Gottlieb Grove, Full Grounds
August 21, 2001

Twilight was setting on Gottlieb Grove when the guests began arriving. Cars had been valeted the entire length of the Grove entrance and the trees lining the driveway strung with lanterns. Beautiful Black couples in black tie and evening gowns, draped in diamonds, pearls and furs made their way through the orchard to the main house, which had been outfitted with a party tent. An ice sculpture in the center of the tent read Lillian-35-Johnathan.

Johnathan sucked in his stomach as tight as he could and hurriedly fastened a waist cinch around his girth. He refused to buy another tuxedo just because the one he had was two sizes too small. He'd manage the night. He was doing this for Lillian. She deserved it. Lillian had been an absolute angel in the last three weeks. He'd never realized how much of the same mindset he and Lillian were. But in days of finding out that Anastasia was pregnant, Lillian had called the police and had her accused of stalking. The ensuing restraining order had ended all contact between Johnathan and Anastasia. Lillian was fierce in her support of him—even though he was wrong. Unlike that witch sister of hers, who'd taken off to comfort Anastasia and never returned, Lillian could be counted on in a rough patch. Lillian's loyalty had cleared up any confusion he'd had about who he wanted to be with. Johnathan had promptly handed over the names of friends he wanted to attend his and Lillian's 35th wedding anniversary party. There was no reason to change horses in mid-stream.

Lindersyl had been an utter disaster. The saying "never the same river twice" kept going through his head. Johnathan could not wait for Lindersyl to get off the Grove. Who the hell did she think she was, judging his situation with Anastasia? Lindersyl knew nothing about how manipulative and deceitful young girls could be. For all he knew Anastasia was faking the pregnancy or carrying some other man's child. It wasn't like he was with her 100% of the time. Lindersyl had proven what was in his heart: she was no longer worthy of his affections. He was just sorry it had taken so long to realize it.

Johnathan shifted his cummerbund first above his stomach, then beneath it. It looked better slightly above, so he made the dismal decision to tighten his girdle just a bit more. He wasn't going to be able to eat very much or bend over, but it was worth it not to have to buy another tux. All that was left to do was retrieve his wife and make a grand entrance at 6:30 p.m. sharp.

Bvlgari had outdone itself in making Lillian's special order diamond necklace. Thirty-five specially cut four-carat diamonds with platinum backing and a center seven-carat black diamond. Someone told her the black ones were the rarest and most sought after—so it became a must-have for the occasion. Lillian pushed her breast up until they sat cushioned atop two inches of foam filler. The black diamond fell dead center her cleavage. In a black satin strapless evening gown, she checked her watch and saw that there were few precious moments alone before it was time to descend the stairwell and greet her guests. This was easily the happiest day of her life. She pulled her satin gloves up to her elbows and took a deep breath when she heard a knock at the door. It was Johnathan. "I'm coming," she giggled. How the tide had turned in her favor. Their mother had always said that Lindersyl had no sense of decorum or loyalty. Here Johnathan was caught in some little slut's ruse to extort money, alleging him to be the father of her unborn child and the woman who professed to love him best, runs out on him. All Johnathan had had to do was tell Lillian that the girl, Anastasia, was lying; he had never slept with her without protection for Lillian to take up his cause. Besides, whether Eisendorff and Grier were hers or not, they were Johnathan's and they should not have to share their inheritance, their legacy with some 19-year-old's bastard. Lillian felt it could be Johnathan's child, but didn't want to believe it. She couldn't afford to believe it. First, Lindersyl, now this girl would have succeeded in giving Johnathan offspring. Were it true, this would be something that she had been unable to do, so she was willing to take Johnathan at his word. Lillian didn't know to where her sister had run off, but was glad for the peace and quiet. Perhaps she missed Ladbroke Mews and had returned. Lillian slid her B.zero1 ring over her gloves, happy also that Harry had evaporated into the night. She opened the door and gleamed at Johnathan who looked like a cool million to her. She took his hand and headed for the stairwell, thinking with each step, "I got my man!"

6:30 p.m.

Johnathan and Lillian gave each other an impassioned embrace, then kissed lovingly for the friends, family and media gathered at the Grove to celebrate their anniversary. They walked down the center stair, draping each other. One of a dozen hired attendants handed a microphone to Johnathan as they reached the bottom step. He surveyed the applauding crowd before speaking.

"I have been fortunate beyond my wildest dreams to have met and married such a beautiful, exquisite woman as Lillian Ebersol Gottlieb. She is dynamic and fearless, gracious and absolutely amazing. She has been a friend, a lover, a confidante," Johnathan spotted Lindersyl and paused. She was in flowing pink chiffon, her hair pulled back in an elegant bun. His heart raced and he was both angered and delighted by her presence. He chose his next words carefully.

"Lillian has stood by me and proven herself loyal, trustworthy—a real woman. She is the kind of rare jewel that knows how to love and be loved by a real man. We thank you for joining us here tonight to celebrate our love. Enjoy the festivities," Johnathan said, before handing the microphone back to the attendant.

He and Lillian kissed again, this time more keenly. Johnathan had intended to go over and curse Lindersyl out, but Lillian had hold of his arm and was ushering him towards a collection of her sorors.

Lindersyl made it inside the main house and through the crowd just as Lillian and Johnathan paused at the bottom of the stair to address their guests. Lindersyl felt the sting of Johnathan's words, but felt more sorry and embarrassed for him than anything. It was definitely over between them and getting to know their children all over again and Anastasia, Lindersyl didn't feel she'd ever trust Johnathan again. He hadn't changed at all; he'd just learned to act his way through the most important issues of his life. Lindersyl wanted to speak with Johnathan about Anastasia and see if she could at least get the restraining order lifted—particularly since Johnathan kept showing up at Anastasia's banging and kicking at her front door. The threats from him had become so scary that Lindersyl had moved Anastasia from her cramped one-bedroom into a luxury two-bedroom with controlled access close to Thaddeus Mosse College. Lindersyl's old friend Bree Babalola's daughter Kemi was a midwife and she had gladly taken on Anastasia care. The restraining order notwithstanding, Lindersyl's time with Anastasia had been a joy. It had also distracted her attention from Johnathan and Lillian. More than anything, Lindersyl was excited about being with Eisendorff and Grier. They were bright, beautiful, smart, funny and now, happy. She also had a grandchild to spoil rotten. The lot had begun going to Bible study and church services three times a week. Keeping with the new family creed of full disclosure, Lindersyl told the kids about Anastasia and Johnathan's impending parenthood. Though unexpected, none were particularly surprised. When they got to know her, Grier and Eisen both adored Anastasia. They'd all doted and marveled at Anastasia's expanding tummy.

"It was bound to happen at some point." Eisen said. Grier just laughed, "How sick, a new father at sixty-two."

No one had been back to the Grove since the Sunday afternoon confessions three weeks earlier. Tonight they had all shown.

Lindersyl looked about the grounds, happy she'd come home, if for nothing else than to exorcize those demons keeping her from moving on. The pool house was empty, and Lillian had all of its contents tossed out. Lindersyl rolled her eyes at Harry's remaining personal belongings setting out on the balcony under a sign that read "Salvage Pick Up". Lindersyl was resting on the thought that Lillian and Johnathan truly deserved one another when Johnathan came up to her from behind.

"What're you doing here?"

"Minding my own business, would you believe?"

"Why are you here? Lillian is right, you can't stand to see her happy. If you're here to disrupt this evening, you think again! It would give me great pleasure to toss your ass right out of here."

Lindersyl walked away without incident, despite Johnathan grabbing at her to stop her exit. She would not fight with him—especially not tonight with him in such a volatile mood.

6:51 p.m.

Eisen watched from the tent entrance the exchange between his parents. His mother was getting over his father, but slowly. Her heart was on her face while Johnathan spoke of Lillian's love and loyalty. Eisen imagined she probably felt it should have been her standing beside Johnathan celebrating their anniversary, rather than her sister. Eisen had done what he could to convince Lindersyl not to attend the party, but she had insisted. His mother and Grier would be heading back to Ladbroke Mews in a few days and this would be Lindersyl's last trip around the Grove for a while. Eisen was sorry she was leaving now that they could finally embrace each other as mother and son. He considered shutting down his practice and flying out with her, feeling a need to be nurtured and hugged by her constantly. Lindersyl had taken to mothering expertly and with great fortitude. His mother had been instrumental in getting Terrie to come around to seeing herself as more than Avery's mother and some body men used as a playground.

"Terrie, no man wants to love a whore. Eisen has seen you in a new light, a respectable one and he wants to take you away from that fantasy lifestyle into something respectable and real," he'd overheard Lindersyl tell Terrie.

Terrie liked Lindersyl and saw the best of intentions in her words. She'd agreed to live with Eisendorff as an engaged couple for six months and if all went well, to marry. Eisen could not be happier. His life on an upswing, until his mother insisted he attend his father and Lillian's anniversary party. These gatherings had always been a sore spot with Eisendorff who saw them as networking opportunities for social climbers and brown-nosers who could care less about his family. His experience had been that truly wealthy people were mental cases: worried about losing their wealth and footing, along with their prestige, their position and their celebrity among people jockeying for a piece of their pie. He'd spent his life avoiding Johnathan and Lillian's soirees, now he'd been tossed by coercion into the midst of the gala of the century. Replete with celebrity entertainment that included Kenny Rogers, Gladys Knight and a highly celebrated jazz band, Eisen was certain he'd vomit at the loving exchanges between Johnathan and Lillian before the night was over. He'd seen his parents part company—Lindersyl heading in one direction and Johnathan in another, so he felt safe ducking back into the tent to find some of the world famous crab claws Lillian ordered and had prepared by Paula Dean.

7:01 p.m.

Harry went through the side entrance of the pool house to the upstairs deck off of what used to be his living room. He'd seen the newspaper article announcing the event and had made his way back to the Grove against every fiber of sanity in his body. Every step he took forward, his conscience pulled him back saying, "You don't belong here." Instead Harry pulled up a wooden crate chucked with his things as a chair and watched the festivities. Lillian seemed at home, or maybe just finally content to have Johnathan to herself. Her display, lavishing him with kisses and loving looks was sickening; saturating Harry with a blind disheartening. "Everybody plays the fool sometime," he comforted himself. When he found himself crying into his shirt collar, he admitted coming had been a mistake.

7:13 p.m.

Grier had her own wedding to get through in a few weeks without turning into Bridezilla, and felt put upon attending the farce ceremony her father and aunt were giving. What were they celebrating? No one had a clue that they weren't even married? After hearing the confessions of all, Grier couldn't get her lips to unpurse at the party. She took Johnathan and Lillian's dramatic sweep down the stairs and speeches as minstrelsy at its best. She wanted to go home, but was there to support her mother. Lindersyl had insisted on coming—so there she and Brice had found themselves as well. The goal was to be seen by everyone else there, except Johnathan and Lillian.

7:30 p.m.

Lillian approached the stage and asked for everyone's attention. She wanted to acknowledge her sorority sisters. Then as an afterthought, having spotted Lindersyl, Lillian decided to go for the jugular. She beckoned Johnathan to her side.

"Johnathan and I also want to thank our children, Eisendorff and Grier, come on up here. We could not have produced two more beautiful children," Lillian smirked, more than smiled.

Neither moved to the stage. Then Johnathan took a freestanding microphone and helped ease the tension. "They're a little bashful. C'mon kids. Don't make your old dad embarrass you by coming out there to get you," he laughed.

Eisendorff and Grier looked at each other from opposite sides of the room and walked towards the stage. Lillian continued, "For those of you who don't know, Eisendorff is a leading psychotherapist with his own practice and Grier, is a design specialist with Xytex. She practically runs the whole of their European acquisitions. Would either of you like to say a few words?"

"No" they both said, walking from the stage.

Lindersyl was sighing her relief the kids hadn't cut a fool. Then Johnathan called out to her.

"Lindersyl Gottlieb, my sister-in-law, ladies and gentlemen is also here. You all know her as the Gottlieb who never quite got it right. Well, gentlemen, she's still available though she's way past her prime. Baby girl, this next song I picked especially for you because hope springs eternal that one day you'll find that special man who'll convince you to retire that loose streak of yours," Johnathan dropped the mic and the deejay began playing Queen's *Somebody to Love*.

The crowd laughed and pointed at Lindersyl whose face registered a mix of utter humiliation and hurt. The jazz band began playing over the deejay, drowning out their sound completely. Lindersyl thought that if she could just make it out of the room before the tears started rolling down her face, she'd be okay. The room of revelers eyed her; some feeling sorry for her, others glad she'd gotten her comeuppance in such a public way and at the hands of her own family. Lindersyl had seen Eisendorff gunning for Johnathan, but couldn't be worried about that. She needed to get outside to her car and safely off the Grove. But the crowd seemed denser and she couldn't make the fast break she wanted. The tune the jazz band played was vaguely familiar, something she'd heard before, but couldn't place—like Muzak. It was loud; louder than it should have been and Lindersyl thought for a moment she was having some sort of anxiety attack where her senses turned on her. All eyes seemed still to be on her and the sound of the band kept getting louder. When she turned around to the sound of the music, the saxophonist was directly behind her. She saw his face and her legs gave way. It was Olivus. He stopped playing and another musician picked up his notes. "Sheer Lindersyl", he said, catching her before she hit the ground.

"Olivus," was all she managed to say.

"Lindersyl, don't talk. Just come to me," Olivus said, beckoning her forward.

Lindersyl cried tears of joy. She jumped and screamed and tore at Olivus' clothes. She couldn't believe her eyes. She wanted to know how and why and when, but couldn't be bothered to ask.

"I've got you Lindersyl, so you can let it go. Let it out. God has enough strength to carry the both of us, love. This is no great personal tragedy. It is our new beginning," Olivus whispered.

Lindersyl just held him and cried, thanking God all the while for His grace and His mercy.

7:48 p.m.

Harry was standing out on the balcony watching Johnathan serve Lindersyl her ass in her hand, when Lillian spotted him.

"Harry Veda, you are trespassing. Leave at once."

"I should kill you!" he said at her coldness.

"I'm going to get Johnathan, then we'll see who gets killed."

"Get him so I can send his ass back to Mercer," Harry said, running down the pool house stairs in anticipation of a fight.

Johnathan was coming out of the main house chiding the deejay for having humiliated Lindersyl when he saw Lillian and then Harry Veda over her shoulder.

"I'll tear him apart!" Johnathan shouted.

As he went for Harry, Eisendorff and Brice came up from behind and jumped Johnathan, tackling him to the ground. Johnathan's frat brothers, old as dirt, joined in the melee, tearing down the outdoor tent with Gladys Knight and half the guests still beneath it. The ruckus continued with Harry punching Johnathan in the jaw hard enough to land them both in the swimming pool. Some guests fell in while others jumped in. By the time the police arrived, all five hundred guests, the servants and musicians were out in the Grove stomping holes in each other's behinds or taking cover in the orchard. There was no order and no calming the crazed and drunken partygoers.

8:03 p.m.

Chasen watched the fighting with deep satisfaction. It solidified his decision to kill them all. He didn't give any more thought to it; he couldn't. Chasen pushed his finger down on a button and released it. The ten seconds it took to detonate the C4 were used driving out of Gottlieb Grove one last time. Chasen watched the explosion and ensuing fire from his rearview mirror.

Chapter Ten
Coming Full Circle

August 24, 2001
3:23am

Lillian pulled the scrunchy from her hair and fitted it around her wrist as she tipped down the side steps and entered the foyer. Seeing two uniformed Mosse Point police officers and a trench coat clad fellow standing alongside them through the glass door; she fastened her silk kimono around her naked body. Bare-foot, the cool night breeze caused her to curl her toes under as she opened the door.

"Ms. Lillian Gottlieb?"

She recognized Sean McAfee in the trench coat as a former high school classmate, now a Lieutenant with the Mosse Point police. He wore the same stern lipped, beady-eyed look when he'd informed her of her father's passing years ago as a young rookie. She stood blocking the entrance, a slight panic gripping her, until she remembered her manners.

"Yes, I am Lillian Gottlieb. Officers, Lieutenant, please come in," she half smiled. "Is there something I can do for you?"

"Ma'am we—", one of the uniformed officers began, but was halted by the furrowed look of his superior.

"Lillian, how you been?" the Lieutenant asked, leading her by the arm into her study.

"Okay I suppose, though I am getting a bit uneasy with you all standing in my parlor at 3 o'clock in the morning. What's wrong Sean?"

"We pulled your son Chasen over around midnight. He was driving erratically along the interstate in a vehicle that had been reported unreturned by Phoenix Car Rental. We identified ourselves and asked that he step out of the vehicle. He did. We asked if we could search the vehicle, thinking maybe he had open bottles or something in the car and we could pull him in to sober up. Instead, we found an explosive making material and a handgun under the passenger seat. Once he realized we were about to arrest him, he started yelling and screaming about how we'd come to stop him. Said that we'd been sent to intercept him by the mighty Gottliebs. Said he could no longer live a lie and that he would have the last laugh. Before we could cuff him, he . . . he wrestled my partner's gun from his belt and put it to his head. He kept saying his mother would not deny him any longer. We tried to stop him. But before any of us could react, he'd put the gun under his chin and pulled the trigger. He's at Shockley Memorial," the Lieutenant sighed and gathered his breath, relieved he'd gotten it all out.

Lillian sat silently for a few seconds before announcing stone facedly, "There's just one problem Lieutenant, Chasen is my nephew, not my son."

"That's pretty peculiar, as we just left your sister Lindersyl, and she said the same thing and sent us here."

"The child is obviously crazy. Can't you see what he's done to our house?" Lillian asked pointing behind her to the out of doors in plain view. The entire back and side of Gottlieb Grove's main house had been blown off.

The End

Epilogue

Johnathan's heart attack was minor and had been the only serious injury from the explosion. Others, 117 to be exact, had been hit by flying bits of Gottlieb Grove's main house-turned—projectiles and shards of glass. Injuries ranged from broken bones and twisted ankles to cuts and lacerations. Of course there were the black eyes, busted lips, and swollen extremities from the brawl that had taken place before the explosion that didn't factor in to the numbers. The entire west side of the house had come undone, blowing the gas line and causing a series of smaller explosions to take place. The grand staircase had fallen and the master and minor suites had been destroyed. Lillian had refused to leave the house though, fearful that some residual guests would sneak in to pilfer what was left of her home. Her friends didn't love her; they were all jealous of her and she knew better than to trust the lot of them. It didn't matter to her that she had officially been labeled a crackpot and counted among the feeble-minded. Lillian had been overcome by grief and loose emotions and there was no one left to hold her and tell her it was going to be okay now that Harry was gone. Harry had left the poolhouse and ironically, Johnathan had taken up residence there. She couldn't stand to even look over at it anymore with Johnathan in there, marking Harry's space as his own. Lillian had heard God's voice as clear as you please, tell her to get out of the Grove and make things right with her sister. But this was her home and Johnathan was her husband and she would not give up either. Even as the east wind whipped against her body as it used to do her home, Lillian refused to budge. Lillian hated Lindersyl for ruining things for her.

It was all her fault. Things were going just fine until Lindersyl decided to show up and start rehashing old, unpopular versions of the truth. They were *versions*, as Lillian had similar stories to tell, but with a decidedly different tinge. Her party had been ruined and the Grove destroyed. It would take months to get that gas line secured. She was effectively homeless, aside from the carriage house. Lillian dug her heels into the debris that had blown into the parlor from exposure and smiled at Johnathan, sitting on the poolhouse balcony, "I am a Gottlieb Girl and I will lead by example," she mumbled. "This is not the end of this by any stretch."

Grier couldn't wait to get out of Connecticut and back to London. She was grateful Xytex executives understood her need to get out of the States and were happy to secure her early return trip. When Grier returned to work in London, there was no burning or gnawing in her belly; only the satisfaction and praise of knowing that being obedient to God was the only way to court victory. Even when it seemed on the surface that she was the weakest vessel of the family, she turned out to be the strongest. This time, Grier rejoiced in the knowledge that she was not running from, but to something: peace. She is still getting use to having Lindersyl as her mother. Some days she is happy, others sad, and still others, angry. Brice wasn't letting her leave without him this time. He shut down shop and sold his condo, determined not to let Grier out of his sights again. The couple began planning their wedding as soon as they returned to Ladbroke, taking up residence in Olivus' old home.

Terrie decided that she couldn't give up her "fantasy lifestyle". She truly enjoyed her sexual freedom, but did recognize that Avery had no business with a mother who did. She gladly gave custody of Avery to a heartbroken Eisendorff, who still believed that there was hope for Terrie as his wife. Eisen took to fatherhood like a champ. He and Avery made it a point to speak to Mr. Thornbush every time they passed the front desk, the first month of his stay and sent him gifts from abroad when they moved away. Eisendorff decided he deserved as much of his mother as Avery deserved of him. After a month of getting certified and credentialed in the UK, Eisendorff opened a practice in Notting Hill. He found a flat close to Lindersyl and visits daily.

Harry cut off all ties with the Gottlieb family and Connecticut. After a semester at Ridgefield Community College, he took a position at The University of California at San Marcos. He and Amelia became a couple. He visited Chasen in the hospital once and apologized to him. He left a photo of himself with Lillian on Chasen's bedside table and a crucifix necklace around his neck. Of course, Chasen was still unconscious then. Occasionally he thought of Lillian and Chasen, but it only moved him to tears, so he spent the majority of his free time composing songs on his compas and comparing the works of the African philosopher Amernemope with the Greek Plato.

Anastasia celebrated her twentieth birthday graduating from Thaddeus Mosse College, with a degree in social work and seven months pregnant. All of her expenses continue to be paid by Lindersyl and Olivus, who came briefly back to the States for the ceremony. Johnathan still refuses to speak to Anastasia and the restraining order remains in effect.

Johnathan remained at Mercer Hospital for two weeks following his heart attack. Doctors kept him as a precaution since the scar tissue from his earlier gun wound complicated his recovery. He moved into the pool house upon his return and hired a housekeeper to tend to his needs. He has not spoken to Lillian since his return to the Grove, though they peer out at each other over the walkway between the rubble of the main house and the poolhouse. Johnathan got a clear snapshot of his life while in the hospital, recognizing the warnings God had been giving him all along. Lindersyl was no longer his wife or his woman, though she had tried to be his friend. Lillian was none of the above. Nor was Anastasia. All had tried to love him and he, in return, had tried to destroy them. Johnathan didn't want friends, he didn't want a woman, and he didn't want pity. More than anything he wanted to be able to sleep at night and not feel smug that he had cheated God out of taking his life each new day. Johnathan started listening for that voice he heard every now and again when he sat real still and concentrated. Before long, he was listening to the ministers on television—he liked that Osteen fellow and a young guy Bryant, out of Baltimore. In due time, Johnathan told himself, he'd build his courage and conviction enough to walk into a sanctuary and let that tiny piece of God he carried in his heart, wash over his whole body. In due time.

Chasen's shaky grip and fear of arrest had been a blessing. The bullet that should have blown the top of his head off and rendered his brain inoperable, had knocked his jaw off track, jamming it into the socket. The bullet had gone out of his cheek, and the sound of the gun blast had burst the eardrum in his right ear. When he was released from the hospital, he was promptly arrested. Only Arthur Collier showed for his arraignment; he'd hopped a plane from London after getting an urgent call from Danker Simmonite that Chasen was in trouble. Arthur arrived at the Grove the day after the explosion. Chasen awaits trial.

Lindersyl toasted hers and Olivus' wedding with a glass of sparkling Voss, having cleared her pantry and her life of all Bollinger remnants. The couple had barely touched down in London before they began telephoning friends and relatives from the airport. "Meet us at the Magistrates' office in an hour," was all either said. They would have a church ceremony later to make it official among the saved, but neither wanted to wait beyond clearing customs to become Mr. and Mrs. Olivus Handy. Lindersyl hadn't thought of Johnathan even once since the explosion at the Grove and counted herself blessed to have made it out of the house when she had. Her heart danced when she thought of Olivus swooping down, like a Black knight, to grip her. Oh, how she loved him. Lindersyl did fret and guilt over Chasen though, and kept contact with Arthur to get regular updates on him. She had also heard from friends near and far that her sister had become a certifiable lunch box, still residing in the ramshackled debris Chasen's bomb had not managed to level. "I can't be concerned about Lillian right now," is what she said, but in her heart Lindersyl knew it was just a matter of time before she'd go marching in to save Lillian. After all, Lindersyl was forever a Gottlieb Girl and only she could set the example Lillian needed to pull herself together.

Spill

Like water spilled on the ground, which cannot be recovered, so we must die. But God does not take away life; instead, He devises ways so that a banished person may not remain estranged from Him.—2 Samuel 14:14

*A*nastasia Harcourt had always had pretty severe menstrual cramps, so the onset of labor felt familiar. She leaned on the mailbox in front of her apartment complex trying to catch her breath. As she inhaled deeply, a sharp pain seized her pelvis causing the air to expel abruptly. She looked down and saw a stream of fluid puddling at her feet. The pain intensified quickly and without warning. By the time she thought to call Dr. Babalola, her contractions were coming every six minutes and she couldn't move. She was lying in her bed, the front door to the apartment ajar, screaming at the top of her lungs when she heard the springs in the door squeak. Someone had entered the apartment; friend or foe, she wasn't sure.

"I'm in here," she screamed between breaths.

It was Johnathan Holland, the sixty-two-year-old, married father-to-be. Her eyes widened when she saw him. Anastasia half suspected he was there to kill her, the baby or both. He had demanded and paid for her to have an abortion twice and he had threatened her life once he found she was still pregnant. When she persisted in trying to reach him, his wife had her served with a restraining order and it had been months since she'd seen him. In fact she had left her old residence, to keep him from stalking her: banging on her door at all hours of the night, or *parking outside her apartment spying on her. Anastasia wasn't sure how he even knew where she'd moved.*

She screamed 'help' when she saw him come toward her.

"I'm right here."

"Get away from me!" she said, smacking his hands away as they reached for her.

"No, Anastasia, I'm here to help you," he looked at her with shocked confusion. He called an ambulance and washed his hands before returning to her bedside.

She had removed her underthings by the time he returned and with her legs spread wide, he could make out the top of a hairy little head. Johnathan's eyes went wide, and instinctively he told her to 'push'. He grabbed a stack of towels from the bathroom cupboard, moving as quickly as he could, when he heard Anastasia holler out. Since he'd suffered his heart attack a few months earlier Johnathan had been forced to rethink every move he made, walking slowly and pacing himself for fear of having another.

Johnathan rounded the corner to her bedside in time to see the head of his child peek-a-booing from his mother's body. Johnathan caught the head in his hands and watched the child squirm its shoulders free. There was a loud suction noise, then the rest of the baby slid out into his hands. Anastasia stopped screaming, the pain gone instantly. Johnathan popped the child on the bottom and it gave a strong cry. Johnathan looked at Anastasia, then back at the baby. It was a girl. "It's a girl Anastasia! It's a girl!"

"Give me my baby," she said, still afraid he was going to harm the child.

"Your baby?" Johnathan said, his face pinched like a fist.

Sweat was pouring off Anastasia like a fountain. She felt nauseous and dizzy, cold and hot. Anastasia could feel her left side go numb, then her right side as the left regained feeling. She took deep breaths like the Lamaze tape had shown, but felt no better for it. The pressure at her pelvis was extreme and she pushed with all she had. Afterwards, she could feel the contractions getting weaker until they stopped. Anastasia could see Johnathan holding the baby. She could hear the child crying. Her left side started going numb again just as she asked Johnathan for the baby. She could feel her body moving but couldn't make it stop. Anastasia felt out of control and knew something was terribly wrong. She didn't fear death. God was with her. She was whispering "Johnathan, please don't kill my baby," when her body began to convulse.

Spill
The sequel to Fester by Shantella Sherman
available 2009

LaVergne, TN USA
23 September 2009
158745LV00002B/8/P